Sybilla

SYBILLA

Joan Hessayon

C

CENTURY

LONDON   MELBOURNE   AUCKLAND   JOHANNESBURG

This book is for my first grandchild,
Ella Cleo Norris

ACKNOWLEDGEMENTS

I would like to thank Constance Barry not only for helping to gather research material but for her careful preparation of this manuscript and her unflagging support. My thanks also to Barry Rogerson of Paul's Malt Ltd., Ware; Geoffrey Harris, retired police officer, Hertfordshire Constabulary; Elizabeth Llewelyn, JP; and to the Librarian and staff of the Cheshunt Central Library of the Hertfordshire Library Services.

First published in Great Britain in 1986 by
Century Hutchinson Ltd,
Brookmount House, 62–65 Chandos Place,
London WC2N 4NW

Century Hutchinson Publishing Group (Australia) Pty Ltd
16–22 Church Street, Hawthorn, Melbourne, Victoria 3122

Century Hutchinson Group (NZ) Ltd
32–34 View Road, PO Box 40–086, Glenfield, Auckland 10

Century Hutchinson Group (SA) Pty Ltd
PO Box 337, Bergvlei 2012, South Africa

British Library Cataloguing in Publication Data
Hessayon, J.P.
Sybilla.
I. Title
823'.914[F]   PR6058.E7/
ISBN 0 7126 1276 9

Typeset by Inforum Ltd, Portsmouth
Printed and bound in Great Britain by
Anchor Brendon Ltd, Tiptree, Essex

1

Napier Drummond left his office, climbed into the Stanhope phaeton, took up the whip and reins and urged the horse to be off before his companion was properly settled beside him.

'I do wish you wouldn't do that,' laughed Francis Babcock as he adjusted his coat-tails. 'I am for ever making undignified exits from Hertford just because you wish to race down St Andrew's Street.'

Napier grinned at the slight, elegant young man seated beside him. 'You're always too much on your dignity to jump into the carriage as you should, old chap. I can't be waiting all day.' He pulled on the reins and expertly manoeuvred his equipage out of the path of an oncoming brewer's dray. He could drive to an inch, but was far too impatient a man to give his passengers a comfortable ride.

Several passers-by on foot acknowledged him as Napier turned from St Andrew's Street into Fore Street. He was an impressive looking man of thirty who had come to Hertford-shire just a year ago and had already established himself as the brilliant and dynamic owner of a maltings in nearby Ware.

Within a month he had purchased Bailton Hall, up Bell Lane from the Salisbury Arms, from its hard-pressed owner and refurbished it at considerable expense. There he entertained the local gentry and business community with no thought for the cost and every attention to creating the desired effect on his guests' sensibilities. He was essentially an actor; his office and his home were his stage, their furnishings his props. This sense of the importance of drama in business was a key part of his philosophy of life, painfully evolved in the school of hard times.

Well above middling height, he gave the impression of being shorter because of his massive shoulders, thick neck and strong features, as well as his barrel chest and muscular thighs that strained the cloth of his tightly-fitting trousers.

Women thought him handsome; he cared not at all. His need was to express power, a force to be reckoned with, and to this end he parted his dark brown curls in the middle and extended his sideburns at a time when most men were still clean-shaven. Thick dark brows, which moved at lightning speed to reflect his every emotion, were part of his facial armoury.

He glanced at Francis. It had occurred to Napier one day that he never employed a man taller than himself. He had examined the conceit, found it soundly based and laughed at his own instinct for dominance. No man needed to be taller than Napier Drummond, anyway, such extra growth being a waste of physical resources.

The two men were very quickly out of the town and the horse pulled against the traces as they travelled up the long hill towards Hertford Heath. Francis sat back in his seat and breathed in with pleasure. The day was perfect. The crocuses might be past their prime, but the daffodils made delightful puddles of butter yellow here and there, glimpsed through the hornbeams, as they lay in wait to please the eye round each bend in the road.

The town of Hertford sat in a valley, but the Heath was higher ground. No part of Hertfordshire rose above a thousand feet, but the land undulated delightfully in gently rolling hills in what Francis always thought of as a thoroughly civilized manner. Hertfordshire was not one of your wilder, more dramatic parts of the country. Its mild climate, its sense of moderation, appealed strongly to Francis' easy-going nature.

'I do believe Hertford Heath is one of the most pleasant places in the county.'

'But not after dark,' said Napier. 'Footpads are a serious problem in this area. Perhaps a county police force will be able to make the Heath safe for travellers. Ah, there's the East India Company's school. The beautiful copper dome will soon be mostly hidden when the trees are fully in leaf. How does it go? The something something of an April day?'

Francis was momentarily startled by the question, then smiled. 'The uncertain glory of an April day, Shakespeare called it.'

'That's it,' said Napier. 'My mother's admirer is for ever spouting poetry. I seldom know what he is on about.'

'I'm afraid Mr Farley flaunts his poetic knowledge in a quite

2

irritating manner,' agreed Francis. He was immensely fond of his employer, but could never accustom himself to Napier's unselfconscious attitude to his own lack of formal education. It was a fine thing to be a self-made man, of course. It showed that one had character and the determination to overcome immense handicaps. Nevertheless, Napier's ability to laugh at his own weaknesses, whether it be his quick-fire temper or his truncated schooling, embarrassed Francis. Thank heavens he was not inclined to be so honest with everyone!

Francis, at twenty-five, was as different from Napier as he could be. He came from an ancient, though far from wealthy Hertfordshire family, one that never doubted its worth nor failed to receive its due. He had been educated at Eton and Cambridge and might have had a successful career at the Bar. His manners were beyond reproach, his form slight but pleasing to the ladies, his voice a tired drawl that spoke of generations of self-confidence. He was a Babcock; there was no need to prove himself in any field of endeavour.

In spite of the differences in their personalities, background, attitudes and prejudices, there was something about his employer's thrusting personality which attracted Francis strongly, and the two men worked well together. The Babcock fondness for tying up loose ends, for instance, dovetailed nicely with the Drummond fondness for swooping raids on their competitors, while Francis' reluctance to confront the more brutal aspects of life made Drummond's aggression useful to him.

Much to his family's dismay, Francis Babcock had invested his grandfather's small legacy in Napier Drummond and Company Limited nearly a year ago, and was now reaping the benefits in a comfortable salary and a share of the ever-increasing profits at the maltings. His work was well within his capabilities and he was in a privileged position to watch the dramas of industrial conflict, while remaining safely out of the firing line.

'Well?' said Napier, breaking into his reverie. 'What have you to tell me? I said I would listen to your report as we travelled.'

'Yes, of course, I was dreaming. At the maltings, the last sixty quarters to be sacked up was of a very high quality. It's on its way to the barge now. We were able to undercut Adams's price, although we're cutting our profits dangerously low. We have had enquiries from two small Hertfordshire brewers; they will order from us next season.'

'Yes, yes, but what about the new purchase? Cass's old maltings. Is work progressing on the renovations?'

'Yes, it is as you directed. The old maltings was in a terrible state. I know Cass sold it to us at a remarkably low price, but I am beginning to wonder if it was such a bargain. The builder finds new difficulties each day.'

'Builders always find new difficulties. That is their profession. Saunders has only been on the site for forty-eight hours. I expect to have many a battle with him before the maltings is converted to my plan.'

Napier's established malthouse had a steeping capacity of sixty quarters – a fairly large house for the area – and was successfully producing good quality Hertfordshire Brown for porter, as well as the finer pale malts. Napier had now acquired a much smaller malthouse in Ware's French Horn Lane, a shambles of a building that had been superseded by newer workings and so had come cheaply. Here he would make malt in a revolutionary new way after the structure had been adapted. He had purchased the patent for this new and secret method, and would now need to make drastic changes to the small house to convert it.

'When we reach Hoddesdon, I will do all the talking to the Widow Hobart,' said Napier. 'I don't want you spoiling everything by being charming to her. This is business.'

'Believe me, I won't say a word. I have no desire to talk about business matters to an elderly widow still grieving for her husband. It's all too distressing. I wish we weren't in-volved.'

'Yet you must agree it is necessary. Tell me what you know about the late Mr Hobart.'

Francis pulled out a notebook from his pocket. 'Departed this life a year and a half ago, in December of eighteen thirty-nine, after a long illness. He was sixty-two. Born in Hoddesdon where he owned a small coach-building business in Lord Lane. Hadn't been able to take part in the running of the business for five years, but seems to have been ably served

4

by his manager. Had owned seven-tenths of an acre of land in French Horn Lane in Ware for the past twenty years, but never attempted to develop it nor showed any desire to sell.'

'We need that land.'

'Indeed we do, but why can't we continue to rent it from the widow as Cass did, instead of buying it?'

'I want to own everything connected with so important a new project. It's good business. Always lay your foundations carefully, check every detail, study every loophole, plan for every disaster, and above all mind your back.'

Francis smiled. 'Micklethwaite?'

'Yes,' said Napier. 'Those are Mr Micklethwaite's aphorisms and very sound too.'

'You know, you have never told me. Who is or was Mr Micklethwaite?'

'Micklethwaite was and presumably still is the owner of a cotton mill in Rochdale. I was sent from home and apprenticed to him at fourteen to learn the business. My father had tired of the sight of me, was certain I would never make a decent gentleman. In any case, there was no money to speak of in the family. He thought the cotton trade would be just the thing for me to make my fortune. Father had met Micklethwaite years earlier and had been very impressed with the man's capacity for making money. I admit Micklethwaite is something of a genius at business and I learned a great deal from him. I hated him, of course. The man was . . . unlovable.'

'Your father sent you from home at fourteen to work in a *factory*?'

Napier smiled. 'You are horrified. Your father would never have done such a thing, I'm sure. My father, I believe was happy to be rid of me. I was for ever getting into scrapes.'

'And had you done something particularly awful that prompted him to send you away?'

'I climbed the church belfry –'

'Well, that's hardly –'

'– and muffled the bells. Then – I can't think now how I dared – I climbed on to the roof where I sat pelting those below with apples. I believe I was feeling at odds with the world at the time. Strangely, I can't remember what grievance I had. Anyway, I found I couldn't get down again and it was some hours before I was rescued. My mother was distraught. Of course, Emmaline and Marianne were too young to realize what a scamp their brother was. There was the devil of a row. Father wrote to Micklethwaite and off I went.'

Which explains, thought Francis, why the mother and sisters are so much more – Francis hesitated over the thought – more *genteel* than Napier. A capital chap, beyond doubt, but one who was inclined to say whatever brutal truth came into his head, something no man of breeding would do. No wonder three gently nurtured females were a trifle afraid of him.

'How long did you stay with Micklethwaite?'

'Two years. I could stand no more. Then I ran away to London and began my career in the drapery business. By the time father died five years ago and I came home to Bury St Edmunds to look after my mother and sisters, I had a chain of sixteen drapery shops which I sold. By the way, I'm telling you this in confidence. My shopkeeping past is no business of Hertfordshire citizens.'

'I would not dream of mentioning it to anyone, I assure you,' said Francis earnestly. He was not sure he wanted to know of it, himself. To be associated with a successful maltster in the heart of malting country was one thing. But he had not realized that Napier had ever been a damned draper! 'We're almost there,' he said with relief.

The road curved down the hill to north Hoddesdon, then rose steeply again towards the hamlet's principal inn, the Bull, in the High Street. Unlike Hertford, Hoddesdon's main thoroughfare couldn't boast paved walkways nor gas street-lamps. The only structure of any interest was the yellow brick clock tower and that was somewhat spoiled by the wooden building that sagged against it.

Trees in yellowy spring leaf lined the road, now deserted but soon to be brought to life; in the distance a coach from London was approaching at speed, all its outside seats unoccupied. The guard raised his horn and blew a melodious warning just as Napier pulled over to the left side of the road and drew to a halt before a rather attractive small Georgian house, its plaster walls painted the colour widely known as Suffolk pink.

'What a dreary little village,' said Napier, tying the reins to a post. 'I prefer a town of some sophistication like Hertford or

6

with soundly based wealth like Ware. I think my brain would rot if I were ever exiled to this peasants' retreat.'

Francis hid a smile. He had just been thinking that Hoddesdon fitted Gray's description of a village 'far from the madding crowd's ignoble strife', where the inhabitants 'kept the noiseless tenor of their way'. He made no comment. His temperament and Napier's were so different that they could never agree on such matters. He also doubted that Napier had ever read Gray's *Elegy in a Country Churchyard*. He couldn't imagine this man of business having the patience to read poetry at all.

The brass furniture on the Widow Hobart's door was highly polished and the front step stoned to whiteness. Nevertheless, Napier's keen eyes spotted several rotting glazing bars in a ground-floor window. Both the windows and their frames needed painting and he even saw – when he looked upwards – that two panes of glass on the first floor had been boarded up! So the lady was hard-pressed? Very well, he would not offer forty pounds for her land. He would propose paying her thirty and raise his price only if necessary.

The door was opened by a surly man, out of livery, who was not even wearing a coat. They were expected; the servant gave them an indifferent greeting, relieved them of their hats and gloves and showed them into the sitting-room.

'Mr Drummond and Mr Babcock,' he announced curtly and closed the door on them.

The room was not large by the standards of Napier's own home, but it was of a respectable size with large windows overlooking a long garden that Napier could see needed the attentions of a gardener. It was a second or two before he took his eyes from the view outdoors and focused them on his hostess. When he did so he experienced a considerable shock.

The Widow Hobart was not above five feet tall and so delicately built that even without tight lacing her waist must have measured no more than eighteen inches. A white lace widow's cap with its flowing white veiling behind sat on sleek yellow hair which was centre-parted and drawn down over her ears before being confined to a bun at the nape of her neck. She was apparently in the second stage of mourning; the fashionably-cut dress was not completely covered in swathes of dull crêpe. The low neckline, closely moulded bodice ending in a point just below the waist at the front, the billowed skirt and tight sleeves with their white 'weeper' cuffs completed the widow's weeds which suited this particular widow very well.

Neither the yards of black material nor the solemn expression of the lady could disguise the fact that the Widow Hobart was not much more than twenty-one or two.

'Good morning, gentlemen, won't you come in and be seated?'

Francis Babcock had been paralysed by surprise but now started forward, only to remember his place and wave Napier ahead of him.

Napier negotiated the large circular table by the front window, skirted the several heavily padded chairs and their accompanying footstools, neatly avoided cannoning into the glass-fronted china cabinet and reached the safety of the open space in front of the fireplace having, with clever footwork, taken care not to be tripped up by the fringed hearthrug.

He introduced himself and Francis curtly, then sat down in the low, soft chair indicated, only stumbling slightly over the footstool which, like its sisters, was beautifully embroidered in Berlin wools. The empty grate was hidden by a folding fan of brass and the mantelpiece was decently clothed in white linen with a lace fringe similar to the sort of things his mother was for ever working on. Resting on the mantelshelf was a particularly ugly collection of vases heavily ornamented with three-dimensional china flowers.

When Mrs Hobart went immediately to the embroidered bell-pull, his heart sank. Surely not afternoon tea at half-past two! He had dined little more than an hour ago on a pint of McMullen's best pale, a quarter of a pound of cheese and several slices of fresh bread. He was not hungry. Besides, as both a repast and a ritual, afternoon tea revolted him. All he wanted was to obtain the lady's signature and remove himself from this stifling room with all possible speed.

'Your letter said you wished to discuss a matter of business with me, Mr Drummond,' said Mrs Hobart softly, her pale eyes studying him with candour. 'But you didn't say what business, so I'm afraid I've no papers to hand –'

8

'Oh, don't give it a thought, ma'am,' said Napier. How frail she looked! 'Babcock, will you hand me . . . '

Francis handed over the sheet of folded paper and Napier looked back at the lady with what he hoped was a reassuring smile. 'It is simply that I have recently bought a derelict maltinghouse in Ware which I shall be developing into – which I shall be developing. For some years, your late husband owned a single acre of land on the same road, slightly less than an acre to be exact. It has never been developed, is waste ground, in fact. Now, I'm willing to take this land off your hands for . . . ah . . . twenty-five pounds just to tidy things up a bit. If you will just sign –'

The door opened and a poker-faced young girl entered with a large silver tray containing all the trappings of the tea ritual. Mrs Hobart stood up and walked over to yet another table, plush-covered, which rested against the wall at the garden end of the house. The maid set down the tray and left.

'Milk and sugar, Mr Drummond?'

'Just milk please.'

'Milk and sugar, Mr Babcock?'

'Yes, please,' said Francis, rising to his feet to pass the cups.

Napier received his tea from Francis and finished it in one go. He was not paying a formal call with its strict rules of proper behaviour. This was business and should have been finished by now.

Mrs Hobart helped herself to a cup, stirred it methodically and finally took her seat opposite him.

'Now then, Mrs Hobart –'

'Oh, but you have finished your tea. I'll get you some more.'

'No, I –' But Mrs Hobart stood up, set down her cup, removed his from his hand before he could properly protest and walked to the table. This time, before returning the cup, she picked up a small tripod table to move it close to his chair. Both men half rose to help, found they were too late and sat down again. Napier's cup and saucer were placed on the table. Mrs Hobart picked up her own cup and sat down.

'Forgive me, Mr Drummond, do continue.'

'Well –'

The door opened and the sullen maid re-entered, this time carrying a three-tiered cake-stand. Plates and napkins were

9

passed. Sandwiches and cakes were offered. To Napier's fury, Francis took his time before choosing a small cake. Napier, weighing the pros and cons of taking anything, out of politeness finally chose a sandwich and put it on his plate, vowing not to touch it until the lady's signature was drying on the paper.

'I'm afraid I don't understand,' Mrs Hobart said, looking at him in her candid way when the maid had departed and she was once more seated.

Napier leaned forward with the paper, and with uncharacteristic clumsiness knocked over the tripod table. The tea soaked into the carpet at once, the sandwich fell open revealing its cress interior and, inevitably, one slice landed butter-side down.

Mrs Hobart rose and jerked on the bell-pull. 'It really doesn't matter at all, Mr Drummond,' she said in response to his repeated apologies. 'Do leave everything just where it is. Only the cup handle is broken off and I'm sure Saul can mend it.'

Napier subsided into his chair, thinking gloomily that the day had not begun well. He gazed out of the window while the maid cleaned up the mess. Francis droned on in his well-bred way about the pattern of the cup, the best way to repair broken china and other cups he had known which had been successfully glued together again.

At last they were alone. 'We must not take up more of your time, Mrs Hobart,' said Napier crisply and shifted his feet as if he fully intended to stand up and depart.

'But you were telling me about this land my husband owned. Do continue. I know nothing about it. Mr Hobart never discussed business matters with me.'

'Have you no sons – that is, perhaps your husband had a family before –'

'Mr Hobart was a widower of twenty years. His only son died ten years before I met him, and we had no children. The land you speak of does indeed belong to me.'

'Well then. This really is a simple matter. I will pay you thirty pounds for less than an acre of land you didn't know you possessed.'

'You said twenty-five.'

'I know, but on reflection I think the land is worth thirty. I

10

have the money with me. You can send me the deed whenever you come across it.' He unfolded the agreement. 'Here, do you see? You just write Mrs . . . ah . . . I don't know your first name . . . ' He looked up; she looked back.

'No, you don't.'

'Well, anyway, Mrs Something Hobart. Just here, please.' She took the agreement but didn't look at it. 'I wonder why.'

'Because we must have it in writing that you are selling me the land,' he said with as much patience as he could manage. 'That is the way business is properly transacted.'

'I meant, I wonder why you want to buy this land? You say you have bought a derelict malthouse. There are dozens of malthouses in . . .' She frowned at him, suddenly suspicious. 'There isn't a malthouse on my property, is there?'

'No, of course not! Do you suppose I would try to purchase a plot of land with a building on it for thirty pounds?'

She smiled sweetly. 'Your first offer was twenty-five pounds. But no, I don't suppose you would do such a thing. I'm sorry, I believe you still haven't told me why you want to purchase my land.'

'Well, you were only getting five pounds a year as rent from Mr Cass . . . ' began Francis helpfully. He tailed off in embarrassment when Napier cast him a malevolent look.

'So that is why I received a bank draft for five pounds last year!'

Napier looked at the Widow Hobart carefully, noticing the delicate nose, the faint, arched brows. Was she a feather-brained little innocent or a shrewd woman of business who realized that she had him in a cleft stick? Something about the smile that played around her lips caused him to decide that she was mocking him. He stood up abruptly.

'Of course, I could offer you more money, Mrs Hobart, but I am persuaded that it won't serve. If you will just return the paper . . . '

Mrs Hobart stood up in one graceful motion and began folding the document along its original creases. 'I intend to think about it for a day or two.' Ignoring Napier's outstretched hand, she placed the agreement on the mantelshelf and rang the bell.

'How kind of you to call, gentlemen. And you mustn't

11

worry about the cup, Mr Drummond. I'm sure it can be repaired.' Relentlessly, she shepherded them towards the door where the manservant was waiting for them with their hats and gloves.

Napier and Francis silently took their places in the carriage and Napier wheeled round so that they could head for Hertford at a dangerously brisk pace. Neither man spoke for several minutes.

'Sybilla,' said Francis after a while.

'I beg your pardon?'

'Sybilla. Mrs Sybilla Hobart is her name.'

'You knew her first name and said nothing?'

'But the lady obviously didn't want you to know it,' protested Francis. 'And you didn't wish me to speak. What could I do?'

'Remember which side your bread is buttered on,' said Napier savagely. 'You did speak, after all. You told her Cass was paying her five pounds a year.'

'But that was only fair.'

'Fair? Do you realize what . . . Listen to me, Francis. You are either my friend or my foe. I will not allow you to take the neutral ground. That woman deliberately chose to discomfit me, which is a fine business tactic, but hardly the action of a poor defenceless widow. If she wishes to deal in a man's world, she must be prepared to sacrifice her finer feelings – or see them sacrificed for her.'

Napier pulled on the reins and wheeled the horse and carriage round on the Ware Road.

'You're not going back?'

'I'm going to Lord Lane. You did say that Hobart's coach-building business is there, didn't you?'

Napier turned right, down Lord Lane, at a spanking pace and drew to an abrupt halt when he saw a faded sign saying 'O. Hobart, coach-builder'. He handed the reins to Francis and jumped down on to the road. 'Wait here.'

The building had large green wooden doors along the roadside which had been folded open to allow the sun and spring air to penetrate the gloomy depths of the single lofty room. Three men were sitting in a corner, but one slowly rose at sight of Napier and came forward.

12

'I'm Mr Puddifoot, manager of Hobart's, sir,' said a fat-bellied, florid man in greasy gaiters, open shirt and waistcoat. 'May I be of service?'

'Possibly. I might wish to have a pony phaeton built in double-quick time. Could you handle the work?'

'Oh, yes sir. We've nothing else on at the moment. If I could know the specifications . . . '

'I shall write to you with all the details,' said Napier and headed for the phaeton.

'Won't you give me your name?' called Mr Puddifoot, but Napier gave no sign of having heard him.

'No business in hand,' he said triumphantly to Francis as he turned the carriage once more and headed for Hertford. 'She will be eager for my money. Send for the pipes and other equipment for the malthouse. Delay will cost us dearly. I shall let Mrs Sly Boots consider my offer for about a week. She will be happy enough in the end to accept thirty pounds.'

'In all probability, Hobart's normally have all the business they can handle,' protested Francis. 'There must be twenty or thirty coaches stopping at Hoddesdon's inns every day, which would provide sufficient work for a small coach-builder capable of doing running repairs.'

'Not enough. And there can be few enough inhabitants of Hoddesdon or its neighbour, Broxbourne, wealthy enough to invest in more than one carriage. The gentry will place their orders with a more fashionable establishment. I don't doubt that the firm is under threat. Hoddesdon is a coaching town, remember. It serves no other purpose and is already past its peak. The railway station in Broxbourne is – what? – a mile and a half away. In another year or two, when the railway reaches Hertford, passengers will board at Shoreditch and bypass that little hamlet altogether. I daresay most of the inns are already relying on short distance trade from Broxbourne station to destinations not yet covered by the Northern and Eastern. Who would choose to spend two hours shaken about in a coach at twopence a mile when the "Puffing Billy" will do the journey in forty-five minutes for as low as one shilling and sixpence? No, I have no worries about Mrs Hobart. She will sell and at my price. It's a fair one. She will be joining the women in the workhouse if she does not.'

Francis didn't reply. The meeting with Mrs Hobart had not gone as planned and one could never predict how Napier would react to being thwarted – with his ready temper or his ready wit. Apparently this fiery man's sense of humour had deserted him today, and Francis knew well enough when to keep his mouth shut. He sat thinking about Napier Drummond as a draper. There was something not quite right there. Francis could not picture Napier as an unctuous shop assistant, even at sixteen. The mystery of his employer's fortune remained.

'What sort of name is Sybilla?' said Napier as they reached Hertford Heath. 'A stupid name. I've always hated it. It's like a hiss. A suitable name, however, for such an insipid looking woman. Nothing to her. Nothing at all. A sparrow masquerading as a blackbird.'

'I thought she was rather pretty,' said Francis, then wisely added, 'but now that you mention it . . . '

2

Sybilla stood in the sitting-room right where the two men had left her and took a deep, ragged breath, then another, but she couldn't stop the fury that was making her entire body shake. She watched them enter their carriage and drive away and still she stood, unable to control the sense of outrage that had her in its grip. The nape of her neck was tingling, a tightening of the skin that spread upwards and outwards until her entire scalp felt as if it were too small for her skull. Clear indication that she had needed every ounce of restraint to keep smiling, to control her voice, to prevent herself from screaming and attacking that overbearing man who had swaggered into her drawing-room and ordered her to sign a piece of paper without even offering a proper explanation of where exactly this small piece of land was. Some place or other in or near Ware. He had behaved as if he were doing her a favour, but her slightest hesitation had increased the offering price by five pounds. Did he think she was a total fool? Of course he did.

She turned back towards the fireplace to have a closer look at the agreement, pushing past the furniture that carried her endless items of needlework, those symbols of her hours of confinement. Four years of tending to the wishes of a sick, demanding old man followed by sixteen months of waiting out the enforced seclusion and idleness of a conventional mourning.

She avoided the area round the chair where Mr Drummond had been sitting just as if he were still there radiating power, assurance and contempt for women, reeking of manliness and the knowledge that he could take whatever he wished. It made her weak to think of him and she would certainly not sit in that chair again. Ever.

The thick paper of the agreement crackled as she unfolded it. It was couched in the sort of legal language that was intended to trap helpless women, but at least it told her that the land was in French Horn Lane. She had seldom visited Ware, near as it was, but she knew French Horn Lane. There was an inn by that name.

15

She neatly refolded the agreement, laid it back on the mantelpiece and began to gather the tea-things. Mr Babcock's cup, saucer, plate and crumpled napkin sat sedately on an occasional table. Strangely, his aura had disappeared with him, an insubstantial man whose features she could not now recall. Fair, dark, smiling, sad? She couldn't remember and it didn't matter.

She looked back at Mr Drummond's chair. Yes, his ghost still crouched there, mocking her. What was the matter with her? She could never remember having met a man whose nearness revolted her so much, not even Mr Hobart's. *His* ghost had been laid to rest with him. Was she now to be haunted by a complete stranger who was bursting with life?

Mr Drummond's clothes were obviously expensive. That waisted frock-coat of blue superfine, the grey-striped trousers held taut by a strap under his instep, the garish yellow waistcoat and black stock might be fashionable wear for a rich man, but on him they looked vulgar. His features were large and coarse, his sideburns too long, although not long enough to hide a brown mole at the angle of his jawbone. Of course, his mouth was too full; he had a most unbecoming small scar running into his upper lip on the left side. No wonder she had taken only the briefest glance at him and been forced to avert her eyes thereafter!

She wondered if Mr Drummond had any idea how much thirty pounds meant to her. Her widow's jointure was one hundred pounds a year and the business had yielded just fifty pounds profit in the past twelve months. A house of this size with three servants seemed to swallow money. Furthermore, she was obliged to send her mother forty pounds a year so that her brother, Robert, could continue his studies in a solicitor's office. That left her just a hundred and ten pounds to pay the servants' wages, heat, light and maintain the home and feed four people – five, if one counted her maid's little daughter, Fanny.

To be given thirty pounds for a piece of land she hadn't known she possessed would lift an intolerable burden and remove a constant source of worry for an entire year. But why not more? Whatever he might think, Mr Drummond would not get her signature on any agreement for less than *forty* pounds.

The pressure in her head was growing; she must get out of this stifling room into the open air. She went into the hall and took up the ugly bonnet with its yards of black veiling, put on the dull black cotton gloves, shrouded herself in the heavy black shawl.

'I'm going to walk over to the workshop,' she said to Cissy who was coming to clear the tea-things. 'I won't be gone long.'

'Shall I come with you, madam?'

'No, carry on with what you are doing. Open the windows and air the drawing-room. I thought it was a trifle stuffy in there.'

The veil reached her elbows, cutting out the sunlight, dimming the colours of spring and hiding her supposed grief from prying eyes. Grief. Dear God!

Her mother and brother had bullied her into marriage with a hideous old man she had met but twice. Mr Hobart, who had rented a set of rooms facing the sea for the sake of his health, had found his way into the Cart and Horses on his very first evening in Portsmouth. There Robert had befriended him, and within the month was congratulating himself on having found a husband for his sister. The old man wanted a bride, Robert had informed her one evening. Hobart wouldn't live long; it was the perfect match.

Sybilla had hated the idea of marrying any chance acquaintance of Robert's. But think of the financial security, they had said, the fine dresses and fancy parties! And remember your duty to your poor, ailing widowed mother and your younger brother who must be given a chance in life. How selfish of you not to marry this decent man when it would be such a help to your family. Worn down by their arguments, she had finally agreed.

After the wedding, Mr Hobart had brought her directly to this pretty house which was at least three times the size of her old home in a main street in Portsmouth. But from the first, she had hated it because it belonged to Mr Hobart, because it was the house he had shared with his first wife, and because it was to be her prison.

Fortunately, her immediate response to Hoddesdon had

been quite different. The old village was quiet, clean, very pretty and surprisingly friendly. Any number of genteel men and women had come to call on the new bride, welcoming her and, she chose to think, feeling some sympathy for her plight; Mr Hobart was known to be eccentric. Before her new husband had become bedridden, there had been "at homes", dinners, dances and card parties to attend which a girl from a poor home had found wonderfully exciting and certainly some consolation for a hated arranged marriage. But Mr Hobart refused to entertain in his turn, even, towards the end, to allow morning callers. Gradually, she had become isolated. Who could blame these kind folk for reacting to repeated snubs and leaving the Hobarts to their own company?

When Mr Hobart died, everyone had been most kind. But the first year of her widowhood had imposed quite different restrictions on her movements, leaving her too much time to brood. At least there was a time limit to her present imprisonment. Already, the burden was lightening. If she behaved herself and controlled her rebellious nature, she might one day be allowed to take her modest place in Hoddesdon society. If, that is, she could maintain her social position by continuing to live in Hornbeam House, retain three servants and return the hospitality of those kind families who, presumably, would one day entertain her.

Mr Hobart had given little thought to her future except to make out a will in her favour – and that had been part of the terms of the wedding agreement. Her financial position was precarious.

The black wool absorbed the sun's warmth and she allowed the shawl to slide off her shoulders. Her petticoats were all stiffened and the one next to her legs was of red flannel which caught against the lisle stockings, forcing her to walk slowly and decorously whether she wanted to or not.

Mr Puddifoot was standing by the road enjoying the day, his greasy hands clasped behind his back. He saw his employer walking towards him and raised his dusty hat in greeting.

'Afternoon, Mrs Hobart. Fine day.'

'Yes, it is, Mr Puddifoot. Have there been any new orders?'

'As a matter of fact, a gentleman stepped in only a moment ago. You just missed him. He said he wanted a pony phaeton buildin' in double-quick time. His very words. Double-quick time.'

'Why, that's wonderful and such a relief! It's worrying to see the men idle. They've not had anything to do for the past few days, I believe.'

'I've kept them busy with odd jobs,' said Puddifoot complacently. 'They're just having a short rest.'

'When must the phaeton be finished? Is the customer someone I know?'

'Oh, it was just an enquiry, ma'am. He said he'd send me the specifications so's I could quote.'

'You will take care to give a proper quote.'

'Got to be competitive, Mrs Hobart.'

'Yes, but the last time you made a phaeton we actually lost money.'

'If you're not satisfied with the way I've been doing things after all these years –'

'No, no, I'm quite satisfied, Mr Puddifoot. What was the gentleman's name?'

'Didn't leave a name.'

'I see.' Sybilla bit her lip. She was twenty-four years old and well aware that she looked younger. She was also totally inexperienced in running a business or controlling employees. She was not, however, insensitive to her fellow creatures. There had been ample opportunity to study mankind and all its weaknesses in spite of the constricted life she had led; she could detect a lie or a brutish will no matter how cleverly such things might be concealed.

Looking at her manager, who was never quite sober, she knew without doubt that she was being cheated. The trouble was she didn't know how he was cheating her nor what to do about it. She gazed at his red face, the small eyes squinting against the brightness of the day and, for the second time this morning, felt overwhelmed by her helplessness, her inability to control any facet of her life. She had been taught to give way, to listen to the opinions of those older and wiser than herself, to say nothing.

'Good day, Mr Puddifoot,' she said dully and turned back towards High Street.

The Misses Harriet and Arabella Sams had a small chemist

and druggist business in the High Street, just three doors from her home. Out of sisterly feeling for two hard-working women, Sybilla gave them all her business. They greeted her with their usual kindness and enquiries after her health, two spinsters in their forties who still retained the air of innocent girls.

Sybilla bought a few grains of laudanum and then, because the sisters were also booksellers, stationers, silversmiths, purveyors of postage stamps and owners of a small lending library, she lingered awhile. She bought a stamp for the letter to her mother that she had just completed and chose a book to borrow. Sybilla had a great deal of time for reading.

She gave the laudanum to Saul when she returned home, with instructions that Cissy should put it safely away with the other medicines. Then she went to her husband's desk in the morning-room and unlocked the drawer that held his papers. The deed was right where it should be, of course, together with other letters pertaining to the land and a plan showing the exact location of the plot in relation to the road and other properties, all tied into a bundle with red silk ribbon.

She rang for Saul. 'I want you to drive me to Ware, please. I have some business to attend to.'

'I'm just working in the vegetable garden,' said Saul mutinously.

'It's going to be fine and dry all day. You can work in the garden when we return.'

'I'm never going to get it all finished as it is, madam. This is the first dry day we've had in weeks.'

Their eyes locked for several seconds, then Sybilla sighed. 'Harness the horse to the gig. I'll drive myself.'

Saul smiled slightly, hiding his sense of triumph as best he could. 'Cissy can go with you, ma'am.'

'Very well and I'll take the child, too.'

'Oh, that ain't necessary. She can stay with her gran.'

Sybilla narrowed her eyes. 'I said I will take Fanny as well. The ride will do her good. Please tell Cissy to get her dressed straight away.'

Saul nodded and backed off. Having got his own way over the gardening, he was prepared to let his daughter's brat have a ride in Mrs Hobart's carriage. That didn't matter one way or

20

the other. Just so long as young madam knew who ruled this house.

Cissy and her two-year-old daughter had not spoken during the twenty-five minute drive to Ware, and Sybilla could be sure that they wouldn't make a sound on the return journey. Mother and daughter seemed to live in a state of trance. The child was excessively quiet for a two-year-old and was today very heavy-eyed, causing Sybilla to suspect that Cissy kept her little girl sedated with Godfrey's cordial. Fanny was illegitimate and Saul could not tolerate the sight of her. The child's docility was probably her best protection against violence.

Ware was four or five miles due north of Hoddesdon and two miles east of Hertford, but the three towns had only brewing and the river Lea in common. Hertford was twice the size of the other two. Ware and Hoddesdon each had about two thousand inhabitants, but what a difference in atmosphere between the two places!

Hoddesdon was somnolent; Ware was always busy, the greatest malting town in the whole country. Its narrow High Street was never free of the huge equipages that transported the malt. Eight shire horses were needed to pull the wagons whose wheels gouged the surface of even the finest of Mr McAdam's roads.

Sybilla, an indifferent whip, nervously negotiated the horse and gig past one of these monsters and was greatly relieved to find a place near the French Horn where she could draw up for a while. She knew exactly which piece of land belonged to her, thanks to the map in Mr Hobart's effects, and now stared through the black veil at it in considerable surprise.

'Excuse me,' she said to a workman. 'Where are those bricks going?'

'To fix up that there malthouse, ma'am. Mr Drummond's just bought it and it's in a dangerous state. Goin' to be nobody knows what.'

Sybilla looked up at the building, all of seventy feet long with small windows set in ranks every six feet or so up its huge side. The kiln at one end was cone-shaped, reaching up perhaps as much as a hundred feet and topped by a white wooden cowl which was badly in need of paint. There were dozens of such structures in Ware and their owners were invariably rich men.

Without a word, she turned the gig and headed back to Hoddesdon. Fanny was asleep by the time they reached the stable; Cissy carried her indoors. Sybilla called sharply to Saul to attend to the horse and went into the house and up the stairs to her room.

It was a little before four o'clock and the western sunlight was flooding into the room, its brilliance bouncing off the long mirror. She had already thrown back her veil and now untied the bonnet strings to toss the hated thing on to the bed.

Standing before the looking-glass, she studied the widow who had been Sybilla Sutherland. A small woman who had listened for so many years to comparisons between herself and her brother that now she fully believed she was stupid, lazy, rebellious and ungrateful, while Robert was hard-working, clever and ordained by fate to bring credit to the family.

And as she looked at herself, the image of Sybilla Hobart, née Sutherland, disappeared from the glass. Just disappeared as if she no longer existed. She turned her head and looked fully at the dressing-table. Now it was gone, but her peripheral vision showed her a mirrored Sybilla in profile.

She closed her eyes, wanting to cry, fingers pressing on her temples. *Oh, no, not today*! But what was the use? A flash of red lightning, glimpsed out of the corner of her left eye on this cloudless day, sent her flying to the bell-pull. *Quick, Cissy, before the pain begins*!

The tight bodice hooked up the back. She couldn't get out of it without help, but she could manage the skirt. She unhooked it feverishly and flung it on to a chair. The petticoats next, one by one, puddling the floor. Auras of red light stabbed her left eyeball. She sat on the bed to take off her boots, already dizzy. Was that Cissy on the stairs? When the door opened, she was fully dressed from the waist up, wearing only her drawers and shift below the black bodice.

'Oh, ma'am,' cried Cissy. 'Shall I get the laudanum?'

'Yes, hurry.'

She tore off the white widow's cap, tugged at the dozens of pins that held her hair. Already the fingers of her left hand

22

were tingling, but that other Sybilla Hobart had returned to the looking-glass, very much the image of the helpless fool she felt herself to be. She was nauseated, but she wouldn't be sick; she never was, although she often thought it would be a relief.

By the time Cissy returned with the laudanum drops dissolved in water, the pain had enveloped one side of her head. It was centred on her left eye but throbbed in her ear and cheekbone, making her teeth ache.

'The curtains,' she murmured, screwing her eyes against the light, but Cissy said she had to be able to see to unfasten the bodice first, and began with deft fingers to release her mistress from the black bodice and finally the boned corset beneath.

Naked but for her shift and drawers, Sybilla waited for Cissy to turn down the bed, to shape the pillows into a back-rest with great thumps of her hands that sounded like thunderclaps.

Slowly, carefully, Sybilla lowered herself on to the bed, reclining against the four pillows, resting her head against the harsh linen with infinite care, gritting her teeth as the coverlet was rasped up to her chin. The rattle of the curtain rings was agony, but darkness brought relief of a sort. The door closed and she was alone with her tormentor, the beast who ravished one half of her head while leaving the other half untouched.

The air of unreality that always accompanied these attacks removed her from the quiet darkness of her own bedroom and plunged her into a boiling cauldron of thoughts, fears and impressions. All the stored-up, sealed-off, shut-away thoughts that never saw the light on good days.

Mr Hobart on their wedding night revisited her, wheezing loudly. *I shan't bother you with all that business. I'm a sick old man. You just look after me and we'll get along fine.* But she'd had to share a bed with him all the long years until he was too ill to bear her tossing and turning next to him. She'd had to endure all the casual touching and tangling of limbs of two people sleeping on four feet of feather bedding.

Mr Puddifoot and Saul made their appearances as she slept, or perhaps during her waking moments; it was hard to tell. In any case, they both displayed to the full the same insolence, that determination to have their own way which frustrated her at every turn.

The hours passed, the daylight faded. Cissy brought her a jug of water and another dose of laudanum. The silent girl turned a lamp down as low as it would go, then put it out of her mistress's line of vision. She said good night in a whisper, uncomfortable to find herself in the same room with one so strangely afflicted.

Eventually, the pain eased as it always did. Sybilla slept deeply, dreamed that Mr Drummond, in a nightshirt like the one Mr Hobart always wore, was climbing into the bed beside her. She woke with a gasp and sat up to look round in terror. A split second later a dagger-blow stabbed her eye and she subsided against the pillows, shaken, disturbed, but in too much pain to ease herself with tears. Then she slept again, mercifully free from dreams.

In the kitchen the Potters – Saul, Cissy and Saul's wife, Mary – sat down to dinner. Fanny was already asleep and the three adults ate largely in silence.

Mary Potter was thirty-eight. She had never cared much for prettying herself up and thought her daughter's obsession with personal cleanliness was an indication that she had ideas above her station. Mary thought it wise to give a warning about grand ideas. *You be grateful for what you've got*, she'd say to the silent girl once or twice a week. *A girl what's got a byblow to bring up is lucky to get any position, let alone a nice place working for a family like the Hobarts*. And Cissy would nod her head and walk away so that her mother never knew if the girl had taken in a word she said.

Mrs Potter was a good cook and an extremely canny shopper, so she was able to steal a shilling or two from the housekeeping each week without Mrs Hobart suspecting a thing.

Saul grew more vegetables than they needed, but what he got for selling the rest usually went on drink. Being always drunk was why he'd been laid off from the Salisbury Arms a few years back. He'd been an ostler, but this position was better, as he never tired of telling her. They could all have been perfectly happy here if Saul hadn't taken against little Fanny.

Cissy had sworn she'd been raped by a street trader named Jack Dark when she was working up in London. But the magistrates hadn't believed her because Dark swore she'd been willing. He was a comparatively respectable married man who smiled a lot, and the magistrates had mistrusted the word of a dab of a girl with a sullen face and no good looks to speak of.

She had lost her place, of course, and had to come home. Saul didn't believe her story of having been raped, and to be perfectly honest neither did Mary, although she never said so.

'You say she's still got the headache?' asked Saul, wiping his mouth on the back of his hand.

'She won't be better this night,' said Cissy.

Mary served up more potatoes. 'She should have a cloth on her head wrung out in vinegar. I never heard of anyone having headaches like that woman does.'

Cissy had never heard of it either. She was genuinely grateful to Mrs Hobart for taking her in, and had never told her parents the odd things Mrs Hobart said about seeing flashing lights and funny things. Mrs Hobart had made a rag doll and had once sewn a complete set of Sunday-best clothes for Fanny. It was after the old man had died and Mrs Hobart had said she did it because she was bored. But it was the finest thing anyone had ever done for Cissy. Nor had madam's kindness ended there.

Most of all, Cissy was grateful for being allowed to have a follower. When Jefferson Smith had come to work at the Bull where he was an ostler, it had been no time at all before he met her father. Papa drank his porter at the Bull most nights and always too much. Jefferson had brought her father home one night, had carried the unconscious man over his shoulder like a sack of barley. He and Cissy had liked one another straight away. Her father said she was nothing but a whore, out after a new man before she had finished suckling the last man's slip on the shoulder.

For once, Cissy had stood up for herself. Jefferson Smith meant too much to be allowed to slip through her fingers just because of her father. She had gone straight to Mrs Hobart and asked if she could have a follower and Mrs Hobart had said yes, of course, and what Fanny really needed was a father and maybe things would work out so that they could get married. So that was why Cissy never talked about her mistress's queer turns. Her folks would surely think madam was crazy.

25

In the morning Sybilla woke up, her shoulders tensed. Sometimes the first few seconds of wakefulness were mercifully free of pain and then it all came back with a sickening rush. She blinked her eyes and waited. It was all right, so she got up and tottered to the curtains. Another beautiful day and she was ravenous.

She rang the bell, knowing that Cissy would bring up tea and bread and honey. A bath would refresh her. She hadn't had so many of these bad turns since Mr Hobart died, but one day of sickening pain could destroy her confidence for weeks, making her nervous about going anywhere for fear the beast would attack her away from the seclusion and safety of her own home.

It had happened once, many years ago in Portsmouth. She and her mother had been at a small party. There had not been many parties in the young Sybilla's life and this one had been very special. They had hardly arrived before she had begun to feel very ill. Everyone had been afraid that her white face and strange behaviour signalled the onslaught of some infectious disease. Mrs Sutherland had been forced to take the girl home immediately, and had railed about it to Sybilla for weeks.

When Cissy had brought the breakfast tray and gone off to fetch the enamel bath, Sybilla poured herself a cup of tea and drank it quickly. Bliss! She was fully recovered now, the hot drink had made her whole. And the first thought that came into the mind of the whole Sybilla was about Napier Drummond.

In their separate ways, Mr Puddifoot and Saul could defy her, but there was a limit to how far they could take their defiance and both men knew it. It was a trying situation which would not get better, but would not be allowed to get worse.

Napier Drummond was another matter. He could be the victim of her resentment against all men because she was in an ideal position to thwart him. What a pleasure it would be to take some sort of revenge on a man who had seriously disturbed her. And the brilliance of the scheme was that she didn't have to place herself in his terrifying presence in order to make him suffer. She could achieve her ends by letter. But oh, how she wished she could be a fly on the wall, to see his face, watch him descend into a rage as he realized what she had

26

done. She would get just what she wanted from this wealthy man of business who was unaccustomed to being denied anything by anyone at all.

Napier stood by the window in his office watching a cart drive down St Andrew's Street.

'Babcock!'

The door opened, but he didn't look round. 'Read this.' He held out a letter and Babcock came over to take it from him.

It was from Mrs Hobart and it said quite simply that all goods and materials must cease forthwith to be carried across Hobart property to the malthouse now owned by Napier Drummond and Co. Ltd.

Babcock experienced the truth of the expression 'to go cold all over'.

'My God!' he said, his mind grasping at straws. 'But wait! Business at the malthouse has travelled to and fro across that land for years without let or hindrance. Perhaps we could –'

Still without turning round, Napier held out another letter and Francis reached for it reluctantly. This one proved to be a carefully written copy of a legal document. Oswald Hobart, it transpired, had yearly entered into an agreement with the previous owners of the malthouse, John Cass and Sons, for the right to cross his land. The sum he had charged for the past twenty years had been five pounds annually, but the agreement was automatically null and void if the malthouse should be sold to anyone else.

Francis passed a hand across his face, devastated. It was his responsibility to check on such matters, to see if there were previous legal agreements, to make sure that when Napier began a negotiation, he was in the strongest possible position. No one knew better than Francis what Mrs Hobart's communication meant. They would have to pull all their men off the malthouse site immediately. The lady could set what terms she wished.

'This is entirely my fault,' he said, 'and I do apologize most humbly, but that doesn't help, does it?'

'Yes, it is your fault and no, apologizing doesn't help. The lady may be willing to enter into a new agreement with us to

27

allow us access for five pounds annually, but somehow I doubt it. We have alerted her to other possibilities. If she fails us, I may be able to persuade Adams to let us cross his land.'

'There isn't sufficient room for a cart. Everything would have to be carried in by hand. Besides, Sam Adams hasn't spoken to you for six months.'

'A misunderstanding. He knows I have a quick temper and don't mean the half of what I say.'

'You called him a fat fool, and since everyone present felt that you had described him to perfection, I don't see —'

Napier turned round to smile wryly at his friend. 'My mother always said my tongue would be my undoing one day. I'm the fool. You're right, of course. We are going to have to deal with the lady and that won't be easy. Did you notice how clumsy I was yesterday?'

Francis, who had developed the art of being deaf and blind when the occasion demanded, now denied that he had noticed anything out of the way. 'And that's not all,' continued Napier. 'I raised the offer for no reason. Did you hear me? Mrs Hobart certainly did. She was on to it in an instant. I underestimated my opponent and I went to her territory instead of inviting her on to mine. She'll bleed me, Francis, and I deserve it.'

'What are you going to do? I know you will think of something clever.'

'At the moment I can't even lick my wound. Who ever heard of being stabbed in the back by a sparrow?'

3

Napier, eating his breakfast alone in the rose-pink morning-room, looked up in surprise as his mother entered wearing a frothy robe and cap of blonde lace, pink ribbons and cream satin. Pointedly, he consulted the clock on the mantelshelf.

'Eight o'clock, Mama! Have you insomnia?'

Mrs Dorothea Drummond was a plump lady in her fifties. Habitually corseted to breathlessness, she looked more attractive than usual this morning in her loosely fitting negligée which disguised her figure while drawing flattering attention to her round cheeks, small nose and blue eyes. No one could describe her these days as pretty, but she had a considerable talent for thinking herself into the part of *grande dame* on occasion, when she could at least *appear* to be quite formidable. Nothing of the *grande dame* about her this morning. Never at her best in her son's presence, she was at this moment looking distraught as she greeted him.

Napier was deeply suspicious. 'May I pour you some coffee? You will surely not wish to eat breakfast at this hour. Will you not return to bed presently?'

'I may, dear. I just thought I would join you for a few minutes.' Mrs Drummond gave a brave smile and, sitting down, took a delicate sip of her coffee.

'I welcome your company, Mama. We haven't seen a great deal of each other lately. It was thoughtful of you to join me this morning.'

Thoughtfulness had nothing to do with it, of course. Mrs Drummond undoubtedly needed some money which she hoped her son would give her. Nothing less important would have dragged her from her bed. He knew her purpose in joining him; she knew that he knew. Nevertheless, they would play out the scene as they had done once or twice a quarter for the past five years.

The door opened again and Napier looked up, expecting the butler. Instead, he saw his two sisters, Marianne and Emmaline, coming towards him, trying with varying degrees of success to look as if they had arisen early quite by chance.

Marianne was twenty-one and bore a slight resemblance to her brother. As dark as he, she had the misfortune to have the same heavy eyebrows and bold features. There was nothing delicate or particularly feminine about her appearance. Fortunately, she was a lively, matter-of-fact girl, capable of appreciating life's little ironies. Napier was very fond of her, proud that so many young men seemed to find her attractive. This morning, however, he glared at her as if she had betrayed his trust. Was Mama marshalling support for her plea of poverty? Quite unnecessary. Napier was not an ogre, therefore his mother did not require the protection or the support of her daughters.

'Don't tell me you just happened to wake early this morning, Marianne.'

This was just what Marianne had intended to claim. She was quick-witted enough to see that the ruse would not serve, however. 'Not at all. I came to join you and Mama, since I knew she planned to breakfast with you.'

Dismayed, Mrs Drummond looked swiftly at Emmaline who was the perfect image of herself at twenty. Emmaline's fair hair was already brushed and pinned into a neat bun. The girl would never appear before her brother with her hair flowing down her back as her sister was doing. A timid girl, Emmaline looked at her brother now as if he were a wild beast and she a helpless maiden about to be devoured. Emmaline invariably brought out Napier's worst side.

'Well, my dear sisters, what do you normally drink for breakfast? Tea or coffee?'

'I prefer tea,' said Marianne, 'but don't trouble yourself. I'll pour my own.'

'I couldn't eat a thing,' said Emmaline.

'You haven't been offered any food,' Napier reminded her coldly.

'I mean I couldn't drink a thing. But . . . I believe I will have a cup of tea after all.' Marianne gave an impatient snort and filled a cup for her sister.

Napier took up his knife and fork, cut into his ham with precise strokes and ate for several seconds while his women-folk watched. When he could bear the silence no longer, he laid down his cutlery with a clatter and sighed loudly. 'Suppose you tell me why you have all gathered this morning. I have a great many things to do and would prefer not to start the day with indigestion.'

'I would not cause you to have indigestion for the world, Napier,' said his mother plaintively.

'I'm sorry, I didn't mean to suggest that you would. But what is the matter? Are you dipped? Is that it?'

'Yes, I've been a trifle extravagant.'

'You have spent your entire allowance so soon after quarter day?'

'A number of pressing bills . . . '

'Bills for what?'

'Well, for a number of necessary items.'

'What items? Can you show me the bills?'

'Don't bully your mother!' said Marianne.

'I? Bully my mother?' asked Napier, as Mrs Drummond murmured that she was certain her son would never do such a thing.

Napier was beginning to feel beleaguered by his family. They did not need to approach him in numbers just because his mother required extra funds. It wasn't as if this were a new departure for her. She always overspent her allowance, was incapable of doing otherwise. He had tried increasing the quarterly sum, but found it made no difference. She spent whatever she was given, and then more. He had the impression that today the entire family had gathered to shame him into unaccustomed generosity, which was most unfair. He was many things, had many faults, but he was not mean. They would discover that this was a poor way to handle the man of the family.

'Will you tell me what you need the money for?'

'Just things,' said Mrs Drummond weakly.

'Will you tell me how much you want me to give you?'

'One – whatever you wish to give your poor mother. You have always been most generous, ever since you came home to us. I'm such a fool . . . '

Mrs Drummond began to cry, which confounded Napier. He had no experience of weeping women. From fourteen years of age, he had spent his life in rougher company, among people

31

who seldom cried even in the face of tragedy. Now here was his
mother weeping daintily over the necessity of asking her
wealthy son for a few pounds. She had adopted several
dramatic poses in her quest for funds over recent years, but
tearfully throwing herself on his charity was a new device. And
quite a disgusting one.

Controlling his anger with difficulty, he folded his table
napkin edge to edge and in half again, matching corners
carefully, and placed it beside his plate. He moved his knife
and fork closer together, lining up the handles exactly. He
turned the handle of his cup until it was perfectly parallel to the
edge of the table. Then, having counted to twenty and finding
himself still angry, he stood up and bared his teeth in a travesty
of a smile.

'I am certain that my sisters have not also spent their
allowances so soon into the quarter. You may borrow from
them, Mama.' He left without another word, without even
bending to give his mother the customary dutiful kiss on the
cheek.

'You would have done better on your own,' said Marianne
quietly when they were alone.

'I know that now, dear. It is easy to be wise after the event.
But I always irritate Napier when I ask him for money. I
thought if you two were present I would be prevented from
saying something foolish and he would hesitate to scold me.'

'Well, at least he didn't scold you,' said Emmaline.

'He also didn't give me any money!'

'I only wish Emmaline and I had enough to give you from
our allowances –'

'A hundred pounds? How could you?'

'Two hundred pounds, Mama,' Marianne reminded her
gently. 'Mr Farley wants you to give him two hundred
pounds.'

It was a rather endearing characteristic of Mrs Drummond's
that she simply refused to acknowledge unpleasant facts. She
didn't want to owe someone two hundred pounds and she was
unable to forget about the debt altogether, so she just forgot
about half of it. Napier, predictably, did not find this an
endearing idiosyncrasy. He found it maddening and often said
as much.

'I am so very tired of these regular contretemps over money,' said Mrs Drummond.

'Then why not exercise a little self-control in future, Mama? Vow never to overspend your allowance again. Show Napier what a nipcheese you can be.'

'Yes, dear. That is a very good notion. And next quarter I will do just that. But in the meanwhile Mr Farley must have the money. Such a simple pleasure! To be part-owner of a troupe of actors when I have been interested in the theatre all my life. If one has responsibilities towards artistes, one must pay up, you know.'

Marianne leaned forward to squeeze her mother's hand as it lay on the cloth. 'Suppose I approach Napier on your behalf. I will tell him about the acting company and your involvement in it. He will pay your debt, I'm sure of it.'

'If you do, I will never speak to you again, Marianne! You must not tell him the reason why I want the money, although I will allow you to plead for me. Surely, you can think up some reasonable excuse why I should want two hundred pounds. If he knew the truth, he would forbid Mr Farley to enter this house, I know it.'

'I'll say you have gambling debts amounting to two hundred pounds. You have paid them off, but now need fresh funds.'

'What are you saying? Napier would never give me any money again. And he would say Florian had led me into bad ways. Florian Farley is the only pleasant man I know. Not that I don't love Napier dearly, but men are so heartless.'

Marianne sat back in her chair; Emmaline poured herself another cup of tea. They knew what was to follow and had heard it many times.

'My father was a stern man and you can be sure I obeyed his every command. And so did my mother. Oh, we knew our places! Then your dear Papa, to whom I gave the best years of my life, sent away my only son to the horrid north and I wasn't even allowed to visit him for two whole years. When that poor desperate boy ran away to London and finally wrote to us, your father refused to ask him to come home. I don't mean to suggest your Papa was a wicked man, you understand, just unable to enter into the feelings of a mother.'

'We understand,' said Marianne.

'I loved him very much,' added Emmaline.

'And he loved us all. So why did he make out a will leaving everything in trust, with Napier as guardian? I am at the mercy of the son your father never wanted to see again.'

'Papa didn't think you would want the worry of attending to your own affairs.'

'Your Papa thought I would be too stupid to conduct my own affairs. And Napier came home to prove to me beyond doubt that I am too stupid. Where am I going to find two hundred pounds?'

'Nowhere. Let Mr Farley pay the money. He was the one who involved you in this scheme.'

'Marianne!'

'Well then, pawn the family jewels.'

'But there isn't a pawnbroker in Hertford and I wouldn't know how to go about it if there were.'

'Marianne was just joking,' said Emmaline wearily.

'Oh, I see. I am boring you both. I do beg your pardon. It is not your worry after all. I think I will return to bed. I'm feeling rather fatigued.'

Mrs Drummond made a martyred exit, downhearted but dignified, not too dramatic, really quite affecting. Marianne mentally applauded her mother's acting skill, torn between sympathy and irritation. What a family we are! she thought.

'I'm hungry. Shall we ring for breakfast?'

'All men are not heartless, thoughtless brutes, surely,' said Emmaline.

'No, and all women are not hopeless about money, but you must admit that the generalities hold good. The more things change, the more they stay the same. Mama is in debt today and she will be in debt next quarter. Napier is angry today and he will be just as angry in a few months' time.'

The door opened and Mrs Drummond re-entered the room. 'I don't know why Napier persists in thinking I am extravagant. He furnished this house from top to bottom. And everything new! Don't you remember? I suggested that some of the curtains from the old house would do in the guest bedrooms, but he insisted on having new ones made.'

'Perfectly true,' said Marianne. 'And I daresay they cost far more than two hundred pounds.'

34

'Well, I don't know if they did because I never saw the accounts, I merely chose the fabric. But, I ask you! Eleven new settees and twenty new armchairs throughout the house. And what about the oak panelling in the library? The room was perfectly acceptable as it was. Now then, wasn't that extravagant?'

'You must tell him so.'

Mrs Drummond smiled. 'I don't think I will, dear. I don't think I would further my cause at all.'

'Oh, please don't criticize Napier,' begged Emmaline. 'He would argue, probably say that he hadn't spent a penny more than he could afford. You two would disagree and we would end with a dreadful quarrel. And you know I can't bear an unpleasant atmosphere.'

'So we will forget I mentioned it. Heigh-ho!' Quite restored to good humour, Mrs Drummond waved her hands in the air and did a little dance step, leaving her daughters laughing at her antics.

'Here she comes!' said Francis with some relief, peering down Ware's High Street. He and Napier had been standing outside the French Horn since eight forty-five this morning on what Francis had increasingly begun to think of as a fool's errand.

But Napier was right as usual. Yesterday Mrs Hobart had refused them permission to cross her land in order to reach their own. Today at nine o'clock she had come to see if her orders were being defied. She was sawing uncertainly on the reins of a small mare as she sat with her maid in a gig that was certainly no advertisement for her coach-building business.

'I knew it,' said Napier, 'come to see if she can catch us out. Stand here by the side of the road. And do try to look anxious. I want her to feel she has the upper hand.'

But she does! thought Francis.

Sybilla Hobart had seen the two men almost as soon as they had seen her, which had a devastating effect on her driving. A flock of sheep being driven down the road was causing difficulties even for wagon drovers. And they, rough men all, were hampering her progress very thoroughly. Cissy was gripping

35

the seat and uttering frightened little mewings which further destroyed Sybilla's concentration.

Mr Babcock and Mr Drummond, she noticed grimly, were maintaining solemn faces. But only with difficulty.

Finally, when it looked as if she would be stuck in Ware's High Street for ever in a sea of fleece, Mr Drummond pushed his way through the panicking sheep to stand on the step of the gig.

'If you will give me the ribbons, I fancy I can get your gig into French Horn Lane, ma'am.'

Without waiting for permission, he took the reins from her grasp and, still standing on the step, deftly coaxed the horse, encouraged the sheep and bullied the drovers out of the way. Sybilla had nothing to do but renew her hatred of the man.

'Good morning, Mr Babcock,' she said when Mr Drummond had helped her to alight. 'I didn't expect to see you here this morning.'

'Hoping you might come, Mrs Hobart,' said the older man quickly, before Babcock could speak. 'Naturally, there are no workmen on the site. However, Mr Babcock and I are desperate to take one last look round the malthouse. A matter of urgency; it's in a dangerous state, you know. My only hope lay in the fact that I was certain a shrewd businesswoman like yourself would come today to see that all is as it should be. May I humbly beg that we may accompany you across your land to reach ours, and that you will be my guest so that I can show you the malthouse whose renovation you are preventing?'

Through her veil, she regarded him cautiously, her heart thudding uncomfortably as if she really were daring to look into the devil's eyes. Had she known he would be here, she would never have ventured out.

'Of course, sir.' She must say as little as possible. The fewer the words, the fewer the opportunities to reveal her ignorance or be caught in some verbal trap. Sybilla had the liveliest respect for Mr Drummond's wickedly devious mind.

Fortunately the ground was dry, but recent rains had softened the earth and she was forced to take Mr Drummond's arm to negotiate Hobart land as they followed cart tracks up to the towering malthouse.

36

Mr Drummond started to open the door, then paused and turned to her. 'It occurs to me, ma'am, that you might prefer to rent your land to me as your husband rented it to Cass. We could come to a better agreement, a slightly larger sum.'

'I'm afraid not, sir. Do let us go in. I've always wanted to see what a malthouse was like,' she said, and immediately wondered if this was exactly the response she had been intended to give. Well, she couldn't help it. What advantage had he gained, anyway? Mentally shrugging, she stepped inside and looked round the eerie, dark stillness of the cavernous building. Empty it might be, but the smell of dried barley clung to every brick.

'Ah!' he said, breathing deeply. 'Smell the malt!'

'Like sour beer.'

'This building has done yeoman service for almost a hundred years. Do you understand the malt-making process?'

'No, I don't –'

'Ma'am, it is too dark in here for it to be safe to wear your veil. Won't you feel free to throw it back? Ah, that's better. Dusty, isn't it? And not much light coming through those louvres. Step over here; mind that piece of timber. At that end was the barley store where the barley was delivered by the farmer and allowed to lie for some time. It was built of wood and since it was rotten, I've had it taken down. Now right here was the fifteen-quarter cistern, now also removed. Barley was steeped for several days in water to allow it to swell. The water was then drained off and the barley spread in a box or couch.

'The upper floors are gone now, but if you look up, you can see where they were, six feet or less from each floor to ceiling and each with its own rank of windows. The barley was later spread on the floors no more than a few inches deep, and allowed to germinate, regularly turned over with wooden shovels. It's a tricky business knowing just when to arrest the germination, and a good man is paid well for his knowledge.

'Now, over here . . . ' Napier Drummond took Sybilla's arm and led her down the long room. 'Here is the kiln where the malt was dried on wire mesh over hornbeam faggots to amber, brown, chocolate or black according to what was wanted. It was sacked up in the next room to await delivery to the brewer.'

Above the furnace, the circular brick dome soared a

hundred feet to the windbreaker cowl. Sybilla looked round her with great interest, then walked out of the kiln. Three ranks of louvred windows in the malthouse walls let in slanting bars of brilliant sunshine, and motes of dust danced in the beams. The room was warm; she felt the eyes of both men on her heated face, and blushed.

'You should have told me that my land was the only means of access to your building, Mr Drummond.'

'It is not the duty of the draper to tell the customer that her curtains will fade, Mrs Hobart.'

She blinked at him. Was he saying that she should have investigated before selling to him? Well, she had done! 'But I found out for myself, didn't I? I didn't sign your piece of paper. I wonder if *you* were so careful before buying this – this white elephant.'

Mr Drummond looked away. 'You have every right to gloat, ma'am.'

She would have felt the utmost alarm at Mr Drummond's sudden humility had not Mr Babcock made a strange noise in his throat just at that moment. She turned to look at him and read consternation on that young face. Still watching Mr Babcock, she said: 'Since you are so well informed about malting, Mr Drummond, I think you should forget your secret schemes and build yourself a proper malthouse somewhere else.'

'I own a sixty-quarter malthouse in Ware, ma'am. That is to say, my cistern can hold sixty quarters of barley at a time. Did you know that Ware is the most important malting centre in the whole of Great Britain? Why, last year alone Ware malt-sters paid one hundred and twenty thousand pounds in excise duty and undoubtedly should have paid more.'

Sybilla was staggered. She had no idea what percentage of the value of malt was paid in excise, but she was well able to interpret Mr Drummond's message. He was a wealthy man who was prepared to pay up.

'You tried to cheat me.'

'Never.'

'You were perfectly capable of paying handsomely for my land and you offered only twenty-five pounds. A paltry sum.'

'Are you suggesting I should pay an exorbitant price merely

because I am capable of doing so? The land is worth no more than forty pounds. That is my offer.'

'If you could reach the malthouse any other way, then the land would be worth only forty pounds. As it is vital to your project, it must have a greater value.'

'The venture is a hobby, nothing more. Besides, Mrs Hobart, you do me an injustice in imagining I'm totally in your clutches. My friend, Sam Adams who owns the malthouse behind this one, will allow me to enter across his land.'

'No, sir, it is you who insult my intelligence. I had wondered about that, but the plan shows clearly – and I can see by the cart tracks – that there is not room to bring vehicles of the size needed across Mr Adams's property.'

Mr Babcock made that strange sound again and Mr Drummond gave him a look that should have stopped his heart. So she had scored another direct hit!

The three of them were standing facing one another in the centre of the vast room. Sybilla, intent on her first ever negotiations, didn't notice that the sunlight struck her face directly. She looked radiant, the black veiling thrown back to frame her pale skin, rosy cheeks and lustrous eyes. The two men stared at her with some admiration, but it was Napier who recovered his wits first.

'What can I say in the face of such perspicacity, except that it would be a pleasure to have you as a director of this enterprise. A seat on the board, you know. Your share of the equity, invested in the funds, calculated with compound interest semi-annually would yield . . . ah . . . three per cent, perhaps more.'

Francis Babcock held his breath. Napier was talking gibberish, absolute rubbish, and it was patently obvious that the lady didn't realize it. It was an old trick of Napier's to sound out the business knowledge of an adversary. Now that he had discovered the extent of this impudent woman's ignorance, Napier would pounce and demolish her with a stream of invective. She would slink away, and Francis could stop feeling so confoundedly guilty about the mess they were in.

'And . . . and how much would you pay me?' asked Sybilla uncertainly.

'Why nothing, ma'am. I should expect you to invest a

39

reasonable sum to buy yourself into the enterprise. On the other hand, I could simply buy the land. Name your price.'

She took a deep breath, moistened her lips and said softly: 'I have no price, sir. I will not sell. You will just have to forget about this project. It's terribly warm in here. Shall we go?'

Francis coughed – he couldn't help it – and gave Napier a helpless look behind Mrs Hobart's back.

They all squinted against the bright light out of doors and began walking back towards French Horn Lane where the patient Cissy was seated in the gig. No one helped Sybilla over the rough ground this time, but then she didn't appear to need help; her steps were resolute. The men stumbled after her, and Francis could feel Napier's fury as if his anger was generating physical heat.

At the roadside, she turned to smile at a gentleman who was raising his hat to her. Dr William Horley was a physician living towards the southern end of Hoddesdon High Street. He had treated Mr Hobart for years and was with him at the end. A kindly man in his sixties, he had shown her much quiet sympathy during the difficult years.

'Good morning, Mrs Hobart. How nice to see you in good health.'

Reminded of her minor indiscretion, Sybilla brought her veil forward and began to introduce Dr Horley to the other two men. They, however, clearly knew one another quite well. All three men said goodbye to her with great courtesy and she drove off without mishap, to her complete surprise and Cissy's evident relief.

What a beautiful day it was! The forsythia was glowing yellow, the willow branches drooped in pale green ropes, her widow's weeds were insufferably hot and she had just turned down the offer of a tidy sum. Suddenly, she felt almost unbearably confined by her corset. Usually the tight lacing gave her a good feeling of control, a constriction that at once governed her movements and assured her that she was living within the proper bounds of decent behaviour. But today she wished herself free of them. She wanted to breathe deeply, sing for joy, wear a red dress and dance all night. Mr Napier Drummond, the epitome of Man at his most ferocious, had been defeated by a twenty-four-year-old woman from a poor

Portsmouth family. Victory – for once – had gone to the righteous.

'How pleasant to see you, Horley, old chap,' Napier said to the Hoddesdon doctor. The two men were magistrates, had met several times in recent weeks and were due to meet again on Monday to choose a chief constable for the Hertfordshire Constabulary. On this matter, as on many others, they were in perfect agreement.

'I'm surprised you've met Mrs Hobart, Drummond. She doesn't get about very much.'

'Just a matter of business, a parcel of land,' murmured Napier. 'Splendid woman. Brave, too. Poor little thing. Unfortunately, I'm not likely to meet her socially.'

'Well, well,' said Horley, right on cue, 'you might meet her at my home. My wife has been meaning to invite Mrs Hobart to dinner for some weeks now.'

'Oh, that would be splendid! But so many of us,' said Napier quickly. 'My mother, two sisters and of course Francis, here. Your wife might not –'

'Why, why, it would be a pleasure. What about Saturday night?' said Horley, wondering what his wife would say when told that she was soon to entertain so many strangers for dinner. 'I fancy you won't wish to wait too long, eh?'

Napier removed a bit of fluff from his sleeve. 'You're too quick for me, Horley. I can't hide my feelings from you. What can I say but thank you and I pray you will give no hint of my . . . er . . . ah . . . '

'Say no more, dear chap. I understand perfectly. It is early days; discretion is the word. You will be hearing from my wife.'

Horley whipped up his horse and rode off before he found himself entertaining the entire Hertfordshire Yeomanry. Still, he told himself, he was happy to do it. Napier Drummond would be an extraordinary catch for the pretty little widow. She deserved a man with fire in his veins the second time round.

'You are outrageous,' said Francis when Horley was out of earshot. 'Why did you bully the good doctor into issuing invitations to us all?'

'Because if I fail to charm Mrs Hobart, my mother or sisters

41

may do the trick. Mama will invite the widow to our house for dinner if I ask her to. *I* could hardly do so. As for you, my friend, you will be present to see that I do not say something disastrous. I am a desperate man. Why else would I take such a dangerous step?'

'I suppose it is a trifle cruel to raise the lady's hopes.'

'Raise her hopes! Do you mean marriage? Why, she'd sooner see me roasted over an open fire than marry me. But I can't let the matter rest here. I must find ways of continuing to see her, because only time will enable me to sort out the Hobart land. She's clever, damned clever.'

'She didn't understand a word of your business cant.'

'No, by God, she didn't!'

'I thought when you –'

'She's not trained to business, but she's naturally talented. Heaven forbid that she should ever learn her way about! Remember my first lesson? Come, come, man. What have I taught you?'

Francis thought frantically, sifting through his mentor's aphorisms. All he could remember were instructions of the sort he had completely failed to follow in the Hobart matter – check every detail, study every loophole, plan for every disaster. None of these did he wish to mention.

'*What have I done to deserve this*?' he cried, suddenly inspired.

'Exactly. What have I done to deserve this? When offered a gold mine for one and sixpence, the first question to ask the vendor is: What have I done to deserve this? She asked me straight away why I was doing her the favour of paying her for a piece of waste ground.'

'Pity we didn't do the same when Cass offered us his malthouse so cheaply.'

'I wouldn't advise you to remind me of my lapse from sound principles, old chap,' said Napier chillingly. 'Two can play at that game and this business has been damnably handled from the first. But I'll tell you where I went wrong with the widow. I was in too much of a hurry to close the deal, I rushed her and, in doing so, treated her discourteously. She is offended and rightly so. But all I require is the time and space to smooth her ruffled feathers. And I fancy I can do that over the next week.

In the meantime, my lad, suppose you double check the patent, the plans, the builder's charges and a few other things.'

Napier went to his home earlier than usual that day and found his mother alone in the morning-room tatting or crocheting or some such thing. She looked up from her work and frowned.

'Napier, dear! Is anything wrong?'

'Why, no, Mama. I've come merely to apologize for my rudeness this morning. You are impossibly frivolous, you know, but you always look just the thing, I must admit.' He removed two large white five-pound notes from his coat pocket and handed them to her. 'Will that make matters better? I am a brute. Say you forgive me.'

Mrs Drummond's eyes filled with tears. 'Oh, my son, you are very kind to us and you must think me the most ungrateful of mothers. I have failed you miserably.'

'Why, what a thing to say! What can you mean?'

But Mrs Drummond was too moved to continue talking. Murmuring something about needing to put the money in a safe place, she left her puzzled son in the morning-room and went in search of her daughters.

'It was so touching,' she said a few minutes later in Marianne's bedroom. 'He was so very sweet and apologetic, and really, ten pounds is a great deal of money for fripperies. How could I tell him that I need ten times as much.'

'Twenty,' said Marianne.

'What's that, dear?'

'You need twenty times as much, Mama. Two hundred pounds.'

'Napier is in such a good mood, let us not say anything to annoy him,' said Emmaline. She was trying on a straw bonnet of Marianne's. It had pink ribbons and looked much better on her than it did when surrounding her sister's strong features.

'You may keep the bonnet. It looks very well on you,' said Marianne and turned her attention to her mother. 'Mama, you must tell Mr Farley that since he beguiled you into this theatre business, he must get you out of it.'

'He would if he had the money to do so, poor dear.'

'Poor dear!' Marianne had been lounging on her bed, but now sat up indignantly. 'He has taken two hundred pounds from you, and now wants another two hundred. You have spent your little nest-egg. If you don't recover, Napier will discover the shortfall in February when he checks over your finances.'

'I know and it gives me sleepless nights. But I have so much pleasure in owning part of a troupe of players. To sit in one's own box and –'

'Which Napier believes to be owned by Mr Farley.'

'– to go backstage and talk to Mrs Mowatt and the other actors. And dear Mr Watts. I have had value for my money; you must agree there.'

'Oh Mama,' cried Marianne. 'I have seen how happy you are these days and, indeed, we all enjoy it. At least Emmaline and I do. Napier isn't partial to the theatre. But you seem to be getting in deeper and deeper and I've begun to suspect Mr Farley of –'

There was a knock on the door and all three women jumped guiltily. However, it was only John, the footman, bringing a note to Mrs Drummond that had been delivered by hand.

Mrs Drummond read it aloud with amazement. ' "Dear Mrs Drummond, Will you and your daughters and son give us the pleasure of your company at dinner on Saturday, April 9th at 8 o'clock. R.S.V.P." And it is signed by Mrs William Horley, Greshams, High Street, Hoddesdon. But I don't know any Horleys of Hoddesdon and if Mrs Horley doesn't know the names of my son and daughters, why does she want to entertain us? Besides, it is dreadfully short notice.'

'You can count on it, this is Napier's doing, Mama. Thank heavens none of us has any other plans for Saturday night or he would force us to abandon them.'

'It's a matter of business, I suppose. I'll go and speak to him. Had he mentioned it to me, I would have been happy to have invited them here.'

Mrs Drummond found her son reading *The Times* in the library. 'Napier, dear, I've had a dinner invitation from a complete stranger.'

'Oh, Mrs Horley has come through, has she? I thought I could count on old Horley. Splendid. You can go, can't you? You're free?'

'Yes, but two days' notice!'

44

'It will only be a small party, I'm sure. Ourselves, Francis and Mrs Hobart.'

'Mrs Hobart? A widow?'

'Now, Mama, don't go matchmaking. It's not like that at all. I don't particularly like the woman and she heartily dislikes me. It's a matter of business. To tell you the truth, she is being very obstructive. I must see her somehow. As a bachelor, I couldn't invite her here, but you can do so once you have met her.'

'And so you prevailed on Mrs Horley to invite you both to dinner. And the girls and me. Well, I will do my best, but if the widow dislikes you, she may refuse my invitation. Has she been a widow long? Was she devoted to her husband, do you think?'

'I shouldn't think so at all. Old Hobart died nearly eighteen months ago. He was sixty-two and she cannot possibly be more than twenty-two or three.'

'A quiet party then, but we can have some music. And this young thing is making matters difficult for you? Napier, I am intrigued!'

'Oh, she's clever. Devilishly clever. I've never met her equal. Not in a female at any rate.'

Mrs Drummond was still clutching the five-pound notes and now waved them at him. 'Had you explained the situation to me earlier, dear, I would have done you this favour for nothing,' she said sadly, and left him to his paper.

She was upset, as always, after the briefest of conversations with her only son. He didn't trust her, would never ask for something directly, preferring to manipulate or even bribe her. He was the most secretive man she had ever met and she couldn't tell if he were, on the whole, happy with his life or not. Yet again she went over the circumstances of his having been sent away at fourteen. Mr Drummond had been convinced that the boy would thrive under the tutelage of Mr Micklethwaite, and no one could deny that Napier was now thriving, a wealthy and respected man. She didn't understand her son as she understood her daughters. The break in their acquaintance had come at a crucial time. The boy had matured into the man under other influences than her own.

It had been a full year after he arrived in London before

Napier wrote a stiffly formal letter addressed, pointedly, to his Mama only. He had given an accommodation address, the Bull and Mouth coaching inn. It would have been possible to travel to London to find him, but Mr Drummond would not consider it. Napier had done a cowardly thing in running away from Micklethwaite. And he had behaved abominably in failing to write and relieve his mother's anxiety for very nearly a year. He would not be searched for; he would not be invited to return to his home and family. She had never even considered defying Mr Drummond and travelling to London to find her son. And that had been a mistake for which she was sure Napier had never forgiven her. They had kept in touch by letter, so at least she had known where to reach him when Mr Drummond had died. She often wondered what the boy had done in London during all those long years.

On the day of the funeral, a scowling man in his mid twenties had turned up on the doorstep, had growled in his deep voice that he was Napier Drummond. The untidy boy with wide eyes and mischievous ways had turned into a hard-eyed man who wore his clothes well, who answered his own questions before anyone else had time to think and took decisions on everyone's behalf.

She and the girls lived in terror of his sneer, longed for his approval and never ceased to marvel at his generosity. He could be amusing; men liked him and many women had set their caps at him. Yet, to his mother, he remained an enigma.

Sybilla sat in the morning-room holding a letter from her mother as if it were a death warrant. And in some ways it was; it signalled the demise of her freedom. She could not deceive her family for much longer; it was a miracle that she had been able to keep the secret of Mr Hobart's death all these months. One of these days someone who knew the truth was bound to meet her mother or brother by chance. Then all her freedom and independence would disappear, because Mama and Robert would prevail upon her to sell her home and business and return to Portsmouth.

Her conscience had troubled her severely these past months. What, after all, was her duty? Was it not enough that she had

46

endured four years of marriage to a hated old man; that she had sent forty pounds annually to those who had sold her into slavery; that she had been forced to listen night after night to her husband's lectures about gratitude for his generosity?

At first, the idea had seemed quite simple. She would keep Mr Hobart's death a secret until she was strong enough to resist the pressures that would be placed on her by her complaining mother and by Robert, whose greed was boundless. Unfortunately, the past months had not made her stronger. Loneliness had weakened her resolve. Inactivity had sapped her energy, so that she had begun to think that the struggle for the right to conduct her own life was not worth the effort.

Then yesterday Mrs Horley had invited her to dinner, and her view of her difficulties had changed radically. Why should she give up her freedom if she could lay her hands on forty pounds to stave off the evil day for another year? Six months into her widowhood, she had sent her entire savings to her mother, but the next forty pounds were now due; Mama was anxious for the money and hinting that she wished to visit her daughter. Fortunately for Sybilla, Mrs Sutherland did not have enough money for the fare and so was unlikely to turn up on the doorstep expecting to see her elderly son-in-law.

By a stroke of luck, Sybilla now had a means of obtaining forty pounds. She might dislike Mr Drummond, but she could not honestly say that she was sorry to have met him. She would enjoy her little triumph over him for a few more days and then she would agree to forty pounds. Or no, since Mr Drummond must have a right of way over her land, she would ask for fifty pounds and have ten for herself. Crumpling her mother's letter, she threw it on to the meagre heap of coals in the grate. Time enough to worry about Mama in twelve months.

She liked the Horleys; when the invitation had arrived yesterday, she had run joyfully upstairs to look out her only black dinner gown. After Mr Hobart passed away, she had sent her finest gown, the simple one of pale blue satin, to Samuel Neale's warehouse in Hertford to be dyed black. She had anticipated scores of invitations to quiet dinners from various Hoddesdon acquaintances. In the event, the gown had hung unused in the wardrobe, its glorious colour dimmed for ever. Saturday night would, at least, justify the expense of dyeing it. She had a box of black bugle beads and some wide black velvet ribbon with which to concoct a trim for the hem of the skirt. The jet necklace and earrings – a shocking extravagance as it had turned out – would be taken from their velvet box at long last.

To the devil with convention and the duties of a daughter! She intended to enjoy herself in the company of these two elderly people, and to take all the pleasure that life might offer in whatever weeks of freedom were left. She put a hand to her thudding heart, trying to still the panic that so often threatened to overwhelm her. The thought of returning to her old life in Portsmouth was almost unbearable.

4

Sybilla had intended to walk the mile to the Horleys', accompanied by Cissy, in order to save herself the aggravation of persuading Saul to turn out with the gig. In the event, Fanny developed a fever; Cissy was very distressed. And by eight o'clock it was not only dark but raining heavily, one of those spring showers that might or might not be short-lived. So there was nothing for it but to battle with her manservant.

Saul made sure he took his time in bringing the gig round to the front door and, as a consequence, Sybilla was late arriving at the Horleys' pleasant house. She urged Saul to collect her promptly at half-past eleven and rang the doorbell, sincerely hoping that she would not be forced to walk home alone.

Mrs Horley met her in the hall, quite out of breath as if she had been running. She was a tall woman with a scrubbed face and the expression of one who will succour those less fortunate than herself, whether they wish it or not. Usually, her formidable height and personality overwhelmed Sybilla, but tonight Mrs Horley was caught up in her own worries.

'There you are, my dear, it was all such a surprise! I've never entertained such important – are you wet? Let me look at your shoes; you'll catch cold if your feet are wet. It's about time you lightened your mourning, my dear. What is it? Fifteen or sixteen months? We are odd, but it can't be helped. Where could I find extra men at such short notice? At least, not suitable ones. Come, dear, we must go in. No, stand here first and take a deep breath. There now! It helps to calm the nerves.'

The manservant opened the door; Mrs Horley took her firmly by the arm and marched her into the drawing-room. 'And here, at last, is Mrs Hobart!'

The men stood at once; three women looked up at her. From the corner of her eye she saw Mr Drummond smiling slightly, Mr Babcock and Dr Horley.

'Mrs Drummond, this is our dear young friend, Mrs Hobart. Sybilla, Mrs Drummond, Miss Drummond and Miss Emmaline Drummond!'

'My dear,' said Mrs Drummond, smiling at her, 'but you are enchanting! How ironic it is that the black which proclaims the grieving widow can also make her look so attractive on occasion. I expect I shouldn't say such things, but it's true. You look delightful.'

'Why, thank you, Mrs Drummond.' Sybilla nodded to the two young women, the elder dark like her brother, the other a younger version of Mrs Drummond. Their smiles were warm; she liked them at once, certain that in other circumstances they could have been friends.

There was not time to say a word; Mrs Horley's iron grip was bruising her arm as she was pointed in the direction of the men. She needed all her courage to take a few paces towards Mr Drummond, her pleasure in the evening's dinner party having evaporated at the sight of him. She had a vague feeling that she was walking into a trap set by this man, one which would deprive her of the vital forty pounds. His eyes were deceptively admiring, his smile warm. Oh, but he was a dangerous man! He had every reason to be very angry with her. Therefore, his apparent pleasure at seeing her was an ominous sign. When the greetings were completed, she hurried thankfully back to take a seat among the ladies.

Mrs Drummond, by skilful questioning, soon had the better part of her life story from her, all that she wished to tell, at least. The older woman's good humour and genuine interest in everything she said made Sybilla glow with pleasure. How extraordinary that such a frightening man could have such a delicious mother! Sybilla thought of her own mother's lined face, set permanently in the expression of one who knew herself to have been ill-used by life. Mrs Sutherland never took an interest in anyone but her son and herself. And not necessarily in that order.

It was no surprise to Sybilla to find herself seated between Mr Drummond and Mr Babcock at dinner. She couldn't imagine how he had achieved it, but the odious Mr Drummond had made poor Dr Horley invite all these people for his own purposes. No wonder Mrs Horley looked flustered. This was quite a party to arrange at short notice.

Mrs Drummond's dress and those of her daughters were stunning and expensive. Mrs Horley's old wine silk and her own plain black made a strong contrast. She felt shabby. Yet, surely Mrs Drummond's compliments were sincere, and what found favour with such a fashionable lady must be acceptable. Sybilla refused to worry about the lack of diamonds round her own throat.

Turning to her dinner partner, she said softly: 'Is Mrs Drummond, by any chance, your stepmother?'

'No, why do you ask?' said Napier.

'It's just that she is so charming.'

Napier laughed appreciatively. 'And therefore no blood relation of mine. I expect I'm a changeling. It's a pleasure to meet you again, Mrs Hobart, away from unpleasant business transactions.'

'Are you ever very far away from your unpleasant business transactions, Mr Drummond?'

'Ma'am, I will not spar with you tonight. We are here to enjoy ourselves.'

'Well, I shan't enjoy myself if you patronize me.'

He laughed aloud, his eyes sparkling as he lifted his glass to her. Good manners demanded that she lift hers to him. And as she drank, she saw Mrs Drummond's eyes on her in a most speculative way.

The party was such a small one that the conversation often became general, the guests addressing one another across the table. Everyone began toasting everyone else and it would have been rude to refuse to drink. By the time the first course of gravy soup, salmon with shrimp sauce and fried whiting had been removed for the entrées of lobster cutlets and chicken patties, she was feeling elated.

The second course of veal, lamb and ham garnished with vegetables had just been arranged on the table when Dr Horley, looking rather flushed, called out to his principal guest: 'My dear Drummond, I hear you have bought a malt-house in Ware which you are intending to turn to some new mysterious purpose. I hope I am not speaking out of turn when I say that any new source of employment in the area is welcome, but I do wish you had thought of Hoddesdon. Apart from the inns and public houses and Christie's brewery, this town has nothing much to offer the working man.'

Napier leaned back in his chair. 'Well, old chap, as a matter

51

of fact, I did buy Cass's derelict malthouse, but have since decided that it won't do. I intend to drop the whole project.'

'Come, come, sir!' cried Sybilla, and even as the words escaped her, she knew it was the wine talking. 'To abandon such a project? You must have spent at least –' she groped for a figure, '– five hundred pounds. An investment of a similar sum in the funds with compound interest calculated semi-annually should yield, surely, five per cent? You won't convince me that you intend to leave so much capital tied up in a derelict building.'

Mr Drummond gave her a small nod as if to say touché. 'Quite correct, ma'am. I expect I'll think of something.'

Sybilla's raillery earned her undisguised admiration from the other guests, particularly Mr Drummond's ladies. In all probability none of the women had the faintest inkling of business matters, and Sybilla certainly didn't know if she was speaking nonsense or not.

'My goodness, Mrs Hobart,' said Mrs Drummond. 'Your grasp of financial matters is amazing in a woman. No wonder my son says you are extremely clever.'

Mr Babcock gave a strangled cough. Napier Drummond's brows drew together ominously, and his mother looked momentarily discomposed.

'To be deemed clever by Mr Napier Drummond is a compliment, indeed,' said Sybilla, enunciating her words carefully. She felt ten feet tall and just a little light-headed. She might be supping with the devil, but she was unafraid.

When the third course arrived, she avoided the ducklings and chose instead a little cabinet pudding with vanilla sauce. Then as the need to absorb the alcohol she had consumed continued to be urgent, she allowed herself to be persuaded into small helpings of compote of rhubarb and orange jelly.

Doctor Horley surveyed his table with pleasure. His wife had been very put out to be rushed into this party, but he had not hesitated to insist. He wished to perform this small service for Napier Drummond who was a strange man, a mixture of ruthlessness and generosity, angry outbursts and acts of quiet kindness. The two men had sat together on the Bench on many occasions; he had learned to respect Drummond's keen, probing brain.

In Horley's experience such men as Napier Drummond were a breed apart, driven by an inner compulsion to achieve something worth-while. Success can be defined in a number of ways, but merchant adventurers generally saw it in terms of money earned. This year I have made "x" number of pounds, therefore I am successful. Next year I shall make twice as much and be twice as successful.

No doubt the nation's prosperity was built on such foundations — the striving for wealth. Nevertheless, this particular obsession could lead to an arid lonely life. These hard-driving men — so visibly strong, so inwardly vulnerable — needed the stability of loved ones, which meant marriage and children. Napier Drummond needed a goal, a purpose in life beyond an ever-increasing bank balance, and had indicated his interest in Sybilla Hobart. So be it. It was his good friend's duty to promote the match.

Throughout dinner, Horley had been asking Drummond questions, choosing topics which were calculated to draw the man out and show him in a favourable light to the widow. He studied Drummond's profile as the young man listened to Mrs Horley, and when the opportunity arose, Horley spoke once again to his principal guest.

'You are a wealthy man, Drummond, and a young one. You have obviously worked hard, but there is always more than that to making a fortune. To what do you attribute your success?'

Napier thought for a moment. 'I think experience counts for a great deal; one learns as one goes along. But I take my lessons in business from studying the lives of great men. Consider Captain Cook. He discovered that citrus fruits and sauerkraut could prevent scurvy among men who were at sea for long periods — as you well know, Horley. But sauerkraut is not to every Englishman's taste. Of course, the Captain could have ordered his sailors to eat it but they would have grumbled and no doubt found ways of avoiding the dish. Being a student of human nature, he chose another way. The first week at sea, he offered sauerkraut only to his officers and forbade the regular seamen to have any. During the second week, he pretended to relent, and allowed every man aboard a chance to eat it if he so wished. His men, who wanted to have anything the officers had, ate their sauerkraut with enthusiasm.'

53

'And what is the lesson you learned from Captain Cook, Napier?' asked Marianne.

'I think I can tell you that,' said Sybilla. 'That you can achieve your aims more quickly by playing on a man's envy than by appealing to his good sense. Which, I must say, is typical of men.'

'Hear, hear!' said Marianne. 'It would not be the same with women sailors, Napier. Captain Cook would only have had to explain the advantages of eating sauerkraut to his women and they would have eaten it without complaint.'

'You believe women are less envious than men?' said Napier. 'Perhaps you are right. I think Captain Cook would have told his women sailors that sauerkraut was more *fashionable* than any other vegetable. That would have been equally successful, I'm sure.'

Roars of agreement rose from the men and everyone began talking at once. Looking down the table, Mrs Horley gave her husband that little nod which said that they had achieved something very special this night – the perfect blending of personalities, an evening where no one was neglected, no one left feeling self-conscious. She doubted that she would ever give such a perfect party again.

Later the women left the men to their port, and Sybilla soon discovered that her few remarks at dinner had earned her considerable respect among her own sex. Marianne assured her, laughingly, that her brother had, in general, a very low opinion of the weaker sex, but that he clearly made an exception in one case. Mrs Drummond remarked that she had seldom seen her son so very much at his ease. Sybilla's feelings towards a man who apparently admired her were bound to soften. Perhaps he was not such a demon after all.

The men rejoined the ladies and all too soon the tea-tray arrived. The evening was drawing to a close. Sybilla had no choice, once the tea was finished, but to ask her hostess if the servants would have her gig brought round to the front of the house.

Mrs Horley's man returned to the drawing-room a minute or two later and announced in what Sybilla thought was an unnecessarily loud voice that Mrs Hobart's carriage had not arrived at all. However, a young person by the name of

Jefferson Smith was waiting in the kitchen and he would be pleased to walk home with Mrs Hobart as protection.

'Certainly not!' said Napier before Sybilla could recover from her embarrassment. 'Have my carriage brought to the front door and I will accompany Mrs Hobart to her home.'

'Splendid idea!' cried Dr Horley eagerly, and Sybilla was left with nothing to say but thank you.

The Horleys and the Drummond ladies took their leave of her with great affection. Mr Babcock bowed deeply and she was soon being helped into the rich interior of the Drummond carriage for the short ride home.

'What happened to your servant?' asked Napier as soon as they were alone.

'Oh, I suppose Saul has been drinking again. Jefferson Smith is his daughter's follower and a fine young man. He often brings Saul home when he has drunk too much. How aggravating; Saul never behaved this way when Mr Hobart was alive. It is very difficult in some ways to find oneself alone.' What to say to this terrifying man? She imagined him crouched in his corner like a predatory animal, ready to pounce. 'How . . . how do you discipline insolent servants, Mr Drummond?'

'That is like asking Lord Salisbury how he replies to a condescending remark. It doesn't happen to me. However, if the advice is of any use to you, I've found that there are some people who confuse rudeness with superiority. The more roughly they are spoken to, the more harshly treated, the more certain they are that they are in the presence of greatness. If your Saul is the scruff who opened the door to me the other day, I would say he came into that class. On the other hand, I think you would be wise to dismiss him. A woman living alone needs a manservant on whom she can depend.'

'It's difficult. His wife is my cook-housekeeper and his daughter is my personal maid. I am dependent upon them. If I dismiss Saul, he would simply lurk about the house, living off his wife's earnings. Here we are, Mr Drummond,' she said a little breathlessly. 'Thank you for seeing me home.'

He stepped out of the carriage quickly and helped her down, holding on to her hand when she would have pulled away.

'It has been a most enjoyable evening, ma'am. I can't

remember when I was so diverted. Undoubtedly, we shall meet again. Good night.'

Not surprisingly, Sybilla overslept the next morning and was very nearly late for church. Saul, she was told, was not feeling well. Since there was no question of taking little Fanny from her bed, Cissy stayed at home while Sybilla and Mrs Potter walked in silence to St Augustine's which was not much more than a hundred yards away.

Saul put in an appearance that afternoon unshaven and wearing a filthy old moleskin waistcoat. Sybilla passed him quite by chance in the hall and ordered him to come with her into the morning-room.

'You lazy, useless, drunken fool!' she began when the door was closed behind them, adopting a stance that bore a remarkable resemblance to Napier Drummond's. 'You embarrassed me before a number of important people last night and I will not be treated in this way. Either you change your ways or you and your family will be out on the street. Do you understand me?'

'Yes, ma'am.' Saul drew himself up a little, straightening his round shoulders and ogling her with bulging eyes. There was no doubt that she had taken him completely by surprise.

'I am involved in business transactions with one of the wealthiest men in Hertfordshire and I will not be humiliated by an insolent servant again. I can find other servants any time I choose, Saul. You are not indispensable.'

'I'm ever so sorry, Mrs Hobart. It won't happen again. I heard that a gentleman brung you home in a fine carriage. Don't be doin' anythin' hasty, ma'am, Mrs Potter and Cissy would cry their eyes out if you dismissed them on account of me.'

'You may go,' she said frostily, and he did, backing out of the door and apologizing every step of the way, leaving his mistress surprised and delighted to be – for once – in control of her servants.

She spent the rest of Sunday attempting to read a few elevating sermons, but found it difficult not to daydream. Pleasant memories of the previous evening led to speculation about her social life in the future. Surely, now that Mrs Horley had invited her to dinner, others would do the same. But should she entertain Dr and Mrs Horley to dinner, inviting, say, another gentleman? Or were widows not expected to invite gentlemen to dinner?

Even more intrusive were her thoughts about Napier Drummond. She had relaxed in company on Saturday night, allowing herself to enjoy the evening without looking too closely into its possible purpose. Dr Horley had been prevailed upon to invite them all to dinner. Why? So that Napier Drummond could continue to try to persuade her to sell her land? Or so that he could tell her to her face that he would rather abandon his plans than pay her price?

She bit her lip in vexation. He mustn't do that! She needed the money desperately. How cruel he was! She gave way to a childish indulgence and spent an hour in imagined conversations with him, giving him weak but vicious lines to speak to which she made brilliantly arrogant replies. It was all very satisfying for a time, but eventually she had to face the truth: either he would buy her land and she could live another year in Hoddesdon, or he wouldn't, and she would be forced to return to Portsmouth. She hated him for the power he had over her happiness.

On Monday morning, to her great surprise, Sybilla received a letter, delivered by a liveried servant. Mrs Drummond and her daughters had enjoyed meeting her, and would she honour them with her company on the following Saturday evening for dinner? They would be only a small party. And, by the way, her son had insisted that the Drummond carriage should be sent for her. It would be waiting at her door at seven o'clock. Sybilla sighed with relief: Mr Drummond wanted to buy.

She scribbled a delighted acceptance and handed it to the Drummonds' servant, then sat down in the morning-room to consider her next move. It was not necessary to go upstairs and search her wardrobe for a suitable gown; she knew she had only one. As she had worn it to the Horleys' home, she could not, would not wear it again the following Saturday. Her attitude might be frivolous and vain but she didn't care. A woman had just one way of expressing her true self and that was in her choice of dress; all women understood this unspoken language, even if their men did not.

Depending on what she wore on Saturday night, Sybilla would be saying to Mrs Drummond: I am Sybilla Hobart, impoverished provincial widow; or if she chose to, I am Oswald Hobart's widow, inconsolably bereaved. In fact, she intended to say something totally different – I am a stylish and wealthy widow who is both proud and independent.

She had better order the new gown immediately. Any costume that could say so much would be not only costly but also laborious to make.

Tired of viewing the world through black mesh, she took a pair of scissors to the veiling on her bonnet, tied the ugly thing under her chin, gathered up her shawl because the weather had taken a turn for the worse, and left the house.

The day was cheerless, with bare branches bending in the wind and most of the daffodils rain-battered and broken-stemmed. She hated the treachery of April with its false promises. Standing for a moment on her doorstep, she gloomily surveyed High Street in both directions. She bought her meat from Gocher's, her provisions from William Sams, her green-grocery from Mr Jones and most other things from the Sams sisters. And not one of them was more than fifty yards from her front door.

In the past five years, she had travelled no more than five miles from Hornbeam House in any direction. Before that, in Portsmouth, she had never once travelled even that short distance from home, except when she left it for good.

Not unnaturally, she was a little nervous about having dinner with the Drummonds. What did she know of the way of life of such ladies as Mrs Drummond? For all Sybilla knew, the Drummonds might be on the same social level as Lord Rosebery, whom she had been told lived in Hertford, except that she thought the Earl of Rosebery would not have graciously attended a dinner party given by Mrs Horley.

Sybilla nodded to Mrs Auber who was walking majestically on the other side of the road, her maid five paces behind. There were three drapers in the High Street, but she was certain that ladies like Mrs Auber patronized none of them. These shop-keepers had probably travelled no farther afield than Sybilla had. What worth-while advice could they possibly give her about the choice of material for a smart dinner gown? For that matter, it was entirely possible that not one of them would have anything suitable.

But in these thoughts she did them an injustice. Christopher Tuck was Hoddesdon born and bred, but not only did he have a fair selection of grey silks, he also offered a good deal of advice based on his experience in selling to the local gentry. It was at his suggestion that she chose a delicate pearl grey with a self stripe.

Esther Pegrum, the dressmaker next door to Tuck's, had a large pattern book; Sybilla quickly found exactly what she wanted, and was determined not to count the cost. Assured by Miss Pegrum that the style she preferred was not in any way incorrect or indecent, she gave free rein to her imagination in the matter of decoration.

She knew she ought not to buy any sort of gown at the moment. If Hobart's last substantial customer, Mr Crockford, had not, only last Saturday, paid his outstanding account of six months, she wouldn't have had the money to purchase the cloth. Mr Crockford's payment had been briefly earmarked for buying coal and lamp oil, but the long warm days were drawing near. She could manage without fuel and light in order to buy a necessary dress. Or at least the cloth for it. Poor Miss Pegrum would have to wait a few weeks to be paid for her dressmaking.

The clock on the yellow brick tower was striking eleven when Sybilla thought she would pay a visit to Mr Hobart's shop in the hope that Mr Puddifoot had received an order since Saturday. The cost of the gown was preying on her mind; it would be pleasant to discover that Hobart's might be making a little money in the near future.

The big green doors were closed against the threat of rain, and she had to let herself in by a small door on the left. The three men were seated in their favourite corner, but none of them rose as she entered.

In Mr Puddifoot's case, the reason became clear as she drew close enough to look into his eyes. At eleven o'clock on a Monday morning, Albert Puddifoot was too drunk to think of greeting his employer properly.

'Stand up,' said Sybilla in the tone of voice that had worked so well with Saul.

The Perkins, father and son, jumped to their feet. Mr Puddifoot made a supreme effort and stood up, swaying slightly, grinning foolishly. 'Morning, Mrs Hobart.'

Sybilla felt almost faint with righteous anger. 'How dare you drink yourself to stupidity on my time? You're not fit to manage this business and I've a good mind to dismiss you.'

Mr Puddifoot, sobering rapidly, blinked several times. 'Here now! I won't be spoken to like that by a uppity young woman scarce out of the schoolroom what married a sick old man for his money.'

'Yet, you have no objections to taking money from the uppity young woman in return for no work at all.'

'What cheek! That does it,' said Puddifoot, by now quite red in the face. 'I can work elsewhere. I got skills. There's many a coach-builder as'ud like to hire Albert Puddifoot.'

'Well, I – '

'Just give me my back wages and I'll be off.'

'Back wages?' cried Sybilla, once more on the offensive. 'I paid you two pounds on Saturday and as you have certainly done no work today, I don't owe you a farthing. You may leave as soon as you have given me the account books.'

The young lad ran to the small glass-walled office to fetch the books as Puddifoot turned away to snatch up his jacket and hat. Sybilla stood frozen to the spot with shock. The only person who knew how to manage Hobart's was about to walk out of the door, and all because she had foolishly listened to Mr Drummond's advice. There was nothing she could say now to mend matters. Perhaps the silly man would realize his folly and beg forgiveness. He had been drinking heavily, after all. He was in the wrong. She certainly would not back down.

Sybilla rubbed her forehead. Only twice in her entire life had she ever spoken sharply to a man; the results had been largely disastrous, and all the fault of Napier Drummond. Why couldn't Saul have taken himself off in a huff while Puddifoot resolved to do better in the future? In the event, Puddifoot made a quite dignified exit, staggering through the small door, his hat at a jaunty angle.

'You'll not find another manager in a hurry, Mrs Hobart,'

said Henry Perkins in the voice of doom. 'My son and me can't do all the work as is necessary to run a coach-building business.'

'What work? I see no work. There has been nothing for you to do these past weeks. Dust those account books for me, Jethro. I don't wish to soil my clothes. I shall put you in charge for the time being, Mr Perkins, but I'll not pay for idleness any longer. Whitewash the walls and paint the woodwork green. Don't forget the doors. And clean this filthy floor! I shall give some thought as to what is to be done about the business later on.'

Perkins, a small man with an unruly shock of grey hair and skin like tanned leather, scratched his head. 'It's going to be difficult, ma'am.'

'Painting the shop?'

'No, ma'am. Building coaches. We can't get the staff, nor I don't have Mr Puddifoot's connections. I don't know as I can rightly take the responsibility –'

'For heaven's sake, don't consider yourself defeated until we actually receive an order. Show a little backbone. Jethro, talk some sense into your father. Remind him that you two will be hard pressed to feed yourselves if you leave me.'

'Yes, Mrs Hobart, not but what me Dad's right,' said Jethro without enthusiasm, and Sybilla received the account books from him with a snort.

Anger carried her all the way home and into the morning-room. It was not until she had looked carefully at the accounts that she began to shake. The figures, names of coach parts and specialists were totally incomprehensible to her. It seemed that Hobart's actually made only the bodywork of carriages. Mr Puddifoot bought the wheels elsewhere. The ironwork and (she thought) the undercarriages were made to specification by a farrier.

All these years, Sybilla had been under the impression that coaches in their entirety were made in Lord Lane. Not that she had any way of knowing. Mr Hobart had never gone near the shop; he had trusted Puddifoot who came to the house each Saturday to collect his wages and discuss the week's business. On these occasions, Sybilla had always left the men alone, but the arrangements had seemed to work perfectly. Of course, in those days, Mr Hobart kept the accounts here at the house and studied them regularly. It was only when her husband had become too weak to do so that Sybilla had asked Mr Puddifoot to take the books and keep them up properly. How naive she had been! She was sure the manager had been an honest industrious man until he had found himself working for an ignorant widow.

Standing up from the table where she had been studying the accounts, she rubbed the small of her aching back, refusing to panic even though fear was constricting her throat. She would not give up. Somehow she must keep the firm afloat, because failure meant a return to Portsmouth in disgrace. It occurred to her with a small shock that Puddifoot's monthly wage and the cost of the silk gown were almost the same. The expenditure on one was cancelled out by the saving on the other. Nevertheless, she must not buy another gown.

For the moment she couldn't think beyond this one resolution: no more new clothes. Her mind was racing round in profitless circles. She had never felt more alone. There was no one to turn to for advice, unless she swallowed her pride and took her queries to Mr Drummond. She might do so, she thought on a rising note of optimism. It might just be possible for a brazen woman to say: I wish to be paid fifty pounds for my land and, by the way, can you please sort out my business affairs? Had he not got her into this tangle by ill-judged advice? She bit her lip at the thought. She didn't know; she would see how matters progressed on Saturday night. If this terrifying man continued to behave like a lamb, she would raise the subject on the way home from dinner, because there was no doubt that he would accompany her home. Why else was he taking such trouble to have her fetched and carried in his own coach, if not to take the opportunity to speak in private with her about the Hobart land?

Napier sat down in a corner of the large room and rubbed his eyes with thumb and forefinger. His head ached a little and he wished that the assembled magistrates of Hertfordshire would not all talk at once. It was half-past eight at night and the day had been a long and trying one.

He had been in court a good part of it. Two women had been sentenced to six months' hard labour for stealing nine yards of printed cotton. Practised thieves, both; he felt no sympathy for them. But a labourer named Roland Cameron had been transported for seven years for stealing a candlestick worth sixpence. He was a known thief, of course, but nevertheless the man might end by paying with his life merely for the stealing of a small household item.

Sometimes a day on the bench depressed Napier greatly, leaving him moody and ill-tempered for a week. It was the self-righteous pettiness of law-abiding citizens that disturbed him most.

Today a boy of ten had been brought before the court for playing pitch and toss on a Sunday. The boy's mother had pleaded on his behalf; she hadn't shoes for him to go to church; he hadn't realized the wickedness of his action; he was sincerely repentant. After consultation, the magistrates had agreed to let the boy go free with no more than a scolding.

Napier thought the woman must be well acquainted with the minds of the sort of men who sat on the bench. She knew better than to say her boy had laboured six days for a few pence and was entitled to some playtime as richer children were, or that surely his parents were the proper people to decide how his Sundays might best be spent. She had been too knowing to give voice to any of these impudent thoughts. Instead, she had wrung her hands, whined and begged forgiveness for her son – and saved him from a birching.

Napier always tried in a quiet way to direct his fellow magistrates towards a just sentence. They didn't understand the poor. How could they? His experiences at the northern mill and on London's streets were almost unique among magistrates.

He looked up from the floor and saw Horley's eyes upon him. Horley detached himself from a group of vociferous magistrates and came over to sit down beside Napier. 'You look very tired, my friend,' he said in his kindly way. 'You work too hard. A young man like you should spend more time in idle pursuits.'

Napier shook his head. 'I'm just a trifle blue-devilled. It gives me no pleasure to pass judgement on my fellow men.'

'Then why do it?' asked Horley. 'Resign from the bench.'

'My experience of life has equipped me better than most to dispense justice,' snapped Napier.

Horley sat back in his chair, raising his eyebrows and looking thoughtful for a while. 'I don't know what your past is, Drummond, nor is it any of my business. I presume you have lived among the poor and learned to appreciate their suffering. But don't you ever run away with the idea that you are the only magistrate capable of feeling compassion.'

'I beg your pardon. That would be a mistake.' Napier looked at Horley speculatively. 'Shall I tell you where I gained my knowledge of the poor?'

Eagerly, the doctor took a nearby chair. He had been curious about Napier's past for some months. 'Whatever you wish to tell me, I shall regard as confidential.'

'Let me see, where to begin? My father, having tired of the sight of me and not wanting me cluttering up the house any longer, sent me to an old acquaintance of his in Rochdale when I was fourteen. Mr Micklethwaite owns a cotton mill and I was to learn the business.'

'Perhaps your father thought he was genuinely promoting your future success.'

Napier raised his eyebrows in surprise. 'It is possible, I suppose. Micklethwaite never married. Perhaps Father thought the old man would make me his heir. I lived very comfortably in Micklethwaite's house and took my meals with him. He made me work hard, but since he was a very lonely man, he talked to me for many hours each night. Even though I was such a young lad and very aggrieved at having been sent away from home, I must admit that I learned a great deal about business principles. If my parents had troubled to explain their purpose in sending me away, and if they had visited me occasionally, I might have settled to the life reasonably well. Father, however, was an indolent man who would not travel north, while Micklethwaite was obsessed with work and refused to give me permission to go home for a visit.'

'Whatever your parents' intentions, you were surely too young for such a life. You would have been better occupied with your schoolbooks.'

'That is also my opinion. At least, I'm not so sure. I was

made for a business life, you know. Try to picture my circumstances – a fine house, soft bed and more food than I could eat. Yet at the factory, there were children my own age and younger to whom Micklethwaite paid scarcely any wages and whom the overseers treated abominably. The contrast between what I enjoyed and they suffered was very great.'

'This would have been before the passing of the Factories Act of '33.'

'Yes, but I shouldn't imagine the lot of pauper children is much better now than it was then. An Act of Parliament is only effective if the local magistrates make it so. During my time in the north, many of the magistrates were factory owners. They will not regulate themselves. At all events, after two years I could stand it no more and ran away. I never considered going home because I was convinced my parents no longer loved me. Instead, I walked to London.'

Napier stared into the middle distance for a moment, remembering. 'It was a difficult journey; I hadn't a complete change of clothing with me and I wore out one of my two pairs of shoes by the time I reached the capital. I had just ten shillings between myself and starvation when I bedded down the first night in Bishopsgate.

'While I slept, sheltering in a doorway, I was robbed of every penny by the very men who had spoken to me kindly and offered to look after me. They taught me a valuable lesson – never trust anyone. For two days I had nothing to eat. Fortunately, a doxy took pity on me and gave me a few coppers every day to act as her protector and see to it that her customers didn't beat her.'

'My word, Drummond!'

'Later,' said Napier, smiling slightly at his friend's amazement, 'I joined forces with a street trader. Billy Barge was an old man in failing health who used to peddle his wares all over London and the southern counties. I can still see him – battered top hat, tattered frockcoat and a huge mole on his right cheek. He carried his yard wand in one filthy hand and rolls of cotton strapped on his back. I was soon carrying the cloth, of course. Do you know anything about street traders?'

'Only what I have discovered from those who appear before me in court. Did the man Barge have a pedlar's licence?'

'Yes, he did. He paid four pounds a year for it and considered himself to be a fairly successful street trader. Barge bought all his supplies from Smith's swag shop in Bishopsgate. I had better explain. A swag shop is a large shop that supplies street traders. The shop usually caters for the servant class as well, but servants pay more for their goods than the street traders do. The swag man is willing to haggle; he would think you a fool if you accepted the first price offered. I loved to haggle with the man at Smith's, and Barge was quite willing to turn that side of the business over to me.'

'I should imagine you were very adept at it.'

'I'm pleased to say I was. Billy Barge got many a bargain because of my quick tongue. I have a knack with figures. I can calculate very rapidly and have always found it gives me a considerable advantage over those who must use pen and paper. Swag shops are always situated in the less elegant parts of town, of course, and they are large dusty places crammed to the ceiling with supplies. Nevertheless, serving in a swag shop is infinitely preferable to walking the pavements with cloth on your back. Besides, I soon discovered that the owners of swag shops hired managers to run them while they lived very comfortable lives. I set my heart on one day owning a swag shop.'

'Hardly to be compared with owning a mill.'

'No.' Napier's face darkened. 'But shopkeepers have a better life than mill children and, besides, I intended to own a swag shop by my own efforts. But all of this is in the future. Billy Barge and I walked all over southern England for six months. Then in Poole, Billy suddenly died. I saw him into a pauper's grave, then took over his licence and trade. Well, street trading is a young man's game. I was strong, hardworking and quick-witted. I'm proud to say, I was able to open my first shop on my eighteenth birthday.'

'Drummond, you should have written to your parents and gone home! They must have been desperately worried about you.'

'I wrote to Mama as soon as I returned to London after Billy died. I gave them an accommodation address and hoped to be invited home. My mother wrote to me, but I was not asked to return. I admit I was too proud, or perhaps too much of a coward to go home and risk a rebuff. By the time mother's letter arrived saying that Father had died, I owned sixteen shops and had a neat house in the City. I seldom entered my shops, but I purchased all the supplies for them, driving very hard bargains, I can tell you. It was an exciting life and I soon learned to appreciate what money could buy. However, I saw that I must go home to look after my family. I sold the shops to a rival and returned to Bury St Edmunds five years ago.'

'Your whole working life has been in cotton. How came you to become a maltster?'

'I'm coming to that. In Bury, I opened an exclusive drapery shop, nothing but the finest silks, wools and cottons. Fashionable Suffolk beat a path to my door. My family spent my money but didn't hesitate to inform me that I had blighted their social lives. Mama said repeatedly that she didn't mind for herself, but as the girls grew up, she became increasingly worried that my involvement in trade was ruining their chances of advantageous marriages. In my travels, I had several times visited Hertford and Ware. Pleasant towns, you must agree. And I liked the malting fraternity. Last year, I decided to become one of them. They are mostly Quakers, as you know, and perhaps it is their religious convictions which cause them to treat their employees well. At any rate, I felt that I would like to own a malthouse. We left our past behind and came to Bailton Hall.'

'And you are a quick study. I'm told you know an amazing amount about malting.'

'Yes, but not enough. I pay my manager well and give him shares in the business to keep him sweet. I must not forget that my prosperity depends on his judgement.' Napier studied his friend carefully. 'Will you still invite me into your home now that you know the secret of my early life?'

Horley smiled. 'It is a privilege to know you. What an extraordinary story! Not one to be told abroad, however. Society foolishly looks down on shopkeepers. Your sisters—'

'Quite. I'm resigned to hiding my shameful past.'

'Oh come, sir. You have every reason to be proud of your achievements. This country needs more men like you.' Horley was greatly moved and very anxious to change the subject. Napier Drummond was a far more complex man than he had imagined, but not so great an enigma when one knew his background. Drummond's spur was his dead father's indifference.

'Now about these candidates for Chief Constable of the county,' the doctor said heartily. 'Will you support Archibald Robertson?'

'He is superior to all the rest. We are doing the right thing in having a County Constabulary, you know. Look how well the new police have conducted themselves in London. It's a fairer system than the old one, fairer by far. Don't listen to Salisbury and his fears of a police state, nor that the landed gentry will be paying the lion's share for a service that will only benefit the town dweller.'

'But that much is true.'

'Never mind. They can afford it.'

Horley laughed, but said nothing further as the magistrates were called to order to indicate their preferences for each of the three candidates. The vote confirmed Napier's judgement. Robertson had no competition to speak of and won the post easily. The magistrates then suggested that a threepenny rate should be raised to pay for the new police force which would have one Chief Constable, four superintendents, six inspectors, thirty constables at twenty-one shillings a week and thirty receiving nineteen shillings.

Later, when members of the Police Committee were being selected, Napier made sure his name was put on the list. Then, with a tired nod to Horley, he left the Shire Hall for home.

5

Jefferson Smith sat in Sybilla's kitchen and drummed his fingers on the table. He was a powerfully built young man whose face bore the signs of a brief, unsuccessful career in the prize ring – scarred eyebrows and a nose which had too often been flattened against his face. He didn't have a full set of teeth; his smile was rather frightening, but his temperament was steady. Mrs Smith, his mother, lived with him in Lord Lane and went daily to clean for Mrs Auber as an extra housemaid. Between them they had contrived for many years to live without hardship.

'Used to have forty-five horses in the stable, the Bull did,' said Jefferson in his deliberate way. 'Coaches coming and going at all hours. Now they've only got thirty-five. They let me go because I'm only nineteen and I ain't been there as long as the others. Don't see what that's got to do with it. I work hard, I don't care for Daffy's Elixir, I'm strong and honest.'

Cissy was sitting on the other side of the kitchen table, cupping her chin in her hands. 'You're a good man, Jefferson, and you didn't ought to of been turned off like that. It's wicked. Your mam must be worried.'

'Cried like a baby. We can't manage without my twelve shillings a week. You know I was going to ask you to marry me, girl, but I can't do that now.'

She nodded glumly. Marriage to Jefferson was a long-held dream, but she had always known that it was a distant one. Stoical by nature, she met this new setback with outward calm.

'How much did you say you'd get if you was to become a constable?' she asked at length.

'Nineteen shillings, but I might get twenty-one in a year or two. I know I can do it, Cissy. Colonel Robertson, he's the new Chief Constable, he said I'm just the sort of man they're looking for. He'll write to me at the beginning of next month to tell me if I get to be a constable. I can read and write: wouldn't be considered if I couldn't.'

'You'd have to go away.'

'Maybe not. They're going to have constables all over the whole county, Hoddesdon too. Maybe I could stay with Mam. We'll get together in the end, Cissy. We're both young. Mam's always saying that to me.'

'Whatever would I do if I left Mrs Hobart?' she mused, more to herself than to Jefferson. 'She lets me keep Fanny with me, and my mam looks after her when I have to go out with Madam. If we was to get a place of our own, I couldn't work for nobody.'

'It would be hard, I know. But if we lived with *my* mam, *she* could look after Fanny. She's right fond of the child and wouldn't treat her like your father does. Then you wouldn't have to feed her Godfrey's cordial. You'll kill that child dosing her one of these days.'

Cissy stood up, blazing with anger. The bench on which she had been sitting crashed to the floor. 'Don't you ever say that, do you hear! I love my girl. I'd never hurt her, I wouldn't!'

Jefferson lumbered round the table to take his love in his arms. 'There, there, I didn't mean to upset you. It's just that the medicine puts her to sleep too much. Half the time she's too sleepy to eat proper. There's good grub here and Fanny needs to grow. I know why you do it. It's because of your old man, but –'

At the sound of footsteps on the back stairs, the young people sprang apart. By the time Saul shuffled into the room, Cissy was looking out of the window and Jefferson was lounging nonchalantly against the mantelpiece, studying the empty grate.

Saul was too absorbed with his own affairs to spare more than a look in his daughter's direction. 'She's give in!' he said.

His wife came out of the stillroom, her sleeves rolled up to the elbow. 'What's Mrs Hobart done now?' asked Mary Potter.

'I'm to have a new coat and white gloves. That's what she's give in about. She didn't want to, tried to say summat about not having the readies, but I just kept on naggin' her. "It's not right," I says to her, "me going round in an old waistcoat, and opening the door to the Lord knows who, looking like a vagrant or summat." "You don't look proper, I admit," says she, "and that embarrasses me. I know a manservant should be in livery. You stay off the blue ruin and one day I'll buy you a coat and gloves to look proper opening the door to my fine guests." "And stockings," says I, quick as a flash. "I got to have white stockings. And I'm sure *I* can't afford to buy them." So she thought a minute and says, "No, you'll have to find your own stockings and another shirt too." I'll have to lay out, I reckon, and you must keep them washed, Mary, and the gloves too. I'm to have a clean shirt every week without fail. She said so.'

'That's right,' said Mary. 'You get fine new clothes and I get more work. That's the way it allus goes.'

'Stop whining, woman. You get aprons.'

'What's that to say to anything? I can't put aprons on my back, can I? And she never gives away her gowns, not a thing since the old geezer died. A nipfarthing, that's what she is.'

Everyone nodded in silent agreement. A rich woman who kept her clothes to herself and never passed on anything to her servants was beyond comprehension. And to the Potters, Sybilla seemed very rich.

'Jefferson's been turned off at The Bull, Pa,' said Cissy after a short pause.

'I daresay he'll get something else,' said Saul, not interested in the least. 'You won't be able to get married now, so don't go thinking of it.'

'Remember how lucky you are,' added Mary, who had not delivered her little lecture this week. 'Mrs Hobart ought never to of let you have a follower. Too soft-hearted by half, that's what she is.'

'Don't count on that.' Saul headed for the gin bottle which had been cunningly hidden in the larder. 'You heard how she jumped down my throat, the little bitch.'

'That was because you didn't turn up to fetch her last Saturday night, I reckon. She might of sent you packing,' said Jefferson. 'Anybody else would of.'

'I know how to do my work proper,' said Cissy in the flat voice she always used to her father. 'She's got no cause to complain. Mam, Jefferson and me is going for a walk over to see his old lady. If Fanny wakes —'

'She never does,' answered Mary, 'but I'll be here. When am I ever anywhere else? Give me some of that gin, Saul.'

Mrs Drummond was the first member of the family to come downstairs. She walked quietly across the parquet floor of the spacious hall to enter the drawing-room. Earlier she had ordered a fire to be lit, and now caught a footman in the act of tidying the hearth. He looked very smart in his brown livery; a handsome, strong young man whose understanding was not great. She wondered if she would ever accustom herself to having so many liveried servants about the house.

'Good evening, James.'

The boy leapt to attention. 'Good evening, Mrs Drummond. I meant to be finished here –'

'That's all right. I've come down early. Take your time and see that you leave everything in perfect order.'

'Yes, ma'am.' The boy had reddened unattractively. He gave the mistress a grateful smile and returned to his chore.

'Is your mother feeling better, James?'

'Yes, ma'am. I seen her for a hour last Sunday and I'm to be let off tomorrow afternoon, thank you.'

'You may ask Cook to arrange a small basket of food. I don't mind, you know, but no one must take food without my permission.'

'Yes, ma'am. She's very sensible of your kindness and so am I.'

He bowed himself out of the room, and Mrs Drummond sighed unhappily. Napier would not have approved. Her generosity was erratic, occasionally excessive and always subject to her mood of the moment. This was most unfair, Napier told her repeatedly, because the servant who whined the most received the greatest largesse, while the deserving servant was penalized for his self-respect and stoicism. Sometimes Mrs Drummond wondered how she had managed to run a home before Napier returned to tell her what she was doing wrong.

She sighed again, more loudly, and restlessly fingered the fringe of her shawl. She was quite out of patience with her son. When they had returned from the Horleys' dinner party last week, Napier had called her into the morning-room to discuss the events of the evening. He had been lavish with praise for her clever handling of Mrs Hobart. Just as if she had calculated her every compliment! At first he had been inclined to regret her revelation that he had described Mrs Hobart as clever. On reflection, however, he had decided that this had been a master-stroke which was bound to lower the lady's defences and give her false confidence.

Now, as she sat awaiting Mrs Hobart's arrival, Mrs Drummond wondered if she would be too self-conscious to speak sensibly to the girl at all. And such a charming, unaffected young person who was apparently capable of standing up to Napier! She wished, rather maliciously, that she might see Mrs Hobart confound him utterly.

The butler ushered in Mr Florian Farley and Mrs Drummond rose at once, coming forward with hands outstretched.

'Florian, my dear! I'm so pleased that you could come to support me this evening.'

'Fair damsel!' He kissed each hand, then drew her towards him to place a kiss on one flushed cheek. 'Never let it be said that Florian Farley failed in his farcical fabrications to felicitate the femme fatale of his fantasies.'

She laughed delightedly. 'I only hope you may be able to say that when the champagne runs out.'

Farley gave a judicious tug to his brilliant red brocade waistcoat that just would not meet the top of his trousers. 'In this house, my dear delight, the champagne never runs out. Napier and I are not the greatest of friends, but I'll allow that he is generous to a fault in the matter of drink as in all else. But not – alas, I can read it in your face – not, I say, in the matter of two hundred pounds to be paid to our dear friend, Henry Watts.'

'I couldn't bring myself to ask him; I'm ashamed to say that I am afraid of my own son. However, if only tonight's party goes well, I may find the courage to broach the subject and he may be inclined to forgive me. He has dealings with a young widow, Mrs Hobart. If he can be made to feel that I have helped him there, he might reward me. Isn't that an awful thing to say? But I am desperate.'

'A young widow, did you say? Is his heart engaged?' Mrs Drummond started to speak, but he cut her short. 'What am I thinking of? Napier has no heart.'

'Florian, that is unkind of you.'

73

'No, Dorothea, that is heartless of Napier. To be serious, my dear, that scamp of yours is young enough to be my son, yet he shows no respect for grey hairs. Or rather, he might, but what hair I have left is, I thank God, still brown. He doesn't like me, but I could bear up under the strain of it, if only he didn't also believe me to be downright dishonest.'

'I'm sure –'

'My angel, let us face it. I should not have tried to persuade him to buy those shares. But, I swear I didn't know they were worthless. My present business affairs are different altogether. Henry Watts is a man of impeccable reputation who manages not one, but two, theatres –'

'One of them is too far away from the West End.'

'Granted, but as I was saying, two theatres, lavishly decorated, everything of the first stare. Both theatres play to full houses –'

'Not the one in Church Street, Marylebone, Florian. Fashionable people will not travel so far for their entertainment.'

'The crowdedness of the one compensates for the . . . ah . . . less crowdedness of the other. And you must admit that, at the Marylebone, plays are extravagantly mounted and the actors are of the – well – almost the highest quality. Henry Watts is as sound as a dollar.'

'But ours is the only box that is occupied. He can't seem to rent the others for the season. And that, I believe, is one reason why Mr Watts is pressing us for the two hundred pounds. If there's nothing wrong, why is he so anxious for our money? Tell me that.'

'I daresay he isn't *anxious* for our money. Two hundred pounds must be as nothing to a man of his wealth. But you know what businessmen are. He will not allow us credit over so many weeks. He is a hard man, of course, just as Napier is.'

'I've never known Napier to be so –'

'Depend on it, he is. You know nothing of Napier's business affairs, after all.' Florian Farley sat down beside her, forgetting his jocular pose for once. 'If I had not outrun the constable this quarter, I would pay the money myself. You know I would. But I live upon a small fixed income and exercise the utmost economy, except in the matter of dress and entertainments.

74

Yet, for some reason, I am always behind with the world. I wish it were otherwise.'

Napier, bursting into the room at that moment, found the couple holding hands as they sat with their heads together on the sofa. He scowled and the two older people looked like naughty children caught stealing birds' eggs.

'Good evening, Napier. How are you these days, old fellow?' said Farley with forced heartiness.

'Very well, thank you. I don't need to enquire how you go on.' Napier flashed an irritated look at his mother. Fortunately, Marianne and Emmaline entered the room just then, and Florian was able to create a diversion by jumping to his feet and complimenting both young ladies on their appearance.

Francis Babcock and one of Marianne's most volatile admirers, Septimus McCann, were announced. In the general conversation that followed, Napier found an opportunity to isolate his mother.

'Why the devil did you invite that old roué?'

'To entertain Mrs Hobart, and lift my spirits. Do not scold me, Napier,' she said with unusual asperity. 'I am in no mood for it.'

Mrs Hobart was announced and entered the drawing-room shyly, a vision in grey. Septimus McCann, seeing the widow's frail beauty for the first time, knew a moment's disloyalty to his divine Marianne.

Napier started towards her, but Farley was nearer. ' "She was as fair as the roses in May",' he said theatrically and brought her mittened hand to his lips with a flourish.

Napier ground his teeth, but was gratified to see that Mrs Hobart looked neither pleased nor flattered, just stunned.

'Mrs Hobart, may I present Mr Florian Farley?'

Napier quickly took her by the elbow and guided her towards Septimus, whose evil genius prompted him to imitate Farley and kiss her hand with enthusiasm. Now she was amused, her eyes brimming with laughter. The Drummond women saluted her cheek in turn and Francis, not to be outdone, also kissed her fingers lightly. Sybilla dared not meet Napier's eyes, but she need not have worried, kissing hands was not part of his social equipment.

Mrs Drummond pressed her to step upstairs to take off her hat and pelisse. Sybilla was whisked out of the room, just as Napier turned to give Farley a judicious set-down. That gallant, however, was in high spirits. Everyone was laughing at his witticisms, and Napier was forced to remain silent. He remembered how entertaining he himself had found the man until Farley had begun openly paying court to his mother. After he had discovered the way matters stood between them, he could find nothing at all amusing in Farley's antics. The attempted sale of suspect shares confirmed Napier in his dislike. Farley was a fortune hunter; why else would he court a middle-aged woman?

Sybilla followed her hostess up the broad staircase, and in spite of her determination to appear the epitome of sophistication, couldn't help exclaiming at the beauty of the house.

'Yes, it is attractive, isn't it?' said Mrs Drummond. 'I'm afraid I can take very little credit for it. My son bought it over a year ago and furnished it largely to his own taste. Then he spirited us away from Bury St Edmunds and deposited us here.'

'But didn't he even consult you?'

'Yes,' said Mrs Drummond, sorry to have brought up the subject, 'but you know what Napier is. All determination and action. We are very happy here. This is a somewhat finer house than our previous one.'

'Your bedchamber is certainly beautiful.'

'Decorated specially for me. Napier's choice, although I protested at the expense. Do you like the wallpaper?'

'It's beautiful,' said Sybilla and meant it. The paper bore a Chinese pattern of brilliantly plumed birds entwined with richly coloured flowers. The mauve of both flowers and plumage was echoed in the silk hangings of the beds, and even in the intricate pattern of several Indian rugs.

'The paper was one and threepence the yard, and my sitting-room is papered with it as well,' murmured Mrs Drummond, knowing full well that she was puffing off her son's wealth in a vulgar way. But surely this extravagance was some sort of proof of Napier's love for her.

When they returned to the drawing-room, Napier urged

everyone to enter the garden by way of the French windows so that they could visit his new stove house. It was quite dark out of doors, but both the path and stove house itself had been hung with lanterns which gave the grounds a fairytale appearance that enchanted Sybilla.

The stove house, built to rest against a south-facing wall, was very warm, and crowded with plants. Among its treasures were four rows of strawberries, forced to fruit weeks in advance of ordinary ones. Gallantly, the men picked some for the ladies of the party.

'Francis, you goose!' cried Marianne. 'You have given me a strawberry with soil on it.'

'Do wash it, ma'am,' said Francis. 'The gardener has provided us with a bowl of water. Such a fuss as you make, madam.' She made a face at him. 'Miss Emmaline, is your strawberry clean?'

'Yes, thank you. I've washed it myself.'

'There, Miss Drummond, see how self-sufficient your sister is?'

' "My Lord of Ely, when I was last in Holborn, I saw grand strawberries in your garden",' intoned Florian in his most theatrical voice. '*Richard the Third*,' he explained. 'I couldn't think of anything more appropriate in connection with strawberries.'

'You are well acquainted with Shakespeare, sir,' said Sybilla.

'Ah, the Bard is my delight and will continue to be until I reach my dotage and memory fails me altogether,' said Florian, and taking her by the arm walked her out of the stove house and on to the path. 'You are chilly, fair one? I found it a trifle too hot in the stove house. "When well-apparelled April on the heel of limping Winter treads".' *Romeo and Juliet.* You see, I have no favourites among the plays.'

'Don't let that silly man steal your guest away,' teased Marianne, as she walked with Napier several paces behind Sybilla and Farley.

'The moment she appears to be bored, you may be sure I shall rescue her. At the moment, she seems wonderfully amused,' replied Napier calmly.

'Well, of course she's amused! Everyone is amused by Mr

Farley, except you. And that is because you have no sense of humour.'

'But a strong sense of what is best for my mother,' he snapped.

'She found my father all by herself before you were even born.'

'Exactly so. You prove my point.'

Marianne took a deep breath, then thought better of her intended tirade. 'My dear brother, I know he treated you abominably, but can you not admit that he was a good husband, and fond father to his daughters? He made mother very happy. That is, I don't mean she was happy that you had been sent away, but —'

'Was she not?' asked Napier coolly. 'Don't neglect your swain. He's looking quite forlorn. Wherever do you find them, Marianne?' On the words, Napier walked away briskly to catch up with Sybilla and take her other arm. Within seconds, Farley had dropped back, much subdued.

The rich blue walls of the dining-room contrasted beautifully with the white moulded ceilings, and showed off the gleaming mahogany furniture to perfection. The table had been set for eight, of course, but Sybilla thought that twelve or more could be seated with the greatest comfort. Silver and crystal glittered in the candlelight; the richly decorated plates looked exquisite on the heavy damask cloth.

Mrs Drummond had sandwiched Sybilla between Napier Drummond and Mr Farley, and a greater contrast could surely not be found. On her one hand she was decreasingly amused by an inconsequential monologue, and on the other plunged into a serious conversation and asked the most searching questions.

Sybilla didn't know whether to be relieved or not when Mr Farley, feeling the need of a wider audience, directed his jokes at the general company. Napier Drummond took advantage of having her full attention. He was pleased to see her in such looks tonight. Her gown was clearly the creation of a woman of taste. (He could have priced the cloth to within a penny, but this he didn't mention.) He congratulated her on having abandoned full mourning. It was a trifle hypocritical to mourn the old man excessively, was it not? Surely, she had been sold into marriage by her parents.

She felt herself blush, said her father had died years ago, tried to convince him that she had most certainly not been forced into marriage. Such a thought was revolting.

'Oh, was it a love match, then?' asked Napier wickedly. 'Don't blush. My guests will wonder what I have said to put you out of countenance. Never mind, the worst is over. As a widow, you may live as you please.'

'A woman can never live as she pleases, sir.'

'Really? You surprise me. What would you like to do that Society and the law forbid?'

She was forced to laugh, and her laughter brought a surprisingly warm smile in response. 'You are outrageous, Mr Drummond. I can't think why I continue talking to you.'

'Perhaps,' he said very quietly, 'because there is no one else with whom you can speak freely. And we must speak freely when I accompany you to your home this evening.'

She nodded. There was so much that she would have liked to say, but this was hardly the time or place to discuss Hobart's.

Very soon Mrs Drummond led the ladies out of the drawing-room, leaving the gentlemen to their port. The drawing-room was chilly after the heat of the dining-room. A servant had just heaped the fire with fresh coals and it would be a few minutes before they glowed brightly enough to throw out any warmth.

'Come sit here, my dear,' said Mrs Drummond. 'Your shawl is a warm one, I see.'

'Well, mine is not,' said Marianne, heading for the door. 'Will you excuse me, Mrs Hobart? I must fetch something warmer, and one or two other things. We are to have some rare entertainment this evening.'

'Oh,' said Mrs Drummond, putting a hand to her head. 'You know, I do believe I have indulged a trifle too much in Napier's wines. My head is spinning.'

'Mama!' exclaimed Emmaline. 'You mustn't say such a thing. What will Mrs Hobart think?'

'Well, I believe I, too, have had too much. I don't know how it was, but no matter how much I drank from my glass, it always seemed to be full. Mr Farley is very droll, isn't he?'

'Yes, he is the dearest man, but my son dislikes him most unfairly.'

Sybilla could quite see how a man of Napier Drummond's temperament might quickly tire of such a fribble, so she said nothing in reply to this.

'He pays you the most outrageous compliments, Mama,' said Emmaline.

'Yes, dear, which infuriates Napier. I know dear Florian talks nonsense most of the time, but I pay no attention to the words, I just enjoy the sentiment.' She turned back to Sybilla.

'Napier is a most unnatural son –'

'Mama!'

'– you have no idea what difficulties I face, dear Mrs Hobart. There is the matter of two hundred pounds, for instance –'

'Mama,' said Emmaline desperately. 'I'm sure Mrs Hobart doesn't wish to –'

'I'm rather frightened of him, you see, and since dear Florian is involved, and Napier doesn't like Florian –'

'I must see what is keeping Marianne,' said Emmaline faintly. 'Will you excuse me?'

Neither Sybilla nor Mrs Drummond so much as looked in her direction as she left the room, but James was startled to see the younger daughter fairly fly up the main staircase a few seconds later.

'Marianne! I've been looking for you everywhere! You must come at once. Leave the costumes, I beg of you.'

'Whatever is the matter now? Here, take these capes.'

'I believe Mama is about to ask Mrs Hobart for the loan of two hundred pounds.'

'Don't be ridiculous!'

'At all events, she is saying the most dreadful things about Napier, and he won't like that. If Mama spoils his business dealings –'

'Well, why didn't you change the direction of the conversation, you ninny? Good God, do you suppose she has drunk too much? She never refused wine during dinner. I was very surprised because she is usually very abstemious.'

'She said her head is spinning, but I didn't know whether to believe her or not.'

When the sisters returned to the drawing-room, it was to find Mrs Drummond wiping her eyes with a wispy handkerchief and her young guest wearing two bright spots of colour on her cheeks.

'Mrs Hobart and I have just been having a cosy chat,' said Mrs Drummond emotionally, patting Sybilla's hand.

Marianne couldn't guess what might have been divulged in such a highly charged atmosphere and had no idea how she could defuse the situation without saying something that would be offensive to her mother. In the event, she had no opportunity to say anything. The men entered the room on a burst of laughter; Napier began to organize the seating for the entertainment which was to follow, and everyone was talking at once. Marianne looked at her sister who was chewing her lower lip, and shrugged her shoulders helplessly.

When everyone was seated, and Napier had arranged for Sybilla to have the place of honour, Emmaline opened the piano lid and played several short pieces. Sybilla was not musical, had never learned to play any instrument and didn't recognise the melodies. Yet it was obvious even to her that Emmaline Drummond was a sensitive, talented pianist. When Francis Babcock joined her to sing several popular songs, the effect was enchanting.

Florian Farley then made his appearance as Hamlet. He had not changed his dress, his only concession to costume being a rather dishevelled yellow wig. The effect was ludicrous, and just was was intended. He declaimed Hamlet's "To Be Or Not To Be" as written, but his gestures were wholly inappropriate to the words and gradually, as the speech progressed, he began stressing quite the wrong places, rendering the lines occasionally hilarious. Sybilla laughed until she cried, and she was not alone. Napier was smiling, too, but his eyes had scarcely left Sybilla's face.

Finally, Mrs Drummond, Marianne and Florian Farley announced that they were about to perform a one-act farce, and that they would be playing all the parts.

As the three dashed in and out of the drawing-room, changing costumes and voices as the many parts required, Sybilla was amazed that dear, oppressed Mrs Drummond could abandon herself in such a humorous way so soon after unburdening her soul. Marianne was an accomplished actress, and Mr Farley, Sybilla thought, must at some time have been a professional actor. This was only guessing, of course. Sybilla had never actually been to a real theatre and was, therefore, no judge.

At half-past eleven, she parted from the Drummond ladies with great warmth, already on first-name terms with the two girls. Marianne, her voice heavy with meaning, promised to call upon her soon.

As Sybilla had expected, Napier Drummond climbed into the elegant carriage beside her, and for the first few minutes the conversation was all about the evening's entertainment: Emmaline's playing, Marianne's acting, and – what Sybilla could not understand at all – Mrs Drummond's willingness to take part in theatricals. Her own experience of mothers had not led her to suppose that any woman of advanced age could be so good-natured.

'Ever willing to play the fool in a good cause,' said Napier.

'Well, I think it's marvellous. I only wish I could play or sing or act.'

'Believe me, you have no need to make a spectacle of yourself to win the admiration of those who know you.'

Sybilla blushed in the darkness. A compliment from Napier Drummond was worth cherishing, because she was certain he never, never put himself out to please. Unfortunately, she couldn't think of a suitably light reply and was forced to change the subject.

'It was very kind of you to send your carriage for me. So comfortable.'

'I put no faith in that servant of yours. Hertford Heath after dark is not safe for an unaccompanied lady. You may have noticed that one of the stable lads is riding the box with a shotgun.'

'Yes, I had noticed and I am grateful for it. But Saul is much improved. I took your advice, you see.'

'My advice? I don't remember giving any.'

'I called him into the morning-room and gave him a firm dressing down.'

'I can just imagine it.'

'You may laugh, but I must have convinced him that I would not stand any nonsense in the future. He has been the pattern of sobriety ever since, and ready to do my bidding.'

'You amaze me. I had never imagined that my words, so casually spoken, would have goaded you into what I am persuaded was uncharacteristic behaviour. You would have done better to take my other advice, however. Find yourself a better man.'

'Oh, we all get along very well these days.'

Napier was greatly amused, persuaded her to repeat what she had said to Saul, thought she had not been stern enough to effect any real change, but decided at last that it was the shock of her having spoken at all which had done the trick. 'For I'm sure you never raised your voice to the scoundrel before last Sunday.'

'No,' she admitted, 'and I hope I will never have to do so again. It was most unpleasant. I like to be upon good terms with everyone.'

'I will give you another, more important piece of advice, Mrs Hobart.'

'Thank you, sir. I was hoping to discuss –'

'Don't attempt the same trick on the manager of your business. He is a different type altogether, and one, moreover, with skills to sell. He'd probably walk out on you, and then where would you be?'

The silence lay heavy between them for several seconds.

Napier sighed. 'You did try the same trick on your manager, didn't you?'

'What would you have done? I found him inebriated at eleven o'clock on Monday morning. Anyway, how do you know what sort of man he is?'

'I once stopped by to enquire about a pony phaeton.'

'So it was you! You raised all my hopes, only because you wanted to check on my financial status!'

'Mrs Hobart, do you really think I am a fool? Business dealings are my life. Of course I checked on your financial status. But never mind that. How could you have been so idiotic as to let that man go? You should have kept him on even if you had to restrain him by force.'

'I'm only a woman trying to do my best in a man's world.'

'Aha! I've heard that whisker a thousand times before. Do you know anything about coach-building?'

'No, of course not.'

'No, of course not,' he mimicked. 'For years you were married to a coach-builder. Were you never curious? You've been a widow for a year and a half. Didn't you think it important to discover as much as you could about the source of your income?'

'Mr Hobart left everything to Puddifoot –'

'Yes, but you can bet your life he *knew* about the business, what was right and reasonable, what was wrong or dishonest. You, dear lady, have succeeded in cutting your own throat.'

She was so stunned by this outburst, that she couldn't think of a thing to say in her own defence. Not that he would have given her the opportunity to say it.

'Women, all women, irritate me beyond bearing. You think it unladylike if you can do simple sums without using your fingers. You whine to be given a carriage of your own, but never make the effort to learn to drive properly. You insist that you must have complete control over your own money – if only heaven or some poor man will provide you with enough – but you are not interested in studying the proper investment of funds. In short, you wish to lead the lives of dressmakers' dummies, while being treated with respect. Allow me to predict that you will be bankrupt within the year if you don't stop playing the grand lady and attend more seriously to your own affairs. Money does not fall from heaven. It has to be earned. At least, it does for people like us.'

The coach had drawn up before Hornbeam House, but Sybilla sat perfectly still, incapable of making a move as her heart thudded painfully against her ribs. A thousand thoughts crowded into her mind, but she couldn't sort them out into a coherent rebuttal.

'Mrs Hobart, forgive me,' said Napier, stricken with remorse. 'I was carried away. We must discuss –'

'No wonder your mother is terrified of you.'

'*Did she tell you that?*'

'No. I saw it for myself. More times than I could count *on my fingers* you glowered, snapped and sneered at the poor woman. I don't know how she bears up under it.'

'I am amazingly tolerant of . . . She might have my respect if . . . How would you like to have Florian Farley as a step-father?'

'I should be so grateful to have my mother – that is, if I knew my mother was –'

'– no longer a burden to you? Exactly. But I wouldn't be relieved of a burden; I would be expected to welcome a millstone. What a fine opinion you must have of me, ma'am. Were you not afraid to ride so far with me in the dark?'

'As it was a straight choice between you and highwaymen –'

She scrambled out of the carriage and hurried to her front door, tugging the bell-pull furiously. First the mother all but asks outright for a temporary loan of two hundred pounds and then the son treats her to a vicious stream of insults. The Drummonds were all mad, and she was not in the mood at the moment to admit that part of Mrs Drummond's charm was her madcap manner. Saul finally opened the door and she stumbled across the threshold. Only then did she hear the carriage pull away.

6

Napier discovered that his mother and sisters had retired to bed when he returned home after taking Mrs Hobart to Hoddesdon. His valet, Kindersly, therefore took the brunt of his bad temper. That long-suffering man said "yes sir" and "no sir" at what he considered to be appropriate intervals and clicked his tongue sympathetically as he helped his master out of his evening clothes and into his dressing-gown. Mr Drummond was not very forthcoming, and try as he might Kindersly couldn't discover the cause of his master's fury. But as everyone below stairs knew that he was paying assiduous attention to a pretty young widow, Kindersly put down this attack of spleen to a troubled heart.

Mrs Drummond was not at all anxious to meet her son on Sunday morning. Her daughters had subjected her to an inquisition after all the guests had departed. She had cried a great deal as she racked her brain for answers to their questions, but none of them were any the wiser at the end of it. Mrs Drummond could not remember if she had actually, in so many words, tried to borrow two hundred pounds from a young woman she hardly knew. On the whole, they all thought she had not. Mrs Hobart seemed to enjoy the entertainments that followed the tête-à-tête, and had gone off in the carriage with Napier in high spirits.

'I think you just allowed your tongue to run away with you a trifle, Mama,' said Marianne finally.

'Well, I had been cross with Napier all week. He was on my mind, you see. It's possible I might have been just a wee bit indiscreet. I really must not drink so much again. I can't think what possessed me to do so tonight, except fretting about Napier. Nevertheless, I'm sure I could never have been so grasping as to ask for money.'

'I think you should not worry, Mama,' added Emmaline helpfully. 'Even if you did approach her for the money, Mrs

Hobart is clearly a wealthy woman and, unlike you, has complete control over her own funds. Don't you envy her?'

'With all my heart,' replied Mrs Drummond. 'But, my dears, I must beg of you to make every effort to be on the best terms with your brother, so that he doesn't suspect anything. Just in case I've offended the young woman, you know. Perhaps whatever business he wished to conduct with Mrs Hobart is now safely concluded and we can all heave a sigh of relief.'

The next morning at breakfast, Napier's pensive mood put that comfortable thought out of their minds. But, as agreed, they smiled and chatted to him with great animation. To their surprise, Napier was also excessively polite to them, putting himself out to be charming. Which, as Mrs Drummond later said, made Sunday's breakfast quite the most miserable meal she could remember eating.

It was not surprising that Napier preferred to fight his business battles in his own office, a spacious room on an upper floor on St Andrew's Street in Hertford. He had taken some care in furnishing it. The room was thickly carpeted, the red pattern glowing in the light from two large windows, the surrounding moat of hardwood floor polished to a wicked smoothness that had unbalanced many an unsuspecting adversary.

The desk, solid oak of course, but not too large, was placed between the two windows. Napier's favourite position was behind it in a high-backed leather chair. When he sat in his accustomed place, his face was in shadow, while those of his visitors received the full glare from the windows as they perched uncomfortably on frail straight-backed chairs. A bookcase hugged one wall and above it hung a handsome painting of an imperious, gold-braided gentleman astride a horse. A small brass plaque on the frame helpfully informed the curious that this was General Napier, but did not mention that the subject of the painting was no relation. Napier Drummond had hung the painting – which belonged to his mother and was the inspiration for his own Christian name – as a reminder to himself never to be pretentious. But that was his secret; he was not in the habit of explaining his motives to others.

'Babcock!' he bellowed.

A side door opened and Francis leapt nimbly over the polished floor to take his place in the sturdier of the two chairs.

'Very enjoyable party on Saturday night, Napier. That ridiculous man can be vastly amusing when he chooses.'

'Mmmm . . . !'

'Your family looked well. Who is that overdressed young cub your sister –'

'Spare me your polite conversation, Francis, and speak your mind.'

Francis laughed. 'Well then, did the lady agree to sell?'

Napier smiled sardonically. 'You know my way with words when I choose to be persuasive.'

'You quarrelled with her,' said Francis promptly. 'Oh, Napier, why?'

'That is an interesting question. I really don't know why. Mrs Hobart brings out the worst in me.'

'I would not have said so, having seen the two of you together on Saturday night.'

'Mere formalities. Besides, I was on my best behaviour. Battle did not commence until we were alone. Until we had almost reached her front door, in fact.'

'I can't imagine such a quiet little thing besting you in a contest of wit and verbosity. I would have expected you to leave her all a-quiver.'

Napier laughed. 'When will I convince you that it is unwise to reduce to a quiver someone from whom you want a favour? As a matter of fact, I gave her the full force of my personality for several minutes and she was indeed quivering. With rage. The lady's style is to deliver one home thrust and then retire from the field of battle. I'm at a standstill, Francis. All my hopes are destroyed and I can blame no one but myself. Leave me to sulk in my lair, old friend. I'll either come up with a new plan of action or I'll do away with myself.'

Francis knew Napier well enough to read deep disappointment beneath the bantering words. He went back into his own office and began a careful review of the company's finances to see how badly dipped they would be by the failure of the malting venture. He had been working steadily for about an hour, and had just decided that they would scrape by, but that there would be no dividends for the shareholders this year, when he heard Napier in the next office.

'Take care, Mrs Hobart!' he heard Napier say anxiously. 'That floor is highly polished. Here, sit in my chair, won't you?'

Francis slipped from his own chair and stationed himself by the connecting door expectantly. Two things were almost immediately obvious to him: he was not going to be invited to attend this meeting; and he could eavesdrop only on Napier's part of the conversation, because Mrs Hobart's voice remained a tantalizing murmur.

Thus he heard Napier's: 'Stand then, if you insist, madam. I am all ears.'

A maddening murmur from Mrs Hobart indicated to Francis only that she was frostily angry.

'What?' bellowed Napier. 'Are you stark raving mad . . . ? No, I'll speak as loud as I choose. How dare you come here with such an outrageous demand? With your brazen greed and your want of delicacy, I'm surprised you are not already as rich as Croesus. Do you take me for a flat? I wasn't born yesterday and no, I won't meet your figure. You may keep your land for ever with my blessings . . . and good day to you, too. Mind the floor!'

Francis was really quite pleased not to have witnessed so violent an encounter. Unpleasantness of that sort distressed and embarrassed him. Poor Mrs Hobart must be completely crushed. He hurried to the window where he was very soon able to see the lady emerge from the building, mount the gig quite calmly and drive off in her customary execrable style, nearly colliding with a brewer's dray.

'Babcock!'

Francis sprinted back across the room and opened the door into Napier's office. 'How much?' he said eagerly. 'I couldn't hear anything she said.'

'Brace yourself. Four hundred pounds.'

Francis dropped into a nearby chair, marvelling at the woman's nerve. To walk into Napier Drummond's office and make such a preposterous demand required a degree of courage Francis did not possess. Or a degree of stupidity he didn't possess either.

'I wonder why she took the trouble to come on such a fruitless errand. She must have known that you wouldn't pay her so much.'

'Yes, but don't you see? She is keeping the negotiations open. The way is clear for me to make a counter offer. We are still in business.'

'You were dreadfully brutal to that poor woman.'

Napier grinned. 'Were you quaking in your shoes? I assure you, she was not. Game little thing. Doesn't know the meaning of fear. I've never known anyone so cool-headed.'

Francis was not at all convinced that the negotiations were still open. But when an attorney arrived in the late afternoon, begging an interview with Mr Drummond and claiming to represent Mrs Hobart, Francis had to admit that once again he was wrong.

'Good day to you, gentlemen,' said the attorney who introduced himself as Mr Wartnaby of Wartnaby and Dampier in Ware, also commissioners for taking acknowledgements of deeds by married women. Napier shot Francis a triumphant glance.

'Mr Drummond, I find myself in a most embarrassing situation,' said Mr Wartnaby. He removed his doeskin gloves, taking his time and revealing perfectly manicured nails on soft white hands. 'I have been approached by Mrs Hobart to act on her behalf as I have done in the past for her late husband –'

'And what sort of man was the late Mr Hobart?' interrupted Napier.

Mr Wartnaby wrinkled his nose. 'Rather coarse, opinionated, difficult to deal with. But he had been ill for many years, poor man, which may explain it. Mrs Hobart came to my office last week to ask a number of strange questions which I felt –'

'About compound interest calculated semi-annually? Shares of the equity, that sort of thing?'

'Why, upon my word, sir! I thought she was mistaken. Did you – have you offered to take the lady into some sort of partnership?'

Napier shook his head. 'Have you come to negotiate the sale of the Hobart land?'

'Why, yes sir. The lady feels that you will not listen to her properly. She should have put these negotiations in my hands much earlier, of course, but better late than never. I fancy I will save her the equivalent of my fee. Such large sums of money . . .' Mr Wartnaby crossed his legs primly, inspected the nails of his right hand and buffed them on the sleeve of his sober jacket. 'And this is what I find so embarrassing, you see. You know what women are.'

'Tell me about them.'

'Well . . . why, you know. Ignorant of business. Inclined to foolishness. It is a pity that such a . . . I must watch my words . . . *young* woman should have been left in sole charge of her own affairs. No one appointed to . . . no trust fund . . . She wants . . . you will laugh, sir, I am persuaded you will laugh. She has asked me to demand four hundred pounds for seven-tenths of an acre!' Mr Wartnaby tried a hesitant laugh on his own account, found he was laughing alone and closed his lips.

'Mrs Hobart has explained the situation to you? I can't reach my building because she owns the access.'

'Yes. Let me apologize on her behalf. So foolish to hold up the wheels of progress. I recollect you have some new venture under way, with a heavy investment of capital.'

'That is perfectly true.' Napier's eyes closed to slits. 'I'm not sure I understand you, Mr Wartnaby. Mrs Hobart has engaged you to act on her behalf. She wants four hundred pounds for a plot of land I cannot do without.'

'Just so.'

'Do you wish me to understand that I can offer much, much less and you will undertake to persuade her to accept it?'

'Why . . . a reasonable offer . . . in a nutshell. I suppose . . . '

'Do you expect *me* to pay your fee? Or perhaps slip some money into your fist?'

'No! Mrs Hobart will pay me in the customary manner. I only wish to do business in a rational way.'

'So,' said Napier. 'Mrs Hobart is to pay for the privilege of being betrayed by her attorney. What a fine upstanding man you are!'

'*Sir!*'

'Are you in the habit of taking advantage of the women who come to you? Mrs Hobart wants four hundred pounds for her land. You should be making every effort to squeeze from me a figure close to that amount. In private, try if you will, to convince the lady of her mistake in asking so much. But don't you dare ever come to me proposing to dupe your own client!'

Mr Wartnaby jumped to his feet, overturning the frail chair which lost a leg, as it had been threatening to do for months. 'You're well known in Ware, Mr Drummond. Everyone knows of your uncontrollable temper. Mad Drummond, they call you.'

'Yes, so I've heard,' replied Napier affably as he stood up. Francis also rose to his feet, his heart pounding with the excitement of it all. 'And everybody is afraid of me,' continued Napier with a note of pride. 'You are not the first man to come crawling through that door. No, sir. But one person is not afraid of me: Mrs Hobart. I will not pay her price, of course, but she is a worthy opponent. Good day to you, sir.'

Mr Wartnaby, half-way to the door, now hastened through it, leaving a glove behind. He saw it fall to the floor, but his nerve failed him and he wouldn't return to pick it up.

'Napier,' said Francis quietly as he picked up the pieces of the chair and the fallen glove. 'Far be it from me to tell you how to go about your business. But wouldn't it have been wiser to have kept your opinions to yourself, made the man a reasonable offer and allowed him to persuade Mrs Hobart to accept?'

'Yes, of course it would, but how could I have overlooked such a piece of effrontery? Did you ever hear of anything so disgraceful? He was willing to act contrary to his client's best interests and then pocket her fee. Mrs Hobart is right, you know. I had never given the matter any thought before. It *is* difficult for a woman living alone to manage her life.'

'Yes. Wartnaby was right to deplore the way Mrs Hobart's finances have been left. There should have been a trust, an executor. Has she no male relatives, I wonder? Women should not be burdened with such worries.'

Napier smiled. 'My mother would be delighted if she had complete control over her pittance. She cannot forgive me for having my tight fist on the purse strings, or my father for having arranged her affairs in this way. Of course, she would have been destitute within six months. Mrs Hobart, I fancy, is rather different. She is neither stupid nor extravagant. She lacks experience, but apart from that, every man with whom she deals attempts to take advantage of her.'

'Including you?'

'Less than others, but she doesn't realize it. She needs a husband.'

'We can't wait that long. It would be unthinkable for her to marry within two or two and a half years of being widowed, and by that time our patent method will either be a resounding success or a bad dream.'

'Ah! We are discussing correct behaviour, are we? I'm afraid I am not conversant with all points of etiquette. Didn't Croxley remarry three months after his wife died?'

'He's a man! Besides, he has young children to care for.'

'And Lady Mandeville. Didn't she marry her husband's cousin just thirteen months after she was widowed?'

'Yes,' said Francis. 'That was some years ago, and the only reason you know the exact length of her widowhood is because the scandal was so great that people still speak of it.'

'Yet the Mandevilles have survived.'

'Their credit is such that —'

'I see. I'm grateful for your advice. You, naturally, know all about such things. One way to get my hands on the land would be to marry Mrs Hobart myself. Wouldn't my credit —'

'Possibly, but hers wouldn't. The world would say she had done very well for herself, and call her a scheming hussy. But you can't be serious. I know I have said often enough that a man in your position should marry, but, believe me, I didn't have the widow in mind. Why throw yourself away on a penniless woman when you could have any one of half a dozen brides of good family and at least modest fortune?' Francis looked into Napier's smiling eyes. 'Oh, it was a joke and you've been laughing at me. What a relief! In any case, even you would find it difficult to bring the lady to the altar within a week or two.'

'Poor Mrs Hobart. She may have no family to speak of, but any woman owning a parcel of land worth four hundred pounds can't be described as penniless.'

They both laughed and the subject was dropped. But later that evening after Francis had dined with the Drummonds and the two men had enjoyed several brandies, Napier gave his friend a meaningful look and suggested they drive out for an hour.

93

'At this time of night?' exclaimed Mrs Drummond. 'But wherever would you – I beg your pardon. It is none of my business.'

'It is merely business, Mama,' said Napier. 'I must see a – gentleman about some land. He lives alone. I'm quite sure he'll be at home.'

'Well, the tea-tray hasn't arrived yet,' said Mrs Drummond, trying to ignore Marianne's stormy face. 'Will you take tea with the gentleman?'

'I'm quite sure tea will be served, Mama.'

'Why can't you settle at home for one evening?' said Marianne. 'You are always off somewhere. It's obvious you find our company boring.'

Since Napier was quite sure that this speech, although directed at him, was meant for Francis, he just smiled and left the room. He heard Francis making profuse apologies as he took up his hat and gloves. The carriage had arrived at the front door by the time Francis finally joined him in the hall.

Mrs Hobart looked more stunned than pleased when Saul showed the two men into the morning-room where she had been reading quietly before a small fire. Saul, she thought, should have led the men into the drawing-room and then come to fetch her. She was a little embarrassed to be discovered in this shabby but comfortable room wearing an old black woollen gown.

'I hope we are not intruding, madam,' said Napier pleasantly. He never carried a grudge, forgetting harsh words spoken by either side five minutes after they were uttered in anger. He was, therefore, unaware of the resentment that blossomed in many a breast for weeks after an encounter with him.

Sybilla was embarrassed to meet him again so soon after their quarrel, but her hopes were high, which helped her over the awkward moment. Curiously, she couldn't meet Mr Babcock's eyes; he seemed to be acutely uncomfortable. She ordered tea to be brought to the morning-room and found seats for her guests. Napier Drummond sat directly opposite her; Francis Babcock preferred a hard chair closer to the door.

'Your attorney paid us a call today, Mrs Hobart. Incompetent man. You should find yourself a more capable representative,' said Napier.

'All men are incompetent when required to work for a woman,' she replied with a hint of bitterness.

'Why, that is just what I was saying to Mr Babcock this afternoon. Life is difficult for a woman living on her own.'

The tea tray arrived, carried by the thin, sour-faced girl who had served them on their previous visit. The conversation switched to the subject of tea, who would take milk and sugar. Mrs Hobart was an efficient hostess, attending gracefully to the needs of her guests. She couldn't hide her tenseness, however, waiting for an opening salvo on the subject of the land.

'I have written to your mother, Mr Drummond,' she said as she sat down with her own cup. 'I enjoyed spending Saturday evening at your home very much.'

'It was pleasant, wasn't it?' replied Napier. 'You and my mother have developed quite a close relationship, I believe. She speaks of you with warmth. And you –' he paused, his eyes alight with laughter, '– are her champion, are you not?'

Sybilla flushed, but met his gaze. 'I admire her; Mrs Drummond is a woman of many fine qualities.'

'She has not your head for business, ma'am.' Napier allowed her to remove his cup from his hand, even though he had drunk only two-thirds of the contents. She was restless, he noticed with satisfaction, and had to be on the move. He watched her closely as she emptied the dregs of all three cups into the slop-bowl before pouring fresh tea. 'My mother would never have demanded four hundred pounds for a piece of waste ground,' he said sweetly. 'She may have her faults, but she is not greedy.'

'No, she is so good-natured that certain people trample on her feelings, wounding her deeply.' The cup rattled in its saucer as she handed it to Francis. He almost dropped it, having caught a glimpse of Napier's suddenly stormy expression.

'Come, madam. We have avoided the subject long enough. As I said earlier today, you are not able to manage your affairs as you ought. Life is difficult for a woman living on her own, for *anyone* living alone. Marriage, even such a one as yours, has much to recommend it. In fact, Mr Babcock is always harping on at me about the need to take a wife. But since you have no marital plans for the near future, no man to whom you would automatically turn, I was wondering –'

Napier heard Francis gasp a split second before he received the contents of the slop-bowl in his face. Only then did he realize just what interpretation she had put on his words. He made no move to dry himself, but smiled wryly, his eyes on his hostess who was pale and breathing heavily. 'For shame, my pretty. Don't you know that violence is the last refuge of the inarticulate?'

He ducked the contents of her own cup since he knew it would be hot. However, his shirt and cravat were now thoroughly soaked. A single tea-leaf clung to his chin as he stood up.

'Mr Babcock, would you excuse us –' began Sybilla as she rose to her feet, but Francis was already out of the door, murmuring something about awaiting Napier in the carriage.

'I must apologize for my behaviour,' she said shakily. 'I don't usually act – I don't know what I was thinking of.'

'Yes, you should be ashamed,' laughed Napier. 'Francis was shocked.'

'Well, it was your fault!'

'He was shocked by both of us. I'm afraid he doesn't understand our fiery temperaments.'

'I don't normally have a fiery temperament. I'm noted for my self-control. At least, I used to be.'

'You have perhaps been forced to keep a tight rein on your emotions for too long. I hadn't meant – that is, perhaps unconsciously I wanted to . . . What I am trying to say is, I hadn't meant to speak at all yet, but now that I have, don't you think there is something to be said for the scheme? I must confess I didn't expect to be scalded in reply to my – er – proposal.'

'Proposal? Is that what it was? I could have sworn it was an arrogant assumption, motivated by greed and determination to have my land at any cost – except the price I'm asking.'

'You are not thinking clearly, my dear. It would be cheaper to pay four hundred pounds than to marry you. My *proposal* was – how shall I word it to be safe from another drenching? My suggestion was impromptu.'

Napier looked at the young girl as if he had never seen her before. She was stunningly beautiful in her anger. Her eyes were filled with tears; she looked very small and touchingly vulnerable. He had never intended to plunge so casually into matrimony, but now that she had so wildly misunderstood him, he felt himself recklessly inclined to carry the matter through. Why not? Certainly, no other woman had ever appealed to him so strongly. He felt rather protective towards her. Poor thing; she would find a safe haven at Bailton Hall. He moved forward confidently to take her in his arms.

She shrank away from him. 'Don't touch me!'

Napier hesitated. 'Come, Sybilla. Take this chance of happiness and security.'

'You are too generous. Get out.'

He took a deep breath, not knowing whether to be relieved or sorry, and turned away. He let himself out of the house, leapt into the carriage and ordered the coachman to spring the horses. The carriage bowled down the empty dark road, raising a cloud of dust and the fury of a stray dog, whose barking echoed in the stillness. Neither man spoke for several minutes.

'Oh, well,' said Napier. 'No man is perfect.'

Francis howled with hysterical laughter, the result of too many minutes spent dreading an ugly scene in the carriage. There was never any knowing how Napier would react.

'You are a great sport,' he said when he could catch his breath. 'What, by the way, had you intended to say following such a rash preamble?'

'Something about asking Horley to advise her. I had some vague idea that her doctor could mediate between us. I trust Horley, you know. It was a sound idea.'

'I'm sure you spoke without thinking, but you were very nearly rolled up. You might have spent the rest of your life tied to a harpy. I was never so disgusted in my life as when she threw the tea in your face. Twice! I must admit I would not have suspected her of such a want of conduct.'

'No, I don't suppose you would.'

'But how fortunate that she doesn't appreciate what a catch

you are. She might have leapt at your supposed offer with tears of joy.'

'There were no tears of joy.'

'What a marriage that would have been! You two can't be in the same room without quarrelling. When the time comes, promise me that you will choose a conformable wife.'

'Yes, of course. All I need is a dull wife to complete my happiness.'

'This is famous. What an extraordinary night, but don't worry, I won't say a word to anyone. I'm so glad you have taken it well. Many a man would not. I was afraid you would be ready to murder someone by the time you entered the carriage, and that I would be the sacrificial lamb.'

'No, my friend. I bear my battle scars lightly and will now run away and live to fight another day.'

Napier maintained a steady flow of patter at his own expense the rest of the way to Hertford, and bade a light-hearted farewell at the gates of Balls Park where Francis rented a small house.

Alone in the carriage, he dropped his cheerful pose and sat with clenched teeth. He was an impulsive man, used to riding roughshod over others. Sybilla's actions in no way discomposed him. But her look of revulsion as he started to take her in his arms was a different matter. He was not accustomed to being repulsed by a woman. In fact, for the past fifteen years he had taken great care never to walk into a situation where he could be hurt in this way. The Flos and Mags and Betties who had assuaged his loneliness over the years had lightened his purse, but he had made sure they never touched his heart nor dented his pride.

Reflections of Fore Street's gaslights glittered in his eyes. He had met his match; a slip of a girl who had exposed all his weaknesses, robbing him of power. She had achieved his defeat merely by her quiet dignity and courage. Her silences left him stumbling over his own tongue. Admittedly, he had spoken thoughtlessly tonight, but at least he had momentarily pierced her diamond-bright reserve. He must take what comfort he could from that fact.

A man who had dodged knives as well as fists in his time could not be disturbed by a little tea – hot or cold. He had his defences: a quick mind, a bold façade and a sharp tongue. None of them had so far served him well in dealing with the widow.

In polite society a tendency to verbal abuse branded a man as uncouth. Yet, although he knew this perfectly well, he had never learned to weigh his words, and until now had little cause to regret his street ways. A snarling dog, he was fond of saying, was seldom challenged to fight.

His frustration over the Hobart land aroused his battle instincts. He could not afford to crawl away like a whipped cur. Failure was a spectre that haunted him. *He must not fail.* Before it was too late, he must find a satisfactory way of gaining possession of the land. The lady would find that she had placed herself in the path of a juggernaut. He would crush her and pass on, unmoved by her cool beauty.

Those who knew him for a ruthless businessman would have been surprised at his restraint tonight, because he never considered destroying the young widow by telling her that she had leapt to the wrong conclusion, that he had not intended to offer her his name, was merely about to suggest she should ask Horley to advise her. He might be furious that she could imagine he would be so clumsy in proposing, or that he would do so in Francis Babcock's presence, but he would never have offered her such a humiliation as she must feel if her mistake were pointed out to her. Napier chose to win his negotiations with a certain style. To inflict the sort of blow to her pride as she had inflicted on his would be foul play.

The carriage turned up Bell Lane towards Bailton Hall, and the sound of revelry coming from the Salisbury Arms jerked him back to awareness of his surroundings. In future, it would be wise to conduct his battle away from the amused eyes of Francis Babcock. That young man would learn of victory when Napier held the deed in his hand, and not before.

The butler, opening the door to him a minute or two later, stared at his damp, stained shirt in puzzlement. 'Has it been raining, sir?'

'Yes, with milk and sugar. Send Kindersly to me.'

*

99

It was the sulky girl who opened the door to Napier on Tuesday morning.

'Take me to Mrs Hobart, please.' He was across the threshold and well into the hall before the girl realized it.

'It's only half-past nine, sir!'

'I know the time, thank you. Where is Mrs Hobart?'

'Still in bed with a terrible headache.'

'Poppycock.' He removed his hat and tossed it on to the narrow table, and began peeling off his gloves. 'I've no time for trumped up excuses. Tell your mistress that I wish to see her immediately.'

Cissy, wide-eyed, turned and ran upstairs, leaving Napier standing in the hall. Within a very short time he looked up to see Sybilla in a light green dressing-gown making her way carefully down the stairs. Her hair hung in a heavy cascade almost to her waist and her face was deathly pale.

'Good God, woman! What is the matter with you?'

'I have a severe headache. What is it you wish to say to me?' She reached the hall floor, but felt too ill to play the well-bred hostess by inviting her guest into the drawing-room. She leaned against the newel post and waited.

'You were overwrought last night. I have come back to talk sensibly to you about the land. This can't go on.'

'Mr Drummond, please go away. I am overwrought *now*, believe me. I don't want to talk. I want to go back to bed. Say whatever it is you have on your mind and then, I beg of you, leave me in peace.'

'Are you sure it's nothing serious? Just a headache? I'd better send for Horley.'

'No, no. There is nothing he can do. It is not, as you have said, anything serious. Just a headache. I shall be well tonight, or perhaps this afternoon.'

'I'll carry you upstairs.'

'No!' She winced at the mere thought of it. 'Please don't jar me. I couldn't bear it.'

'Sybilla, my dear —'

'And don't call me Sybilla.'

'It will be quicker and easier if I carry you. I won't jar you, I promise.'

He picked her up swiftly and started up the stairs. After a

short but heartfelt groan of agony, Sybilla was unprotesting. She clung to the lapel of his coat, each step a torment. The man was like a lumbering elephant, clumping heavily on each tread. And the stairs stretched upwards for ever.

'If you'd ever had a headache like this –' she began.

'Never had a headache in my life. No time for them.' He swung her round. 'Is this your room?'

'Yes. For God's sake, put me down.'

He set her on her feet by the side of the bed and looked round him. 'No wonder your head aches. The room is stuffy. I'll open the curtains and let in a little fresh air.'

'Don't you dare, you dreadful man,' she said bitterly and put her fingers to her temples.

'Here, I'll do that.' He crossed the room, setting each floorboard bouncing, brushed her hands aside and began massaging her temples vigorously. Concentric rings of brilliant colour radiated from her right eye. She saw him through a haze of pain, a strong healthy man, enjoying the sharp spring day, arrogant and unfeeling. She devoutly wished she had the strength to hit him. In fact, even the resonance of her own voice within her skull added to the pain. She was forced to low-voiced monosyllables when she wanted to shout.

'What has caused you to succumb to this affliction, ma'am?'

'Not what, who!'

He dropped his hands and stepped back a pace. 'I see. So this suffering is to be laid at my door. I told Babcock that you were not afraid of me, but –'

'Of course I'm not afraid of you. But I do wish you were not so – so rough in everything you do.'

To his surprise, he was deeply wounded. 'In that case, I must truly apologize. Go to bed. You look dreadful.'

She laughed briefly. 'Thank you for the compliment. That was just what I needed.'

'Oh, Sybilla, can I never say the right thing? I shall go away, I promise.' Taking her face in his hands, he gave her a hearty, friendly kiss on the forehead. A shower of stars assailed her optic nerve. She was half blind; the world was coloured orange and smudged almost beyond recognition, so she felt the vibrations of his going rather more clearly than she saw the departure.

With infinite care, she removed her dressing-gown and slid between the sheets, seeking escape from the pain. The kiss burned on her forehead. A few moments later, the closing of the front door gently rattled the windows in their frames. Sybilla winced.

'The gentleman wrote you this letter, ma'am,' said Cissy softly as she came into the room.

'Put it here on the side table. Come to me at noon.'

Cissy laid the letter on the table as instructed and departed, deeply shocked. The mistress, she thought, should have been more upset by the rude man's behaviour. Picking her up and carrying her upstairs, indeed! She had never seen the like. Cissy was disappointed that Mrs Hobart, whom she idolized, had not at least screamed for help as any decent woman would. Not normally a communicative girl, she couldn't wait to reach the kitchen in order to tell this tale.

Sybilla reached out for the letter. Her head ached too much to allow her to read and, in any case, it was too dark. However, she had no trouble at all in discovering that the single sheet of writing paper enclosed a bank draft. Sighing happily, she sank on to the pillows and slept soundly for several hours.

When Cissy entered the bedroom at noon carrying a tray with a light luncheon, Sybilla sat up with pleasure. She was hungry, and impatient to be dresseed so that she could deposit the money at the bank in Ware.

After the first cup of tea and the second slice of bread and butter, she picked up the letter to gloat over the bank draft properly. And read the amount with horror and outrage. Two hundred and fifty pounds! She had been cheated! She wouldn't accept it. He had taken wicked, but typical advantage of the fact that she had been unable to think clearly.

She fumed inwardly for a full minute, but following this first flush of justifiable anger, her temper cooled. The bank draft, representing so much money, was too precious to be destroyed in a fit of pique. After all, she had originally planned to demand just forty pounds for the land. The sum of two hundred and fifty pounds seemed, on reflection, to have an almost mystical significance. It divided itself neatly, indicating to her how it should be spent.

Mr Drummond might think himself clever. She had to admit

he was a formidable man. It was highly unlikely that there was another person in the whole of Hertfordshire who could have wrung so much from him in return for so little; she was entitled to congratulate herself on her achievement. And the best was yet to come, because she would use his own money to take a very subtle form of revenge.

Only when she had considered her next move carefully did she pick up the sheet of paper to read what he had to say. The letter was short. There was no greeting and no signature. Just two words: Forgive me.

Of course she wouldn't. More importantly, would he ever forgive her? She hoped not.

7

In the early afternoon, Napier ushered Wartnaby's clerk from his office, then walked quietly into Francis Babcock's room.

'There you are, Francis. Never underestimate me.' He tossed the deed to the Hobart land on to the desk.

'Good lord! You did it! I congratulate you. How much did you have to pay in the end?'

'Fifty pounds. I wrote a draft on my personal account before she had the opportunity to change her mind, so the company owes me fifty pounds.'

'I'll see that the money is transferred to your account. I still can't believe that she was so ready to settle.'

'The bargaining was carried out in a most unpleasant atmosphere,' said Napier blandly. 'She looked quite drawn by the time I left, I assure you. But that was a near miss, Francis. Promise me you will rap my knuckles – or put your handkerchief in my mouth – the next time I look about to say something rash.'

'But that's the trouble,' laughed Francis. 'You never look as if you are about to say anything rash. You just speak out when I least expect you to. Of coures, you are seldom so hilariously misunderstood. Hadn't we better busy ourselves with our plans?'

'Immediately. Get in touch with the workmen as soon as you can. I'm going directly to Ware and may well work through the night. Too much time has been wasted already.'

Mrs Drummond received a scrawled note from her son at three o'clock, telling her not to expect him for dinner that evening. At ten minutes past three, she despatched James with a fond invitation to Florian Farley, asking him to join her for dinner, explaining that her son was away from home.

Florian rented a small cottage, belonging to Sir Hugo Mandeville, on the Hertingfordbury road. Although he knew that Mrs Drummond dined at eight, he walked into Hertford and arrived at her home at five o'clock, confident of a warm reception.

'There's no point in suggesting that we take a turn in the garden,' said Mrs Drummond, meeting him in the hall, 'because it is bitterly cold outside. And the girls are sewing in the morning-room, so shall we take advantage of Napier's absence and sit cosily in his library?'

'Surely it is as much your library as his, my dear.'

'No, I don't think so. The room bears the . . . the stamp of his character, don't you think?'

'Perhaps you're right,' said Florian thoughtfully. 'In which case, let us sit elsewhere. Your son's personality is so strong and so different from my own, that what suits Napier must make me uncomfortable.'

In the end, they decided to go upstairs to Mrs Drummond's own sitting-room. The Chinese bird wallpaper decorated this room from the ceiling to the white-painted chair-rail. The room was bright, comfortable and so entirely her own that Mrs Drummond felt easy at once and began to tell Florian her news.

'I have the two hundred pounds in notes for you.'

'Upon my soul! How did you come by them?'

'Well that,' admitted Mrs Drummond, 'is a cause for worry. Mrs Hobart called on me this afternoon and offered to lend me two hundred pounds on the understanding that I pay it back next quarter day. So I have the money and I need not approach Napier until June. Who knows? A miracle may occur before then. It seems – although I don't remember perfectly – that I complained bitterly about Napier to her last Saturday night and even told her about Mr Watts. I would have told you about it, except that I haven't seen you.'

'But, my dear,' interrupted Florian, 'you *could* not have asked her to lend you two hundred pounds, only because you were afraid to mention the debt to your own son!' He looked at his companion doubtfully. 'Could you?'

'I over-indulged on Saturday night. I've no clear recollection. In fact, I quizzed Mrs Hobart about my asking for the money, and she grew quite pink. She insisted that I had not, that she had merely put two and two together. She grew rather upset when I hesitated, so that I couldn't refuse her. And anyway, I've been so worried about Mr Watts, that I am quite glad to be able to give you the money. Do you think he would have carried out his threat to approach Napier? He was rather sharp with me the last time we attended the theatre.'

'He would meet his match in Napier if he did speak out,' replied Florian, 'but, needless to say, I would no longer be welcome in your son's home and our visits to the theatre would soon be only a fond memory. If Mrs Hobart wishes to lend you two hundred pounds, I don't see why she should be denied the pleasure. She will surely not expect interest on the money, but I think it would be a fine gesture if we were to take her to the theatre one evening.'

'Oh, yes! Napier won't mind, I'm certain, but he has to be considered, you know, because although I – or rather you – have a box, all the other expenses are his.'

Florian tugged at his waistcoat. 'Napier has a generous nature. You can't deny that, Dorothea. Don't you think it would be wisest . . . '

'If you are going to suggest that I bare my soul to him, you can hold your breath. Napier is generous with his wealth; also with his scorn. I could not bear it, I tell you. And it wouldn't matter how he came to hear of our arrangement, I should be forced to agree never to see you again.'

'You are a grown woman, as well as being his mother.'

'I am also fifty-three years old and set in my ways. I have always obeyed the men in my life. First my father, and what a tartar he was! Then dear Drummond, who was the kindest man who ever lived, except on one subject. And now Napier. I'm too old to disobey. How I wish I were a different sort of person. Strong-minded and clever.'

'I understand, believe me. Did you know? Florian is not my real name.'

'Never!' said Mrs Drummond in mock surprise.

He smiled. 'My real name is Fidelio.'

'Now, Florian.'

'I jest. My baptismal names are Thomas Isaiah. Be honest with me. Do I look to you like a Thomas Isaiah?'

'Not now, dear, but you may have done so in your cradle.'

'All my life I have wanted to be someone else. Anyone but the man I am.'

106

Mrs Drummond took his hand and held it between hers. 'I've never asked you, Florian. Were you ever an actor?'

'For three months only. I ran away when I was eighteen and joined a troupe of travelling players. I took the name of Florian then. My father found me and brought me home. I was set to studying the law, because he wanted me to join him in his practice. When I was twenty, he died, leaving me a small income. My mother had departed this life two years earlier, so I thought my opportunity had arrived. I sold the house and land and took the mail coach to London.'

'Just like Napier!'

'There were many temptations: I gambled, I speculated, and, inevitably, for I am no businessman, I lost all the money I had received for the property. By that time, I had also met Isobel. After we were married, we bought a very small house in Baldock with the money her grandmother had left her and we lived modestly on my inheritance. We never had any children to bless our old age and, as you know, she died five years ago. I felt my whole life had been wasted. Nothing to show for it. I decided to enjoy what years were left to me, and when I met Henry Watts, I thought that at last I had found my place in the world. Unfortunately, the acting company has given me more worries than joy. If I had not met you at the Gibson's party . . .'

'Oh, Florian. What a sad life. Are you bitter that your father took you away from the acting troupe?'

'Excessively.'

'Well then! Napier ran away and no one forced him to come home. He became very successful, so why is he so bitter towards me?'

Florian smiled fondly at her, unruffled by the knowledge that her thoughts were never very far from her son. 'He felt rejected, perhaps.'

'Well, he was! Dear Drummond totally rejected him. But in my heart, I never did. I do so regret it all. Napier has suffered from the lack of female influence in his life.'

Florian stood up and took a turn round the room, keeping his thoughts on that subject to himself. He was certain that Napier had enjoyed his fair share of petticoat company. On the other hand, he did understand what Dorothea meant. Napier had missed the softening influence of his mother.

Florian also had long ago formed his own opinion of "Dear Drummond".

At half-past seven, Mrs Drummond sent him down to the drawing-room so that she could change for dinner. So it was that when Francis Babcock was shown into the drawing-room by the butler, Florian had to play the part of host, asking the young man if he had been invited to dinner.

'Well, no,' said Francis ruefully, 'although to tell you the truth, I was hoping to be invited. Napier is having something sent in to him, but I've never developed a fondness for scratch meals.'

'And who can blame you, dear fellow?' Florian pulled the bell. 'I'll tell Scrimshaw to have another place set for dinner. The ladies will be delighted to have you join us.'

Scrimshaw opened the door almost at once. 'Yes, Mr Farley?'

'Mr Babcock will be dining with us this evening,' said Florian.

'Yes, sir.' Scrimshaw closed the door carefully. When the cat's away the mice will play, he murmured to himself, and headed for the back staircase. Cook *would* be pleased.

'Quite an attractive woman, that Mrs Hobart,' said Florian casually as he sat down in a deep chair. He had to spread his legs to accommodate his paunch. Even so, low chairs gave him indigestion.

'Yes, I suppose she is, although she is not the type I prefer. Rather too strong-minded for my taste.'

Florian rubbed his chin. 'Wealthy woman?'

Francis laughed as if at some private joke. 'She certainly couldn't be described as penniless.'

'I believe she has business dealings with young Napier.'

To Francis, 'young' Napier was as old as the trees – and sometimes as wise, but never as silent. 'That is all finished to everyone's satisfaction, I believe. We should be seeing no more of Mrs Hobart. Oh, I know Mrs Drummond is very fond of her, and Emmaline – that is, *Miss* Emmaline – thinks her something wonderful. But Napier need never see her again.'

'Hmmm.' Florian was well pleased with himself. He had elicited all the information necessary about Mrs Hobart, and wanted only the opportunity to be alone with his dear lady so that he could pass it on.

Emmaline and Marianne entered the room in an excited swish of silken skirts, surprised and well pleased to find that they were not to dine alone. Marianne immediately took charge of the conversation, hatching plots for their amusement after dinner. Everyone would be put to work on some new songs for which Emmaline had recently bought the music. She had been practising for several hours and Marianne thought her sufficiently adept to play while they all sang. And Mr Babcock must learn one piece as a solo; Marianne would not take no for an answer. He had a very pretty voice when he put himself out to try, and she was determined that he should perfect it. She would coach him on the proper rendering of the words which were very affecting.

She turned her attention to Mr Farley and began listing his tasks for the evening; and, not surprisingly, was firmly put in her place. Mr Farley had not been at all pleased with Marianne's own performance the other evening. She must not move when others were speaking; professional actors considered this to be very bad form. Marianne was at once contrite, quite prepared to listen to advice.

Francis and Emmaline felt themselves fortunate to have been forgotten. 'You must not do anything you don't want to do,' said Emmaline softly. 'My sister's enthusiasm sometimes runs away with her.'

'She never allows her appreciation of *your* finer qualities to overwhelm her, I notice,' said Francis, eyeing the dark young woman with disfavour.

'That is her way. I'm not quick and clever as she is. She loses patience with me.'

Francis smiled. 'I suppose it would be expecting too much for her to appreciate how lovely you look this evening, ma'am. Pink – do you call it rose pink? – suits you perfectly. But then, everything you do and wear becomes you.'

'Shh. Don't let them hear you.' Emmaline put her hands to her rosy cheeks in a gesture that invariably made her sister snort scornfully. 'You are too kind in your praises, sir! I don't know what to say!'

'Tell me only that you will come for a walk with me on Sunday if the weather is fine.'

When Napier was not present, Mrs Drummond was invariably more at ease. She had an excellent carriage and, away from her son's censorious eyes, was capable of moving across a room in a style that Mrs Siddons would have envied. She had that sort of fine English skin, like tissue paper, which folds itself into hundreds of creases with age, but beneath the lines and the excess flesh her bones were good. Given an admiring audience, she would be a handsome old woman one day.

Looking almost regal, she paused in the drawing-room doorway tonight, whale-boned into an acceptable shape in her turquoise, bell-shaped gown which was cut to reveal quite beautiful shoulders.

'Mr Babcock! What a pleasant surprise!' she said with unfeigned pleasure. 'Well, aren't we a cosy party. If only Napier were home to complete the circle. But he lives for his work, I know.'

'Yes, he does, Mrs Drummond,' said Francis. 'I hope you don't mind my staying for dinner. I really came only to tell you that your son does not expect to arrive home before midnight, and you are not to worry.'

'We shall all practise tonight, Mama,' said Marianne, 'and amaze Napier with our performance at some later date.'

And, despite Emmaline's sighs and Francis' glowering looks, that is just what they did all evening. Marianne issued instructions to one and all, until Florian grew tired of it and began playing the fool.

As the evening wore on, Francis, his eyes on Emmaline, became increasingly irritated. 'Your sister has been seated at the piano for hours, Miss Drummond. I think it is time we stopped. I must go home, too. I have a long day ahead of me —'

'Oh, Emmaline,' cried Marianne, 'just one more song. I want to hear Mama and Mr Farley sing "My Heart's Away". Please play it.'

'Marianne, you are a tyrant,' said her mother. 'I will sing just this one song and that will be the end of tonight's work. Come along, Florian. Do you ever get the feeling that all the world's a stage?'

The song was a sentimental one, with cloying lyrics and a

110

difficult melody. Florian and Dorothea Drummond could not resist the temptation to ridicule it. The second verse was rendered with gusto and, as the tempo increased, each succeeding verse received rougher treatment. The sixth and final verse was a quite professional burlesque.

Napier, his hair disarrayed, his hands and clothing dirty, stood in the doorway, an unsmiling witness of the last two minutes of this rowdy performance.

'Napier!' said his mother, dashing forward as the last chord died away. 'We didn't see you come in, dear. Come and sit down. You look quite tired. Florian, you know where the brandy is. In the library. Will you fetch a glass?'

'With your permission, Napier,' said Florian punctiliously. The young man looked to be on a devilishly short fuse; Florian didn't wish to be the one to provoke an outburst.

'I'd be much obliged, Farley,' said Napier, and he sat down in an armchair. 'But I'm just a trifle tired, you know, not ill.'

'I know what will revive you,' said Marianne. 'We'll entertain you. Emmaline, come back to the piano and –'

'Don't be such an idiot!' said Napier brutally. 'Can't you see I'm in no mood for caterwauling? Leave me in peace.'

Marianne was unmoved by his anger. 'Well, you needn't bite my head off. We're all tired of your being as cross as a bear.'

'Well, I'm not!' said Mrs Drummond stoutly.

'Not tired of my being as cross as a bear, Mama?' quizzed Napier, and laughed at her confusion.

Mrs Drummond left the room to help Florian find the brandy; Marianne and Emmaline relieved their nerves by indulging in a low-voiced squabble that had been brewing all evening; and Francis, at last, had a chance to ask what was amiss. 'For your face tells its own story, Napier. Some disaster has occurred. What is it?'

'When we were moving the equipment into place, a flywheel slipped and crushed the legs of one of the workmen. He died about an hour later. He had a wife and seven children. I was the harbinger of death, you might say. The cottage smelt of cabbage and bad drains, and the wife's grief was pitiful to see. We will have to do something handsome for the family. I won't allow them to be sent to the workhouse.'

111

'And here was I all evening, enjoying myself while you –'

'I don't begrudge you your pleasant evening. Do you seriously think I would have been pleased to discover that something terrible had happened here, and that you were all as miserable as I have been this night? My sisters have nothing more serious on their minds than a petty quarrel, my mother and Farley worry only that I have found them together, and you, silly fellow, feel guilty because I came home to find you laughing. Believe me, I rejoiced to see such normality and good cheer in this room.'

He rubbed his eyes, then smiled at Francis. 'Innocent pre-occupations will restore my spirits eventually. Thank God, I don't live in such a house as I have seen tonight. Occasionally, a black mood descends on me, you know, and I wonder why I have fought so hard all my life to acquire wealth and a measure of power. Tonight I was reminded of the reason – so that my family will be provided for no matter what happens to me. And so that I can help a family like the Drews. That's the sort of power worth having, Francis.'

'Now, if I had my new coat, we'd look very fine driving to Broxbourne station house, Mrs Hobart.'

'I know, Saul, and I have promised to order the coat for you soon. Please be patient. I've a great many things on my mind at the moment.' Sybilla and Cissy were crowded next to Saul on the single seat of the old two-wheeled gig. The springing was poor, the cold April wind was cutting their faces painfully, and the road held any number of potholes which Saul seemed determined to drive over. Fortunately, the journey to the railway station was less than two miles. Sybilla was certain that no matter how terrifying the new trains might be, they could not be as uncomfortable as the gig.

She was glad to be on the move, doing something positive. Mr Puddifoot's departure had left Hobart's rudderless. Henry and Jethro Perkins were two of the sorriest men she had ever met. A small repair job had come their way the day before yesterday, and the men had experienced no difficulty at all in doing the work. It was after the work was finished that father and son seemed capable only of standing round looking

112

foolish. Henry Perkins didn't know what charge should be made, couldn't imagine how it ought to be calculated, didn't feel he had a good enough fist to write out the bill. Jethro assured Sybilla with stunning honesty that anything his father couldn't do, he couldn't do either.

With growing impatience, she had dragged from these two lugubrious men the information that the repairs had taken them six hours. She doubled the hours and calculated the cost in wages, then added in the cost of materials. Finally, she doubled the total to arrive at the charge to the customer. She had almost finished making out the bill when Henry, looking over her shoulder, began to suck his teeth loudly.

Henry thought the charge was excessive. Henry didn't know what the charge should be, but he was in no doubt what it should not be. In the end, Sybilla added just one pound to the expenses, saying that this could not go on. Something must be done!

'Have you ever travelled on the railway, ma'am?' asked Saul, breaking in on her thoughts.

'No, I haven't. Cissy and I are going to enjoy this adventure, aren't we, Cissy?'

'Yes'm,' said Cissy with a sigh of resignation. London held terrifying memories for the young maid who had hoped never to go there again. There were thousands of people in the great smoky place, but she could never be sure that Jack Dark wouldn't leap out at her and attack her again.

Besides, she was frightened to ride on the new railway; she was sure such great speed would turn her brain. And, as if that weren't enough to worry a body half to death, she was desperately concerned about Fanny who had not yet fully recovered from her recent fever. Because of this mad trip to London, Cissy was forced to leave the child all day in her mother's careless charge, with no one to protect her from Saul's casual cruelty. Dear Jefferson had promised to visit the house on some pretext and if Fanny was well enough, he would take her over to visit his own mother for an hour or two. Jefferson had nothing else to do these days since he had been turned off by the innkeeper, and Mrs Smith would make a fuss of the child, cosseting her as she never was in the Hobart house. Jefferson would have a chance to accustom himself to the role of father, and Fanny would be happy enough. Nevertheless, Cissy did wish she could have stayed at home.

She had been so bold as to suggest that her father was the proper person to accompany Mrs Hobart on a perilous journey of nearly twenty miles to London, but the suggestion had fallen on stony ground. Mrs Hobart didn't like her father; Cissy could tell the signs. People thought Cissy was simple, but she noticed things that others didn't. Long ago, she had decided to keep her observations to herself, however. Nobody wanted to hear the opinions of a silly girl.

The fourth train of the day started from Broxbourne station house at half-past nine. The engine was already puffing steam, noisy enough to make both young women highly nervous. There were two coaches linked by heavy iron fixings which Sybilla devoutly hoped would be strong enough to last the journey. On each coach there were fixed what appeared to be three closed carriages minus their wheels. Six people might sit in each carriage, three facing the engine and three more, kneecap to kneecap, facing backwards. The first and third of the three carriages had the numeral "one" painted on the side, the second the numeral "two", indicating the class of carriage. Servants normally sat in the second-class carriage while their masters travelled in the first-class carriages, but Sybilla had no intention of being parted from Cissy on this, her first real outing without the chaperonage of either her brother or husband. She had even briefly considered travelling third class which cost only eighteen pence per ticket, but two difficulties forced her to abandon the scheme. In the first place, third-class passengers stood in wagons which were entirely open to the elements. In the second place, the railway companies had no intention of providing such a cheap means of travel except on rare occasions. Today, for instance, there were no third-class wagons hitched to the engine.

Opting, finally, for comfort and safety, Sybilla paid over twice the third-class charge for herself and Cissy, and they hurried to find places in the very last of the first-class carriages, as far away from the hissing giant as possible. Sybilla had dreaded being forced to travel with her back to the engine, but in the event, they were the only occupants of the carriage.

With a terrifying blast of the whistle, the driver unleashed the steaming monster and they were off. Sybilla glimpsed Saul waving to them as if they were to be away from home for years, and turned her head to find Cissy crying bitterly.

'Come, come, Cissy. We are going to be perfectly safe, you know. Accidents seldom occur on railways and this is a great adventure. Why, we will be whisked to Shoreditch in just forty-five minutes. Can you imagine travelling so fast? I can't, I assure you.'

She looked out of the window to see the trees skimming past. The tracks were laid within sight of the river and travelled for many miles in the valley of the Lea. The land was low and marshy; willows flanked the line, their silvery-backed leaves shimmering in the breeze. Not many trees liked to have their toes in water a good part of the year as willows did.

The noise of the engine and the jarring of the heavy iron wheels over the rails kept the women silent for some distance, but the rhythmic bump and swing soon exercised a soothing effect on Sybilla, so she was rather startled when Cissy spoke.

'I don't see why you should give my father a coat. Mam works harder and she don't get nothing.'

'Well, you must see that your father has been trying very hard to break himself of his bad habits. A new coat is to be his reward for good behaviour.'

'And them as ain't got bad habits gets no reward.'

'Besides,' said Sybilla, remembering a dinner party not too long ago, 'servants in the best houses are dressed very finely.'

'Fine houses have fine servants. It's right for them to be dressed proper.'

Sybilla sighed; the Potters had a way of wearing down all opposition. 'I'll give you and your mother a dress length each of printed cotton.'

'You don't have to give me nothing. You gave to Fanny.'

'I know,' said Sybilla, 'but I'll give you a dress length for your bottom drawer just the same.'

Cissy lapsed into silence and Sybilla was free to consider the state of her finances. Two hundred pounds had gone straight to Mrs Drummond so that at an appropriate moment (as yet to be decided) Sybilla could announce to Mr Drummond that his miserliness towards his mother had been noted, and Mrs Drummond's distress alleviated by someone else. Forty

115

pounds had been despatched immediately to her own mother. And if it occurred to her that she was happy to lend two hundred pounds to Napier Drummond's wealthy mother while she begrudged forty to her own, she told herself quickly that the two hundred would be returned to her come quarter day.

She was left with just ten pounds of the money she had received for her land, and there were so many little luxuries she would like to spend it on. There was never anything to spare for herself these days. Her widow's mite barely covered the expenses of running the house. Instead of indulging herself, however, she could see that she would be paying out most of it to the Potters. What would Mr Drummond say to that if he knew?

The first time the train had ground to a halt, Sybilla and Cissy had clutched one another in terror. The noise! The screech of wheels! The shuddering to a standstill! But at the second scheduled stop, Sybilla had her nerves in hand, which was fortunate because the train became quite crowded, and four City gentlemen squeezed into their small carriage. The two young women knocked knees with three large men sitting opposite, and it soon became very stuffy in the enclosed space.

With a perfunctory 'by your leave', the men lowered the small windows on their leather straps. Within minutes, Cissy and Sybilla were covered in black smuts. By the time they reached High Street station house in Shoreditch thirty minutes later, Sybilla's gloves were soaked with sweat. She had done her best to control her fear of travelling on the iron devil and was now weak-kneed with exhaustion. She tried to forget for the moment that it was all to do again if they were ever to reach Hoddesdon. Cissy, less proud, had cried unselfconsciously all the way, much to the amusement of the men.

When they emerged from the station house, Sybilla was totally unprepared for the noises of the street. She and Mr Hobart had avoided London on their bridal journey to Hoddesdon, so she had no idea what the great town was like. Of course, pedlars and packmen had been an important part of her existence in Portsmouth as well as Hoddesdon, but she hadn't imagined so many of them crowding every London thoroughfare. Pedlars, vagrants, beggars with huge sores or

116

crying babies, men hung about with pots and pans, women selling eels or hot potatoes. A ballad singer, having collected a sizable crowd, was bellowing a new ditty, prior to selling the sheet music for it. But even his penetrating voice was almost drowned out by the rumble of handcarts over cobbles and the repetitive cries of costermongers, knife grinders and pie-sellers.

Shoreditch bore all the signs of a once-fine neighbourhood gone to seed; Sybilla didn't care to approach any of the rather ill-kempt passers-by to ask the way. St Leonard's church gave them a bearing and they began walking, but when she and Cissy had been jostled several times by odorous men and endured a few catcalls, her eyes began to fill with tears. So this was the London she had longed to visit! A hateful place.

Cissy was not too nice in her notions to ask the way of a woman who was selling old clothes and shouting her wares in a croaking voice. Grudgingly, for the woman could see she would get no business here, she told them to carry on walking for a few hundred yards more, and then to ask again. 'Dun-nings Alley is well known,' said the filthy woman, beginning to push her laden barrow again. 'You can't miss it.'

As they moved farther and farther away from the haven of the station house, Sybilla wished she had hired a hackney cab when they had disembarked as some of the men had done. The trouble was, she had never in her life ridden in one, and was afraid of being cheated or made to feel foolish. They paused for breath at the corner of Sun Street and Bishopsgate Street Without, and Cissy asked a beggar the way to Dunnings Alley. 'The next turning on the left,' he told them civilly enough, and Sybilla gave him a farthing.

'I'm going to visit a coach-builder, Cissy,' said Sybilla when they had found the road at last. 'That may seem a strange thing to do, but I want you to show no surprise no matter what I say. Do you understand?'

'Yes'm,' said Cissy. 'Is that the place straight ahead? Joseph Richards and Company?'

Sybilla had planned this outing with the greatest care, certain that it was absolutely necessary. Now that the moment had arrived, however, she was regretting it. She straightened the bodice of her black gown and fiddled with the bow of her bonnet. She was dipping in and out of deepest mourning from day to day, a fact which would no doubt have incurred Mr Drummond's scorn if he knew of it, but she couldn't help it. She had too few clothes to make the transition to half mourning fashionably gradual. In any case, full mourning suited her purpose today. Well aware that her youth was a handicap to her, she had decked herself out in black from head to toe in an attempt to look older. The heavy black veil, resewn to the bonnet, would help by hiding her face.

How different was this coach-builder's premises from her own. A neatly dressed man greeted her in the doorway with a deep bow. Beyond him she could see two small carriages, their poles resting on the floor, gleaming in the light from a large front window.

'May I be of service, madam?' asked the man deferentially.

His dignity was almost Sybilla's undoing, but she stood her ground and spoke boldly. 'I wish to purchase a Stanhope gig of the finest quality. I will pay a proper price, but I do not intend to be cheated. I want you to prepare an itemized account of every part of the carriage and send it to my home.'

The man looked thunderstruck, fingering his watch-chain as if telling the beads of his rosary, before he finally spoke. 'Can you tell me exactly how you would like the gig to be designed, madam? Any modifications from the one you see here?'

Sybilla ran her tongue over dry lips. She hadn't realized that the elegant little two-wheeled carriage before her was a Stanhope gig. 'I shall inspect this one. Have you any drawings of other styles?'

'I have some catalogues. Excuse me.'

Sybilla walked over to the gig and inspected every inch of it, trying to memorize each detail of body, paintwork, upholstery and springing.

'Better'n what Mr Puddifoot makes,' hissed Cissy, and Sybilla gave a forbidding shake of the head.

The man returned with several cheaply printed sheets pinned together. He handed her one set, pointing with a stubby finger at plans for a Stanhope gig. 'Does this model meet with madam's requirements?'

'Yes,' said Sybilla. 'I like this.' The plans were virtually meaningless to her; she couldn't tell if the gig resting on its poles in front of her differed in any way from the plan she was holding. 'I should like to take this home to show . . . his lordship who is my trustee.' She began folding the sheets of paper small enough to fit into her reticule, aware that the man was gaping at her.

'Madam, I'll just have to see if we have another copy of those plans!'

He dropped a sheaf of papers on the sloping seat of the gig and turned away to go back to the office. On the pretext of picking up the papers which had scattered, Sybilla took a careful look at each one. '*Gadsons,*' said the first, '*wholesale coach ironmongers, varnish, japan and colour merchants. We supply everything required by the coach and cart builder.*'

The man returned with his order pad; Sybilla was forced to leave the scattered papers, but noticed that Cissy was tidying them carefully.

'Yes, that's all right. You may take that set of drawings with you, madam. Now, may I recommend the standard four-foot-seven-inch wheels with a one and a quarter inch Collinge axle? We supply the Woodhouse forecarriage and shafts of five feet eight inches, ironed up complete for a sturdier cart. Would madam care to choose the carriage lamps and body colour?'

Sybilla was shown a page of carriage lamps and, with some relief, pointed out the lamp on Mr Drummond's fine carriage. The man raised his eyebrows. Discomposed, she pointed to another more modest variety and raised her eyes for his approval. 'And I'd like to have it painted blue, please.'

'That is a wise choice, madam,' he said. 'Now, may I have your name and address, please?'

On their way back to the station house, Cissy opened her capacious bag and drew out some folded papers. 'He had lots of sets of them catalogues and I thought you might want to have a few, Mrs Hobart.'

'You took them?' asked Sybilla, eyeing the white sheets greedily.

'He had lots of them. All exactly the same. I daresay he won't notice his loss.'

'You shouldn't have taken them of course, but I won't deny I am grateful. I can't explain, but it's important.'

119

'Seeing if Mr Puddifoot is up to snuff,' said Cissy simply.

'Mr Puddifoot no longer works for me.'

'I know,' said Cissy. 'But he don't work for nobody else, and I reckon you could get him back if you tried. His wife's made his life purgatory since he left you.'

Seeing that there was very little point in trying to keep a secret from her maid, Sybilla explained that she hadn't realized so many parts of a carriage could be ready-made, instead of being created specially by a carpenter or a farrier. The savings gained by buying ready-made parts would make Hobart's more competitive.

'Teach Mr Puddifoot a thing or two,' added Cissy with satisfaction.

They went into the station to await the next train, and it was not until the noisy thing was actually on the move that Sybilla forgot about coach-building and remembered her terror.

8

Jack Dark made his way into the crock shop. He was a tall man with a neck like a bull, and as dark as his name suggested. He hadn't shaved for a week nor put on a clean shirt in over a month. A spotted handkerchief, tied round his neck, served as both collar and cravat. His waistcoat of red plush was bald in places and his frockcoat, with its capacious pockets, had had the Lord only knew how many previous owners. His trouser legs were frayed at the bottom, but his boots were sturdy; they needed to be. He had a heavy wicker basket on his arm and a dented top-hat on his head.

The top-hat would soon be removed in favour of a cap padded with straw. Jack had come to purchase crocks to peddle that day, and as the laden basket could weigh up to seventy pounds, the best way to carry it for many hours was balanced on his head with his top-hat resting on the crockery.

The shop was actually a dirty warehouse. Large opened crates full of cheap crockery covered the floor space, pushed so close together that it was difficult to walk between them to see what was on offer. The light was poor, and there were already about twenty men and women peering into the crates, making their selections and squabbling. Jack thought they had probably already snapped up the best buys. He should have come for his wares the night before, but when he'd done his business for the day, he usually stopped to have a pint or two before going to his home, too tired to think about stealing a march on his competitors.

Now it was half-past eight in the morning and he hoped to be knocking at his first door by nine o'clock. Tobias's was the only crock shop in Shoreditch, so although old Toby was a thief and a rogue beyond doubt, Jack was forced to trade here. He picked out some blue-edged plates at one and eightpence the dozen (but a dozen plates numbered thirty in the trade), teacups and saucers, cruet sets and rummers. On the chance that they might go down well, he also bought four mugs with 'For a Good Boy' painted on the side. In all, he filled his basket with fifteen shillingsworth of crockery, paid his money and left the shop.

He would have been very surprised, indeed, to learn that the shop had a turnover of four thousand pounds a year with a mark-up on the crockery that averaged out at fifteen per cent. But he would not have been surprised in the least to hear that Toby wasn't the real owner of the shop, but just an employee who was paid on commission. Everyone knew that when a man could afford to open such a place as Tobias's, he found someone else to do the work.

Jack had planned to work a short route today, swapping the crockery on his head for old clothes which he would then carry on his back. By bartering instead of selling, he avoided the necessity of buying an expensive hawker's licence for four pounds a year.

Tonight, around six o'clock, he would make his way to the Clothes Exchange in Houndsditch where he would haggle with dozens of other street traders for the best price for his clothing. It would be a long and tiring day. To walk fifteen miles carrying such heavy loads day after day aged a man very quickly. He was thirty-one now and would soon have to find some other way of scratching a living.

A man like Napier Drummond, thrust amongst the street poor by chance, had quickly found his way to the top of the hierarchy. Jack Dark had been bred to his trade, but he was of low intelligence and had no imagination whatsoever. He never looked beyond tomorrow.

By tonight he should have sold his fifteen shillingsworth of wares and earned himself two or three shillings profit. This was barely enough to meet the rent on his room and buy a bit of food. Come what may, he had to pay a shilling a week insurance for a proper burying, because Jack and his wife had no intention of being flung into paupers' graves when their days were done. Tomorrow, as always, he would have only enough hard money to buy a further day's wares, and so the hopeless cycle would continue. He could never get ahead of the game.

He decided to go up Hoxton way this morning, where he would work the larger houses, calling at kitchen doors in the hope of taking a few items of clothing off one or two of the maids who were collecting crockery against the day when they got married. Perhaps he might also make a sale to the house-keeper if she needed to replace a few broken cups or plates. The best customers of all were the owners of lodging houses who often had clothing given to them. They didn't know the value of what they had been given, and sometimes Jack could make a tidy profit. There was no question in this business of a fixed price for anything. It was a dog-eat-dog world; he took what advantage he could of the ignorant, and expected to be ground down by those who were wilier than himself.

The basket load had lightened very promisingly by mid-morning. Jack lifted it off his head in order to get himself through the doorway of the Crown, down Dunnings Alley. He ordered a pint of porter, exchanged a few bantering words of greeting with some of the regulars and made his way over to the window. Alternately rubbing the back of his neck with one hand and lifting the tankard of dark beer to his lips with the other, he began to feel a little less weary. The tankard was almost empty, and he was wondering if he could afford another, when Cissy Potter and a fine-looking widow walked right past the window towards Bishopsgate Street Without. Had there been no glass between them, he could have reached out and touched Cissy, yet she hadn't seen him.

He gulped down the dregs of his porter and, with a rattle of plates, took up his load to follow them. He kept his distance as they walked up Bishopsgate, wondering what on earth had brought the widow and her maid to Shoreditch.

At the station house, Jack hung back. It was obvious to anyone that the two women were going to board the next train, that they could only be travelling in one direction since this was the start of the line, and that the last stop was Broxbourne. Cissy, therefore, lived somewhere to the north, between Shoreditch and Broxbourne, but maybe miles from the railway line, to the east or west. Tracking her down would be like finding a needle in a haystack.

He studied the widow carefully, trying to memorize every-thing about her. Try as he might, he couldn't make out her features beneath the heavy veiling, but he could see she had bright yellow hair. If he ever saw her again, he'd know her. Maybe this particular needle *could* be found in a haystack.

As for Cissy, the girl was no longer much to look at; she'd

gone sour and sullen before her time. She used to be always singing and full of saucy chatter, he remembered with pleasure. It never occurred to him that her loss of youthful bloom might have anything to do with him or his ruthless rape. Fleetingly, he felt a yearning for lost opportunities. With a little coaxing, perhaps a trinket or two, he might have enjoyed something more lasting than . . . But regrets buttered no parsnips. There was Betty sitting in their room at home, never smiling, hardly speaking as she stared out of the window; no use to him in his work, no comfort to him in his bed. It would be tricky, bringing up the delicate subject of Cissy Potter; when the row broke out and he was arrested for rape, Betty had known straight off that the girl hadn't been willing. But Betty'd kept her chaffer shut because she hadn't wanted him flogged.

Betty must be brought to see the importance of finding out where Cissy lived. A month or two after his appearance in court, Jack had turned up in his regular way at the house where Cissy had worked. To his very great surprise, they set about him with brooms, dish clouts or anything else that came to hand. He would never understand women. The housekeeper told him crossly that Cissy had been dismissed and gone home to her parents to have her baby. What sex? he had asked. A boy, she'd said after a moment's hesitation.

The sight of Cissy a few minutes ago had brought on a sudden wave of fatherly feeling – a new sensation to be sure. He'd have that lad to raise as his own. The boy was his, legally. He was the actual father, wasn't he? All right then, he'd have the boy. Betty would make a better mother by far than Cissy, foolish young girl that she was. He would need every penny he could get his hands on if he were to find the child, but he would contrive somehow. With his spirits amazingly revived, Jack hoisted his basket on to his head and began calling his wares.

After an early and very plain dinner, Sybilla sat down in the morning-room to study the catalogues Cissy had pilfered. Their pages were a revelation. She didn't know whether to laugh or cry, but thought that a few tears were probably in order for the fool she had been.

Mr Puddifoot's accounts showed that fulcrum plates (whatever they were) were made to order by a farrier in Ware for five shillings the pair. But Gadsons sold them, 'filed and bored', for two and sixpence a pair. Or, if one purchased them in bulk, five *pence* the pound. She was at a slight disadvantage in that she didn't know what a fulcrum plate was, how many were needed for one carriage, or how much a pair might weigh. But if they could be bought for five pence a pound, wasn't it worth taking the risk of being left with a few at the end of the year?

And what about foot plates, rein rails and whip sockets? Even coach bodies, it seemed, could be ordered by post and sent by rail. The possibilities for saving money were endless if one bought from stock instead of having things made to order. Mr Puddifoot ought to be able to see the advantages, yet he hadn't done so before. Was it that her husband and his manager were so old-fashioned that they actually didn't know about ready-made parts? Or were these parts dangerously inferior? She thought not, otherwise Joseph Richards and Company would not be using them. Sybilla suspected that other coach-builders were more up to the mark, and that was why she was not attracting any business these days.

With pen and paper, she sat down and laboriously began to cost out a Stanhope gig, comparing the figures in the account books with those prices offered for parts in the catalogue.

Many hours later, she sat back in the chair, defeated, and rubbed her burning eyes. She was too ignorant of the details of coach-making to produce proper calculations; an itemized estimate from Joseph Richards and Company would certainly help.

The other problem was the one so cruelly mentioned by Mr Drummond. It was true that women had only the scantiest knowledge of arithmetic. It was considered unladylike to be able to add any but the simplest of sums. Girls were kept well away from the subjects which occupied so much of their brothers' time.

Small sums were simple; everyone knew that two and sixpence plus two and sixpence made five shillings. But really large figures pushed a well brought-up girl into the realms of the unknown.

Tonight Sybilla had drawn up a column of sixty items in

pounds, shillings and pence, and could not be at all sure if she had added them correctly. One added the pence column first, of course, then the shillings and finally the pounds. All of this was very difficult and laden with opportunities for error. Yet Sybilla had met packmen selling pins and sewing cotton and needles and a dozen other items, all for odd sums, who could reckon the total quicker than you could blink an eye. And many of them couldn't even write their own names! Men, Sybilla had been taught, were naturally clever at sums, just as women were not.

As in every aspect of her late husband's business, Sybilla was hampered by having no one to turn to who could advise her. Yet, if she were to rehire Mr Puddifoot and work with him successfully, she must appear at all times to be more know-ledgeable than she really was. That would be quite a strain at first. So far as she knew, there were no books on the subject of coach-building. Boys were apprenticed to the trade at an early age, and that was how the secrets of coach-building were passed down from one generation of males to the next.

She closed the account books and put them carefully away, together with her penned calculations and the catalogues. She must wait upon Joseph Richards and Company. If they sent her an itemized account, she could certainly learn from it, and then use it to show Mr Puddifoot how she wanted him to operate the business in the future. After that, she would just have to trust him.

It was late and she was depressed, but she ought to be feeling just a little pleased with herself, as well. After all, she had conquered her fear of the railway, of travelling without the guiding hand of her brother or husband, of dealing in the business world. Instead of being happy, however, she felt restless, imprisoned and, as always, lonely.

She picked up a cushion from a low chair and looked at it critically, remembering how many boring hours she had spent embroidering the cover in bright wools. She hated the design of stylized flowers worked in vulgar colours. She squeezed the cushion hard and then, on impulse, threw it with all her strength at the settee. It landed on the seat with a soft thump and, to her surprise, Sybilla felt better. Two more cushions followed the first. Now seven cushions rested on the settee and she had no more to throw. Crossing to the settee, she gathered all of them in her arms and walked to the farthest corner of the room.

Thump! Thump! How good it felt. Some landed on the floor, one toppled over the back of the settee. One particularly wild throw hurtled a cushion towards a carved Indian table which fell over. She didn't care, didn't even bother to set it on its legs. She picked up the cushions again and threw them around the room in a frenzy.

Now she felt warm all over. And *strong*. Her breathing was fast and shallow, her head buzzing pleasurably. The relief to her nerves was beyond anything she could have imagined. Massaging her throwing arm, she noticed that the right sleeve of her dress had come loose from the armhole. She was not surprised. Dress sleeves were designed to keep the shoulders well back and the arms almost immobile. Ladies simply did not throw cushions.

Throwing cushions was developing into a mania for Sybilla, however. She couldn't stop herself. The satisfaction she felt when one of them plopped on to the settee was beyond description. She had discovered a near silent form of rebellion.

And it was not only cushion throwing that gave comfort to strained nerves. Tea could be satisfactorily thrown on occasion. Often she had longed to throw the contents of her cup into Robert's face when he had been smugly recounting some expensive prank he and his friends had got up to. The other night she had actually done the deed, thrown tea in a man's face. Mr Drummond, who was an extraordinary man by any reckoning, had seemed to understand the impulse. Her fiery temperament, he had called it. That was not a satisfactory description of Sybilla Hobart. Not by a long chalk. Sybilla Hobart was a woman of iron self-control. She *never* lost her temper, no matter what the provocation. That was why she had been contrite at once, and still could not account for her action the other evening.

No one knew better than she that marriages were often contracted for purely practical reasons. She hadn't thrown tea in Mr Hobart's face when he proposed, after all; it had never occurred to her to do so. Why, then, had she reacted so strangely to Mr Drummond's businesslike proposal? It was a

127

far more attractive offer than Mr Hobart's had been. She shook her head to clear away the cobwebs of tiredness. The answer to that question lurked at the back of her mind, too painful to be fully examined at the moment.

Turning down the colza lamp, she carried it upstairs to her bedroom. It was late; half-past twelve, the clock said. Cissy had probably gone to bed, which was highly inconvenient. The bodice of the dress hooked up the back and she really couldn't get out of it without help, yet she was loth to pull the bell. It wasn't concern for her servant's sleep that stayed her hand so much as a most peculiar reluctance to have Cissy fussing around her.

Every stitch in the bodice had been set by hand. Careful back stitches, they were, close together and pulled tight. Still, she must put them to the test. Reaching behind her neck, she grabbed two handfuls of cloth and pulled. There was a slight ripping sound and she felt cool air on the upper part of her back. It took many more tugs, and she was becoming very hot and frustrated, before the stitching broke far enough to allow her to slip out of the bodice by pulling it down over her hips. She picked up the torn mass of black wool and balled it in her hand to throw it; but that particular madness had mercifully passed. The earlier exertion had brought her some measure of inner peace.

Deliberately, as an exercise in self-discipline, she folded all her clothing neatly on a chair before she turned out the lamp and got into bed. A few night sounds filtered through the open window — a horse whinnying, the high-pitched howl of a motherless puppy. She turned from her left side to her right, pulling a plump feather pillow over her head. Hot and restless now, she pushed the pillow out of the bed and sighed heavily, wide awake despite an aching tiredness.

Voices below, hoarse whispers, travelled upwards and sorted themselves out: Jefferson and Cissy in the garden. Sybilla couldn't hear their words, just the cadence of their speech: his deep and slow, hers skittish. Once a stifled giggle. *Cissy giggling?* But then why should the poor girl smile for her employer? Why not save her laughter and good humour for the man she loved?

Sybilla blinked back a few tears, having just made a profound discovery. Being in love was sharing laughter in the dead of night. Unlike marriage which was a matter simply of doing as you were told. Being in love was making plans for the future together. Marriage, especially an arranged marriage, meant not daring to plan at all. Being in love was something the maid knew well, and the mistress had never experienced.

When Sybilla had been fifteen, small for her age and as flat-chested as a boy, she had conceived a secret passion for the new curate. There had followed a sudden interest in religion that had surprised her mother no end. Just the sight of the curate striding down the road a hundred yards away could rob Sybilla of the power to breathe, could bring on a giddiness that was close to a miracle, so glorious did it feel as it tingled down her thighs, almost making her too weak to stand.

One fine Saturday in May, the curate had called on Mrs Sutherland, and Sybilla had been summoned to the parlour to make her curtsey. The curate had stood, had shown his strong white teeth in a warm smile. Sybilla remembered nearly suffocating with the agonized joy of his manly nearness.

'Good morning to you, Miss Sybilla,' he had said. Not the most original greeting, to be sure, but hardly exceptional in the circumstances. Yet in speaking it, he had destroyed all the beauty of his being, the perfect Adonis of Sybilla's imagination. And all because his voice was high-pitched, fully half an octave higher than Sybilla had expected. On such small details, do infatuations falter and crumble to dust. Tears had pricked her eyes as she waited for the moment when her mother would release her from the disappointing presence of a perfectly decent young man. Poor Mr Grimes. He knew at once that he had upset her, but would never, now, discover what had brought that stricken look to her narrow little face.

It had been a year or two before she had fully comprehended that infatuation and true love were not the same thing. Real love was built like a house, brick by brick, and you valued each brick whether it be rough or smooth. If you didn't, if you hated the pitch of a voice and let that small thing spoil the whole, then the emotion that held you in thrall was something else altogether, the nonsense of schoolgirls. Sybilla had set aside the nonsense of schoolgirls that day in her mother's parlour. Strange then, that she could still recall the beautiful curate with clarity, when most other sights and sounds of her youth had faded. She had matured beyond the abandonment of infatuation, and found nothing to take its place.

The eleven o'clock post the next day brought the estimate from Joseph Richards and Company. After studying it carefully, Sybilla told Saul that she was going to Hobart's shop, seeing no reason to tell him her real destination. She was relieved to find some excuse to make her escape from the house. The Potters were driving her mad. Cissy's reaction on finding the torn bodice the next morning had been swift. Why ever hadn't madam called her? And surely madam would no longer be requiring the black dress, would she? Did madam wish for Cissy to get rid of the horrid old thing for her?

Sybilla, not having intended to part with the dress just yet, reminded the girl of the promised dress lengths for herself and her mother. Cissy had not forgotten, but she clung tenaciously to her original theme, that madam would no longer be requiring the black bodice and skirt. The result was that within the next hour Sybilla was relieved not only of the black dress, but also of two dress lengths from Christopher Tuck, a ready-made brown coat and two pairs of cotton gloves.

Mrs Potter had pursed her lips critically when shown her new dress length of brown printed muslin, and pronounced herself partial to Cissy's material which had the same flower pattern on a maroon background. Unequal to the manoeuvring that was about to take place, Sybilla left the kitchen. Later, only Cissy bothered to thank her for the gifts, adding as she left the room, that she preferred the brown, anyways.

Sybilla had scarcely left her own doorstep when she was hailed by Mr Crockford, a recent customer. He had just been coming to call upon her, he said, because his conscience was bothering him. He had given the matter serious thought and knew he could get no peace until he confessed. Thrusting thirty shillings into her hand, he told her a story that nearly caused her to change her plans completely.

He left her after several minutes standing statue-like in front of the Misses Sams shop, and both spinsters watching her through the small panes of their bow window, probably wondered what was causing her to look so shocked and angry.

130

She was in two minds whether to go on or not, but decided finally to press ahead. Knowledge was power. She would have the upper hand from now on.

Mrs Martha Puddifoot answered the door promptly to Sybilla's knock. 'Mrs Hobart! Do come in, ma'am. What a pleasant surprise! You'll be wanting to see Mr Puddifoot, I've no doubt. Come into the parlour. I'll just fetch him.'

Mrs Puddifoot was a small, extremely intense woman in her late thirties, who liked to thrust her face right up to anyone she was addressing. Sybilla always had to resist the urge to back away. Mrs Puddifoot often managed to drive her listeners into corners, and there her tongue was given full rein. She had a piercing voice and an animated way of speaking that emphasized every other word, regardless of meaning.

If Albert spent his life saying 'yes, dear' and 'no, dear', he could at least take heart that his wife was a spirited champion in his defence. She would tell anyone within earshot that her Albert was the finest coach-builder in the whole of England. Never mind that she had never met another coach-builder in her life, she just knew it was true.

Sybilla waited in the neat, never-used parlour while Mrs Puddifoot went in search of her man. The house was the end of a row of brick terraces on Lord Lane, two up and two down, comfortable and warm. The Puddifoots had several children, but Sybilla could see no evidence of them in this room.

Suddenly, the door opened and Albert was thrust into the room by his good wife with her hand on his back. 'Morning, Mrs Hobart,' he said, struggling to find an attitude between bluster and embarrassment. Sybilla had no chance to reply.

'You've come to invite Albert back to work, I dare say. When he told me you'd laid him off, I said, "Never!" Just like that. "Never!" and I stamped my foot.' Albert's loyal wife stamped her foot to show Sybilla how it had been done. 'I said, "Why, that's monstrous," for I don't mince my words, Mrs Hobart. "That's monstrous, and you the best coach-builder in the whole of England. Whatever was Mrs Hobart thinking of," I said, "for she don't know the first thing about building coaches as everybody knows." '

'Now, Martha, why don't you –'

'I know a few things, Mrs Puddifoot,' said Sybilla coolly. 'I

131

know that Hobart's coach-building methods are out-dated and expensive. I know that Hobart's has not been run competitively for some time.'

'My Albert using out-dated methods?' squeaked Mrs Puddifoot. 'I'm certain he does no such thing, and if he does it's because the old ways are the best. You'll understand that when you are a little older, I dare say. Whatever can you be thinking of, ma'am?'

Sybilla stood up. 'I am thinking that I made a serious mistake in coming here to talk to Mr Puddifoot, because it is perfectly clear to me that the poor man will not be allowed to speak at all. Whatever can you be thinking of, Mrs Puddifoot?'

Martha Puddifoot looked momentarily stricken. Her husband's glaring eyes were on her, and she took a defensive step backwards.

'Why don't you go and make us some tea, Martha, while I talk business with Mrs Hobart?' said Albert placatingly, and his wife showed every sign of being eager to leave the room.

'I'm not sure I've got any tea left,' she grumbled. 'Can't afford to buy tea when there's no wages coming in and five mouths to feed.'

Albert sighed with relief when the door closed behind his greatest admirer. He turned his eyes to Sybilla expectantly.

'Mr Puddifoot, I have just had a most interesting conversation with Mr Crockford. I understand now why I have lost business to my competitors and why I have sometimes lost money on an order.'

'Now, Mrs Hobart –'

'It's because when it comes time to present the account, you say the price is so much, but as a special favour to a valued customer, you will give a discount of ten per cent. The customer says thank you very much, tips you handsomely, and *I* am the only loser!'

Puddifoot put his head in his hands. 'I don't know what to say.'

'You might try making amends.'

Puddifoot's head came up with a jerk. 'I can't, ma'am! I've spent it all. It wasn't much. Really it wasn't. I didn't think it would matter. I'd been drinking rather too much and, well, it was drinking money. Sometimes I just added on a few shillings to the account. I had to have the drink, you see. But these days at home have cured me, I swear it.'

Sybilla took a deep breath, wondering if she were doing the right thing. If there were any other way she would certainly have taken it.

'Mr Puddifoot, have you ever heard of Gadsons?'

'Don't believe I have, ma'am.'

'They make all sorts of parts for coach-builders. Ready-made parts, do you see? So that you don't have to order everything made specially. It is much cheaper that way.' She handed him the catalogue, and he flicked through it, his eyebrows rising in surprise.

'Of course, I've heard of ready-made parts. Never had any use for them. Mr Hobart, he didn't like –'

'Times are changing, Mr Puddifoot, and I must change with them. I am certainly not succeeding in my present way of going on, so I may as well try something different. Now here is an itemized estimate from a well-known London coach-builder. I went to Shoreditch to see these people, pretending that I wished to order a Stanhope gig. They sent me this estimate.'

'Well, I'm bound to say that you've been very clever, Mrs Hobart. I can see how much cheaper they're able to make the gig than we would be. I suppose it's because they buy parts in bulk. But Hobart's couldn't do that. The shop don't get enough trade to warrant it. You'd be laying out for parts and they'd rust in the shop.'

'Well, of course, my first priority is to drum up business. I know that perfectly well and I have a plan that should do the trick. I'm willing to take you back, provided you give up the drink. I want you to build a Stanhope gig for me.'

'But you got a gig! That would be throwing good money after bad and take up time that we might use building for someone as would pay.'

'I'll decide about that. It's my money and my risk, remember. If you come back to Hobart's, you would be completely in charge of all the building work,' said Sybilla as they heard Mrs Puddifoot approaching. 'But I would take responsibility for finding new customers. And I will decide what to charge. Another one of your tricks and I'll go to the law. Is that understood?'

Puddifoot would have liked to appear just a little reluctant for the sake of his pride, but as had happened many times before, his wife destroyed his best laid plans for a dignified retreat from an untenable position.

'Well, now. I did find *some* tea in the caddy. Not the best, mind you, but now that Albert has got his old job back – and with more money, I've no doubt, for you must be very sorry for what you done to him, Mrs Hobart, and no hard feelings on either side, I'm sure – I think we can celebrate. Can't we, Albert?'

'Mr Puddifoot will receive the same money as before,' said Sybilla, her eyes on a fat cushion that was just aching to be thrown at this dreadful woman. 'Provided he cuts costs and uses more efficient methods. That is, if *you* will allow him to return,' she added, enjoying Puddifoot's look of black fury directed at his wife.

Although May was almost upon them, the weather was still unseasonably cold. Sybilla said goodbye to the Puddifoots, but instead of returning home, she walked on down Lord Lane. It was not necessary to go very far before reaching lonely woodland.

Despite being town bred and more accustomed to the pounding of the sea than the stillness of woodland, Sybilla occasionally liked to walk alone in Broxbourne Woods, exploring little-used paths. These acres of trees were all owned by great landowners who managed them well so that they grew to give a constant supply of wood. Some were coppiced – cut off at the base – and allowed to regrow from ground level. Others were pollarded – the branches pruned back to the trunk at about head height so that deer couldn't eat the young regrowth. Recently coppiced acres made a boring walk; the rolling land looked as if some great disaster had overtaken it. On the other hand, trees that had been coppiced a season or two ago impeded the way, their branches catching on one's clothing.

She preferred to walk in the old pollarded groves where bluebells and anemones, primroses and other pretty plants flourished until the leaves were fully out and the overhead canopy grew too dense for anything very much to survive. The ground was soft. Would it ever stop raining? Her boots and skirt hem soon became caked with mud. And because she had taken off her bonnet at the first opportunity, her hair began to come loose from its pins and branches entangled themselves in the yellow strands.

She walked for two hours, turning back only when she was pleasantly tired. As soon as she reached the first houses on Lord Lane, she paused to repin her hair and replace the bonnet, then walked on quickly to Hornbeam House.

Mrs Potter had prepared cold ham and bread and butter, which awaited her in the morning-room. Sybilla ate ravenously, drank two cups of tea, then spying a cosy, soft chair, fell asleep in all her dirt.

Emmaline and Marianne had decided to take the closed carriage for their visit to Mrs Hobart's home because one could not depend on the weather at this time of year. Changing clothes was one of their main occupations during the day; they had exchanged their simple morning gowns for elaborate visiting dresses. Emmaline's was her favourite rose-pink silk with a plethora of blue frills encircling the sleeves and layering the bodice. Her bonnet was very large. The blue crown soared skywards behind her, while the face-framing brim was lined in matching pink silk.

Marianne's bonnet was even more extravagant and set even further back from her face, so that it looked as if it might fall off at any minute. It was white with a froth of white lace veiling trailing down her back. Her skirt of billowing white figured silk was topped by a tight green velvet jacket. The sisters knew themselves to be looking very fine as they arrived in Hoddesdon to visit the rich widow.

'Are you sure this is the address, James?' asked Marianne of the footman as he opened the carriage door.

'Yes, Miss Drummond. Hornbeam House, Hoddesdon.' He pointed to the pink-washed house sitting tight upon the gravel pathway.

'It is hardly what we expected . . . ' began Emmaline and, as usual, was given a quelling look by her sister.

Saul was very impressed when he answered the knock on the door to find a liveried footman on the step and two grand ladies waiting expectantly in a handsome carriage. Now she'll be glad she bought me a new coat, he thought, and invited the ladies to come into the drawing-room while he fetched the mistress.

Emmaline and Marianne entered the narrow hall, their eyes politely focused straight ahead, their minds racing in calculations about Sybilla's income and possessions.

The drawing-room was overcrowded, but they had spent too many hours with their needles not to appreciate Sybilla's skills which were displayed round the room. They sat down to wait, and because they dared not discuss the one topic that interested them most at this moment, didn't speak to one another at all. It was fully eight minutes by Marianne's pocket-watch before they heard Sybilla coming down the stairs. Of course, they had heard her racing upstairs soon after they arrived.

She greeted them affectionately, apologizing for keeping them waiting, and expressed her pleasure at their unexpected company. She almost convinced them that they had not thrown her into a panic. But if the sisters knew little else, they knew the signs of a woman who was unaccustomed to receiving afternoon visitors.

Sybilla had slipped fresh white lace cuffs and a huge lace collar on to her dark blue dress. Her hair was brushed neatly and she was only a little out of breath.

While Marianne and Sybilla soon fell into easy conversation – the fashions, their few mutual acquaintances, Mrs Drummond's invitation to attend the theatre in the near future – Emmaline looked surreptitiously around her. Mama could not have intended to accept two hundred pounds from a woman in Sybilla's circumstances. Mr Babcock had misled them. The house was well enough, but it needed repairs, redecoration and totally different furnishings. These cheap pieces could not be Sybilla's choice. Emmaline tried to imagine what it must have been like for the beautiful young girl to marry an old man and come to live among his first wife's possessions.

Emmaline's one talent, apart from playing the piano, was sniffing out the exact social status of those she met, placing them accurately in the hierarchy of her acquaintances. She observed absolutely everything, picking up clues wherever she might. For instance, Sybilla's grey silk gown had been quite new and was, therefore, an expression of Sybilla's own taste, not a reflection of her husband's taste or generosity. It had been expensive, which had fooled them all, but Emmaline could draw other conclusions about the servant who opened the door.

Nothing so clearly indicated the woman of fashion as the style and number of her male servants. Sybilla, it would seem, had only one man in the house and he not properly trained. A number of emotions struck Emmaline at once: pity for Sybilla's poverty, embarrassment on account of her ignorance of the finer points of polite life, admiration for her courage. In Emmaline's view, Sybilla was that greatly-to-be-pitied specimen, the genteel impoverished widow. Mrs Drummond had had any number of such women among her acquaintances at one time. But that was all long ago when Emmaline had been a little girl.

When Napier had come home to Bury St Edmunds, everything had changed. The circle of her mother's friends and acquaintances had altered irrevocably. All sorts of people came to the Drummonds' home after Napier returned. They were none of them from the top drawer of society and they were none of them poor.

After years of rubbing shoulders with wealthier sorts, of being able to purchase almost anything she wished, Emmaline now found herself uncomfortable in Sybilla's simple house. She wondered what Napier made of the widow. It was impossible to read his mind. Thanks to her mother's wayward tongue, however, there could be no doubt what Sybilla thought of Napier. To correct this undoubtedly bad impression was the purpose of the sisters' visit. Emmaline wondered when Marianne would tackle the subject.

After the tea-things had been removed, apparently. The little maid had scarcely closed the door behind her when Marianne said: 'Mama was rather distraught the other night, Sybilla. I'm afraid she may have said . . . may have been rather indiscreet.'

'She said very little,' replied Sybilla. 'That she is afraid of her son and finds herself unable to converse freely with him is evident.'

'That's true. I can't deny it and Mama is most grateful for

137

your timely intervention, but I can't allow you to harbour uncharitable thoughts about my brother.'

'I've no wish to . . . It's none of my business, Marianne.'

'Nevertheless, I think it might be wise to tell you a little about Napier's past life. He was a scamp by all accounts, always getting into trouble. Papa warned him that if he didn't attend to his books and stop getting into scrapes, he would be sent away. Well, one day – Emmaline and I are too young to remember it – he somehow managed to get himself on to the roof of the church belfry. It took several hours to get him down. Papa carried out his threat. He had met a Mr Micklethwaite from Rochdale many years before. Mr Micklethwaite was a childless widower who owned – owns – a textile mill. Papa apprenticed Napier to the mill owner to learn the business. He was fourteen and travelled alone to Rochdale. We never saw him again as a boy. Mr Micklethwaite wouldn't let him come home for a visit, and my father never got round to visiting him.'

'But didn't your parents want to see –' Sybilla broke off. 'I'm sorry. I didn't mean to interrupt.'

'Well, I suppose it does seem odd. But anyway, one day when Napier was sixteen, he ran away to London and didn't write to my parents for almost a year. Father was furious. He refused to have Napier's name mentioned in the house, that I *do* remember.'

'But what did your brother do in London? A boy like that? Had he any money?'

'I really don't know what he did,' said Marianne complacently. 'You know what my brother is like. I expect he managed very well. Eventually, he did send Mama a letter giving an accommodation address of a London coaching house. Mama wanted my father to go to London immediately to track Napier down, but Papa wouldn't consider it. So there was nothing she could do.'

'If my son had run away,' said Emmaline, taking one of her intense turns, 'I would travel half the earth to find him.'

'You!' said Marianne scornfully. Then recollecting herself, said to Sybilla, 'Napier seems to feel that Mama might have made a greater effort, but there was never any question of her defying my father.'

Sybilla didn't propose to discuss that point. 'When did your brother return home?'

'Five years ago. When my father died, Mama wrote to him. He came home a wealthy man in his mid twenties. A complete stranger to us. He has looked after us ever since and I must say in his favour that he is excessively generous.'

'He arrived in London at sixteen and made his fortune within a few years without help from anyone?' asked Sybilla incredulously.

'Apparently,' said Marianne. 'I assume he did so by honest means.'

'But if he is as generous as you say and as wealthy as you say, why did *you* not ask your brother for the money your mother needs?'

The sisters' expressions of horror spoke volumes. 'But the investment in the acting troupe was probably an unwise one,' said Emmaline breathlessly, 'and Napier would be so scathing.'

Sybilla felt a trifle giddy. Would she ever see her two hundred pounds again?

'You don't know how unpleasant Napier can be when he is cross,' said Marianne calmly. 'He is usually in the right of it, I must admit. But that just makes it worse, don't you agree?'

'Yes,' said Sybilla faintly. 'Oh, yes.'

9

On the day that Sybilla went to Shoreditch, Napier summoned his manager to his office.

Scrope was in his late forties, a wiry little man of amazing strength for his size. He had been a maltster all his working life and came from a malting family. He could still carry one and a half hundredweights of barley on his back and mount a narrow ladder to an upper floor as sure-footed as a goat, but these days he was not required to do so. Napier had promoted him to the position of manager, given him power and higher wages, setting him slightly apart from the other men of his family.

He had brushed the dust from his clothing, put on his frockcoat and hat and polished up his shoes for the meeting. Mr Drummond might know next to nothing about the ancient art of malting, unlike other owners, but he was worthy of respect all the same.

'They're talking of bringing the railway to Ware, Mr Scrope. They should be starting to work on the tracks very soon now. Can't say I'm pleased.'

'It'll be a good thing, sir,' said Scrope, crossing his legs. 'Must help our business.'

'In what way? Don't you think we're well enough as we are?'

'Why, Mr Drummond, sir! It's well enough to send malt down river to London; Ware has done so for generations, but think about our country customers. If only we could get rid of some of the horses and wagons and send malt by railways! A horse costs as much as a maltster, and the horse don't make malt. He just eats his head off and needs to be looked after. Railways will be just the thing, specially when there's lots of them and we can ship to our customers all over the country. Of course, that won't happen for years.'

Napier studied Scrope's grizzled face. He might know very little about malt, but he knew a great deal about the minds of men. And he had heard that Scrope was a fanatic on the subject of railways. 'Great noisy things,' he said quietly.

'Noisy? Why yes, I daresay they are. But they don't clog up the roads the way wagons do. Sometimes you can't move about at all in the town. Railways are the nation's future, sir.'

'You're a modern man, Scrope.'

Scrope sat back, straightening his shoulders a little. 'Can't stand in the way of progress,' he said simply.

Well satisfied with the words he had led his manager to speak, Napier changed the subject. 'We're still malting, aren't we?'

'Cuckoo malt,' said Scrope scornfully.

Every maltster in Ware, perhaps in the entire country, had stopped malting on 31 March. Everybody knew you stopped malting about the time the first cuckoo could be heard, no matter what the weather. Napier Drummond, who must be excused on the grounds that he was new to the business, had insisted that malting should continue at his malthouse so long as the weather was cool enough. Barley germinated at fifty to sixty degrees, and germination had to be arrested at just the right moment. All it needed now was one hot, sunny day and the temperature in the malthouse would soar; the barley would germinate too far and become useless for good quality malt. Of course, it could be mixed with the better stuff and sold just the same; Scrope knew the tricks of his trade. But that wasn't the point. No matter how many extra quarters you might be able to make in April, you didn't do it. You stopped on 31 March.

Scrope had discussed this important matter with Mr Drummond right at the first. He had told him how owners of maltings didn't care if their malthouse did lie idle for six months of the year earning no money. They made enough money from October to April not to have to worry about such things.

Maltsters, those men who actually made the malt, were a breed apart, almost like gypsies. When the malthouses closed down, they took themselves and their families off somewhere else, to Hitchin, perhaps to make tiles, or even further afield. They understood kilns, that was what mattered. They could stand the heat. Those who had stayed behind to make cuckoo malt would lose out on the best summer jobs. Scrope's men

141

weren't happy. He'd kept them at it by threatening not to re-employ them in October. But they weren't happy.

Napier, knowing perfectly well what thoughts were going on behind that hard-eyed stare, promised his manager this week would see the end of malting for the season. This was Monday; he would like to see Mr Scrope on Wednesday at one o'clock.

When Wednesday came, Scrope arrived looking a little happier. The weather was still as cold as be damned, they were still steeping twice a week, and Mr Drummond had seen to it that everybody from the beer boy to Scrope himself had received a bonus. The boy had got a shilling and the four maltsters seven and sixpence, which was very generous. Scrope's own bonus had been substantial. They had all drunk Mr Drummond's health in the beer they consumed so freely whenever they worked in the kiln – and, for that matter, whenever they weren't working in the kiln.

'Sit down, Mr Scrope, I have some great news for you!' Napier was on his feet, walking round the desk to perch on the edge so that he could wave a document in the manager's face.

'This is a patent taken out by a man named Patrick Stead which will completely change the method of manufacturing malt. I have the right to implement his new methods.'

Scrope looked sceptical. He reared back in his chair as if to distance himself from the mysterious document, already wary of the unknown.

'First of all we will use a blower to pass air currents against falling grain to screen it. Now that is not so strange, I admit, but we will heat the air to about one hundred and ten degrees to cleanse and purify the grain before steeping.

'Then when I build the floors of the house in French Horn Lane, they will be double and house water pipes between the two layers. By running hot or cold water through the pipes, we can control the temperature of the floor and keep the barley germinating at between fifty and sixty degrees.

'I ask you. Why do we stop malting in March?' continued Napier, ignoring Scrope's bulging eyes. 'Because the air gets too warm, causing the barley to germinate too far and too fast. By this method –'

'Pipes in the floor? Hot air on the barley before steeping?

142

No!' If Scrope had possessed a cross at that moment, he would have held it up to ward off evil.

'But that is not all.' Napier raised his voice to overcome objections. 'We will use a steam pipe under the kiln floor occasionally, to give moisture to the malt whenever you think it necessary. Then, during kilning, if you should so wish, you may employ dry air. Provision will be built into the kiln.'

'You can't do it,' said Scrope and Napier's eyes narrowed. Francis had entered the room silently a minute or two earlier and now stood tensely at the back, waiting and watching.

'We can double our turnover and our profits by malting all year round,' said Napier. 'It is a logical thing to do. No one knew how to do it before, that's all. Not only that. I plan to modify malthouses for other maltsters. Two businesses, do you see? Remember the railways? They were thought to be a mad idea at one time by people who couldn't see the advantages. But *you've* seen the advantages of railways, haven't you? We were just talking about it the other day.'

But Scrope had not been attracted to railways in their experimental days. He hadn't given them a thought. Like thousands of other men, he had taken to the idea of railway travel and transporting – and become fascinated by steam engines – long after railways had become a fact of commercial life. He was a follower, not an innovator, a man who recognized progress after it had passed him by and become part of the everyday scene. Besides, he was quicker to advocate change in other fields than in his own.

'The men won't do it, Mr Drummond. Why, for one thing, they wouldn't be able to take up their summer jobs.'

Napier sighed. 'They only take up summer jobs because there is no work in the maltings.'

That wasn't quite true and Napier knew it. To be sure, the summer migrations had begun all those years ago because there was no work in the maltings. But these days the men moved on because travelling had become an established part of their life cycles. They took different work because they wanted to, not because they had to.

Napier tried again. 'It must come. We cannot stand in the way of progress. If we don't do it, someone else will'.

'I tell you, Mr Drummond, sir, other maltsters won't buy

143

them modifications. They won't take the chance of spending all that money on a system that might not work. And even if they did, brewers wouldn't buy the malt made that way. What would you do then, sir? Brewers want plain floor-made malt. They know the old ways are best. The British man likes his beer to taste like British beer.'

Napier returned to his seat, rested his head against the high leather back and thought about what to do next. He could see Francis from the corner of his eye, the lad's whole body poised on the balls of his feet. Napier knew that Francis was waiting for some stroke of genius, a collection of carefully chosen words which would destroy Scrope's objections.

In Napier's direct line of vision was Scrope, also tense, afraid and worried for his future, utterly convinced of the validity of his case.

'I value your opinion, Mr Scrope. You know malting. You know the minds of maltsters and brewers. I don't. If you say I'm holding a worthless piece of paper, then I believe you. The idea is right, you know, this is the way it will one day be done. If I had time enough and wealth, I'd make others come round to my way of thinking. But changing men's minds is a lengthy process, sometimes lasting years. I admit I haven't the stomach for it. I have remodelled Cass's old malthouse; it is in sound condition now. I'll put in two more floors and next season we'll make malt there in the old way. I hope you will manage both my maltings.'

Francis could hardly believe his ears. Disappointed beyond all words, he collapsed back against the wall, knocking General Napier, in his heavy gold frame, out of true.

'It's a wise man as listens to good advice,' said Scrope, handsomely. He stood and thrust out his hand to his employer, aware of Mr Drummond's loss of face and of his own increased power. He had just won a battle of ideas with a man reckoned to have the sharpest mind in Ware. He felt a tremendous sense of warmth and affection for this fiery stranger. Later, he would feel a certain contempt, a certain wariness of one who could harbour such silly ideas. But at the moment, only genuine regard was reflected in his open features.

'One thing I would ask, Mr Scrope. Don't tell anyone about

Patrick Stead's patent. I would be very angry indeed if some other maltster took up my discarded plans. Especially when you have advised me so strongly not to touch the new method.'

'Oh, I won't do that, sir,' said Scrope, taking in the gentle threat. 'That would be terrible. Besides, anybody would think you'd run crazy.' He nodded goodbye to Francis and stepped carefully over the polished floor as he left.

'But what is this?' cried Francis. 'Why did you have to change your mind so suddenly? One word from Scrope . . . All the investment, the time I've spent –'

'Wasted, Francis. Largely wasted. It was a hare-brained scheme. The right idea at the wrong time. Fortunately, Scrope enabled me to see disaster ahead.'

'But he's only one man!'

'Yes, and I'm gambling that his reaction is typical of the trade, that he speaks for others. But most of all, I'm gambling on the fact that he understands the conservative attitudes of the brewers. We might have been able to make the finest malt in the country, but if the brewers wanted something else, we would have been bankrupt.'

'But to perform an about face, humble yourself before the likes of Scrope . . . I never thought I'd see the day.'

'I may have gone mad, my friend. I feel very strange at this moment. I have to ask myself what I want most from life. The answer, I'm afraid, is success. Success, and the money that proves I'm successful. I don't love the malting trade enough to want to improve it.'

Francis sat down and stared at the carpet. 'All the hours of hard work I put into this scheme. That's not to say that you didn't work hard also. It's just that I'm a lazy fellow and don't like to waste my time. Besides, you should have slept on it. You took the decision too quickly.'

'I am always a man for quick decisions. When I see what has to be done, I do it. We have learned a valuable lesson from all this, I think. Did you ever hear about the hound who got so far ahead of the pack that he was savaged by the deer? We might – we *would* have been savaged by the brewers. We have had nothing but trouble on this venture.'

'The Hobart land,' agreed Francis. 'It was an omen, I suppose. Still, to look on the bright side, we will have a new fifteen-quarter malthouse which is sure to make a profit. I expect you are right. You've saved us from disaster. To tell you the truth, I was always a little sceptical of our chances. Now I think of it, the whole project was a mad start. A hare-brained scheme as you have said. I feel quite relieved. But I had better go at once to French Horn Lane and give the men their new instructions.'

The next day, Napier entered his larger malthouse through a side door. The sixty-quarter house was one of the largest in town, situated handily beside the river. Colourful barges were standing by at this moment to take his sacks on board for a slow journey to London. Napier supposed that several sacks of barley had been hidden in these waters until the latest excise man had taken his leave, but he chose not to enquire too closely into these tax evading pranks.

It was six o'clock in the morning and the cool early light sifted its way between the louvres of the small windows; not enough to work by. Primitive rushlights were here and there spiked against the walls. Not even a colza lamp hung from a beam. Maltsters were like pit ponies, accustomed to working in semi-darkness.

The last batch of germinating barley was spread out at the far end of the large room, leaving the rest of the floor bare. Two men, graceful as ballet dancers, moved in step across the floor, scooping barley into their large wooden shovels, tossing it in a sweeping movement so that it drifted to the ground in an even carpet. The air was heavy with dust; no wonder maltsters sometimes suffered from the lung disease that afflicted the farmers who grew barley.

Napier made his way to the kiln and found Scrope and three others stripped to the waist, silhouetted by the burning embers of hornbeam faggots. They had to turn the germinated barley as it lay above the heat on wire mesh, a hot and difficult task. They were not working at the moment, however. Six o'clock was apparently the time for what the men called beaver.

A few faggots had been raked from the fire bed on to the hard brick floor and a large frying pan rested on them. The smell of bacon frying was strong here, mingling with the cloying scent of malt. The beer boy had tankards ready for those who were sweating away their bodies' fluid.

146

Scrope and his men greeted Napier in a friendly way and offered him some of their food. He refused, but gladly took a tankard. He was already so hot he had to strip to his shirt-sleeves. One of the men took his outer garments to hang them on a hook while he retreated, beer in hand, to the coolest corner.

The talk flowed unselfconsciously and was all about the latest encounter with the excise man, how the forces of the law had been outwitted. Napier was applied to for a comment now and then, or an occasional opinion, but mostly he drank in silence. How different it all was from the Rochdale mill that dominated the countryside, with its brutal overseers, over-worked women and children, strict timekeeping and everlast-ing, mind-destroying noise. There was a permanent state of war between master and men, each refusing to trust the other.

In malthouses, the men worked until their day's tasks were finished. Then they went home. They started at four in the morning and left in the early afternoon, stopping to make beaver whenever they wished. Malthouses were primitive places, dusty, dark and sometimes incredibly hot, but no one complained, because these working men had been allowed to keep their dignity.

And that, primarily, was why Napier had wanted to be a maltster. A sentimental reason reinforced by the good fact that malting was very profitable. He had no wish to own men's souls. He just wanted to make money – and, of course, to enjoy the challenges that making money brought. Perhaps Patrick Stead's progressive methods would destroy these independent men. Wasn't it progress that had created fiendish mills? He didn't know. In fact, to be perfectly honest, he didn't know anything at all. He had been running as fast as he could since he was sixteen, chasing a dream, sustained by hatred of his father. Hard work had been a way of escaping deep thought.

Now he had been brought to a standstill. He chose to see the collapse of his plans as defeat, stark and humiliating. Napier Drummond was not a successful man. He had failed. The very condition he had feared most had overtaken him. In some ways it wasn't as bad as expected. The sky had not actually fallen on him; people didn't shun him in the streets.

In other ways it was a greater calamity than he could have

imagined, because it took from him his direction, his certainty of purpose. He had always known what he was going to do next week, next month, next year. Now the future was a perfect blank.

He knew that he had no feeling for malting. He was a visitor here, an owner of a large malthouse who was never allowed into the charmed circle of malting owners; an outcast.

How different it had been at the mill. Whether he liked it or not, he had belonged there. He took a deep breath of the hot air which seared his lungs. Bacon and malt smells hung about him in the close atmosphere, but it was the remembered smell of size in the cloth that suddenly pricked his nostrils and burned his eyes. And the looms. The clack and clatter that deafened those who spent their lives working on them. He had developed a sixth sense about cotton mills, had learned to sniff trouble in the very air.

Then, from his days with old Barge, he had learned which cloths the ladies liked and which they wouldn't touch. He'd followed his protector's advice, and never questioned the vagaries of taste and fashion. What difference if he thought the latest fashion stupid? He supplied what was wanted today, shunning those cloths which had been loved the day before yesterday. By the time he opened his first swag shop, there was little you could tell him about the making and selling of cheap cottons. Much later, in Bury St Edmunds, he had mastered the better quality woollens and silks.

On the other hand, what did he know about malting? Like a fool, he had left the field of his expertise to become the manufacturer of a product which depended entirely on the experience and judgement of other men.

The most important stage in the malt-making process was the buying of the barley, a task no owner ever delegated – except Napier Drummond who had no choice. Malting barley carried a premium; only the finest quality would make good malt. Maltings owners went into the fields to see the growing crop where they bargained and bullied the farmers who grew for them. Napier had to depend on Scrope to say to the farmer: 'Cut this section, leave that one for two weeks. We'll pay forty shillings for this barley, less for that.'

He should never have bought a malthouse. No, that wasn't

true either. The money was good; he liked Hertfordshire and its people; he would stay – and, eventually, he would learn.

He said goodbye to his workers for the season. Outside, the sky was lightening, but the sudden change in temperature from the kiln to the bitter spring air made him shiver. He settled his hat on his head which ached a little. He was unaccustomed to so much introspection, didn't like facing himself and had always thought it was rather self-indulgent, like prinking before a mirror.

The failed venture would always rankle; there was no shying away from that. And intimately connected with the failure was the tiny figure of Sybilla Hobart who had thwarted him over the land. Like the bad-tempered witch she was, she had added insult to injury by throwing tea in his face, just because she thought he had dared to propose marriage.

Suddenly, like being struck by a bolt of lightning, he saw that particular incident as it must have looked to Francis. My God, how that woman had made a fool of him! He was not surprised that Francis had given way to a fit of hysterical laughter. And what would Francis say if he ever discovered how much that land had really cost?

Sybilla Hobart was the symbol of his declining powers, bad luck. No, that was stupid. He tried to reject such an atavistic response, tried to tell himself that she had not cursed his endeavours, was not responsible for his misjudgement. But in spite of himself, he still believed it. He never wanted to see her again.

And yet – he had assented to a visit to the theatre and had undertaken to host the outing since the entire party would have to stay overnight in a London hotel. Napier cursed his foolish generosity in giving way to his mother's persuasions. He would be in Sybilla's company for hours. She would be alluring in a low-cut gown, beautifully controlled, having herself well in hand: the cool widow. Hopefully there would be no flashes of temper, no fleeting looks of uncertainty to tempt a man into feelings of misplaced sentiment. He would have to be on his guard at every moment.

Attempting to thrust Sybilla from his mind, he set out to walk to Hertford. Earlier, he had walked to Ware to clear his brain, and had not succeeded in doing so. Perhaps the return journey would do the trick.

Sunday afternoon was a blustery day, cold and threatening to rain. Francis had already exchanged views about the weather with half a dozen people on his walk from Balls Park to Bailton Hall. When Scrimshaw opened the door to him, he had to agree once again that yes, it was too cold for the first day of May.

Emmaline met him in the hall as he removed his hat and gloves. 'Shall we go into the drawing-room?' she asked, and hurried ahead of him to open the door, anxious to get him safely hidden from prying eyes.

'Emmaline.' He took her hand as soon as the door closed behind them. He kissed the palm and she didn't draw away, nor was she displeased. On the other hand, she was afraid of being seen in such embarrassing circumstances, of being chided for her forward behaviour. Propriety played no part in her attitude towards Francis. She loved him; he might do as he wished with her if only no member of her family should discover them.

'You misled us about Mrs Hobart,' she said by way of casual conversation.

Francis dropped her hand in some surprise, but smiled at her warmly. He knew her little ways, always attempting to maintain a flow of inconsequential chatter when she was most agitated.

'In what way, dearest?'

'You told us she was rich.'

'I don't believe I ever discussed her financial status with you at all.'

'Well, you must have said something to Mr Farley. Marianne and I paid her a call and I was never so mortified in my life. Everything she has is so shabby.'

'But what difference can that possibly make to you?'

She sighed, looked out of the window, sighed again and sat down on the settee. 'We won't be able to go for a walk in this weather. It is going to rain, I'm sure.'

'Then let us go into the glasshouse. It will be warm in there and no one will discover us.'

'But what if they did? What could we say if Napier were to walk into the place? He knows we are neither of us interested in the study of botany.'

'Emmaline, I love you. I sympathize with you, circumstanced as you are here, and I know that your family do not value you as they should. But this furtiveness cannot go on. The solution rests with you. Let me speak to Napier. Let me ask him for your hand. He won't refuse, I promise you.'

'You don't know what it would be like. I'm afraid. That may seem strange to you, but my family, and Napier in particular, make me feel like an idiot. Napier would frown and ask questions and pace the floor. He might raise objections and just as we were answering them suddenly change his mind as if he thought the engagement would teach me a salutary lesson. Within half an hour, I wouldn't know my own mind. and I do love you! I'm sure we should be happy for ever if only I weren't afraid –'

'But we could spend the rest of our lives waiting until you are no longer afraid. I would not suggest speaking so soon, but I can't even spirit you away from this *prison* long enough to show you the neat little estate my uncle left to me in Broxbourne Woods. The place needs a good deal of work, repainting and refurnishing. I want everything to be as you wish, so we must become openly betrothed. I assure you, I am fond of every member of your family. I have the deepest regard for Napier, as you know. He is a splendid fellow, although he wants careful handling. Your mother is a darling. And Marianne – is a vivacious young woman whom I can admire even when she does not behave towards you as I would wish, or you deserve. But they are all the most gregarious people I have ever met. They never leave us alone.'

'Would you call it gregarious? I always thought they were ready to spy on me. It's not fair. No one knows what Napier does when he is not working. Marianne has her secrets, and Mama conspires for hours with Mr Farley. Only I –'

'Dearest one, I promise you that when we are married, I will respect your privacy.'

'Oh, not you!' she cried. 'I want no secrets from you.'

'And I,' said Francis with some heat, 'want nothing more than to remove you from this house. The sooner the better.'

151

'What has occurred to Napier to put him into such a filthy mood?' asked Emmaline, which wasn't the *non sequitur* it appeared to be.

'The failure of a business venture. Has he taken out his ill temper on you?'

'On us all. No, that is unfair. He has quite cut up our peace, but not because of anything he has said. He's so distracted and looks so unhappy that Marianne is forever trying to amuse him with her play-acting.'

'And driving him mad with boredom. Poor Napier. He has my sympathy.'

'My sister has a restless nature, but a good heart,' replied Emmaline sharply. 'You must not be unkind about her.'

'Oh, my dear, you are too generous.'

Francis took her by the elbows and lifted her from the settee. She rose willingly, looking at him with such trust that he couldn't resist kissing her. She had just broken away from this passionate but brief embrace when the door opened and Marianne strode into the room.

'Emmaline, you wicked girl. Why didn't you call me when Mr Babcock arrived? If Scrimshaw hadn't mentioned it to me, I should never have known.'

Emmaline blushed and Francis vowed to have a word with Scrimshaw. He customarily pressed a coin into the butler's hand on arrival. Today he had forgotten.

'Good afernoon to you, Miss Drummond. I expect Miss Emmaline didn't think to inform you, since I called on *her* to invite her to take a walk with me this afternoon.'

'In this weather? My sister will not venture to put so much as a toe out of doors on a day like this. You had better ask me to accompany you if you are determined on walking today. I don't mind what the heavens may send.'

Mrs Drummond, hot on her elder daughter's heels, entered the room through the open door, took in the situation in one glance, and tried to think of some excuse for removing Marianne from the room.

'Oh, Marianne, my dear, I had thought we might go into the country for a ride.'

'If you plan to see Mr Farley in Hertingfordbury, and I

152

suspect you do, I shan't come with you, Mama. I would find it excessively boring.'

Francis looked helplessly at Emmaline, but she refused to meet his eye. He wished fervently that Marianne *had* caught him kissing her sister. That, at least, would have brought matters to a head. Emmaline, he knew very well, would not let him come within ten feet of her again, so narrowly had she missed being discovered.

Napier, coming out of his library, heard voices in the drawing-room and joined the company. 'Well, Francis, have you come to see me?'

'No, of course not. I can see you every other day of the week. I came to invite Miss Emmaline to take a walk with me.'

'Well, you won't tempt Emmaline out of doors on a day like this.'

'That is what I have been saying,' said Marianne.

'I'm quite sure that Emmaline would love to go for a walk this afternoon,' said Mrs Drummond, looking at her younger daughter anxiously.

'Well, you must put on your boots if you are to join us,' said Marianne briskly. 'I warn you, I won't wait for ever.'

'I don't –' began Emmaline.

'Oh, for God's sake, girl, don't be so poor-spirited,' said Napier. 'The walk will do you good.'

Emmaline's eyes filled with tears, and Francis turned to Napier furiously. 'I asked Miss Emmaline to go for a walk with me. Miss Emmaline and only her. If she does not care to walk, then we will stay in this room and play draughts. *If* I have your permission, Napier.'

Napier shrugged his shoulders, a shrug that implied permission for Francis to follow any odd start that occurred to him. Then, too, it was a shrug of incomprehension.

'Thank you, Mr Babcock,' said Emmaline faintly. She was very pale and her eyes held a warning: he must not speak. 'But I'm afraid I have the headache. Will you excuse me?' She walked past him to reach the door, never lifting her eyes from the floor.

'So much for Emmaline's company.' said Marianne scornfully.

'Well, I think . . .' began Mrs Drummond. But no one wanted

153

to know what she thought, so she left the room to find Emmaline.

'Don't look so cast down, old fellow,' said Napier. 'I'm tired of studying my papers. I'll come with you two for a nice brisk walk. No complaining or turning back if it rains, Marianne.'

'Not I,' she laughed. 'I'll be two minutes.'

As Napier also wished to change his footwear, Francis was left alone in the drawing-room. Downcast? He was furious. Sometimes – just occasionally – he wished the woman he loved would show a little more spirit.

10

Sybilla flung herself into her work; she studied the catalogues, wrote out orders for parts as she and Mr Puddifoot agreed the need, and visited Lord Lane every day to check on the progress of her new gig.

The Perkins' found increased interest and enthusiasm in their work. And if Perkins senior was still inclined to imagine disaster lurking round each corner, Jethro's excitement more than made up for his father's gloom.

Sybilla wasn't willing to pay for all new parts on a gig that was to be primarily for her own use, so the men stripped her old one and used whatever was still in working order. The body was new, however, shipped by rail from the supplier, and the paintwork – Mr Puddifoot's speciality – took several nail-biting weeks to complete.

After the final coat of varnish had been applied, Sybilla ordered a small celebration. She had seen the raw wood transformed into a glowing coach body with a finish like satin, had come to appreciate her men and to understand the work as well as the costs – the terrifying costs – involved in making a coach. Thirty pounds, she thought, would be the cheapest she could offer a Stanhope gig. And that seemed to her to be a high price for Hoddesdon people to pay for a vehicle which seated only two, or at best, three persons. Would anyone pay it?

Jethro was fully occupied these days with making repairs. That side of the business had unaccountably increased, and while she welcomed the extra income, she now needed another man for the coach-building, always assuming that they did receive a few orders.

On the day the gig was ready to be driven, she asked the men which of them would volunteer to teach her to drive it properly. There was some shuffling and a bit of rough teasing among themselves before it was settled that Mr Puddifoot should give her a few lessons. Everyone agreed that it was important for Sybilla to drive the gig well if her little jaunts were to serve the purpose of drumming up business.

She was surprised at how quickly her driving improved when Mr Puddifoot taught her a few of the tricks used by acknowledged whipsters. For his part, Mr Puddifoot was surprised at how quickly his employer could learn, but then she had already shown that she had a quick mind whenever they discussed the purchases for the business.

Inevitably, the bills began to arrive. Sybilla had stocked her business well with parts, paints, varnishes, brushes and gold size against the moment when they would be inundated with orders. And for her own gig, she had employed the services of a good coach upholsterer. Now, all at once, her suppliers wished to be paid.

'You'll be borrowing from the bank, I suppose,' said Mr Puddifoot, and Sybilla said that yes, she would, although she hadn't thought of it before.

Refusing his offer to accompany her, she set off early one morning to drive to Samuel Adams's bank in the High Street, Ware. On the way, she caused quite as much of a stir as she had hoped. Everyone turned to stare at the handsome two-wheeler gig, its flawless blue surface decorated in gold with the legend: 'Hobart's, coach-builders, gigs £30'.

She wore her very best navy blue ensemble with white collar and cuffs, and a large hat which she was sure made her look both intelligent and businesslike. A clutch of ragged boys gathered to stare as she tied the reins to the hitching post. Fearing for her precious paintwork, she gave them a halfpenny and a stern look before entering the bank.

The manager, coming out of his office, invited her in with unctuous smiles and quite a show of bowing and dashing forward to help her to a chair. The room reeked of damp and self-importance.

'I am Mrs Hobart,' she said, hoping that the very slight tremor in her voice would strike this man as nothing out of the ordinary. 'And I would like to borrow some money, please.'

The manager's smile slipped slightly. She thought his stare hardened. 'What for?'

'Is that any of your business?'

A wintry smirk curved his thin lips beneath a straggly ginger moustache. 'Yes, madam, it is, if you wish to borrow money from this bank.'

'Well, I want it for my coach-building business. I've had a great many bills arrive all of a sudden and –'

'Have you a full order book?'

'Why no, I haven't any orders at all. That is why I want to borrow some money. I intend to place announcements in the *County Press* and *The Reformer*. I'm certain that when my notices appear, I will have enough business to keep my men occupied, but we needed supplies, you see –'

'So you bought supplies because you think you *might* receive a good deal of business in response to your announcements?'

'Yes, sir.'

'Mrs Hobart,' he said rather sternly. He was about as old as Mr Hobart had been when she married him, and the similarity didn't end there. The manager had the same way of speaking to her in a tired voice which implied that she was too stupid to understand anything at all. His greying hair extended down to his jawbone, leaving his ears marooned in a sea of curls. For some reason, all this facial hair drew attention to his nose which was too small and snub for so prominent a role.

'Mrs Hobart,' he began again, clearly at a loss as to what to say to her. 'You tell me that your business is stagnant and that you have rashly ordered large supplies without any hope of definite business. But you have not told me how much you want to borrow or what you will offer as collateral. Now if it is just twenty pounds or so –'

'Well, it isn't. I need two hundred pounds. And as for the other thing, I have nothing to offer. If I had anything to offer, I wouldn't be here!' Now he was grimly amused; she wished she had the nerve to get up and walk out, but faint hope kept her seated.

'Your husband?'

'Dead these past eighteen months.'

'Your business is managed by –'

'Mr Puddifoot. He wanted to come with me today, but I preferred to come alone.'

'Madam, I suggest you bring your manager and your account books with you next week, and perhaps we can come to some arrangement. In the meantime, have you an acquaintance, a man who could vouch for you?'

157

She straightened and lifted her chin a little. 'Why, yes I have. Mr Napier Drummond will speak for me.'

It was gratifying to see the heavy eyebrows lift in surprise, to see the frosty manner change to one of intense interest. It seemed Mr Drummond could be useful on occasion.

'In that case, the situation is altered.'

'Will you lend me the money?'

'Not today, of course, but if you will leave your address, I shall write to you.'

He stood up; there was nothing for Sybilla to do but follow. The interview was over. She must wait, but with improved hopes. How fortunate that she had thought of giving Mr Drummond's name!

The manager saw her to the door, eyed the gig with its brazen lettering on the side, and shook his head. He was shocked, of course. Well-bred women did not behave in this hoydenish fashion. Nevertheless, he was intrigued and amused. Not a great deal happened at his bank to make life exciting. This bit of tittle-tattle deserved to be conveyed at once. He returned to his office and penned what he modestly believed to be one of his wittiest letters to the owner of the bank, Samuel Adams.

Not two hours later, a letter was delivered by hand to Napier in his office. He read the signature first – Samuel Adams – wondering what his old enemy had to say to him.

The contents of the letter left him in a cold rage. He shouted for Babcock.

'That damned woman has done it again!' he growled when Francis had come into the room. 'She has tried to borrow two hundred pounds from Sam Adams's bank to bolster her failing business, and had the audacity to give my name as reference. Adams, of course, puts the worst possible construction on her actions. Thinks my connection with the woman is intimate and that *I* sent her. Has she no sense at all? Will she never stop haunting me? I'll give her a piece of my mind she won't forget. I'll make her wish she had never been born.'

Francis had been reading the letter and now dropped it on to the desk. 'This can't go on, Napier. She clearly has no sense. Borrowing money! And just after you gave her fifty pounds for the land. She is obviously both extravagant and irresponsible. You must speak to her, of course, and without delay. Unfortunately, I have some important papers to attend to –'

'I won't be needing you,' said Napier brusquely. Francis' mention of the money he had paid for the Hobart land, reminded Napier that she had not spent just fifty pounds in the past few weeks, but two hundred and fifty. Only Sybilla Hobart, of all their female acquaintances, stepped beyond the confines of propriety, blundering about in the world of business which was the proper concern of men. Napier picked up his hat and gloves and left the office.

Francis, with a shrug, returned to his own room, vaguely unsettled by the Hobart woman, who seemed to be challenging all his assumptions about the fair sex. He thanked God that Emmaline didn't see the widow too often, although he doubted that she would ever be unduly influenced by such radical behaviour. Emmaline was, if nothing else, properly conventional.

In Hoddesdon half an hour later, Napier banged loudly on the Hobart door. 'I wish to see Mrs Hobart,' he said roughly, his eyes travelling over Saul's stained white stockings, unshaven face and bloodshot eyes. 'You ought to be horsewhipped,' he added cryptically and pushed past the dumbfounded servant.

Sybilla opened the drawing-room door at the sound of his voice, smiling broadly. 'Mr Drummond! I never expected to see you so soon! How kind of you to call.'

'Now see here, Sybilla –' began Napier, but her warm greeting had spoiled his momentum. Turning to Saul, he glared ferociously. 'Here, you drunken oaf, bring me some madeira at once.'

Sybilla blinked in surprise, but was too relieved to see her guest, to wonder what had put him in such a foul mood. She closed the drawing-room door behind them. Saul, shaken nearly to sobriety, trotted away to fetch the decanter and glasses.

'I wouldn't have had you see Saul in that condition for the world. He has been so good lately. I even bought him some clothing as a reward. I can't understand his backsliding.'

Napier prowled the room, picking up an ornament here, patting a cushion elsewhere. 'Can't you? I told you to get rid of him. You need a sound man working for you.'

'I know, but –'

The door opened and Saul shuffled in, tightly gripping a silver galleried tray. He set it down with extreme care and began to pour the madeira into the glasses. His hand was unsteady; he had never in his life exerted so much energy in an attempt to appear sober.

'So you're thinking of giving this rogue his marching orders?' said Napier suddenly.

Sybilla gasped. 'If . . . that is . . . I *am* disappointed . . .'

Saul served a glass of wine to Sybilla, giving a spendid performance of injured pride and unfair betrayal. She looked away. Saul might deserve a dressing-down. Well, undoubtedly he did, but Mr Drummond could be unaccountably brutal in affairs that had nothing to do with him.

With greater trepidation, Saul approached Napier and proffered the tray with one glass on it.

'Shave your face before I see it again,' said Napier softly and Saul nodded vigorously. Sybilla shot a look heavenwards; no wonder the Drummond women were afraid of him!

'I suppose your unkind words *have* been a salutary lesson to Saul,' she said doubtfully when the poor man had taken himself off to shave.

'The benefit will be strictly temporary, I'm afraid. But my tongue will have to serve, since you have apparently lost yours. What has happened to half the furniture in here?'

'The room was too crowded.'

'Sent your predecessor's belongings to the sale rooms?' he asked quizzically.

'Mrs Hobart's taste was . . .'

'Lamentable. Well done. You have lived in her shadow for too long.'

'I've put the pieces in the attic. When Cissy marries, I shall be able to furnish some rooms for her and Jefferson. She is going to marry Jefferson Smith who has joined the county constabulary. We are all very proud of him.'

Napier finished his wine and helped himself to another with quick angry jerks. Saul had spilled madeira on the base of the glass. Now Napier's hands were sticky, as were the tray and the neck of the decanter. Angrily, he took out his pocket handkerchief to wipe his fingers. He had come to give Sybilla a raking down for her presumption and stayed to discuss her maid's nuptials, or so it seemed.

He turned to her. 'Now look here, Sybilla –'

'Did the bank contact you? The manager was so unpleasant. He reminded me of Mr Hobart. Oh, I don't mean . . . But he asked me rude questions about collectables or something.'

'Collateral.'

'Yes, that's it. I told him if I had anything to give, I wouldn't be needing to borrow money. I could hardly say I had never heard the word before, could I? I was ready to sink, I assure you. Then he asked me if any man I knew would give me a reference. Fortunately, I remembered that you had said Samuel Adams is a friend of yours, so I was very relieved to be able to give him your name.'

Napier couldn't help laughing. 'I lied, Sybilla. Sam Adams is my worst enemy. He was furious at the mention of my name.'

'So I have spoiled my chances completely.' She looked at him curiously. 'Do you often lie?'

'Only when it suits me. Sam thought I had urged you to borrow money from his bank.'

'I wish I had given Dr Horley's name.'

The westering sun fell gently on Sybilla, brightening her hair, accentuating her pale smooth skin. The same light played cruel tricks with the interior of the room. Napier saw peeling brown paint, and wallpaper brilliant only where a picture had recently been removed. The window glass had a bloom of dust.

'Why do you need money so soon after I gave you two hundred and fifty pounds?' But he said it more gently than he had intended to, and was moved in spite of himself when a delicate colour suffused her cheeks.

Sybilla said nothing for several seconds, then murmured something about family responsibilities, a brother and widowed mother, pressing, but unspecified debts. There followed a painful silence, and with sudden inspiration, she jumped up from her seat and fetched a parcel wrapped in brown paper which had been lying on a chair in the corner.

'Your mother has been so kind as to send me some cloth which she had no need of during her own mourning.' She tore at the wrappings and revealed a large quantity of lavender silk. 'Isn't it beautiful? I shall have it made up for the evening when

161

we go to London to the theatre. It was very kind indeed of you to invite me. I'm most grateful.'

Napier fingered the cloth; he knew it well. Lavender twilled silk, four-and-eleven the yard. A good quality cloth that he had sold successfully for years in Bury St Edmunds. 'You should have enough here for a matching pelisse. It will suit you, but keep the decoration to a minimum. Let the cloth speak for itself. Full sleeves, I think, with bare shoulders, worn with a simple pearl, or perhaps jet, necklace.'

Later she would be surprised as she recalled this knowledgeable speech. At the moment, her mind was taken up entirely with the abortive attempt to borrow money. 'What can I say to you, Mr Drummond? I would never have gone to the bank if I didn't need the money very badly. I'm not extravagant and I'm not foolish. But surely every business needs some capital? That dreadful man told me to bring my manager with me when I come again, and my account books, which I cannot think are any of his business. Besides, I don't want Mr Puddifoot to know all about my affairs and, above all, I don't want him to discover how ignorant I am.'

'I thought you dismissed your manager.'

'He was happy enough to come back, and for the same wages.'

'That was clever of you,' he said and actually smiled slightly, which encouraged her to continue.

'He has made me a most beautiful gig which says: "Hobart's, coach-builders, gigs £30" in gold letters on lake blue. I drive it everywhere to let people know what I am offering. Oh yes, and I've taken a few driving lessons from Mr Puddifoot. I could hardly hide from him the fact that I had never been properly taught how to manage a horse and carriage.'

'And you drive about with this blatant message on the gig? That is most unladylike of you, Sybilla.'

'Yes, I know. But I don't care. I really don't care about such things. I *must* stay in business. Don't you see? I must. And I believe I can. I have taken small announcements in the newspapers and I'm just certain that someone will see how reasonably we can make good quality gigs. I have discovered that it is far cheaper to purchase ready-made parts than to have everything bespoke for each order.'

162

'So, in the hope that commissions will flood in, you have ordered large quantities of parts, and now your suppliers want to be paid.'

She was delighted at his quick understanding. 'Yes, that is it, exactly. But not large quantities, just the smallest orders they would sell us. I did the right thing, didn't I?'

'Have you the account books? I can give you no advice until I have seen them. Do you object?'

'Not at all. I won't be a moment.' She almost skipped out of the room, leaving Napier to wonder how she had manoeuvred him into the position of adviser when he had intended to be a scourge. He told himself that he could not bear to hear of a badly-run business, that Sybilla had shown considerable initiative and courage, that he was curious about what the account books would reveal.

She hovered anxiously while he turned the pages of the large books. To her surprise, he had insisted on starting five years back, tracing the fading fortunes of Hobart's, clicking his tongue occasionally, sometimes laughing out loud but refusing to explain why. When he, at last, arrived at the pages written in her hand, he reared back, then removed a pencil from his pocket and made certain corrections to her arithmetic. She was embarrassed at first, but his altered totals differed by only a few pounds from hers. She didn't see that it mattered all that much.

'In costing the gigs, you failed to take any notice of overheads, of depreciation, rates, rent and so forth. It will actually cost a little more for each gig than you imagined. In fact, if you complete only one gig a week, your overheads will be much higher per gig than if you have several going out each week. Do you understand that?'

She didn't. 'Does that mean that the bank won't lend me any money?'

'There was never any hope of that. What collateral could you offer? The deeds to this house, for instance, would be collateral. The bank would hold the deeds and keep them until you paid the loan.'

'And if times were hard and I failed to pay?'

He shrugged. 'I don't advise you to return to Sam's bank, and I don't think you would have any greater success at another bank until you have a full order book. By that time, you might be in rather serious straits.'

'Then what am I to do?'

He had known all along, of course. There was only one alternative. Whatever Francis might say if he were to hear of it, Napier intended to lend two hundred pounds to the widow. 'You may borrow the money from me. It will be a formal agreement, just as if I were a bank.'

'And will you hold the deeds of this house?'

He had no confidence in her steadiness. The Lord only knew what mad start might yet occur to her. Therefore, the deeds would be safest in his care. 'Yes,' he said, 'and I will charge you interest on the loan.'

'Interest?'

'One year from today, I will expect you to pay me two hundred pounds plus the interest due.'

'And how much is that?' Her mind was racing. She had heard such dreadful stories from Robert about moneylenders. She wondered if she would be in debt for the rest of her life.

'Bank lending rate has been five per cent for many years, but it has fallen recently and I believe the trend is downwards. I will lend the money to you at four point nine per cent.' She looked both dismayed and confused. 'A little under ten pounds,' he said helpfully and saw her frown disappear.

'Do people always charge interest?' she asked, pursuing her own line of thought. 'Even among friends?'

He was angry. 'Yes, Sybilla, they do. In money matters it is wisest to behave in a strictly businesslike manner. Then there can be no misunderstandings or broken friendships. I should think you would appreciate that. This loan is impersonal. Papers will be signed. Would you really want to be beholden to me?'

'No, oh no,' she said faintly. Now was the moment to stun him with the news that his mother had borrowed money from *her*, and there had been no talk of interest or signed papers. Napier Drummond would be too proud to do otherwise than to pay Sybilla the two hundred pounds immediately. She couldn't do it, however. Whatever mad scheme of revenge had prompted her to give Mrs Drummond the money in the first place, she could not carry it through, because she needed this man's guidance. Besides, she couldn't hurt Mrs Drummond. The secret must remain a secret.

Another thought occurred to her. What would she say to Mr Drummond when she suddenly acquired two hundred pounds on quarter day? There could be no plausible explanation. He would be bound to discover the truth. The only solution was to hide the fact from him and continue to accept his loan; a ludicrous situation. On reflection, she realized that she was worrying unnecessarily. She was sufficiently well acquainted with Mrs Drummond and Mr Farley to realize that there was no possibility of their returning her money this coming quarter day, or probably any other day.

Napier had been watching the fleeting expressions on her face with interest. He couldn't guess what thoughts were crowding into her mind. He was prepared to believe that she was ungrateful for his intervention and unaware of the time and trouble he would be taking on her behalf. Again, he wondered why he was helping her. Perhaps it was because her small business worries were so easily solved. If he could not decide what to do about his own affairs, at least he could watch her business thrive. It gave him a curious sense of power over someone who seemed to exercise power over his fortunes. Fanciful? Perhaps. The reasons for his involvement didn't trouble him unduly now that he had decided to help her. Of course, her business *must* suceed. He could not bear for *two* projects to founder under his guidance.

'Now then, Sybilla, suppose you show me this gig of yours and how well you can drive it.'

They left the house by way of the kitchen. Sybilla ordered Saul to fetch the gig. The poor man, who had, in the last half hour, cut himself several times with his cut-throat razor, left the kitchen and loped off towards the stables at the bottom of the garden.

Sybilla presented Mrs Potter to Napier; the two exchanged knowing looks, each well aware of the steel in the other. Cissy curtsied mechanically and returned to peeling potatoes.

Napier's attention was held by the little girl seated on the flagstone floor, a rag doll lying unloved on her lap. The child blinked slowly back at him, her mouth slightly open. Her eyelids were networked with fine red veins, her eyes sunk deeply into the small skull. Her pinched face was so pale that the skin appeared to be translucent and faintly blue. She wiped her dripping nose on the back of her hand, then wiped her hand on her dress. Apart from the fact that her hair had been brushed that day and she was wearing reasonably clean clothing, albeit without shoes and stockings, he had not seen such signs of deprivation since his days on the streets. There was food aplenty in this house and money, too. He never doubted for a moment that Mrs Potter helped herself by way of the household accounts. There was no excuse for the child's condition.

'Who is the mother?' he asked sharply.

'Cissy is the child's mother. Her name is Fanny. Come, Fanny, make your curtsey,' said Sybilla gently. Fanny continued to sit. Cissy dashed forward, scooped up her child and left the kitchen with a mutinous glare at Napier. At that moment, Saul entered the big room to say that the gig was ready and that he had brought it round to the front door.

It was several hours before Napier returned to his Hertford office. He had prepared several ingenious and plausible excuses for his long absence, all of them carefully constructed away from the truth, but in the event he didn't need them.

Francis poked his head round the door of Napier's office the instant he heard movement there. 'May I have a word with you?'

'Of course, come in. What is troubling you, my friend? You look very worried.'

Francis took a seat, crossed and uncrossed his legs, then leaned forward to put a hand on the desk.

'Napier . . .'

'Francis,' said Napier in some amusement. 'Come on, lad. Out with it. Been tampering with the accounts?'

'No, of course not. How can you joke at a time like this?'

'A time like what, for God's sake?'

'I wish to marry your sister.'

'Good Lord! Is that all? I'm absolutely delighted. I thought you would never get round to it. Mind you, Marianne will lead you a merry dance. I warn you now. You must take a strong hand.'

'Not Marianne. I'm asking your permission to marry Emmaline.'

Napier looked thunderstruck. 'Don't be ridiculous, old fellow. Don't offer for Emmaline. Insipid girl. Take Marianne.'

Francis kept a tight rein on his temper; he really had no choice. 'Marianne is a fine woman,' he said carefully. 'Very much like you.'

'There you are! You like me well enough, don't you?'

'Not enough to marry you, Napier.' The two men looked at one another across the desk until Francis could stand the silence no longer. 'Believe me, I wouldn't be asking for Emmaline's hand if I didn't love her very much.'

'By God, I'll bet you wouldn't!' said Napier, suddenly very angry. 'What has your exalted family to say to this misalliance?'

'They will love Emmaline for herself. I'm not trying to get my hands on your money, you know.'

'Thank you,' said Napier sarcastically. 'That was, naturally, my first thought.'

'Damn it, Napier. Can't you wish your sister well? You and Marianne make it plain how much you despise her. Won't you be relieved to have her off your hands and out of your house?'

'I shall make her a generous settlement, no matter what I think of the marriage or of Emmaline. I only hope your family don't make it abundantly clear that they despise a tradesman's sister.'

'You misjudge them,' said Francis, already regretting his outburst. This was no way to handle Napier. 'Anyway, you aren't a tradesman, are you? You are an industrialist. You are too sensitive, Napier.'

Napier did a most uncharacteristic thing: he began to suck the ball of his thumb. 'No,' he said softly, at last. 'I'm not a tradesman. Nor would I ever do anything to stand in the way of Emmaline's happiness. I don't despise her, I promise you. Perhaps I have not been made aware of her finer qualities. Let's go home. You will be wanting to tell Emmaline that all is well. Does my mother know?'

'Even Emmaline doesn't know that I have asked you at last. She was terrified that . . . what I mean is . . .'

167

'Never mind,' said Napier, standing up. 'I know exactly what you mean.'

Unfortunately – in Napier's view – all three women were in the drawing-room together. The expression on Francis' face told Emmaline that her loved one had approached her brother successfully. She turned to her mother and squeezed her arm excitedly.

'Mrs Drummond,' said Francis, 'I have just received Napier's permission to pay my addresses to Emmaline. I hope you are pleased for us.'

'Delighted, my love,' she said warmly and rose from the settee to plant a fond kiss on his cheek. Turning, she gave Emmaline a hug, and spoke over her daughter's shoulder. 'Bless you, Napier. I've seen this coming for weeks and I just held my breath. I was so afraid that you would disapprove.'

Marianne was on her feet, ready to shake Francis by the hand, speaking loudly, embracing Emmaline too fiercely. She avoided Napier's eyes, but nearly lost her hard-won control when he approached her and surreptitiously squeezed her arm in the sort of brotherly gesture he had never made before. She had not thought him so perceptive. It was now even harder to play the fond older sister, although she was grateful for his unspoken support.

The dinner that evening was the liveliest the five of them had ever enjoyed. Everyone talked at once except Emmaline who radiated a quiet happiness, seemingly in a daze. Several times she smiled her gratitude at her brother. It was all he could do to manage a slight smile in return.

Much later that night, he knocked softly on Marianne's door and was let in immediately.

'The man's a fool,' he said without preamble.

She had been crying and now made no attempt to hide her tears. 'I've been the fool and have no one to blame but myself. I was so sure of him, you see. In my conceit, I thought he was trying to tease me by paying attention to Emmaline. How could I have guessed that he actually preferred her simpering company to mine? What do you suppose ails him?'

'Moonstruck,' said Napier without hesitation. 'I hope you won't dwell on it. You have half a dozen other beaux, after all.'

'Yes, calflings. They're not Francis' equal laid end to end.'

'An intriguing thought, but I'm forced to agree. I'm very sorry, my dear. There's nothing more I can say.'

'Don't pity me, I beg of you. I don't care that my younger sister has found a husband before me. I've no intention of going into a decline. Do you think that's all there is to life?' she challenged him. 'Marriage?'

'Yes,' he said bluntly. 'If you love someone, that's all there is that matters.'

'Well, I'm not defeated. I'm twenty-one and my life is just beginning. I was completely mistaken in the man. Already I love him less. Any man who –' She couldn't continue. Napier came over, kissed her gently on the forehead and left her alone. It would be a long time before he forgave Francis for this.

11

Jefferson Smith wiped the grit from his eyes. It was eleven o'clock at night and he had been up since six. Fortunately, the weather had changed and this early May night was warm and clear as a bell. That, in itself, posed problems, because if he and constable Grizzard could see clearly for several hundred yards, then so could they be seen by others if they were not adequately hidden. They lay in the undergrowth, two hard men in full uniform, watching a farm gate and a short stretch of dusty road. Neither man spoke.

As the minutes passed, Jefferson felt his head nod several times, but jerked himself alert at once. His life had changed dramatically in the last few days, but so had his perspective on life. Before, he had been grateful for any sort of work, willing to do a good job, but relieved when the day was over.

Then, just last week, he had joined the new police, been handed a uniform worth nearly six pounds and, with it, a set of rules and regulations that fairly took his breath away. Being a constable in the Hertfordshire constabulary was to be his whole existence, not a job. For nineteen shillings a week, he had signed away his waking hours, his free will, his every independent thought. He would have just four non-working days a year; he was to work every day and every evening; he was to stay in his own home when not on duty; he was to wear uniform at all times; he was never to enter a public house except in the line of duty; he might take his midday sustenance at an inn, but he must eat it standing at the bar. Constables of the new police did not sit down.

Jefferson, who had never owned a pair of gloves, now had a pair in dazzling white which he must wear at all times. Jefferson, who had never visited a magistrate's court, must now give evidence before magistrates whenever called upon to do so. There was even a regulation about what he was to do with his gloves while giving evidence – tuck them into his belt, fingers on the inside facing downwards.

The old system of parish constables had sometimes worked

well enough, but it was a slack, occasionally corrupt arrangement. Colonel Robertson, taking his lead from the Metropolitan Police, ran his constabulary on military lines with an emphasis on honesty, hard work, and (quite revolutionary, this) crime *prevention*. It was not Jefferson's prime purpose in life to arrest as many people as possible. It was his duty to stop the crime from happening. How he was to do this when he had a large parish to patrol single-handedly, he didn't know. He knew he would try his best.

To his intense disappointment, he had been removed from the Hoddesdon-Hertford area to Bishop's Stortford. On Tuesday, Wednesday, Thursday and Friday he had patrolled night and day in that busy town. On Saturday, he had been removed to Sawbridgeworth, three or four miles away. Sunday morning had seen him touring the beer houses before attending church in Sawbridgeworth. Monday he had been all day in Sawbridgeworth and in the evening with Grizzard, patrolling Allens Green. It had been their good fortune to apprehend Maryann Speller while in the act of stealing a gold locket. The next day, of course, they had taken her to the jail in Bishop's Stortford. The following week they would have to give evidence against her in court.

Tonight, after a full day in Sawbridgeworth, he and Grizzard were waiting for the vandals who had been regularly unhitching Mr John Clark's farm gate and laying it in the middle of the road. Sheep had escaped; a horse and farm cart had suffered an accident by virtue of running over the gate in the dead of night. These desperate men, who caused mischief for no discernible reason, must be caught – that is, apprehended. Jefferson was learning a new vocabulary.

Barnaby Grizzard was only just tall enough to qualify for the new police. He had a slight build and was ten years older than Jefferson. Colonel Robertson had recruited him, as so many others, because he had served in the army for many years. He was used to discipline, long hours and the mind-numbing boredom that was an inescapable part of police work. It was Grizzard whose keen eyes and ears first detected some movement down the road. Jefferson, alerted, felt his back hairs prickle as he looked across to the gate. Four men had approached with muffled laughter and were drunkenly lifting the heavy wooden gate from its hinges.

In unison, the constables rose to their feet, truncheons in hand, and charged across the intervening space. The four men were momentarily startled; one decided to run, then changed his mind when he saw that his companions had chosen to make a fight of it.

Jefferson bided his time, not swinging wildly, not rushing things, just waiting until he got the chance to make a telling blow. His truncheon connected with a bare head and the man went down like a stone. Two others leapt on Grizzard, bearing him down with their combined weight. Jefferson concentrated on the fourth man. He took a few blows himself, one a direct hit on the nose. He remembered cursing the man for causing blood to flow on his precious uniform. Jefferson didn't know what the regulations said about blood on uniforms – or on gloves for that matter.

By the time he was able to turn his attention to his companion, Grizzard's tormentors were free to attack Jefferson. Poor Barnaby lay groaning, half conscious, in the road. It never occurred to Jefferson to run. He stood his ground, not even feeling the multitude of blows that rained down on him, any more than he had done in the old days in the prize ring.

He hadn't sufficient handcuffs, even with Grizzard's pair, to handcuff all four men, but he tied them all up with their own belts before his fellow constable had finished retching into the bushes.

'You stay with them, Barnaby,' he said, patting his friend roughly on the back. 'They can't do nothing now. I'll run back for our wagon.'

Jefferson set off down the road to run the mile and a half to the hidden wagon and its single horse. They hadn't been able to bring their transport closer to the scene of the expected crime for fear of frightening off the villains. He returned with the wagon as quickly as possible, and by that time, it was not only Grizzard who had recovered a bit of spirit.

The two constables struggled to get their charges, no more than boys as it turned out, into the wagon and then whipped up the horse to get them safely locked away as quickly as they could. It had been a good night's work. Jefferson's left peeper was closing fast, they had tapped his claret and no mistake, and there was a certain amount of pain round his ribs every time he breathed deeply. None of it mattered. The mill had set his blood coursing, bringing out the old fighting spirit that had won him much admiration, and no money at all, in the prize ring. His chest was bursting with pride. Surely Colonel Robertson would hear of this night's triumph.

Colonel Robertson, in Hertford, certainly did hear of it. And even though Sawbridgeworth was ten miles from Hoddesdon, everyone in Jefferson's home town knew of it by sundown the following evening. Cissy nearly wept for joy. The elder Potters felt some awe combined with uneasiness. Like many citizens, they disliked this new force of men, strangers who paraded around the parish in their top hats and blue frockcoats. Six shiny brass buttons down the front of their uniforms ending with showy belt buckles on wide belts made constables readily identifiable. No one had learned to trust them yet. They very quickly became the scourge of vagrants, beggars and gypsies, but they stepped deferentially into the gutter when the swells walked by. Boys followed them about shouting, 'Lobsters', 'Crushers' or 'Peel's Bloody Gang'.

Robertson found that his early problems echoed those of the Metropolitan Police which had been set up in 1829; a large proportion of the men got drunk on payday. They were dismissed immediately. That meant a rapid turnover of men in the force, and unlike crowded London, Hertfordshire had comparatively few suitable men from whom to draw recruits.

Therefore, a great deal was made of Jefferson's bravery and Grizzard's staunch support. Grizzard had suffered concussion as a result of the affray, so it was several days before a little ceremony could be held to compliment the two men on their performance, and inform them that in future they would receive twenty-one shillings a week instead of nineteen.

Robertson was no fool; he invited the new police committee to hear his brief but fulsome praise for two of his better men. That should go some way, he reckoned, to still the criticism that continued to come from the landed gentry, who reckoned they were being heavily taxed to pay for the townsmen's protection.

Napier was there, of course, saying little, but finding a way to have a quiet word with Jefferson. He was a friend of Mrs

173

Hobart's, he said. He would tell the lady about what he had heard the Colonel say; she would be extremely pleased to learn of Jefferson's excellent progress.

By the time the Drummonds, Francis, Sybilla and Florian Farley were due to set off for London and a night at the theatre, the air at Bailton Hall was so thick with hurt feelings, pregnant silences and secret conversations that separate carriages for opposing factions were an absolute necessity.

Napier and Mrs Drummond had discussed in the most wounding terms why one of them thought the coming marriage would be a disaster and the other felt sure the match had been made in heaven. Napier had been boorishly blunt and Mrs Drummond had publicly worn her lacerated feelings for days. After that, Emmaline cried frequently and dashed dramatically from any room Napier entered.

At the office the atmosphere was cool. It was inevitable that Francis, knowing Napier wanted him to marry Marianne, should feel extremely uncomfortable. The two men, who had once spent hours discussing every facet of their joint ventures and every other subject under the sun, now began to accumulate secrets from one another. Whenever possible, Francis called for Emmaline and took her for long rides in his new carriage.

Florian Farley was quite prepared to give Mrs Drummond every support, as he frequently told her, but he would not take sides. Both Emmaline and Marianne were charming girls; Emmaline had won the prize, which was surprising but rather reassuring, he thought. Dorothea might accuse him of cowardice if she chose; Florian was a careful man, as anyone continually in debt was forced to be. Stay friendly all round, that was his motto.

As for Marianne, she veered from relentless gaiety to what her mother termed 'making herself interesting' by keeping to her room and refusing to allow anyone but her maid to enter. No one saw very much of Marianne, and even Napier came to be grateful for her absence.

On the afternoon that the two carriages stopped in Hoddesdon to pick up the last member of the theatre party, Sybilla came to the door and invited everyone to come in for a refreshing glass of lemonade before they started a journey that would last almost two hours.

Mrs Drummond announced the betrothal of the happy couple as soon as they were all assembled in the drawing-room. Sybilla said all that was proper to Emmaline and Francis – said it with great sincerity, furthermore, so she was rather surprised at their muted response. She looked at once to Napier who was innocently studying a foil picture, just as if he had not helped her choose its new position only the day before yesterday. It was distinctly odd that he had not so much as mentioned that his sister was to be married in the autumn.

Marianne, bright-eyed and loud, said she thought it was all just wonderful, but hadn't they better be on their way? Sybilla agreed readily enough and was relieved to learn that she was to travel with Napier and Marianne. She assumed she would be told very quickly by the brother and sister what was wrong; and she was not mistaken.

'My brother believes that I have a *tendre* for Francis Babcock, Sybilla, and so imagines that I am distressed by Emmaline's betrothal. You know that I could not *possibly* be interested in any man so *insipid* as Francis, don't you?' said Marianne before they had travelled a hundred yards.

'But, of course I do,' said Sybilla quickly. Napier sat opposite her, slouched in his seat. She couldn't read his expression. 'You would not wish to be for ever tied to a man who is afraid of you.'

'*Afraid of me?*'

'Why yes. Afraid of your quick wit and active mind. Dear Emmaline will suit him very well, you know. He can protect her, guide her thoughts, help her to make decisions.'

'You needn't laugh, Napier,' said Marianne. 'It's true. I see it now. Francis *is* afraid of me. I wonder I didn't notice it before.'

'You are very wise, Mrs Hobart,' said Napier. 'Your advanced years and vast experience of the married state have given you great wisdom in these affairs of the heart.'

Since her first remarks were such a success, Sybilla expanded on her theme, and the three of them were soon laughing loudly as they invented wicked but ever more ludicrous circumstances in which Francis forcefully came to the aid of his beloved. Sybilla knew they were all being childish and rather ill-bred, but the engaged couple would never hear about their jokes, and Marianne seemed to find considerable solace in these scurrilous remarks.

'I believe, don't you, Sybilla, that marriage is not the only suitable life for females,' said Marianne, suddenly serious. 'The single state can be most rewarding for a strong-minded woman.'

'Especially for a woman of one and twenty years,' added Napier.

'No, I mean for ever. Don't you agree, Sybilla?'

'Being alone is preferable to being unhappily married, certainly.'

'Oh, Sybilla!' cried Marianne. 'Was it dreadful? I don't mean to pry into your personal affairs, really I don't, but was it dreadful? Did you hate Mr Hobart? I'm sure I would have.'

'Please, let us talk of something else,' said Sybilla.

The silence lengthened. Marianne was plainly embarrassed by her outburst of vulgar curiosity. Sybilla could almost sympathize, could certainly understand why the girl was finding it impossible to hit upon another less emotional topic. But what of Napier Drummond? Why didn't he say something? The exuberance and self-confidence that had struck her so forcibly the first time they met had been absent recently. He was subdued, polite but withdrawn when they met. She had been wondering if there was some personal tragedy in his life. Now she was forced to conclude that he was extremely upset because Marianne, the sister he loved most, had been passed over in favour of Emmaline. There was no other explanation for such a change in his personality.

'Have you had any new orders since I saw you last?' he said.

'Yes, one. We now have seven gigs in various stages of building. I have had to take on an extra man, but I'm very pleased with our progress. And we've eliminated two coats of paint in the finishing as you suggested. It certainly saves on time and paint, but I wonder if it is quite fair.'

'Perfectly fair. You are quoting a competitive price, giving the customer an inexpensive gig, not one of the best quality. You are not cheating anyone.'

'I think I would like to have my own business, Napier,' said Marianne. 'I can't think what sort of business, but it must be challenging and fulfilling and must make me very rich.'

'You can have no idea what you are saying, my idle sister. Mrs Hobart has worked very hard learning many things in order to achieve her present financially sound position. For instance, in order to show off her gig, she has learned to drive to an inch. I know, because I've ridden with her. While you, lazy puss, refused to allow me to spend even one hour in improving your driving. I worry every time you take out the gig.'

'Well, I don't take it out very often, because it is so much more pleasant to be driven by the coachman. Anyway, I don't see what that has to do with anything. Just because I want to do one thing doesn't mean I have to learn to do another. That sounds rather muddled, but I know what I mean, even if you don't.'

'I know exactly what you mean,' said Napier. 'You are a hopeless dreamer of dreams.'

'I may surprise you one day,' she said archly, and Napier, pleased to see his sister's spirits revived, refrained from further teasing.

Sybilla said that obstacles were constantly put in the way of women who wished to do anything at all. Marianne supported her contention, and Napier allowed himself to be the object of a spirited feminine attack. It seemed there was no wickedness that he, as representative of the male sex, had not perpetrated.

It was not until the coach approached Marylebone that the conversation changed to the sights around them. Napier pointed out the landmarks, although there was not a great deal to see that was of any interest so far from fashionable London.

In the leading coach, Mrs Drummond and Florian entertained the young couple with tales of weddings they had attended, and the small but amusing little things that had gone wrong on these supposedly happy occasions. When that topic had been done to death, Emmaline and her mother began a spirited discussion about the trousseau and how many dozens of handkerchiefs, shifts, nightgowns, tablecloths and napkins

177

would have to be embroidered before the wedding at the beginning of September.

Florian endured this chatter for as long as he could bear, but at last turned to Francis. 'I believe you have introduced your bride-to-be to your family, old chap.'

'Yes, and they adored Emmaline as I knew they would.'

'Oh, Francis,' said Emmaline. 'You are embarrassing me.'

'But they did, my love. My mother wrote to me the next day. She said that you were all she could have wished for in a daughter-in-law.'

This was perfectly true. The Babcocks had assembled in strength at Hebdens to meet the youngest son's bride-to-be. There were twenty-three of them representing four generations. Grandfather Slocumb had persisted in calling her Emily, but had declared loudly to anyone who would listen that she was a pretty behaved young miss. Tarquin, the five-year-old son of Francis' eldest brother, had also liked Emmaline, but that was because she didn't subject him to the usual catechism: can you read, have you a tutor, what are you studying, how do you like your new baby sister?

Emmaline, who had studied the mannerisms as well as the manners of the landed gentry for years, gave a superb performance, neither awestruck by her great good fortune in marrying into such an exalted old family, nor putting on a show of aggressive wealth. She listened attentively to everyone who spoke and agreed with everything that was said; or when opinions differed, invariably and unhesitatingly took the view expressed by her future mother-in-law. She was appropriately but not extravagantly dressed. The Babcocks were able to welcome her into the family as a pretty, well-bred young woman without once referring to the money she would bring with her.

Earlier Mr Babcock had met Napier briefly to discuss the financial arrangements. He had reported to his wife that Drummond had been damned generous – and there was really no need ever to entertain dear Emmaline's brother at Hebdens.

So now, as Francis recounted his dear one's social triumph, Emmaline could demur, safe in the knowledge that if her own family failed to appreciate her finer qualities, the same could not be said of the Babcocks.

'Emmaline – you must allow me to praise the woman I love, ma'am – Emmaline knows just what is right to say or do. She never oversteps the line,' said Francis.

'Well, I should hope not,' said Mrs Drummond.

'But, ma'am, you must admit that the same cannot be said for every young woman. Forgive me, I cannot wish for Emmaline to spend too much time in the company of Mrs Hobart, the widow's company causes Emmaline acute distress.'

'Oh, Francis.'

'But why, dear boy?' said Farley in some surprise.

'She is too bold. Surely no woman of sensitivity would care to ride about the town in a gig *touting* for business. She passed me in Fore Street the other day as I was talking to Sir Rafe Bilkeston and she *waved* at me. I was very embarrassed, I can tell you.'

'Yes,' murmured Mrs Drummond. She was prepared to love her future son-in-law, but just occasionally she did find him a trifle stuffy. 'But she is a woman alone and must be anxious to keep her business going.'

'Indeed she is! Why, she went to Sam Adams's bank the other day to ask for a loan and had the effrontery to give Napier's name as a reference!'

'Good Lord!' said Mrs Drummond, and Emmaline said 'Oh, Francis!' yet again.

'I beg your pardon. I've been terribly indiscreet. I should never have spoken. Only, Napier received a rude letter about it from Sam Adams within the hour. He went to Hoddesdon immediately to tell the lady just what he thought of her brazen behaviour. I'm very much afraid, however, that he may have stayed to lend her the two hundred pounds. I say, Mrs Drummond, are you ill?'

'The swaying of the coach,' she said, swallowing loudly. 'I shall be all right in a moment.'

'Here is the Marylebone theatre, Dorothea,' said Farley. 'Put all unpleasant thoughts from your mind and enjoy the evening. Come now, Emmaline, no need to blush. Let us not show by our manner that we have been talking about poor Mrs Hobart. There they are, getting out of their carriage. Come, come, ladies. Let's see your smiles.'

It was obvious at once that some dramatic change had

179

taken place in Napier's and Marianne's moods since leaving Hoddesdon. Napier rested a friendly hand on Francis' shoulder when he asked if the journey to London had been a pleasant one.

'Yes, quite pleasant,' said Francis distantly. He was disinclined to forget weeks of sulking bad temper, orders barked at him through the door, confidences withheld. But Napier's forceful personality and his assumption that when he wished to be friendly his overtures would meet with success, won Francis over. The younger man smiled, passed a friendly remark, and heaved an inner sigh of relief. He so hated to be surrounded by *atmosphere*.

Mrs Drummond and Emmaline were both pale and subdued; Francis felt his heart constrict whenever he looked in their direction. He had offended against his own code of behaviour and distressed his dear bride and her mother. He wished he could discuss his indiscretion with Emmaline and ask her forgiveness, but he didn't know her well enough. He knew her well enough to marry her, to take her into his bed, but not well enough to discuss his social gaffe. He probably never would. His parents had always maintained a certain reserve, a shrinking from emotional intimacy, and Francis expected his own marriage to follow the same lines. He knew perfectly well that Emmaline refused to confront unpleasantness. She ran away from all emotional displays and quite frankly, this was a great relief to him.

He made mechanical replies to remarks by Napier and Sybilla Hobart, but he watched morosely as Florian was engaged in a whispered conversation with Emmaline and her mother. All three exhibited signs of deepest agitation.

'The poor woman is obviously in serious difficulties,' said Mrs Drummond. 'We must do something, Florian.'

'If you ask Francis for the loan of two hundred pounds, Mama, I shall never forgive you. And I can see it in your eyes. That's what you want to do.'

'Well, but he is soon to be a member of the family, my dear.'

'Hush, both of you,' said Florian as they walked up the carpeted stairs to their box. 'Think a moment, Dorothea. Francis despises Mrs Hobart. How can you tell him that we

180

had the effrontery to borrow money from her? What would he think of us?'

'Oh, I suppose you're right,' said Mrs Drummond wearily.

'Besides, Francis would probably tell Napier straight away,' said Emmaline, then gasped. 'What if *she* has told him? Perhaps that's why he is so cross these days?'

'Rest easy, my dear,' said Florian. 'We would have heard from him in no uncertain terms if Napier knew of the loan. Leave things as they are. I've not seen your brother so cheerful for weeks.'

The fine appointments of the theatre impressed Sybilla. She had nothing to compare them with, of course, since she had never entered a theatre in her life. Napier had told her that Mr Watts had lavished money on his theatre, and she could well believe it.

The box was comfortable, set to the left side of the stage and giving a perfect view of the crowded pit below, the gallery and the boxes on the opposite side of the theatre. She had been told that the Marylebone theatre was never filled to capacity, but tonight seemed to be an exception. It was Saturday night, and if there were few diamond tiaras among the theatregoers, there was, nevertheless, enough wealth being paraded to keep Sybilla entertained the entire evening.

When the curtain rose at last, she gasped with delight. The scene was a drawing-room in the home of Sir John Vesey. It was beautifully appointed with folding doors at the centre opening on to another drawing-room. To the right was a table containing newspapers and books, to the left a sofa writing table. It might have been the private drawing-room of any well-to-do London home, and Sybilla felt herself to be actually on the stage with the actors.

It very soon transpired that the hero, Alfred Evelyn, was acting as secretary to Sir John, and living upon that gentleman's charity. He loved Miss Clara Douglas, who was also poor, a companion to the wealthy Lady Franklin. The play was called *Money* by Edward Bulwer-Lytton.

Sybilla did not want the curtain to close on the first act, didn't want to hear Florian Farley and Marianne discussing the performances of Mr Macready and Mrs Mowatt. To her it had been real, a window on experiences greater than her own.

The theatre held a kind of magic for her and she didn't want the secret feeling destroyed by chattering voices.

Mr Watts joined them in their box, a dandified young man prone to extravagant gestures and colourful speech. She thought he had been drinking, but didn't notice the particular attention he paid to her, the eyes he made, the drolleries he uttered expressly for her amusement. She just wanted the curtain to rise on the second act.

As was to be expected, Alfred Evelyn, the hero of the play, gained money and power before the final curtain. The incredibly sweet and self-sacrificing Clara received her due reward: Clara and Evelyn would be married. The curtain closed to loud applause, and opened almost immediately so that the actors could take their bows. Sybilla wanted to stay, to applaud until the curtain no longer parted. But Marianne was quickly on her feet.

'Come on, everyone. Let's go to Mrs Mowatt's dressing-room. I must tell her what a wonderful performance she gave. She is such a splendid actress, don't you think, Sybilla? Did you enjoy it? Well, come on then. Hurry!'

Mrs Mowatt's dressing-room was crowded with well-wishers, bubbling with the exhilaration of another performance completed. The actors teased one another, jokes that only they understood. The illusion was totally destroyed. Here, Sybilla could see the paint on Mrs Mowatt's face, could tell that the actress was a good deal older than the character of Clara was supposed to have been.

Mr Watts managed to manoeuvre her into a corner. 'Do you like my theatre, Mrs Hobart? I fancy I have done the thing proud. A little gem, isn't it? Not that I'm appreciated here. Too far from the West End, they say. The *ton* won't travel this far out. Never mind, I love it. Of course, I have another theatre which I fancy you will appreciate. Please be my guest one evening.'

Sybilla said that would be very pleasant. If it were possible she would visit the theatre every evening, but she didn't say so to Mr Watts. She could smell the whisky on his breath. His smooth cheeks were babyish, but his eyes were those of a man who had looked into hell. She didn't like him.

Napier squeezed up beside Mrs Mowatt. 'It's time we were

going, ma'am. I have a room reserved for supper and we are all very hungry. We enjoyed your performance very much and hope to see you again soon.'

'Oh, don't take Marianne away, Mr Drummond,' said Mrs Mowatt, whose natural speaking voice was undramatic but very musical. 'Let her stay with me. I promise you I will feed her well and return her to your hotel personally. Trust her to me for just a few hours. She loves the theatre, you know.'

'There's no harm in her staying with you for a while,' he agreed. 'She's had the mopes lately. Your company will revive her.'

Supper in a private dining-room was another new experience for Sybilla. The evening had been a glorious one, making her wish for more. She did not fool herself, however. Such evenings were vastly expensive. No matter how long Mr Puddifoot worked, nor how many gigs they produced, she could not imagine herself ever being able to afford such entertainments.

'You're looking tired, Emmaline,' said Napier.

'Yes, I am. I must go up to my room presently. It's very late. I hope Marianne won't disturb me when she comes in.'

'But you're not tired, are you, Mrs Hobart?'

'Not particularly, I –'

'Splendid, because I have arranged for you to have a little ride round London. It is very beautiful on a fine warm night like this. London is a city of lights and they are not yet out.' Napier rose and held out his hand to Sybilla, bade farewell to the others who were too surprised to say much at all, and left with the widow on his arm.

'Most peculiar,' said Mrs Drummond. 'I had been afraid he would be unpleasant all evening, but he's been charming.'

Mrs Drummond and Emmaline went upstairs to their rooms. Francis detained Florian for a moment. 'When I said . . . what I did about Mrs Hobart borrowing money, I didn't mean that I think a small loan between friends is at all exceptional, you know.'

'Of course, dear fellow,' said Florian heartily, unconsciously patting the pocket that held the last of Francis' twenty pounds. 'And I hope *you* know that I will pay you back come quarter day.'

183

'Did you enjoy the play?' asked Napier as soon as the coach was on the move.

Sybilla turned from the window. 'Oh, so much, so very much. I'm fortunate to have seen such a good play this first time. It was a good play, wasn't it? Mr Farley said so.'

'It is quite well thought of by the critics, I believe. The theme was an interesting one, I thought. A perfectly decent young man is despised by everyone – by almost everyone – until he comes into money. Which he hasn't earned, incidentally. Then he is quite the gentleman. But that's not the way it is in real life.'

'Oh, please don't be cynical. This was my very first experience of the theatre. Don't spoil it for me. It seemed so real, so true.'

'Why, Sybilla, I wouldn't destroy your pleasure for the world. It's just that the play gave me unpalatable food for thought.'

The silence was charged with emotion; she felt his bitterness fill the space between them. 'What *did* happen to you when you ran away to London?'

'You know about that?'

'Yes, Marianne told me some time ago. She didn't know what you had done all those years in London, and neither of your sisters was the least bit curious. But I am.'

'They don't want to know for fear the truth will distress them, and nor does my mother. But I'll tell you, since you ask. I lived and slept in the streets. I met a street pedlar named Barge who sold cloth, and travelled the countryside with him. When he died, I carried on alone until I had enough money to open a shop selling cloth to other pedlars. Eventually, I had many shops. When I received word that my father had died, I sold all of them and opened a very fine drapery shop in Bury St Edmunds, though I never served behind the counter, of course.'

'So that is how you knew so much about the material in this gown! I did wonder. You have been very clever.'

'Do you think so? To be in trade –'

'As I am.'

184

'As you are, is not so fine an occupation for a man if his sister intends to marry a Babcock of Hertfordshire. What do you suppose Francis would say if he knew the whole of it?'

'Well, first of all, he would be very angry with you for presenting him with such a dilemma. He would much rather not know, I'm sure. Then he would be in a pelter lest his family found out. But I shouldn't say these things. I hardly know the man.'

'I think you know him very well,' laughed Napier. 'But aren't you shocked by my disgraceful past?'

'No, of course not. When I was young and my father died, we were very poor –'

'*Poor?* You don't know the meaning of the word. I have rubbed shoulders with the raff and scaff, Sybilla. And not just occasionally, they were my friends and companions for years. Are you not ashamed to associate with me?'

'Don't be absurd.'

'I'm an industrialist now. A wealthy man. As Alfred Evelyn said in the play, to make us tolerably happy, we should not be without plenty of money. However, it would take more money than I will ever possess to make my past acceptable to the Babcocks.'

'Then you had better get Emmaline married as quickly as possible, before they have a chance to find out.'

'Is that your solution?'

'It makes sense, surely.'

'Yes,' said Napier. 'Your common-sense is a delight to me. You are not just in the common mould, you know. Most people wouldn't react as you have done.'

'And your mother has never asked how you managed?'

'Never a word.'

'Well,' said Sybilla. 'You can laugh at them all now, because you are amazingly successful and very clever. You do have plenty of money and I expect you are tolerably happy.'

'Not really. I've reached my limit, you see. I don't know why I'm telling you this – that was Oxford Street by the way. Pity you missed it. I'll show it to you another time. You know the malthouse I was so determined to have on French Horn Lane?'

'I could hardly forget it.'

'Well, I was going to make malt there in a revolutionary

way. I won't bore you with the details, but it was very sensible and clever. I had the patent for the method, so I intended to convert other owners' malthouses for them at a price, as well as make my own malt the new way. But my manager was horrified. He said the enterprise would be bound to fail because brewers wouldn't buy malt made in a new way. I had to abandon my scheme. He was right, I fear, and I would have lost money on it.'

'Well, I never thought I would hear you say such a cowardly thing! If you believe in the new method, why not try it? Can't you afford to lose a little money? Must everything be done for gain? Good heavens, when I met you, you were full of your secret schemes, enjoying yourself. I wondered what happened to destroy your – I don't know – your *energy*. If you believe in it, do it!'

'Sybilla! Perhaps . . . But no, everyone would call me a fool.'

'They call you "Mad Drummond", I'm told. Would it be so much worse to be called a fool? I'm surprised and disappointed in you. I may not be able to afford to take chances, but you certainly can.'

He sat up and pounded a fist into the palm of his other hand. 'Madam, I think you have just changed the direction of my life. Of course, I should have pressed ahead! It doesn't matter if I fail! Let them laugh. I'll do it! Driver, turn round! Back to the hotel!'

Sybilla sat back in the carriage and ruefully smiled to herself. She had given this man new heart. Now he had forgotten her in thinking of his schemes. She had seen nothing of London and might never get the chance. All the way back to the hotel, she listened to his plans, his hopes and fears. She added a word now and then, but doubted if he heard her. He was lost in thought and scarcely remembered to help her from the carriage when they reached the hotel. It was no more than fair, she reckoned. He had saved her business; she had restored his confidence. A fair exchange and no robbery.

12

The return journey to Hoddesdon had been very pleasant. Napier had set aside his own preoccupations to keep his promise to Sybilla of showing her round London. There really was so much more to see during daylight hours that Sybilla was permanently stretched forward to peer out of the window. Marianne, who wanted to get home as quickly as possible, threw herself into a theatrical sulk, but her companions took no notice of her.

It was early afternoon before the carriage drew up at Hornbeam House. Napier leapt out to hand Sybilla from the carriage and waited with her until Saul opened the door and took delivery of her small grip. She thanked him sincerely and asked him if he had changed his mind, yet again, about the malthouse.

'No, Sybilla, I have not,' he said in a low voice. He never called her by her Christian name in front of others. 'I shall never lose faith in my vision again. Please don't tell anyone about my plans, will you? The element of surprise will be very valuable. Besides, I want the pleasure of confounding my fellow maltsters with a dramatic announcement at the right time.'

'I won't tell anyone, I promise you. But I'll wager someone tells *me* about it within the week.'

'A wager? Done! Shall we say half a crown?'

'Why, certainly, sir. But you must know that everything you do is of intense interest to the whole of East Hertfordshire.'

'I wonder why. Never mind, I shall win that wager. When I choose to keep a secret it remains a secret.'

The secret certainly took Francis by surprise on Monday morning. '*Changed your mind*? But you can't do that. The floors are almost completed. They would have to be torn down again. What about the equipment for cleaning the grain before steeping, the kiln floor? Napier, you're mad.'

'You told me yourself that I had given too much weight to Scrope's opinion, that I had changed my mind too quickly. You urged me to sleep on it. Well, now I agree with you. You were right after all.'

It was Francis who paced the floor on this occasion while Napier sat behind his desk. Napier Drummond had a way of walking right over a man's logical objections, of trampling on the feelings of others and dashing their hopes. Francis had just got over the disappointment of seeing the project cancelled. Now what could he say? He knew he was a poor debater. How then could he express himself? He wasn't sure which of his bitter thoughts he wanted to put into words.

'You are making a fool of me,' he said petulantly and knew at once that he had said the wrong thing.

'You don't enter into it. I haven't considered your feelings one way or the other. I have considered what we might do if we dared. Come, old chap, the venture is on again. We'll show the world. And if not, we'll fail gloriously.'

'You're mad, I swear it,' said Francis, He had flopped into a chair on the far side of Napier's desk. The two men stared at each other and, of course, it was Francis who dropped his eyes first. He addressed his further objections to the floor.

'There was a chance before, but the cost of tearing up what we have just done virtually ensures that there can be no profits in the next twelve months.'

'I don't care about that. This is sport not business.'

'Well, I care! I haven't your cavalier attitude towards money. I'm soon to be married and must think responsibly. Besides, I shall look like an idiot if I tell the labourers that all their work is to be torn up.'

'So now, at last, we have cleared the air,' said Napier stiffly. 'You have a responsible attitude towards money and I have not. Well, I shall fund this project from my own money. I'll buy out your interest in the French Horn Lane malthouse. You think me volatile, Francis, but that is because you haven't taken the trouble to know me at all. I lost my way temporarily, I admit. But no more. In future, I'll follow my own star, no matter where it leads me. I'll march to the drumbeat in my own head, no other. As for making a fool of you, that no longer applies, since I shall go myself to give orders to the men. Good day to you.'

Napier left Francis staring at the office carpet, skidded on the polished floor and slammed the door as he left.

Francis sat on, wondering what to do next. Two men could not continue in business together if they disagreed about everything. There had been a happy time when he and Napier saw eye to eye on all points. Then he had fallen in love with Emmaline and, naturally, some of his loyalty now belonged to her. And most of his confidences; Napier, unlike Emmaline, was not a good listener.

As for Napier, he had not been the same since meeting Mrs Hobart. Francis looked up suddenly. Could she have . . . No, he assured himself. What possible influence could the widow have in the matter of malting barley?

It had been a long, unseasonably hot and frustrating day. Napier was accustomed to leaving all details in the capable hands of Francis. He was not the best man to explain his ideas to labourers, to coax from them the work he wanted done. Or to supervise it. He couldn't understand why they needed to be told anything twice, much less five times.

He arrived at his own front door that evening with nothing more than pleasant thoughts of a large brandy on his mind. He was greeted by his womenfolk. They charged at him in the hallway as he was handing his hat to Scrimshaw, all talking at once – screaming really – and all three of them crying. He was tempted to bolt.

'For God's sake, let us go into the drawing-room and discuss whatever it is quietly and in private. Mama, please don't distress yourself if these girls have been tormenting you, I'll soon sort it out. You know what they're like.'

'It is something far worse than you could ever have imagined. I trust you will be able to talk some sense into your wicked sister, Napier. I wash my hands of her,' said Mrs Drummond, and Napier knew at once that it was Marianne who had transgressed.

'Well,' he said, turning to her. 'What have you done?'

'Mrs Mowatt has invited me to join the troupe. They are going to travel round the country for several months in the autumn.'

'Forget it,' he said brutally. 'You are not going anywhere with a troupe of actors.'

'I am to be an actress. I am to have a small part in the last play to be performed at the Marylebone before the season ends. I mean to do it, Napier. I shall run away if necessary.'

'She hasn't a thought for anyone but herself,' said Emmaline. 'I would die of shame if my sister went on the stage. What would the Babcocks say?'

'Damn the Babcocks,' said Napier. 'This family does not organize itself for the benefit of the Babcocks.'

'Francis will be furious.'

'And damn Francis.'

'I knew it!' cried Mrs Drummond. 'You intend to take the girl's part. Nothing is beneath you. Nothing too disgusting. I've lost control of my own little girl.'

Like a baited bull, Napier rounded on his mother. 'Yes, I'm quite beneath your touch, am I not? Pity you've had to enjoy the fruits of my labours for so long when you would have preferred poverty.' Mrs Drummond clutched her breast and practically fainted on to the settee.

'Does that mean you'll let me go?' asked Marianne.

'She's running away because I'm to marry Francis,' said Emmaline, and in saying what she had been thinking for so long, ensured her sister's freedom.

'I will speak to you in private, Marianne. As for you, Emmaline, you are beneath contempt.'

Marianne led the way into the library where she felt no need to adopt dramatic words and gestures.

'It isn't because of Francis, Napier, I promise you it isn't. You know I've always wanted to be an actress. Emmaline needn't tell anyone if she is ashamed of me. Anyway, the Babcocks are never likely to attend the Marylebone, are they?'

'Do you want to be an actress enough to break your mother's heart?'

Marianne hesitated, then lifted her chin. 'Yes, I do. I'm sorry but it's true. I want to be an actress more than – more than breathing. Mrs Mowatt is respectable, you've said so yourself.'

'Two things only,' he said after a moment. 'You will take a reliable maid with you and you will not leave this country. Mrs Mowatt is an American. I'll not have you taking off to that

God-forsaken place. Do you understand?'

'Oh Napier, bless you!' She threw her arms around his neck and kissed him on the cheek. 'And you do know that I'm not running away.'

'I ran away years ago and never regretted it. You will be meeting all sorts of people. Some of them will tell you what a splendid person you are, and they will say these things for their own purposes. Don't listen, Marianne. Be wary. Turn to Mrs Mowatt for advice.' He ran a hand through his hair. 'God help us all. I hope I'm doing the right thing.'

'Well?' said Mrs Drummond when Marianne and Napier returned to the drawing-room.

'She is to travel with Mrs Mowatt for a few months.'

'Oh, no!' Emmaline ran from the room; her door slammed a minute or two later, but by that time Mrs Drummond had made a tearful exit from the room. Marianne and Napier heard her door slam a few seconds after Emmaline's.

Napier put a hand on her shoulder. 'Take my advice and have your dinner served to you in your room. When are you planning to leave?'

'I'm going to Mrs Mowatt's home on Saturday.'

'Make yourself invisible until then. I shall arrange for you to draw money on my bank as you need it. This is your opportunity to show me that you can handle your own affairs. Don't disappoint me, please. I'm not the most popular person in this household at the moment.'

'I know,' said Marianne sadly. 'I have dragged you into my quarrel and I'm very sorry. But, oh so grateful to you. At least I feel there is some purpose to my life. Does that seem silly?'

'No, not at all. But you must remember the sacrifices others are making for you. Never mind Emmaline. I'm referring to Mama. She will not know a minute's peace while you are away. Many would say that you are being selfish to make her suffer, that your duty lies here. I have set aside her authority, because I believe that you should have a chance to put your dreams to the test. Now, excuse me. I'll go upstairs and see if I can make my peace with my mother.'

'Come in,' said Mrs Drummond in a weak voice in answer to Napier's knock.

He found her seated in a chair in her sitting-room. She

looked old and a trifle faded; he felt an unexpected surge of pity and approached to kiss her swiftly on the cheek.

She shrank from his touch. 'You needn't think to come in here and talk me into accepting Marianne's behaviour, for it won't work. I cannot forgive you, Napier.'

'Well, I suppose that is plain enough. I had thought to explain why I've let her go, but I see it's useless.'

'There is *no* explanation, except that you know I don't want her to go, and you are determined to do whatever I will dislike.'

'Do you really hate me so much?'

She looked at him in surprise. 'I don't hate you at all. You are my only son. *You* hate *me*.'

'If you say so, Mama. Perhaps we are not as close as some mothers and sons, but whose fault is that? Certainly not mine. I hardly know you.'

'Oh, you wicked boy! Do you really think that I wanted you to stay away so long? Your father would not go to London to fetch you. What could I do?'

'Come yourself?' he asked quietly.

'When will you understand? I did not defy my own father; I didn't defy yours and I can't defy my own son, even when he sets out to ruin his sister.'

'I see.' He was standing awkwardly in the middle of the room and now looked round for somewhere to sit, uncertain whether he wanted to leave or stay. However, he had never run away from a quarrel in his life. And, there were a few things he wanted to get off his chest.

'And was it my father's idea that I should be given the ridiculous name of Napier, pretending kinship with a famous man?'

'Oh!' She sucked in her breath and put a hand to her heart. 'So you blame me even for your name! Can I do nothing right? I named you for General Napier in a superstitious fit. I wanted you to be as brave and clever as he was. By giving you his name, I hoped to endow you with his qualities. Stupid of me, I admit, but not pretentious.'

Napier bit his lower lip in surprise. His next words were spoken in a much quieter voice. 'Life was hell at Mickle-thwaite's, Mama. I hated it. But since you and Father never

192

came to visit me nor appeared to want me to come home to visit you, I had no one to turn to, so I ran away. It was pointless to come home, or so I thought. That's why I went to London. I missed you, but being a proud young boy, I couldn't bring myself to say so.'

'Oh, Napier, I loved you and missed you so much. I begged your father, but –'

'Then can you really say, as I've always been led to believe, that Father was a fine and decent man? Can you?'

'I can't tell you whether he was good or evil. He was just my husband and the father of my children. I know he was wrong about you, which is a different thing. Can't we – can't we try at this late time in our lives to understand one another better?'

He smiled ruefully. 'I had hoped so, but what can I say to you? I'm determined that Marianne shall have this little adventure. You are determined that she shall not.'

Mrs Drummond was always willing to give way in the face of masculine determination. She dabbed her eyes and looked at him pleadingly. Pleading silently for him to make Marianne's adventure acceptable to her.

He saw his advantage and took it. 'Mama, I intend that she will take Mrs Scrimshaw with her as her maid. You must admit that the old dear is quite a tartar and won't let Marianne get into trouble. Old Scrimshaw will be delighted to have his wife's eagle eye trained elsewhere for a few months, and you can do without a housekeeper for a while. I'll make sure Marianne is adequately funded. I will find out every town they plan to visit and see to it that some man of my acquaintance visits her there to make sure that all is well. I'm not so foolish as to think that a pretty twenty-one-year-old girl should be set entirely free, as I was at sixteen. It won't do. But Marianne will never realize that she is so protected. This adventure will help her to mature.'

'But she might develop a taste for the theatre! She has considerable talent, you know.'

'Then we must let her make her way in the world as she chooses. She's entitled to that.'

'Are you sorry that you ran away to London and lived there all those years?'

'No,' he said after a moment's reflection. 'Not if I can

genuinely feel that I have my mother's love now.'

'Oh, Napier, I'm going to cry again.'

Impulsively, he came over to kneel on one knee, to kiss her hand and receive a kiss in return on his cheek. Now was the time for Mrs Drummond to tell her son about the loan from Sybilla. The sum was almost trifling to him; he could put everything right in minutes. And eventually, she knew, he would forgive her foolishness. Before that, however, she feared he would be angry, that this wonderful new bond between them would be endangered. She stayed silent; the moment passed and the debt remained.

Napier coaxed her downstairs for dinner. He *summoned* Emmaline. However, at the table he put himself out to explain Marianne's plans to the girl, to try to make the scheme acceptable. Emmaline, showing greater forcefulness than he had ever known, laid down her conditions. She wouldn't say another word on the subject, provided the Babcocks did not discover the horrible secret. Francis must be told, of course, but Napier must tell him, for she had no intention of being the bringer of such bad news. But the Babcocks –

Yes, said Napier, he did understand. He would tell Francis. All would be well. He was even pleasant to Florian Farley who arrived in time for tea. But in this matter he showed his shrewdness, because Florian was all in favour of Marianne's treading the boards.

By the end of the evening, Napier felt quite limp with spent emotion. Florian dragged him from his reverie by making some bantering remark to him; Napier replied in kind; everybody laughed. The door opened and Marianne stood on the threshold. She looked quite beautiful for once, hesitant and considerably less aggressive than in the past.

'I heard voices . . . laughter. May I come in?'

'But, my dear, of course!' Mrs Drummond rose to her feet and led her daughter into the room. Warily, conscious of being watched, the sisters touched cheeks. Then, giggling, they embraced, vowing eternal devotion as they used to do after a quarrel when they were children. They were sweet girls, thought Napier. No harm in them at all. Emmaline was becoming more positive, Marianne less bombastic.

Three days later Marianne paid a call on Sybilla and was

194

disappointed to find the drawing-room crowded with other visitors. Before long, however, they took their leave and the two young women were left alone.

'First of all,' said Marianne, 'I am to give you this half-crown. I gather you had a wager that Napier could not keep his plans secret. He lost, of course. Even I know what he is up to. I have long since become accustomed to the fact that my friends' servants speak knowledgeably of his affairs. Why is everyone so interested in him, I wonder?' Sybilla laughed, shaking her head as she accepted the coin. 'And then I have come to tell you my good news. I am to stay with Mrs Mowatt, I'm going to her home on Saturday and I will be acting on the stage!'

Sybilla was so stunned that she was hard put to say anything at all. 'Why, that's ... marvellous! And what does your mother say?'

'Oh,' said Marianne, pulling off her half-mittens, 'she was very unhappy about it at first, but Napier cleverly made her see that it was just the thing. There are conditions to my going. I must take our housekeeper, Mrs Scrimshaw, as my maid. She's delighted, I can tell you, and so is her husband. And, can you believe it, I must write to Mama every day! So Mama is content now. Emmaline is afraid of what the Babcocks would say if they knew and Francis has been very poker-faced about the whole thing, but I don't care for that.'

'So your mother is to lose both her daughters! She must be very distressed. How could she not be? But surely you will come home for your sister's wedding in September.'

'Yes, of course. Oh, Sybilla! I had thought you would understand. You of all people. But I can see it in your face: you disapprove. You are making your own way in the world. Why shouldn't I?'

'That's quite another matter. I have no choice. But you –'

Marianne stood up to leave, feeling very sorry to have come. 'I see. You think Napier should marry me off to some wealthy suitor.'

'Certainly not. Marianne, don't leave. Sit down and tell me all about it. I'll ring for some more tea.'

Reluctantly, Marianne took her seat. She was feeling quite out of charity with Sybilla. She had misjudged her. 'You did tell me that your mother is still alive, didn't you?'

'Yes, I did.'

'Well then, why do you not have her come here to live with you?'

Marianne was hoping to put her friend out of countenance, and succeeded magnificently. Sybilla clasped her hands in her lap. 'I should do so, I know I should. I am a wicked daughter. But, oh you don't know what she is like, so critical of everything I do. *Your* mother is delicious, and she loves you very much. The situations are different.'

'No, Sybilla,' said Marianne triumphantly. 'The situations are not different. No matter what our mothers are like, there comes a time when we no longer wish to share a home with them. Most young women are not so selfish as I am, or else they don't know what they wish to do with their lives, so they stay at home. But I'm sure they feel just the same as I do. Just the same as you do. You want your home to yourself. Don't look so miserable, dear, I understand perfectly. Now, let us not quarrel. Promise me you will be my brother's guest in two weeks' time to see the last play of the season. I am to play a small part and may even speak a line or two.'

After Marianne had gone home, Sybilla took up her embroidery and sat by the open window to catch the afternoon sun. Pink cabbage roses, coaxed into unfurling their petals after weeks of scorching sun, bloomed lushly as they trailed over an old trellis. She could catch their heavy scent every time the wind blew. She *was* a wicked daughter. Her mother's plight was weighing heavily on her conscience. Fortunately, Hobart's was making a respectable profit these days, which enabled her to send a little money now and again to Portsmouth. But as her horizons expanded, with new friends and greater satisfaction with her work for the business, so the thought of once again being under her mother's censorious eye seemed unbearable. She couldn't invite her mother to Hoddesdon. They would be pulling caps within a week. What would her mother say, for instance, if Sybilla were to announce that she intended to visit the theatre and stay overnight in London as the guest of an unmarried man?

She laughed aloud. In fact, she had no idea what her mother might say to such a scheme. Expensive evenings in London were totally beyond Mrs Sutherland's experience. Sybilla

196

wondered if Robert ever went to the theatre. Did he spend his small income on such frivolity? If he did, then Mrs Sutherland would approve of play-acting. Robert's behaviour was her yardstick.

Sybilla laid down her embroidery, unable to set another stitch. She would fetch her writing materials and write a long affectionate letter to Portsmouth. And she would send her mother a small present, some gloves, perhaps. Why hadn't she thought of it before? And answered: because she had not been made to feel quite so guilty before today.

Jack Dark and his wife, Betty, stood in a corner of the Crown down Dunnings Alley and drank their porter in silence.

Betty was looking better these days than she had in months, which was odd because they hadn't found Cissy, though they had been looking everywhere. He had forced Betty to travel with him, instead of moping in their room as she had become used to doing. They had taken the train from Shoreditch and got off the first time it stopped. For several days they had worked the neighbourhood, asking questions wherever they went. At night they slept rough and, when they were sure they had covered the area thoroughly, moved on one stop down the line.

All the way to Broxbourne station they'd gone, and back again. They visited many houses. With them both carrying crocks and exchanging them for clothes and sometimes money, they'd done real well. Tonight they would sleep in their own bed, but not until after they'd gone to the Horse and Feathers to meet a few friends and drink gin until they couldn't hardly stand. Well, what was the point of earning good money if you couldn't go out and enjoy yourself?

'Let's give it up, Jack,' said Betty now. 'I'll come out with you like we always used to do. We could maybe even move to a better room. I'm happy now. Let's give it up.'

Jack sighed. 'Listen, old gal. If we finds Cissy, I know she'll be glad to have the brat taken off her hands. She's young. She'll be able to find some bloke what'll marry her. I know you can't have no babes, but this kid will be half mine and that's something, ain't it? He'll be what – two years old? Soon he can come out with us. You and me will have somebody to help us out in our old age. You want a babe to love, don't you?'

Betty's eyes filled with tears. Yes, she wanted a babe to love, but in ten years she had never fallen for one. Jack's bastard would be better than nothing to still the longing that haunted her. She'd love the boy and it was true what Jack said about a lad to look after you when you were old. She wiped her eyes and finished off her porter.

'But how are we going to find Cissy? We already asked everywhere.'

Jack had been thinking hard. He had come back to this inn in Dunning's Alley, just where he had been that time he had seen Cissy. He went to the window and looked out, just as he had done on the other day. They had been coming from *that* direction . . .

Smiling broadly, he set down his tankard and left the Crown, ignoring Betty's surprised face peering at him through the glass. There weren't too many places down this alley where a fine lady might go. After a moment, he came back indoors.

'I done it, old gal. Figured it out. They was at the coach-makers! Now listen. You go down there and I'll tell you what to say.'

Several minutes later, Betty, having left her crocks at the inn, entered Joseph Richards and Company rather timidly.

'What do you want?' said a swell as he came out of the little office at the back. 'No begging here. Get out.'

'Oh, please sir. I ain't begging, only I've gone and lost my daughter. She ran away, see? And we don't know where she's gone. My husband was told she was seen coming out of this place with a widow. We figured she was the widow's maid. A young widow, pretty as a picture with yellow hair. I just want to talk with my girl, sir. She might be able to help us out and the Lord knows we been having a hard time.'

The man fingered the fine links of his watch-chain as he studied the slut cowering before him. Dirty-faced and largely toothless, she had on a black bonnet that was so faded it looked bronze green. She smelled of old clothes and stale sweat, enough to turn your stomach. On her feet were a pair of men's lace-up black boots several sizes too big.

He knew whom she was seeking. He had himself, personally, written twice to Mrs Hobart, asking her in a most deferential manner if she would care to place an order. The lady had declined. Besides, there was a catalogue missing after she left. She probably wasn't a widow at all, maybe not even a lady.

'You mean Mrs Hobart of Hoddesdon,' he said at last. 'I don't know her address, but how many widows named Hobart can there be in Hoddesdon?'

'Only one, I'm sure, sir. I thank you ever so much. Thank you kindly. Good day to you, sir.'

She was out of the door like lightning and flying down the alley, a young girl again.

'Well?' said Jack as she walked into the inn, smiling widely. 'Well?'

'Mrs Hobart in Hoddesdon.'

Jack's face fell. 'That old buffer at the station house lied to me. "Any young widows in this town?" I says to him. You heard me say it. "Any young widows with yellow hair?" He didn't even ask me why I wanted to know. Just said to me there warn't. He didn't say there was one down the road in Hoddesdon, did he? Never mind. We got her name now. I'll go tomorrow, not too early. I'll have a wash, that's what I'll do, and I'll have me a shave. Not too much celebrating tonight, Betty. I'll need the groats for travelling. We got any clothes today what are better than I'm wearing? I'll smarten myself up before I goes a-calling. Got to look respectable.'

13

Napier bowled into Hoddesdon as the clock in the old brick tower tolled three. The road was not only crowded but dusty; it hadn't rained for days. Market day in Hoddesdon was as colourful a sight as anywhere else, and there was a great deal of noise. This was the high point of the week, a social as well as a commercial occasion. The heat of the sun had brought the men out of the public houses and inns to drink in the open air where they stood about in small groups, laughing and talking loudly. There was a carnival air abroad as stall-holders shouted their wares. And so many equipages, wagons and horses were drawn to a halt by the roadside that Napier had difficulty manoeuvring his phaeton close to Sybilla's front door.

He dropped the whip into its socket, climbed from the high seat and looped the reins at the hitching post. He was not looking his best and knew it. With a pocket handkerchief, he tried to brush and slap the dust from his face and clothing. His collar and cravat had surrendered to the heat; they had wilted so much that there was nothing he could do to smarten himself up.

It was Sybilla's fault; she could hardly complain if he came into her drawing-room looking like a navvy. He had been at the malthouse stripped to the shirtsleeves when her note, delivered by Saul, had reached him. Would he please come at once on an urgent matter? He hadn't stayed to wash up; he had ordered his carriage and driven at the trot to Hoddesdon.

It was Cissy who answered the door, which didn't surprise him. Saul would take his time returning to his duties here. Napier told the girl to have his coach driven to the Hobart stable as soon as her father returned, and assured her that he would announce himself.

'Oh, thank you for coming so quickly,' said Sybilla, rising from her chair. 'There was no one else to turn to.'

'Of course you must always send for me when you are in difficulties. What is it, my dear? I will do anything I can to help. You must excuse the state I'm in, however, I didn't take time to clean myself up.' He took both her hands and led her to the small settee where they could sit down together.

'It's not for myself. I would not have sent for you so urgently in the middle of the day to solve a problem of mine. It's because of Cissy.'

'What? You took me from my work because of your maid?'

'This is very serious. Who else would understand the dangers a young girl faces in life better than you do? I had no hesitation in sending for you. She is in desperate trouble.'

'You are an amazing woman, Sybilla. Hasn't it occurred to you that I would more readily protect *you* from the world's iniquities than take upon myself the task of sorting out the life of a young woman I find singularly depressing?' Releasing her hands, he leaned forward to rest his forearms on his knees. 'Come on, then. Tell me. How can I help this sweet, innocent young maid of yours?'

'I had a visitor a short time ago. He said his name was Jack Dark and that he had come for his child. He told me he was the father of Cissy's infant, but he didn't appear to know that Fanny is a female. He referred to her as the little nipper. I told him there was no person named Cissy Potter at this address and that he had been amazingly careless to have mislaid his own child. He wasn't fooled. He said he would come again this evening and Cissy had better be prepared to give him the nipper, beause he was the child's legal guardian.'

'And is he the father of Cissy's child?'

'Yes, of course he is, but —'

'But she had been a most unwilling lover. It's a tale often told, Sybilla. Take my advice and stay away from the whole business. That little girl might well be better off with her father. He has a legal right to her, I'm sure.'

Sybilla stood up. 'In that case, you had better leave at once. Goodbye, Mr Drummond. I might have known how you would react, what you would think before I even had a chance to put the facts before you.'

'I'm not going anywhere. Suppose you sit down and tell me what happened.'

Despite an apparent reluctance, she was happy enough to do so. 'Cissy knew this man Dark, it's true, but he was a much older man and married besides. There was nothing beyond an exchange of pleasantries between them. She was thirteen then, remember –'

'She looks a great deal older. Go on.'

'This man Dark caught her one night in an alleyway as she was coming home from visiting a friend, a servant girl in another house in the neighbourhood. Without a word, he raped her. She was very frightened, but she did go to the magistrates in the end. Would you believe it? They arrested Dark and then found him not guilty! Right there in the magistrates' court! I'm disgusted that such a miscarriage of justice could occur.'

'Magistrates are only mortal, you know, they're not gods. Perhaps they had their reasons for deciding as they did.' He stood up and tugged on the bell-pull. 'We'll see what the girl has to say. Where did all of this take place, by the way? Here in Hoddesdon?'

'No, no. In Bishopsgate. Both members of my husband's staff, a very elderly couple, died shortly after I married Mr Hobart. The Potters were taken on, and then Mrs Potter asked me if I would have her daughter to live here as the girl had suffered a misfortune. Cissy was a kitchen maid in a large establishment in Bishopsgate.'

'Bishopsgate is a ward of the City. The Lord Mayor and Aldermen sit alone on the bench, which can mean one man's prejudices and impatience or, simply, a failure to probe deeply. But it doesn't matter what the system is – the single professional stipendiary of the London boroughs or the pairs of gentlemen who sit regularly in the counties – we are all capable of making mistakes. Unfortunately, magistrates are all of one class. We own property, we have rank and position, while those who are brought before us are almost always of the lower orders. I had many years to discover what those poor devils think of us.'

'Then why did you become a magistrate? You obviously disapprove of the system.'

'To redress the balance a little, I suppose. I was reminded not so long ago that people of all ranks are capable of compassion. And that's true, of course, but I think I also bring the sort of understanding that is denied to other magistrates.'

202

'I'm sure those people who come before you are grateful that you do understand.'

'No, why should they be? It's their right, after all,' said Napier. 'There is another reason why I became a magistrate. I have always felt that the wicked have an unfair advantage over decent citizens when they appear in court. The villains have invariably made a study of magistrates and the best way to influence them, while law-abiding folk have never given the courts a thought. As a consequence, honest people are often struck dumb with awe or else they take a notion in their heads and repeat it to the exclusion of more important points. That is why I think there could have been a serious miscarriage of justice in Cissy's case. But no one can be tried twice for the same crime. As far as the law is concerned, the matter is closed. Come in!'

Cissy, red-eyed, entered the room timidly, but refused the offer of a seat, preferring to lean against the door.

'This is Mr Drummond, Cissy, whom you have seen before. He is a magistrate and is here to help you.'

'You ain't gonna give my baby away!' the girl bawled, and Napier threw up his hands impatiently.

'No, I'm not. Try to trust me for a few moments. What does this man Dark do for a living?'

'He's a pedlar, sir. Sells crockery. He lives in Shoreditch, but he goes all over.'

'Why do you suppose he has suddenly decided to claim his child?'

'I don't know. I can't think why. He never give me no money for the baby. He told the magistrate – a regular nob *he* was – that I had been willing, and that we had . . . done it many times. Mr Dark said as how he'd look after me, but he never give me a farthing.'

'How old were you then?'

'Thirteen, sir, well, going on fourteen. It was the day before my birthday. A fine birthday that was.'

'Did the magistrate ask you your age?'

'No, sir. Nobody asked me nothing.'

Napier looked at the small girl pressed against the heavy mahogany door. She was clean, which surprised him. Her hair was carefully brushed and fashioned neatly into a small tight

203

bun; her apron was heavily starched and without a stain. She was not pretty; her pinched young-old face had nothing whatsoever to recommend it and her plainness was compounded by an expression of mulish rebellion. She would have made a most unappealing witness. He was quite certain that she wouldn't have faced the necessity of approaching a magistrate until her pregnancy was obvious, too late to make a good impression when she laid her complaint. She had, he was sure, done and said all the wrong things from start to finish.

'What did you say to the magistrate?'

'About what happened? I said Mr Dark caught me in a passageway off Cow's Lane late one night when I was coming home from a friend's house. I said I was that surprised at first that I didn't cry out nor tell him not to, and then –' The sullen face suddenly crumpled, tears overflowed and ran unchecked down her cheeks. She turned her face away to rest it on the polished wood of the door, her shoulders heaving as she tried to control her sobs.

'In the magistrates' court, Cissy. Attend to me. Did you cry there the way you are doing now?' The girl nodded her head. 'So much that you couldn't speak any more?' Another nod. 'Did you say to the magistrate only what you have said to me?' Again a brief bobbing of the head. 'And did Jack Dark smile and talk a great deal?'

Cissy turned round in considerable surprise. 'Yes, sir, he did! He talked and talked. He said I was willing. He said he'd look after me. He said he never forgot his responsibilities, but he couldn't marry me because he already had a wife.'

'And you said nothing more?'

'No, sir.' She thought a moment. 'I did say Mr Dark should've give me something to help me with my baby. I knew I'd get my notice. I didn't know then that Mrs Hobart would take me in.'

Napier rubbed his chin, studying Cissy carefully. 'Will you answer my questions, Cissy? I promise you I only want to help you.'

'I've been answering your questions already. I'll answer anything you want.'

Napier looked at Sybilla, wondering if he should ask her to leave the room, decided against it and returned his attention to

Cissy. 'When he did this thing to you, did you both lie down?'
He heard Sybilla gasp; Cissy now had her emotions well in
hand. It was clearly a relief to be able to speak of her ordeal.

'He pushed me against a wall. He pushed me hard. My head
hit the back of the wall. Then . . . he started to pull up my
skirts.'

'You knew he was doing wrong. Why didn't you scream for
help?'

'He had his hand over my mouth. I didn't even know what
he was doing at first. He said no harm would come to me
because he was standing up. Then he hurt me.'

Napier could see Sybilla's brilliant flush from the corner of
his eye. He should have sent her away after all, but had
thought it improper to ask Cissy such personal questions
without Sybilla's presence as chaperone. 'Thank you for your
honesty, my dear. I do believe you. Now then, Jack Dark is
coming back this evening. Where do you suppose he'll go until
then?'

'Down Rye Meads, maybe, or a public house.'

Sybilla stood up, twisting her hands together, her distress at
this moment almost as great as Cissy's. 'Mr Drummond, Cissy
has the chance of marriage to a good man. Should she not go to
him immediately?'

'Jefferson Smith, do you mean? Certainly not. Marriage is
out of the question at the moment. She must stay away from
Jefferson lest she ruin him. I shall go now to find this man. I'll
come back when something has been sorted out. Both of you
stay here and do nothing foolish while I'm gone. By the way,'
he turned in the doorway. 'What does this fellow look like?'

'Black-haired and clean-shaven,' said Sybilla. 'He is wearing
an old red velvet waistcoat and a frockcoat that is too big for
him.'

When Sybilla and Cissy were alone, the maid wiped her eyes
on her apron and smiled wanly. 'Thank you for trying to help
me, Mrs Hobart, it was good of you. Only there ain't nobody
as can do nothing for me. I just got to look after Fanny as best I
can. Seems like even Jefferson can't help me.'

'Don't despair, Cissy. Trust Mr Drummond. I'll speak to
him about Jefferson when he returns. I don't understand his
attitude, I must say. Just try not to worry for the next hour or so.'

Cissy shook her head sadly and left the room. She knew better than to trust the gentry, or anyone for that matter. It was no use looking to others to help you; you just had to rely on yourself. She knew what must be done now.

It took Napier more than half an hour to track down Jack Dark. Wisely, he had begun his search in the drinking establishments and found his man at last in The Bell. Dark was drinking porter, seated by himself in a corner. Napier studied the man as he crossed the tap-room. He had met a thousand Jack Darks in his time – sly, ill-fed and ill-clothed, slightly desperate. The pedlar would be cunning without being in any way intelligent, more skilled in manipulating magistrates than in staying out of the courts.

'Jack Dark?' Napier pulled up a chair to sit down. The pedlar half rose from his stool, then sat down again, very much at his ease.

'You the governor from Hornbeam House? I'll wager that Mrs Hobart sent you. Well sir, I'm ready to take my lad. I'll bring him up proper. Better than Cissy could. Why, I daresay she'll be glad to be free of him. My wife, now, she can't have no infants and she wants this boy. He'll have a good home, sir.'

'You raped that girl.'

Jack was prepared for the accusation. 'That's what they all say, ain't it? I mean, man to man, that's what they all say. Anyways, the magistrates didn't think so, didn't have to think twice about it. No case to answer.'

'Save your fancy airs for nobs who don't know what's going on in that filthy head of yours. I'm no Johnny Raw. You did it, all right, and I imagine you knew perfectly well that she was only thirteen. You raped that girl.'

'Believe me, guv, if I'd of waited, done things a bit different, she'd of been willing.'

'She was still only thirteen. You raped her and I'm not going to let you have the child. Cissy wants to keep the baby with her.'

'I'll go to the law! That child's mine!'

'You've taken your time about discovering that. The child's very nearly two years old.'

'Don't matter,' said Jack. 'I want him and the law will back my claim. I know what's what.'

206

'You would be ill-advised to try it. Did I mention that I am a Hertfordshire magistrate? I suppose it slipped my mind. The point is, you would have to approach a . . . but you can guess what I should say if you went to the law. New evidence. A different charge. You know I could do it. Your claim would fail.' This was not true; Dark stood every chance of being able to take Fanny away. Napier was hoping the man would not realize the strength of his case.

'I could make life very unpleasant for quite a few people,' said Dark menacingly, although he hadn't the slightest idea how he would go about it. The last thing he wanted to do was enter a courtroom. And now that there were toffs involved . . .

'It might, as you say, be unpleasant all round. Cissy might demand maintenance, for instance,' said Napier. 'I have a better idea. The child would be a burden to you. I suggest you renounce your claim to the infant. I'll write out something and you can sign it.'

'Why should I do as you ask? Tell me that.'

'For ten pounds,' said Napier, standing up. 'Ten pounds are better than a squalling brat, aren't they? Come, we'll ask the landlord for the use of a private room. I'll need paper and pen also.' He turned round to stare down at Dark who was still seated. 'Well, come on, man, I haven't got all day.'

Dark sat gaping, his mind in a whirl. Ten pounds in exchange for a child he had never seen. Why not? Betty might cut up rough, though, especially as it had been his idea to hunt for Cissy all these weeks. He had raised the old girl's hopes, that he had. Never mind, he'd buy Betty some little trinket and she'd be merry as a grig. Ten pounds was a bloody fortune to the likes of Betty and Jack Dark. Still somewhat dazed by the unexpected turn of events, he rose and followed the swell gentleman to a back room.

Napier spent some time in composing the document. He had no legal training and had no idea what value this piece of paper might have if tested in the courts. But he felt reasonably satisfied that Dark would take such an official looking paper quite seriously.

'There now, this says you renounce all your rights to the child of Cissy Potter. Put your mark just there, and hereafter stay away from Cissy.'

'This ain't a confession, is it?' asked Dark, suddenly suspicious.

'Certainly not. Shall I call in the landlord to read it to you?'

'No, he can keep his nose out of my business,' said Dark as he made his cross at the bottom of the page.

When the document had been exchanged for the ten pounds, Napier drove the pedlar to the railway station. There was a train about to leave and Napier bought one second-class ticket to Shoreditch. 'By the way,' he said, as Dark was about to board the train, 'the child is a girl. She wouldn't have been much use to you in your old age, would she?'

About half an hour after Napier left Hornbeam House, Mrs Potter knocked on the drawing-room door where Sybilla was attempting to concentrate on her embroidery.

'I've just come to tell you, ma'am,' said Mrs Potter, 'that it'll have to be me in future what looks after you. Cissy's taken Fanny and run off.'

Sybilla jumped to her feet. 'Oh, has she no sense? I told her to wait.'

'All this ain't your affair, Mrs Hobart. It would have been better if Jack Dark had of taken Fanny. Saul don't like seeing the child around and –'

'Oh, do be quiet while I think. Where might she have gone? Not to Jefferson, surely.'

Mrs Potter heaved a theatrical sigh. 'I suppose she run off to her gran's up in Broxbourne Woods. Over close to Broxbournebury. But leave her alone, ma'am. It's all for the best.'

Sybilla did not agree. She had the horse put to and set off in pursuit. She hadn't far go to. Ten minutes later, she saw Cissy ahead of her almost at the gates of Broxbournebury, and whipped up the horse to draw the gig alongside.

'I'm not going back, Mrs Hobart,' said Cissy. She was holding Fanny's hand and it was plain the child was so tired she wasn't capable of walking much farther.

'Fanny is exhausted, Cissy. She won't be able to go on. Put her in the gig and we'll all go home.'

'I know she's tired. You could give us a ride to my gran's, if you would. My arms ached that much, I couldn't carry her no more. Let me go to gran's where we'll be safe.'

The child was pulling on Cissy's hand. 'Ride, mam, ride!'

'You have been very brave all these years,' said Sybilla. 'Now, at last, a man of consequence, like Mr Drummond, has taken an interest in you. Why won't you give him a few hours to see what he can do?'

With a sigh of resignation, Cissy lifted Fanny on to the seat of the gig. As always, Sybilla was struck by the child's pallor and huge, sad eyes. She took out her pocket handkerchief to wipe Fanny's nose as Cissy pulled herself up into the gig. Fanny immediately clutched her mother's skirt and began to whine miserably.

'She wants her Godfrey's,' said Cissy. 'I ain't give her none today. I'm not giving her up, Mrs Hobart. Fanny is the best thing that ever happened to me, her and Jefferson. If I have to give up Jefferson like the man said, I will, but I ain't going to give up Fanny and that's a fact.'

The sun beat down warmly on their heads as Sybilla manoeuvred the gig round to face towards home. It was a beautiful day, but the young maid and her fretful child seemed incapable of enjoying even so simple a pleasure as a ride in the fresh air. Cissy's depression was so intense that Sybilla felt the waves of despair reaching out to her. She had to force herself to remember her faith in Napier Drummond's powers. The acceptance of defeat and misery, which were so much a part of Cissy's nature, were alien to Sybilla who refused to believe in the inevitability of failure.

All the way home, she kept up a brisk monologue which was intended to lift her maid's spirits. Cissy was unmoved, while Fanny grew increasingly restless. The child wriggled on her mother's lap, cried persistently and kicked out her thin legs with surprising strength when Sybilla was unwise enough to reach over to pat her.

By the time the gig was safely in the stable, Sybilla's nerves were very finely strung. They could see Napier's furious face at the drawing-room window as they walked up the garden path. Cissy refused to be parted from Fanny even for a moment, so the three of them entered the drawing-room to be greeted by Napier's scolding voice.

'Of all the empty-headed tricks!'

209

'Just you leave me alone!' cried Cissy in despair. 'Nobody can help me.'

'I've spent a good deal of time trying, nevertheless, you foolish girl.'

'What news have you for us?' asked Sybilla wearily.

'It took me half an hour to track Jack Dark down, but at least the matter is now settled. I've given him ten pounds and he has given me a signed paper renouncing all claims to his child. He'll not trouble you again.'

'Oh, sir, thank you,' said Cissy, blinking back her tears. 'I can't thank you enough. That's ever so kind of you.'

'*Kind?*' cried Sybilla. 'No, it isn't! You paid that man? How could you? I've never heard of anything so wicked. Cissy, how can you be happy when the man who ruined you has been given ten pounds for his trouble?'

'But he won't bother me no more, Mrs Hobart. That's the important thing. I can't say he *ruined* me, not when I've got Fanny. She's give me something to live for.'

'The man must be brought to justice. This won't do.' Sybilla turned to Napier. 'I suppose you didn't even give that man a telling off.'

Napier snorted impatiently. 'No, since I'm not one to waste my breath. And I hadn't my horsewhip handy either. Dark is a brutal, stupid man who probably has very little conception of right and wrong. He appreciates a little money, however, and fear of the law is strong in him. He'll give us no trouble.'

'I think you are carrying your understanding of rogues just a little too far. I appreciate that he was brought up in a brutal environment and that he didn't have the advantages in life that others have enjoyed. But there are many poor people who do know right from wrong. Your tolerance is an insult to them.'

'I know that, Sybilla, but I can't put the world to rights. I have dealt with one man in the best way I could. I cannot single-handedly save civilization.'

'I don't see why I can't marry Jefferson,' said Cissy. '*He's* a good man, you have to admit that, sir.'

'Yes,' said Napier, turning his attention to the girl. 'He is a good man and I'm sure you wouldn't want him to be dismissed from the police force.'

'No, sir, but why should he be?'

210

Their raised voices had frightened Fanny who now began to cry louder than ever. Sybilla had never imagined how irritated she could be with such a helpless little thing. She plucked Fanny from Cissy's arms and took her into the hall, calling for Mrs Potter to collect her grandchild straight away. When she came back into the room, Napier gestured the two young women to chairs and stood over them like a stern father as they sat down.

'Listen to me carefully, for I shall not repeat this. I've been away from my work too long already. As a police constable, Jefferson must obtain Colonel Robertson's permission to marry. He must be able to show that he has twenty pounds in cash, or furnishings to the value of twenty pounds.'

'Oh, Lordy,' cried Cissy, hugging herself and rocking to and fro in the chair. 'We ain't never going to get married then. Where would I ever get that sort of money?'

'That's monstrous!' said Sybilla. 'Colonel Robertson has no right to interfere with the lives of his men in this way.'

'Everything is monstrous to you, Sybilla. According to you, we live in a very wicked world. For my part, I find the rule unexceptionable. The old parish constable system was lax, poorly organized and open to corruption. Robert Peel, in setting up the Metropolitan Police, tried to gain the public's confidence in his new force by imposing strict discipline. Gradually, the people will begin to trust the police because they will see that they aren't corrupt, drunk or inefficient. Jefferson is a fine example of the type of man Robertson wants in the Hertfordshire Constabulary. The lad can do very well for himself in the future. He is only nineteen, after all, and has made a good start. For that reason, I don't want anything to spoil his chances. He is one of the poor you spoke of, a man with a strong sense of right and wrong. He should be cherished, not destroyed.'

'I do love him,' said Cissy forlornly.

'And you shall marry him soon.' Napier drew out his pocket book. 'I will give you twenty pounds as a bride present. Or –' He looked down at Cissy, thinking of her grasping father. 'On second thoughts, I will give the money to Jefferson. He can then apply for permission to marry. Try to be patient, Cissy.'

'I don't know what to say, sir. I'm that choked. Would you

excuse me now? I must go and tell my mam about it.' She headed for the door, but turned with an afterthought. 'I don't care what anyone says. You are a good man, Mr Drummond.'

Aware that Napier's eyes were on her, Sybilla looked up at him and slowly came to her feet. 'I must add my thanks to Cissy's, and I know you meant everything for the best, but . . . '

'But what?'

'But you are in a position to do great things and you have not done them. You are a powerful and influential man. You might have brought Jack Dark to justice. And you might have argued with Colonel Robertson that he is being too harsh with his men. Why, he is so strict with them, I'm surprised any man wants to be a policeman.'

'Yet, they do, my dear, which suggests to me that you don't know much about the minds of men. I'm not a reformer, Sybilla, I never pretended to be. I'm not a philanthropist, either, always chasing some dreams of Utopia. I'm a rough man and I deal with those problems that cross my path in a practical way. I confess, however, that I don't know how to deal with your monumental ignorance.'

'Oh, that was a wicked thing to say.'

'In keeping, perhaps, with my wicked deeds this day. I inhabit the real world. I don't exist between the covers of a three-volume novel. In the real world, I must face the fact that Jack Dark's case came before a magistrate and was dismissed. I believe that to have been a wrong decision, but the charge cannot be brought again. I'm no legal expert, heaven knows, but I think that Dark is actually the legal guardian of Fanny. I took advantage of his ignorance to deny him his fatherly rights. I'm sorry if my methods distress you.'

'Well, I admit I know nothing at all about the law, but it seems unjust that a man can rape a woman and then claim the child she has been forced to bear.'

'And another thing,' he continued. 'Police rules forbid members of the force from consorting with, let alone marrying, a woman of the criminal classes. They are very strict on this point, and rightly so. If Cissy had run to Jefferson to hide Fanny from her father, it might have been enough to cause Jefferson to be dismissed. I wouldn't have cared to chance it.

212

This way, Cissy and Jefferson can marry with the Colonel's blessing. Surely, that is the best thing. I like the lad. I think he deserves better than to saddle himself with Cissy at the tender age of nineteen, but that is his business. You must admit the Potters are hardly the most admirable family, yet I have done my best to bring the girl some happiness. Still, you choose to criticize.'

'Well, how was I expected to know all of this? It is all too bad. Something should be done about the law which gives a rapist such power. And I still think that if you cared enough about injustice you would stir yourself to put a word in the right place.'

'I didn't expect gratitude from you for my efforts today, but I didn't expect a high-minded lecture either.'

'My goodness, you do have a cruel tongue, don't you? I *am* grateful for your efforts, I said as much. But you have taken the easy way – that is to say, you wouldn't have been satisfied with today's events if Dark had harmed Marianne and Emmaline.'

'No, I wouldn't. But some things are better settled out of court, believe me. Saul should have found Dark years ago and thrashed him senseless. That is what I would have done. I would not wish a sister of mine to go through – but never mind. You have never attended court. You can't know how distressing it is for victims of rapes to give evidence.'

'No, I suppose I had never considered that part of it.'

'Of course it is unfair that mothers have no legal rights over children they've borne, but so the law decrees. You are a strong-minded woman. Suppose you persuade Parliament to change the law. I'm not a member of that gentlemen's club; I've better things to do.'

Distantly, Fanny's cries reached Sybilla and she gritted her teeth. What an appalling day this had been! She was exhausted by the emotion – by the variety of emotions – she had felt during the last few hours. She almost wished she had not sent for this hard man. She had made a fool of herself and been made to see how stupid and ignorant she was. Cissy's gain had been her loss. Her self-esteem, never high, was now as low as it could be.

Napier was walking away from her, but he suddenly whirled round. 'And while I think of it, you're no paragon.'

213

'I never said –'

'You criticize me, yet when cruelty exists in front of your very eyes, you choose to look the other way. I'm not sure that Dark would have treated the child as stupidly as Cissy does. Opium, given in large doses to a young child, can be fatal. You do know that, don't you?'

'Of course, but you don't understand.'

'You do know that Fanny is kept permanently, dangerously, sedated with Godfrey's cordial. You can tell by the child's eyes. If I had my way, giving Godfrey's would be a criminal offence. The desperately poor give it so that babies won't cry while their mothers are out at work all day, or so that the children will not feel hunger and cry for the food there is no money to buy. There's no excuse here. Yet you have done nothing to stop this disgraceful behaviour going on under your own roof.'

'I didn't want to interfere –'

'*Interfere*? In God's name, woman, what do you suppose we have been doing all day? I don't understand you at all.'

Sybilla rubbed a hand over her face as if to wipe away the extreme tiredness. 'If you will just give me the chance to explain. It's because of Saul. I do know that Cissy gives the child Godfrey's cordial, but she does it so that Fanny won't be an irritation to Saul who might do her an injury.'

'And you condemn Dark for one act of lust while Saul poses a continual threat to that little girl! Never lecture me again, Sybilla –'

'Stop it! I won't listen to another word, do you hear? Go away. Get out!'

'You're so smug and self-satisfied –'

Maddened beyond rational thought, she picked up a cushion from the settee and swung it at him. He caught it head high, laughing explosively, his anger completely gone. 'Oh, no you don't, you little vixen! These days I am prepared to defend myself at all times in your presence. Anyway, you were too slow. Here, let go of it.'

'No!' She tried to wrest the cushion from him to swing again, but he was too strong. Her temper was rising; she didn't care what she did or how undignified she looked while doing it. 'Let go of it! I want to hit you and I will!'

He put his arms around her, pinning her own to her sides as he bent his head to kiss her on the mouth. Sybilla's heart swooped to her knees, a totally unexpected, delicious sensation which took her completely by surprise. She couldn't be angry with him while enjoying his embrace so much all at the same time, so she gave herself to the kiss – it was not a conscious decision – and leaned against him hungrily. It was several seconds before she came to her senses. Then she moved in his arms and he released her reluctantly. To her amazement, she wasn't angry at his presumption. She didn't demand an explanation for his outrageous behaviour, but she was exceedingly puzzled.

'Why is it that when I lose all my self-control and behave like a hoyden, you find me amusing? Why do you laugh? Just now you were scolding me and I suppose I deserved it. Well, I know I did. Then, just because I was trying to hit you for speaking the truth, you . . . that is, you showed you were pleased with me.'

He smiled ruefully. 'I don't know, I can't explain.' Her cheeks were still flushed. She was breathing hard and her hair had begun to shed pins. She looked adorable and he wished he could kiss her again. But he saw that she was still holding the cushion, hugging it as a means of preventing him from coming so close to her a second time. This was not the moment to attempt another kiss, to try to awaken in her emotions he sensed she was not yet ready to acknowledge.

She shook her head. 'I'm sorry for my bad behaviour. I don't know what has come over me recently. It's as if –'

'You have had much to try you. Don't be too hard on yourself, Sybilla. I really don't blame you for being angry with me. I was inexcusably rude and quite carried away with the sound of my own voice. Now it is my turn to ask a question. Why is it that you are unwilling to face up to most men and speak your mind? In all your dealings with others, you are a most gentle lady. Indeed, I would say you are too timid. Yet you are not afraid of me, although many men are. When you are angry, you will argue with me, even attack me. Am I not a fearsome beast? I've been told I am.'

Now it was Sybilla's turn to say: 'I don't know, I can't explain.' She set the pillow down on a nearby chair, but moved beyond his reach as she did so. 'I do know why I turn to you whenever something is troubling me. You are a most generous and resourceful man. Do you know? You are thirty pounds poorer as a result of answering my appeal this afternoon. I feel guilty about that, but I think I have found you out. You are not as fierce as you would have people believe. You are a good man even though you *are* inclined to scold rather harshly. Kindness is not a sign of weakness, you know. Rather, it is an indication of your strength.'

They stood smiling at one another for several seconds. He thought it was time to go. There was nothing more he could say today. He consulted his watch; he talked himself politely but impersonally to the door and said goodbye, but not before reminding her that they were all to attend the theatre on Saturday. It wasn't until he was half-way to Hertford that he remembered he would be unable to ride to London with Sybilla and the others. He would be in London all day on Saturday and would have to join the party at the theatre.

Sybilla went immediately to the kitchen, dreading the task before her, but determined to make up for her past cowardice. She made no excuses for herself; she had been doing so for too long.

The Potter family looked up at her in surprise when she entered the kitchen. Even Saul seemed pleased to see her, which made it harder. She took a deep breath.

'Cissy, in future you are not to give Fanny another drop of Godfrey's cordial. It could kill her. She has had too much already.' Cissy gaped at her, then began to howl excuses. Fanny, frightened, joined in the chorus. Sybilla turned to Saul. 'Saul, no matter how tempted you might be to strike that child, you will not lay a finger on her ever, do you hear me?'

Saul began to bellow that he would treat his grandchild as he chose and Mrs Potter joined in the row, although Sybilla could not hear what she had to say.

'If you harm Fanny, Saul, I will take a horsewhip to you or get someone to do it for me. That is all I have to say to you.'

The entire Potter family was in uproar, all of them crying or shouting at her at once. It was the sort of scene Sybilla usually dreaded, but they couldn't upset her today. She had been shouted at by a master of the art; she would never be frightened of raised voices again. She knew she was in the right of it and simply turned on her heel in the midst of the noise and returned to the drawing-room. She had a great deal to think about.

14

As the coach rocked to a halt, Sybilla closed her eyes for a split second, pinching the bridge of her nose. Raindrops still clung to the small window panes following a sudden downpour. The world outside the coach was smeared, making a blur of the filth in the streets, heightening the brilliance of the theatre-goers' luscious dresses. Inside the coach, Mrs Drummond and Mr Farley were still talking with great animation. She had endured their company for two long hours, not at all what she had anticipated.

'Here we are at last!' said Mrs Drummond. 'My dress is dreadfully crushed. I should have worn my blue, but how was I to know the weather would be so close? At least it has stopped raining. Tell John to open the door, Florian. Are there puddles? Must I be on my guard against puddles? Florian, I'm so nervous! I'm afraid I look a fright.'

'You are the fairest rose that ever bloomed,' said Florian for the tenth time as he helped Mrs Drummond from the coach.

Sybilla ground her teeth. The fairest rose that ever bloomed had talked non-stop all the way from Hertford to Marylebone. Mrs Drummond was anxious about Marianne's first appearance on the stage, of course. Sybilla understood that. And Florian Farley was doing his best to help the woman he admired to control her nerves. Sybilla understood that, too. But, oh, how she wished for the sort of conversation that could not be predicted by the yard, every whimsical, inconsequential word of it! In this confined space, she had heard enough cosy chatter, enough question and reassurance, ponderous platitudes following hard upon coquettish utterances, to last her a lifetime.

She would have given much these past hours for a little abrasive company. If only someone had barked out a cutting witticism about a mutual acquaintance, something cruel but amusing, or mused about life in a way that illuminated a mystery of human nature that had always puzzled her! She would gladly endure the odd thundering home truth that cut to the quick if, just occasionally, a few casual words of praise were thrown away on the wind to be caught and cherished.

The evening had begun badly, full of false promises, because Mrs Drummond had invited her to Bailton Hall for an early dinner before they all set off for the theatre. It was reasonable, wasn't it, to suppose that their host would be at home to greet her in the drawing-room, as he had always done before? She had steeled herself for the thrilling ordeal of this meeting, the first since he had kissed her and, surely, altered the course of her life. But he had not been there, and it was left to Francis Babcock to mention off-handedly that Napier was in London where business had called him; he would join them at the theatre. They were all kind to her, this tightly knit group of sweet, decent people, men and women who would never knowingly give offence by word or deed. Four well-bred adults who could not be brought to understand that an honest appraisal of one's faults now and then was an essential part of life. How they must shrink from the blunt character analyses of the head of the house of Drummond!

Francis Babcock, on the other hand, never uttered a sentence before he had chewed it over half a dozen times. Each remark was carefully tested for propriety, appropriateness and the reflection it would cast on the speaker. Emmaline, growing daily more regal, spoke more often than she used to do – and said even less that was worth hearing. Had her loved one told her bluntly that she was becoming foolishly precise in her every word and deed? Of course he hadn't. Sybilla would take no bets on Napier's having allowed her affectations to go unnoticed, however. But perhaps the girl had been too much criticized in her youth. She was a delicate flower and the adoration of her fiancé had, understandably, thrown her a little off balance. Emmaline was a sensible girl, thought Sybilla, who would eventually tire of playing so dull a part.

When it was time to leave Bailton Hall, Sybilla had been forced to choose to travel, as it were, between the devil and the deep blue sea. Whatever she did, she would be cast in the role of gooseberry. She had chosen Mrs Drummond's and Mr Farley's company, mainly because it was obvious that Emmaline and Francis wished so very much to be alone.

Sybilla gathered the skirts of her gown and stepped down

from the coach with as much grace as possible. The lavender silk was sadly crushed. She had wanted to make some small change to the gown for this, its second outing, and had therefore sewn silk violets in heavy swags four to six inches from the hem, and also along the deeply cut neckline. The violets had cost a fortune and the work had been tedious, but the effect was quite dramatic, or would be if the flowers had not suffered so. They had been an early casualty of the small coach space. Now she felt as if she, too, were a wilting violet. She nodded to Emmaline and Francis who were just emerging from the Babcock carriage; Emmaline was dazzling in yellow satin. Ruefully Sybilla gave a half-hearted tug to the violets in her corsage, but nothing could be done here and now to revive them.

It was approaching curtain time and the crowded pavement was seething with theatregoers who suddenly felt an urgent desire to enter the building, the result being a reasonably good-natured crush. The Drummond party must also make haste, but first Sybilla looked up at the structure which, a lifetime ago, had seemed like an enchanted palace of illusion. Tonight, she saw it as a freshly painted barn of a building, flat-faced and pierced by three sets of doors. The plasterwork was freshly painted in dull grey. Why, then, did it have such a tawdry air about it?

Perhaps it was her imagination, but she fancied that the theatregoers tonight were not quite so genteel nor so numerous as on the last occasion. Mr Farley had told her that tonight's play could not compare with Edward Bulwer-Lytton's *Money*. *When Duty Calls* was an old play, written nearly twenty years ago by an author long forgotten. The sole purpose of performing it, so Mr Farley had informed her, was to provide good parts for several comic actors of the company. They would improvise and change the lines to suit their particular talents, making broad comedy even broader. The playwright, fortunately long since dead, could hardly complain about such butchery, nor demand royalties. Anyway, had said Mr Farley, the better sort of theatregoer had already left London for the summer. *When Duty Calls* was good enough for those poor citizens who had no country homes to retire to, and certainly good enough as a first play for Marianne.

220

Inside the doors, Sybilla was struck anew by the richness of the furnishings. The brightly patterned carpet was thickly woven, the blue velvet curtains at each doorway were of the finest quality. Strange that she had not noticed on her first visit how dusty everything was. On the high ceilings, chubby cherubs, trailing swirls of blue ribbon, hovered incongruously round three-quarter portraits of impossibly beautiful women. Money had certainly been lavishly spent. Sybilla couldn't help wondering if Mr Watts was enjoying a proper return on his investment.

Their box was empty. She had been so sure that he would be there! It was also surprisingly dirty. There was even a long white kid glove lying in the filth of the floor. Mr Farley, hot on Sybilla's heels, vented his nervousness in an outburst of outraged indignation. This would not do; this was disgraceful. Someone else had been using their box. Mr Watts had no right to place others here. What had the man been thinking of? And why had not the box been cleaned properly? Mr Farley had a good mind to seek out the manager and send him away with a flea in his ear. Fortunately, Mrs Drummond and Emmaline had no trouble persuading him that this was not the best policy on the night that Marianne was making her debut.

After much discussion, the small uncomfortable chairs were arranged to suit everyone. Three were carefully spaced out next to the padded edge of the balcony for the three women. Three more chairs were then positioned behind them for the gentlemen. Every seat in this second row had to be tested. Many minutes were wasted as first Francis and then Mr Farley sat in each of the three chairs, because no one's view of Marianne's entrance must be obstructed.

Sybilla, far too much on edge to cope with the nerves of other people, flipped open her fan and waved it idly as she studied the crowd below. The house was scarcely half-filled, but what the audience lacked in numbers they certainly made up for in noise. Several men in the pit below her were quite drunk. Mrs Drummond leaned over to hope, in a loud whisper, that the young bucks would be polite when Marianne was on stage; Sybilla, silently, doubted it. Emmaline said several times – once to her mother and twice to her fiancé – that she was mortified to be here in such vulgar company just waiting for the moment when her sister would step on stage to be insulted by the mob. Mrs Drummond was near to tears, Francis was tight-lipped. Manfully, Florian Farley tried to soothe everyone's sensibilities at once. They all dreaded to think what Napier would make of this evening, but only Emmaline put the thought into words.

A hush of sorts descended on the audience as the house lights were turned low and the curtains parted to reveal two rustics in smocks. Their accents were broad West Country and their actions eccentric, but not, thought Sybilla, in any way amusing. For that reason, she was startled when a woman somewhere in the circle began to cackle not only on the occasions when the audience found something to laugh at, but also when everyone else was silent. Her high-pitched caw was building to hysteria. Perhaps the woman knew something that was not yet revealed to the rest of the audience. Since the play couldn't hold her attention, Sybilla began scanning the seats, way over to her right, looking for the laughing woman. Instinctively, she searched for a fat woman of middle age and found her in the second row of the balcony.

The door of the box opened, followed by a little flurry of movement behind her and a whisper of an apology. Mrs Drummond turned her head to scold her son for his late arrival. Sybilla kept her eyes riveted on the actors, although not seeing them at all. She had thought of no one but Napier Drummond since they had last met, had lived with the memory of his lips, the sound of his – usually angry – voice and the warmth of his gaze as he had left her that day. She had pined for days just to see him again, yet now that he was seated within a yard of her, she couldn't bring herself to turn round and smile as good manners demanded. Nothing more was required of her, after all, just a smile of welcome. She couldn't do it.

The entire first act, the entrance of each of the main characters, the comic turns, the foundations of the plot, all passed her by as if in a dream. She could be certain of only one thing: Marianne had not made an appearance. Mercifully, there had been no need to exclaim and applaud, to assure Mrs Drummond that Marianne was brilliant. At long last, the curtains closed, the lights were turned up, and now there was nothing to do but stand, smooth the creases of her skirt and turn to smile with as much composure as she could manage.

Her effort was wasted; Napier had been the first to leave the box. His attention was elsewhere as he helped first his mother, then his sister and finally Sybilla down the step from the box. Now she looked up, very much afraid that her expression was telling him too much of what she felt. He smiled, gripping her gloved hand with his bare one as he led her down the corridor a little way so that they could speak privately. Napier Drummond always departed from his home wearing expensive gloves like a gentleman should do, but he hated having his hands covered, so invariably the gloves travelled in his pockets. She could feel the heat of his hand now, burning through her netted mitten.

'How are Cissy and the child?' he asked as soon as they had found a quiet spot for themselves. Sybilla smiled at the question. Not so much as a polite *good evening, I'm sorry I arrived late* or even *you are the fairest rose that ever bloomed*. He said – always – just what was on his mind.

'Poor Fanny is in a dreadful way. She cries all the time and Cissy has been distraught. Well, we all have. I had to send for Dr Horley. He is a saint, you know. He said it will be difficult to wean Fanny off Godfrey's cordial. It will take time and patience. He sensed the tensions in the household and insisted that Cissy and Fanny should come to stay at his home so that he can keep an eye on the child. As you can imagine, I was very grateful, but afraid that his servants would all hand in their notices. And what poor Mrs Horley made of it all, I haven't dared ask.'

'But why has Cissy finally decided to stop dosing the child?' He knew the answer; he wanted to hear her say it.

'Because,' said Sybilla, 'I told her she must never give the medicine again. And I told Saul I would horsewhip him if he so much as touched Fanny.'

'Foolish girl! Did he threaten you or laugh in your face?'

'Neither. He looked a trifle surprised, I must say. Then he told me he would do as he pleased. However, I doubt it. I'm ashamed it was necessary for you to point out my duty to me. I've been irresponsible, but –'

'Never! You were blameless! I can't forgive myself for the

223

harsh things I said to you the other day. What a bad-tempered oaf I am! And now, because of me, you have no maid. Can you manage?'

'Napier,' said Francis, stepping between them. 'I'm just off to purchase some champagne for the ladies. Are you coming –'

'Take Florian with you,' said Napier curtly. He didn't so much as flicker his eyes in his friend's direction. Francis hesitated, sighed, gave Sybilla a mutinous glare and turned on his heel, calling to Florian.

'I too have been busy,' said Napier. 'Since I had to be in London today, I took the opportunity to call upon several Members of Parliament whom I've met briefly. Sybilla, none of them was the least sympathetic about the legal rights of mothers over their children. I failed you; pleading causes is not my forte.'

'No, you should not have attempted it. When I spoke so rashly the other day, it was the result of foolish anger. Of course, you can do nothing. Please, don't think of it again.'

'I don't like to fail,' he said. 'I stated my case to each one, giving my arguments for greater sharing of responsibility between mother and father, but I was like a fish gasping on the river bank, starved of air. I am accustomed to bargaining, to offering something I have for something I want, such as money. But I had no bargaining counters, you see. I could hardly promise all of them my vote, and it wouldn't have been enough anyway. I came to beg and, like a beggar, I was turned away.'

'Promise me, don't ever try –' said Sybilla, distressed.

'Mrs Hobart, your champagne,' said Francis. A very young maid hovered beside him holding three stemmed glasses on a tray. Francis handed the first to Sybilla, the second to Napier and dismissed the maid as he helped himself to the third. His movements were very deliberate and just a trifle aggressive. Plainly, he had no intention of returning immediately to Emmaline's side.

'I hope you had an uneventful journey to town,' said Napier coolly.

'Yes, quite uneventful. Emmaline felt rather unwell, but I suppose . . . Yes, uneventful. Napier, may I have a word with you?'

'Won't it wait?'

'No, it won't. It's important. I'll only take a moment of your time.'

Napier looked at Sybilla. 'I'll be with you in a moment, Mrs Hobart.' He turned away slightly and inclined his head towards Francis, who clearly wished for greater privacy.

'Emmaline and I have discussed the matter most thoroughly and I have given it many hours of careful thought, I assure you. Napier, I have decided to join you in the French Horn Lane venture. I know we disagreed, but . . . old friends and that sort of thing . . . it hasn't been easy for you, I know. I wish to help carry the burden of –'

'Francis, you're a good fellow, but you must know that the whole of Ware is splitting its sides laughing at me. I know you don't enjoy such bear-baiting and you cannot want to risk your money at this time.'

'I'm determined to share with you –'

'– the humiliation? Forget it. Believe me, I appreciate the offer and admire your courage in making it, but you and I are different men. You would hate it. Indeed, I'm persuaded you hate to hear *me* decried. What such public derision would do to you and Emmaline, I can't imagine. Don't you see? I don't dread their laughter at all. I'll make them eat their words one day.'

Francis lifted his glass to his mouth, taking nervous little sips. 'This is a nightmare. Give up this folly, Napier, and close the maltings. You are going to lose a great deal of money.'

'Have you two set the day for your marriage?' said Napier. 'We must have a talk, you and I. I shall put the money in trust for Emmaline straight away before I lose it all in mad speculations.'

Francis shook his head, finished the champagne and absent-mindedly held out his glass as if to set it down on an invisible table. Miraculously, the maid appeared just in time to whisk the empty glass away, unaware that her efficiency only served to increase Francis' fretful mood. 'I don't understand you and never will.'

Napier laughed. 'There is Emmaline looking quite lost. Go to her, my friend, and tell her all is well. Your sacrifice was not required. Then forget all about my maltings.'

225

In spite of the noise round her, Sybilla had heard every word. When Napier turned to smile at her, she said: 'It's all my fault. I brought this on you.'

'Yes, I believe you did, my dear. Drink your champagne. We must return to our seats presently to await Marianne's big moment.'

'I've ruined you.'

'You have done a great many things to me, but you have not ruined me, nor have you made me unhappy by your strongly worded – one might almost say *interfering* – advice. Francis couldn't hope to understand me, but I had thought you would. I am eternally grateful to you for not allowing me to run away from this battle. I'm not going into the fray unarmed, you know, and I can duck and weave with the best of them. Did I ever tell you my theory that merchant adventuring was invented by warriors who hate the sight of blood? I'm engaged in a fight to the death; it's what I was bred for. It doesn't matter, I promise you, whether I win or lose.'

'How can you possibly win? I hadn't understood perfectly or I wouldn't have suggested that you continue –'

'What? You're not changing your mind, are you? Let me explain to you exactly what will happen. I can see it all now. No respectable brewer will buy my new-method malt. However, all the rogues and those on very tight budgets will buy it because it will be cheap. I shall lose whatever prestige I had, while making a handsome fortune. Then forty years from now, when every other maltster is finally making malt more efficiently, I shall be hailed as a pioneer. Of course, I'll probably be in my grave by then.'

'But you said that everyone is laughing at you.'

'Are you laughing at me, Sybilla?'

'No, of course not.'

'Then nothing else matters. Come, there's the bell. Give me your glass. I hope we are all strong enough to endure whatever is to come in the next hour. Marianne doesn't like to be laughed at, except when she is attempting to amuse. Let us hope, for her sake, that the audience understands the difference.'

The curtains opened on a stage bare except for a large scrubbed kitchen table. Two men were seated at it playing

226

cards. It was obvious from their dress and the number of times they 'damned' this and 'plagued' the other that they must be servants and, therefore, figures of fun.

Marianne entered wearing a muslin gown, apron and mob-cap. She walked boldy enough across the stage to place a hand on the shoulder of one of the men – and then froze. Her stricken expression was clearly visible to those in her family's box. Mrs Drummond reached across to squeeze Sybilla's hand. A female voice from off-stage, so loud it set the entire theatre laughing, hissed: 'There's a couple of you, indeed!'

Marianne seemed to come to life at this prompt, but by this time the other players had turned to stone.

MUSLIN: There's a couple of you indeed! You're so fond of the vices of your betters, that you're scarce out of your beds, when you must pretend to imitate them and their ways, forsooth.
WILL: Pr'ythee, be quiet woman, do.
MUSLIN: Have done with your foolery, will ye? And send my lady word –
WILL: Hold your tongue, Mrs Muslin, you'll put us out.

Marianne was attempting a rustic accent, something she had done very well in her own drawing-room on many occasions. Tonight the trick of it seemed to have eluded her. Her body, stiff and slightly bent from the hips like a marionette, betrayed her nervousness. Her voice was barely audible as she and the servant, Will, continued to abuse each other.

The audience, at no time this evening having shown itself capable of quiet attentiveness, became increasingly restless. The fat lady laughed continuously. The young men in the front seats began to catcall, and Sybilla's eyes filled with tears of sympathy. She quickly lost the thread of the play as her heart ached for Marianne. Had Napier really known to what purgatory he was sending his sister?

WILL: I tell you, a wife is out of date now-a-days; time was – but that's all over – a wife's a drug now; mere tar-water, with every virtue under heaven, but nobody takes it. [Stands up]
MUSLIN: Well, I swear I could slap your impudent face.
WILL: Come and kiss me, I say –

Mrs Drummond gasped and clutched her throat. Sybilla could see Emmaline searching her reticule for the sal volatile.

MUSLIN: A fiddlestick for your kisses!
WILL: Come, throw your arms about my neck.
MUSLIN: Ay, as I used to do, Mr Brazen! Hush! My lady's bell rings. O lud! Come, now give me a kiss. [She kisses him] There now, let me be gone. [Exits.]

Marianne's playing had strengthened as the scene progressed; it could hardly have got worse. But she had not covered herself with glory this evening, and she had given the various members of her family much food for thought. Sybilla was stunned. There was no denying it, when actors kissed each other on stage, it was merely amusing. When Marianne, masquerading as an actor, kissed an actor on stage, the result was quite shocking. How on earth could the girl have brought herself to do it? Not for the first time, Sybilla was struck by the old adage – it takes all sorts. Perhaps Marianne had actually enjoyed appearing on the stage; Sybilla devoutly hoped so. Judging by the footscraping that was taking place behind her, the men of the party were distinctly restless and displeased. Mrs Drummond, of course, was crying openly.

The play limped along for another forty minutes, but no one in the Drummond box listened to it at all. Marianne made another brief appearance to deliver a love note to the heroine and left, accompanied by ironic applause.

Mrs Drummond, in deep distress, was on her feet as the curtains began to close. 'I must get out of here. Napier, open the door, I'm suffocating. Where's my hartshorn? Never mind, I'll have another glass of champagne to revive me. Florian and Francis must go for some champagne. Napier, I have a few things to say to you.'

'I thought you might,' said Napier, holding the door open. The two other men left the box with indecent haste, and Sybilla brought up the rear.

When they were in the broad corridor, Emmaline clutched Sybilla's arm. She had her own tale of woe, her own long list of grievances against her brother, because now she thought of it, poor Marianne could not be blamed. Marianne was but an innocent girl while Napier was a man of the world.

'Do you think that is what Marianne will say?' asked Sybilla. 'Because when she visited my home, she was quite certain in her mind about what she wanted to do. Surely, she won't complain now, just because the debut has not turned out as she wished.'

Emmaline looked down her pert little nose at Sybilla in the *grande dame* manner she had recently adopted. 'My dear Sybilla, Marianne will know that Napier has failed in his duty towards her. She will know where to place the blame, and she will know who were her best advisors. Why, Francis was quite blunt with her, but to no avail because Napier had already spoken. She will know better the next time.'

'The next time she wishes to do something adventurous, you mean? What a pity. Had it been me –'

'Had it been you, my dear, you would have brazened it out, I know, but Marianne is made of more delicate – that is –'

Sybilla narrowed her eyes. 'I'm beginning to dislike you, Emmaline,' she said in a low voice. 'Let me tell you that twenty is too young for such pomposity.'

Emmaline's royal façade disintegrated. 'Oh, *dear* Sybilla, forgive me! I didn't mean to say such horrible things to you. It's just that everyone knows you are adventurous and would dare to do so many things that other people –'

'I would not dare to appear on a public stage,' said Sybilla. 'Please! Don't explain further what you meant to say! I would rather remain friends. Here is Francis, so I'll leave you.'

But it was not to be. Francis handed her a glass of champagne and began talking at the same time. He, too, was aggrieved. 'I feel for Mrs Drummond in this bleak hour. To her must go my sympathy. Poor woman! Forced to see her daughter *debased* in the presence of hundreds. I don't know how she is to support the embarrassment. And Florian, wretched fellow, goes in fear of his life, because, you know, he gave a cautious word of encouragement. But only after he had learned that Napier was urging Marianne on in this folly.'

'I should think,' said Sybilla, 'that the only cause for distress was Marianne's poor performance. It was amazingly bad considering how often she has acted at home.'

'Ah, yes, and for that I really must blame Mrs Drummond. She encouraged this play-acting,' replied Francis.

'Tell me, Mr Babcock, is there anything for which you blame yourself?' asked Sybilla sarcastically. But he answered, quite seriously, that yes, there was. He should have indicated more strongly what his family would have thought of this little escapade. He fancied that would have carried some weight.

'Yes, indeed!' said Emmaline, and Sybilla walked away from them both, too furious to continue speaking to them.

A piercing laugh behind her caused her to turn round sharply. It was the fat lady from the balcony. Her gown was of purple satin, cut dangerously low and dripping with ruching, flowers in pink satin, tucks, folds and pleats, but the shortest of short sleeves which revealed acres of mottled flesh on her arms, shoulders and neck. Three purple feathers waved from the back of her greying hair and a diamond necklace was half hidden in her chins. That this creature should have seen Marianne make a fool of herself was very galling.

Sybilla strolled a short way on her own, but soon became aware that she was being ogled by several raffish young men, and turned back towards the Drummond box. Now she could see Mrs Drummond and Florian Farley, both quite flushed, and Napier looking more drawn than she had ever seen him. Large business losses couldn't affect him, she knew, but Marianne's débâcle was another matter. And his mother had not yet finished scolding.

Pacing back and forth on a stretch of carpet not more than ten yards long, Sybilla was unwilling to join in the conversations of the other members of her party. The hall was so warm that she was forced to fan herself rapidly. Down the hall, a small crowd had gathered round a woman who was slumped in a chair. If they would all move away, the poor thing might recover, thought Sybilla angrily. She was taken by surprise when Napier suddenly joined her as she was walking away from the direction of the Drummond box.

'What must you think of me?' he asked in a low voice.

'Why, that you are a good and loving brother, a man who actually believes that women are members of the human race and therefore entitled to lead the lives of their choice. You are bound to be misunderstood.'

'Bless you! I was sorely in need of one comforting word. But oh, my dear, what have I done to my sister? I've committed the

230

greatest folly of my life and Marianne is paying for it.'

'Nonsense! You must not listen to your family. They talk too much.'

He laughed. 'I was told you had quarrelled with Emmaline and Francis. And in my defence, I gather. But it won't do, Sybilla. I can't fool myself that it doesn't matter, or that it's all Marianne's fault. It is *my* fault.'

'There you go!' She turned to confront him and now looked earnestly up into his eyes. 'When will men allow women to make their own mistakes and enjoy their own triumphs? If Marianne has made a mistake she must take the consequences. Her life is not entirely spoilt, you know. She is still in one piece, a pretty, lively girl who will probably make a great many mistakes before her day is done.'

'You are very eloquent,' he said gently, but the pain had not left his eyes. She had never seen him this way before.

'Oh, Napier, don't be upset!' Impulsively, she reached out to squeeze his hand. She heard him suck in his breath as her own breath was suddenly squeezed away, just as it had been all those years ago whenever the curate had walked by. Only, this feeling was a thousand times more wonderful. She wanted to tell Napier so, but couldn't speak. They stood looking at one another with a pleasure that blotted out everyone else and every sound. They were alone. Alone, that is, except for the bell which began to ring for the third act. The press of people, all intent on returning to their seats, pushing, laughing and talking, destroyed the spell. Without a word, she dropped her hand and they turned together to walk back to the box.

The third act was the shortest of all, but to Sybilla it seemed interminable. The theatre had become oppressively warm and she began to fan herself quickly. Just when she thought she could bear it no longer, a hand touched her arm and she half turned.

'Mrs Hobart, are you too warm? Would you care to leave the box?' asked Napier. She would. Together they slipped from their seats, let themselves out and stood in the now empty corridor.

Napier pulled her by the hand towards the unoccupied box next door. Mercifully it was unlocked. He opened it and within seconds they were inside, as far away as possible from the Drummond box and well hidden from the audience. Without a word, he put his arms round her and kissed her, just as the two menservants began a humourous duologue on stage. He was still kissing her when the sketch was finished, but then they both had to stop to catch their breath.

'Damn these corsets! I want to hold *you*, not whalebone!' he whispered.

'Don't! You mustn't unhook me, for God's sake! No, my darling. Kiss me again.' He did. On the shoulder, the neck, the ear.

On stage, the hero and heroine entered to play their last big scene. There was a smattering of applause for Mrs Mowatt, posing outrageously as a timid young woman of twenty.

SIR BASHFUL CONSTANT: Permit me, dear madam, to throw myself on my knees, for on my knees I must address you, and in that humble posture, to implore your compassion. [Kneels]
MISS LOVEMORE: Oh, sir, what can you mean?
SIR BASHFUL CONSTANT: May I kiss these sweet fingers? [Takes her hand]
MISS LOVEMORE: You put me to the blush, sir. You are too eager, I swear it.

Napier bent to kiss Sybilla's cleavage. She threw back her head and closed her eyes, her skin burning with his touch. Despite the intensity of her joy, she was reluctantly aware of the progress of the play. Even her scant theatrical knowledge was enough to warn her that the final curtain was drawing near.

'My love, you mustn't! The play will be over soon.'

'Have you any idea how much I desire you?' whispered Napier in her ear. 'Here, Sybilla, and now!'

The pins were falling from Sybilla's hair, but she couldn't bring herself to care. When he held her head forcing her lips hard against his, the head-dress began to come adrift. Sybilla raised her hands to her hair, and he swiftly cupped her breasts, lifting them to kiss the exposed flesh again.

SIR BASHFUL CONSTANT: You see me now with tender, melting, supplicating eyes, languishing at your feet. Can you find it in your heart to persist in cruelty?
MISS LOVEMORE: Stop! You must not speak so, sir.

SIR BASHFUL CONSTANT: You should no longer hesitate in gratitude to reward him, who, still on his knees, here makes a vow to you of eternal constancy and love.

'Napier, we must go! You wicked man, you have unhooked me. Quick! Do me up before we are discovered.'
    'I don't care if we are. Tell me you don't care either.'
    She laughed, nuzzling his cheek. 'Well, only a little, because your family have had enough to shock them for one night.' She put her arms round his neck and kissed him, pulling him closer. The head-dress finally came off and joined her shawl on the floor.

ENTER LADY BELLMORE: What is this? Are we to wish you well, dear friends?
MISS LOVEMORE: I – I don't know what to say.
SIR BASHFUL CONSTANT: Say you will be mine, fair one.

Breaking away, Sybilla tried to repair the damage she had caused to Napier's collar and cravat. One of her violets had entangled itself in his diamond shirt-stud. Her fingers were trembling too much to make much headway, and Napier was having similar difficulty with the two hooks at the back of her dress which he was attempting to close with his arms still round her. In any case, there was much interruption because of their frequent need to kiss and kiss again.

ENTER SIR BRILLIANT FASHION: And there's a fine end to this story. If this business were known in the world, it might prove a valuable lesson indeed; the men would see how their passions may carry them into the danger of wounding the bosom of a friend; the ladies would learn that after the marriage rites, they should not suffer their powers of pleasing to languish away.
ENTER THE ENTIRE COMPANY: To win a man, when all your pains succeed, the way to keep him is a task indeed.

As the curtains reopened for the first curtain call, Napier reluctantly stooped to retrieve the head-dress, the shawl and as many hairpins as he could find in the near darkness of the box, while Sybilla made frantic adjustments to her hair, hoping that half the pins would do the work of all.
    'Oh, my little love, such delicate skin as you have,' he

laughed, standing up. 'For heaven's sake, keep your shawl about you. My fingertips are glowing white against the pink. Not bruises, I assure you, but nevertheless . . . '

Still pinning her hair, she looked up at him saucily, and he kissed her again. Only the increasing light in the house brought them to the realization that they really might be discovered. They stepped into the hall just as a liveried box-opener swung open the neighbouring door and Mrs Drummond came towards them.

'Oh, there you are, my dear. Did you see Marianne at the end? No, how could you? Poor Sybilla, it really is very hot tonight. You are looking dreadfully flushed, I must say. Perhaps it will be cooler backstage, because you know we must visit Marianne to persuade her to come home with us tonight. Are you sure you're well enough, or will you go to the hotel immediately?'

Sybilla flicked a look at Napier who shook his head, so she pulled her shawl more tightly round her shoulders and said she was well enough, thank you, and was looking forward to seeing Marianne.

'Yes, I must have a word with her,' said Napier, more to Sybilla than to his mother.

Later, Marianne greeted her family on the stage where the cast and their friends had begun to gather. She was still wearing her make-up, but had changed into her own smart full-sleeved dress. The make-up ended at her chin, leaving her neck and shoulders quite a different colour. The total effect was not only ageing, but extremely cruel to Marianne's vibrant looks.

Mrs Drummond walked in a stately fashion right across the stage before saying in ringing tones: 'My dear, you were very creditable indeed, considering it was your first effort.'

'Oh, thank you, Mama!' Marianne's eyes filled with grateful tears as she embraced her mother with great affection.

'But you must come home with us tonight,' whispered Mrs Drummond in her ear, and Marianne didn't argue. At that moment, Mrs Mowatt joined the Drummond party who were, without exception, warmly congratulating Marianne.

Napier clasped Marianne's elbow to lead her off to one side, as Florian launched into a spirited appraisal of the play. He knew a great deal about the theatre and certainly won Mrs Mowatt's respect. She talked to him at length and, therefore, had no opportunity to comment on Marianne's performance until long after Sybilla, Francis and Emmaline had drifted away.

'Oh, Napier, take me home!' whispered Marianne, clutching his arm. 'I can't bear it any more.'

'It must have been very embarrassing to be so ill-used by the audience.'

'I can't tell you! Acting is not at all as you might imagine. The costumes *smell*, Napier. I had never thought of that, had you? Of course, my costume, being cotton, has been freshly laundered, but the breeches and jackets of the men are revolting. Mrs Mowatt's dressing-room is splendid, but you can see, if you look about you, in what conditions *we* are forced to work – ugly, dirty and upleasant. And the same can be said for some of the actors. The worse thing is that one is expected to join in. You know, help with the cleaning and mending. You may smile, but I have not been used to such treatment. I will be very glad to leave here tonight.'

'I'm sorry, my dear, but that isn't possible. You asked to be allowed to travel with Mrs Mowatt for several months and that is exactly what you are going to do.'

She blinked at him in amazement. 'I see. You intend to punish me for my folly. Why shouldn't I run away from here? You ran away from a place you hated.'

'If I remember rightly, not long ago you threatened to run away from home to Mrs Mowatt. Now you want to run away from her. Yes, Marianne, I did run away – but only after two years. I shall not force you to be an actress for so long a time. Think now. Your performance was abysmal tonight –'

'Napier!'

'– and I'm sure you would not wish to remember *that* all the rest of your days. You would always wonder if you could have been better. No, you must face failure and try hard to improve before you give up the actor's life for ever.'

'So I must go on stage every night for a week and make an ass of myself – Oh!' She clapped a hand over her mouth briefly. 'And that is another thing. The language employed by actors is so salty that one cannot help but pick up the odd word.'

235

'One will just have to resist the temptation,' said Napier sternly. 'I also hope that your next part will not require you to kiss a man on stage.'

'Yes, it is mortifying. Richard is an odious man who has been very unkind to me and was quite rude about my forgetting my lines after we came backstage. I would much rather have kissed James who played the other servant.' She sighed, looking at her brother carefully to see if she might bend his will. 'Must I stay?'

'Yes, you must.' He looked very much the disapproving older brother.

'You think it will be good for my character, don't you? Well, I suppose you are right, but Mama is going to be very angry with you.'

'I can bear it. It would help me greatly, however, if you were to tell her that the decision is yours.'

Marianne shrugged in defeat and squeezed his arm as she stood on tiptoe to kiss his cheek. 'Was my performance really terrible tonight?'

'Really terrible. I'm sure you will be much better at the next performance.'

'Well, dear brother, there is nothing more to be said. Let us tell Mama what *I* have decided.'

Mrs Drummond responded to the news in just the way her children had known she would, but, once again, Florian came to the rescue by urging the good sense of Marianne's decision. And Mrs Mowatt added that she had never expected dear Marianne to run off so soon; Marianne must work hard in the coming weeks. Eventually, Mrs Drummond, always eager to please her menfolk, decided that it was all for the best.

After a few minutes Napier took her arm, as well as Sybilla's and walked between them over to the buffet tables that had been arranged on one side of the stage. The spread was lavish and there seemed to be no end to the champagne.

'You know, Mama. I think you have been very wise in agreeing to let Marianne stay with the company,' said Napier. 'She will get the whole business out of her system and never pine for the theatre again.'

'Yes, my dear. You were right, as usual. Everything is for the best. Have I said that already? Will you just look at this buffet?

I don't think I've ever seen such a gorgeous supper. It occurs to me that I shall feel very much better for a little food. Put a good helping of cold salmon on my plate, dear, and cucumber. I do love cucumber. How about you, Sybilla? Are you hungry?'

'I shall help myself to everything, ma'am,' said Sybilla, and *sotto voce* to Napier, 'You can't manipulate me so easily.'

'I know, but it's not for the want of trying,' he said, smiling. 'There's Mr Watts, as dandified as ever and, if I'm not mistaken, rather drunk.'

Sybilla looked round. 'Yes, I believe you're right. Where does he get all his money, do you suppose?'

He had time to tell her only that rumour spoke of large gains speculating on the stock market, while others favoured the view that Watts was a successful gambler.

An accordionist and two fiddlers began playing, forcing everyone to talk louder to be heard. Some of the younger people began to dance in a rather rowdy manner, and the party took a downward turn. Napier didn't intend to ask Sybilla to dance, having no wish to involve her in this mêlée. When they had finished their supper, he preferred to watch her from a distance as she moved among the throng with great confidence.

Later on, he was treated to an entertaining pantomime when Mr Watts, all unsteady bows and flushed cheeks, attempted to engage her in conversation. She demonstrated her cool, inscrutable manner at its most devastating. Napier laughed out loud when Watts finally bowed with a very stiff back and sidled off in search of better company.

Napier would have approached Sybilla then, except that his attention was caught by the next object of Watts's gallantry. Marianne received him in a very different manner. Flushed from her recent dancing, she laughed up at him flirtatiously, listened attentively as he spoke at length and then slipped her arm in his. Napier started foward to follow them, but they went no further than a pair of chairs at the side of the stage. He could keep an eye on them very well from his present position, and even managed to talk for some time to Emmaline and Francis, while never removing his eyes from Marianne.

The champagne and rather Bohemian atmosphere reacted favourably on Emmaline. She was safe by the side of her beloved, secure in the knowledge that she could not do anything which would offend against good taste. She could afford to relax and enjoy the evening. The Babcocks, after all, were safely tucked into their beds in Hertfordshire.

It was half-past two before the Drummond party reached the hotel. Napier was forced to say a formal good night to Sybilla, watched by his sleepy family, and went to his bedchamber seething with plans. Half an hour later, he knocked on Florian Farley's door and walked inside as soon as the door was opened.

Florian, immense in a brocade dressing-gown, trotted after him. 'Your mother is in her room, sir!'

Napier turned round, laughing. 'I never doubted it, old chap. Did you think I've come spying? Nothing could be further from the truth. I want to chat with you. May I sit down?'

'Oh, yes, yes, of course. I suppose you wish to talk about Marianne's future on the stage.'

'No, your future. What are your intentions towards my mother?'

Poor Florian gripped a chair back and rolled his eyes. 'What . . . that is . . . ' He cleared his throat. 'What do you want them to be?'

'I was hoping that you are not trifling with her affections, Farley.'

'Never! I love her.'

'But you don't intend marriage?'

'I do, I do, but – that is – dear boy, how could I afford her?'

'You couldn't, of course, but if my mother remarries, I shall make her a handsome allowance.'

'Nevertheless – you will permit me to be seated?'

'This is your room,' said Napier with amusement. 'Sit down, by all means. It wasn't my intention to upset you.'

'Wasn't it? By George, I'm surprised to hear it. You love to upset me, Napier. I don't understand you at all.'

'Not many people do.'

'You're not cozening me? You would really welcome my marriage to your mother?'

'I am persuaded she would be happiest living with you away from Bailton Hall.'

238

'Yes, yes. Perhaps a wee house in London so that we could attend the theatre often. We are both addicted, you know. London's hustle and bustle would suit us very well.'

'It could be arranged. Ask Mama for her opinion. Now, I do wish to speak briefly about Marianne, or rather about Mr Watts who showed her a good deal of attention this evening. What do you know about him?'

Florian took out a handkerchief and wiped his sweating face to give himself time to think. Devil of a man, Napier. First one thing then another. Sitting there, looking so pleasant. But all a chap had to do was say the wrong thing – and mention of the four hundred pounds would certainly be the wrong thing – and Napier could turn nasty.

'Seems a decent chap,' he said at last. 'Has treated Mrs Mowatt and her company very well. Everything first rate, you know. Perfectly proper.'

'Yes,' said Napier. 'It's obvious he is wealthy. What I really wanted to know is, do you think he will travel with the company when they take to the road on Monday?'

Florian let out his breath in a glorious sigh of relief. 'I doubt it, my boy. Henry Watts is a director of the Sphere Assurance Company and is most assiduous in performing his duties. He is to be found at their offices every day from ten to four. I know it for a fact.'

'Sphere Assurance? Good Lord! I've shamefully underestimated that young man. Well, you've now put my mind at rest on two counts. I'll leave you to your night's sleep. You look all to pieces, not at all like a happy bridegroom.'

Florian shuffled towards the door in his slippers, anxious to be rid of Napier before the man gave him any more shocks. 'You've quite stunned me, you know. I never dreamed that Dorothea and I would ever be able to marry. It's too good to be true.'

'I shan't call you papa, you know,' said Napier, stepping into the hall.

Florian closed his bedroom door and leaned against it. 'Shan't call me papa? Thank God for small mercies!' he muttered weakly.

15

The next morning Napier was up early. Kindersly had him dressed by half-past nine; a cup of coffee and a roll sufficed for his breakfast. While eating, he penned one of his notoriously curt notes to Sybilla and pushed it under her door on his way out of the hotel.

Napier had never met the chairman of Sphere Assurance, but he did know Angus Tite the deputy chairman, having met him several times in the City within the past twelve months. Tite's house was a splendid one within the City boundaries. Napier sent his phaeton round to the stables and demanded to see the head of the house.

Tite kept him waiting for no more than a quarter of an hour while he finished his breakfast, and came into the library with his hand outstretched in a warm greeting. His rounded shoulders robbed his figure of dignity and caused his clothes to hang on him most unattractively. He had shrewd blue eyes which were marred by a yellowing of the whites. Orange-peel skin hinted at the ailing liver of a man who drinks too often and too much.

'Tite! Good man! I was afraid you would deny me on a Sunday. I realize that I'm imposing on you, but I won't take much of your time. I wish to enquire about the character of one of your directors. I believe he might also be a large shareholder – Henry Watts.'

'Watts?' said Tite vaguely. 'Oh, young Henry! His father was a clerk with Sphere for forty years. Good man. We found a position for the son about six years ago when old Watts died. But he's not a director, nor, I'm reasonably sure, a shareholder. He is a clerk, like his father before him.'

'I can't believe it!' exclaimed Napier. 'I was told he was a director.'

'Stop pacing the floor, old chap, and sit down. I think I can explain the mystery. The rumour about his being a director may have arisen because Henry came into a great deal of money about five years ago. I'm not sure of the source. Some

240

say that he has some special connection with Louis-Napoleon which enables him to speculate brilliantly in stocks and shares. Others speak of his many successes on the turf.'

Napier, sitting in a straight chair, crossed one leg over the other and massaged his ankle. 'Do you actually expect me to believe such a faradiddle? I wasn't born yesterday, though I begin to think you were.'

'Steady on! Why shouldn't it be true? You don't know that it isn't. I admit it is an odd situation, but stranger things have been known to happen. The older I get –'

'That the son of a clerk has access to the French Pretender? Oh, a very common occurrence! I'm told Watts comes to work regularly from ten to four each day. Is that true?'

'Perfectly true. He is spoken of as being very conscientious.'

Napier snorted derisively. 'I don't know anything about the insurance business nor about Sphere Assurance Company. But I do pride myself on knowing something about the minds of men. And I have met this particular young man. If he had acquired his wealth by legitimate means, be it inside information, speculation or gambling, he would not come to work regularly, if at all. Furthermore, if his fortune depended on the stock exchange, he would haunt the place.'

All these conjectures were slowly sifting through Tite's sluggish mind. He had never seriously considered the business of Henry Watts before. There had been so many other problems requiring his attention. Now he could think only that responsibility for any mistakes would fall ultimately on him. The chairman was Lord Worford, the appointment a mere courtesy. For all practical purposes, Angus Tite was the chairman, the man who would have to take the blame for any mismanagement.

'What are you saying? That he has been stealing from my company? I won't believe it. Why, he rents two theatres! He has become an important figure in the theatrical world. It's said he has set up his own stables, that he has a magnificent house in St John's Wood and another in Brighton. We would have noticed a shortfall big enough to cover these expenses.'

'We can soon find out. Your offices are not far from here. If you have the keys, let us walk over and put our minds at rest. I want to know the truth for personal reasons. And if you value

241

your business reputation, you had better find out the worst as soon as possible. The scandal would be bound to affect you disastrously, no matter how much you might protest your innocence.'

Tite, knowing Napier was speaking more of the truth than he realized, overcame his dread of facing bad news and sent word to his wife that he would be busy for the better part of the day.

Once inside the building, the two men went directly to Watts's desk. A cursory glance at the man's books and papers was sufficient to show that large abstractions had been made. While Napier scanned the books and other documents which were fetched for him, Angus Tite sat motionless with shock in a nearby chair. When Napier triumphantly said he had discovered considerable inconsistencies in the accounts, and that not less than eighteen thousand pounds had probably been spirited away during the last fifteen months, Tite knew he was done for. He would be lucky if he were allowed to resign quietly.

Napier, on the other hand, was enjoying himself immensely. The thrill of discovery, the pitting of wits against Watts's own to uncover the truth, was a challenge which he was perfectly suited by temperament and training to meet. He put his worries about Marianne aside for the moment and concentrated on his work. After about an hour, he asked that the chief clerk be sent for, and Tite wearily dispatched his servant in search of the man.

John Harper was attending a nearby church and was with them very quickly. He was not more than thirty-five and appeared to be a deeply religious man of upright character. Not surprisingly, he was devastated by Napier's revelations. He recovered enough, however, to remind Tite that he had been with the company for only six months, that his first act had been to reprimand Watts for his untidy work, and that he had written to the Board suggesting that a new system of checks and counterchecks be put into practice immediately. Tite winced at the memory; the suggestion had been ignored.

'Hmm,' said Napier, still working. 'The erasures cease after the date of Harper's arrival. I believe no money has been stolen since then.'

'Thank God!' said Harper.

'Yes, you have cut off Watts's main source of income. He must be desperate by now. I have seen how freely he spends money. Tite, you must send for Henry Watts immediately.'

'But if I write a letter demanding his presence here, he will guess what is up and run away.'

'Possibly. But if you tell him there has been a robbery and you merely wish him to help identify what has been lost, I think he will come readily enough in order to ensure that no one else looks at these books. In fact, I don't see that he would have any choice but to come as quickly as possible.'

It was well over two hours before Watts reached the offices of Sphere Assurance, and by that time Napier had discovered one of the many devices Watts had used for obtaining money.

'He seems to have gained part of it this way,' said Napier. 'A cheque for £554 10s. for annuity number six was drawn, paid by the bank and entered by them in the pass book. When Watts got his hands on the money and the pass book he erased the two fives, making the payment appear to be £4 10s. Here. You can see quite easily how the two fives have been erased. This was annuity number six, but to add to the confusion, he turned it into annuity number sixty-four. Why else would the four be written in different ink from the six?

'Now, how is the man to pocket the five hundred and fifty pounds without being discovered? He takes a fire loss payment of £7 10s. which was paid some time ago and makes it £557 10s. You don't even need a magnifying glass to see the changes. Thus the fraud is covered – at least from the blinkered eyes of this Board and all of Watts's superiors.'

'So, it's all over. I can't say I'm entirely sorry,' said Henry Watts. 'How clever of you, Drummond.' They all turned to see the young man standing in the doorway. He was impeccably dressed but very drunk, needing the door-frame as support. 'Old Harper here came along and spoiled my game.'

'You haven't been all that clever,' said Napier, eyeing the man with disgust. 'Rather, it's a case of Sphere Assurance having been criminally negligent.'

'Hear! Hear!' said Watts.

Tite and Harper, not unnaturally, didn't join the cheering. There could be no excuse for such appalling laxity and they both knew it. Harper would earn himself a severe reprimand and at least the threat of dismissal, despite the fact that he was on record as having wanted a change in the accounting system. Angus Tite was, of course, ruined. For a split second, he even contemplated putting his pistol to his head and pulling the trigger. It was a fleeting thought only; he couldn't leave his dear wife to face this scandal alone.

'Sit down,' said Napier to Watts. 'I want the answers to some questions.'

'I daresay you do, old chap,' laughed Watts, sitting down heavily. He appeared to be taking his imminent ruin with great sangfroid, but his hand shook as he removed a silver hip flask from his pocket and drank deeply for several seconds, before offering it round with an ironic half bow.

'How much have you stolen altogether?' asked Napier.

'About seventy thousand pounds, but you'll never get a conviction against me. I know I would be transported, but it won't happen.' He blinked slowly several times, his eyes glazed. 'I won't let that happen.'

Tite had begun to calculate all the terrible consequences of this affair. He wished the young villain would walk out now and just disappear for ever. But no, that wouldn't do. Harper knew, and Drummond – who seemed to be revelling in all this – knew also. Angus Tite's only hope was to expose Watts immediately and take credit for the discovery. He didn't believe Drummond would object to that. Tite would play the angry, deceived man, intent on putting his company right – and would hope that his performance saved his skin.

'You must have grown very short of the readies during these past few months,' Napier Drummond was saying.

'Devil a bit! The end of my dreams. You see, I discovered how the business might be done here five years ago. Sphere is really very badly managed, you know. No one cares what goes on. There is a sickness in this business that starts at the top and filters down. Damn it, Drummond! The company was just asking to be defrauded!' Napier absently nodded his head in agreement. 'I had always wanted to be associated with the theatre, and at least for a few years I achieved my ambition. Not many men can say as much at twenty-eight. Playwrights have dedicated their works to me. Did you know that? Mrs

Mowatt, an actress of impeccable reputation, has honoured me by appearing in my theatres. Everything I have touched has been done well, with no expense spared. Everything has been of the finest. Only the general public has failed me.'

'By not buying tickets,' said Napier. 'The theatre was filthy last night. An economy measure, I presume.'

'Not a feather to fly with, old boy. I've closed the Marylebone and Olympic for ever. Mrs Mowatt knows.' Watts gave Napier a malicious grin. 'Too bad about your mother and Farley. I thought at first that you, of all people, would rumble me. Then, I discovered that your dear mama is too afraid of your temper to discuss her finances with you.'

Harper and Tite gasped; Napier stared at Watts's grinning face for a full half minute. 'What about my mother and Farley?' he asked softly.

Watts giggled. He couldn't seem to stop. 'I needed money so I sold your mother shares in the acting company for two hundred pounds. And the best of it is, Mrs Mowatt's husband owns the company. The shares weren't mine to sell! In exchange for the money, I gave Farley the use of a box at the Marylebone. I couldn't rent the damn things anyway. Later, Mrs Drummond promised me another two hundred pounds when I told her the company needed more funds. But I had to threaten to tell you all about it before Farley finally coughed up. I believe Mrs Hobart lent your mother the money. Farley doesn't have a farthing to bless himself with and never will have.'

'*Mrs Hobart?*' Napier cleared his throat, then said more calmly, 'You sold my mother shares in an acting company you didn't own?'

'Ha ha! If looks could kill, dear boy! Don't go running away with the idea that you can have me up on a charge. I signed nothing. No paper changed hands. You really must teach those two innocents a little bit about the proper way to transact business. As for Mrs Hobart, I don't know what arrangements she made –'

Napier stood up and reached for his hat. He was half-way to the door when Tite asked rather desperately, 'Where are you going?'

'To my home, of course. You have no further need of me.

Send for the police immediately. I wish I thought this scoundrel would hang. Many poor souls have had their necks stretched for less, but the courts are powerless to do more than transport him, so you might care to hang him yourself with my blessing.'

Despite his parting remarks, Napier didn't go immediately to his home. He fetched his carriage and drove for several hours round London, through the parks, anywhere. Finally it became necessary to rest and bait his horse before heading for Hertfordshire.

He ordered a meal and a bottle of wine in a hostelry and thought about the woman who had responded with such passion to his kisses the night before. And all the time she had been laughing at him! *Your mother is afraid of you*, she had once said. With a groan, he remembered that Sybilla had borrowed two hundred pounds from him. And he had charged her interest! He didn't suppose for a moment that she had charged his mother interest, and she must know by now that she would never receive the money from either Farley or his foolish parent. Yet no one had approached him to sort the matter out. And why? Because Napier Drummond was such an animal that everyone went in fear of him.

He felt himself flush with shame. He would never forgive Sybilla. Come to that, he would never forgive any of them. Did the girls know? Francis? *My God*! But no, not Francis. Francis would have said something. Francis would not have been afraid. Then, on the other hand, Sybilla was not afraid of him either, was she? He stabbed his food viciously and finished off the bottle of wine with great speed. He would drive to Hoddesdon, tell Sybilla just what he thought of her and then never see her again.

Sybilla had been more than a little disappointed when she read Napier's note: *Must resolve something concerning Marianne. Will wait upon you in Hoddesdon at one o'clock*. However, she fastened her thoughts on their coming meeting in the privacy of her home. When she had packed her few possessions, she was, she discovered, the first member of the party to be ready to leave. The Marylebone hotel was a small establishment; there was no reception room where she could with propriety wait for the others. So she sat tapping her foot in her room for an hour. By eleven o'clock, when Mrs Drummond's maid knocked on her door, she was feeling very irritable and in no mood to hear the *Affaire Marianne* discussed by Mrs Drummond and Mr Farley for two hours.

In the event, the subject was scarcely mentioned. The couple seemed to share a very special secret to which they would refer obliquely from time to time. Clearly, there was much that they wished to say to each other. Sybilla felt even more the unwanted third party than she had done on the journey to London.

At five minutes to one, she waved them on their way from her own doorstep, half expecting to find Napier already installed in the drawing-room. When he was not there, she hurried upstairs to change into a loose – and she hoped, becoming – wrapper and returned to the drawing-room to wait. At two, she allowed Mrs Potter to serve her some cold meats which she ate quickly, not wishing to be discovered by Napier with a mouth full of food.

By half-past three, she had passed through the stage of imagining the loved one laid out on the side of the road following a terrible accident. Then came the doubts about her own behaviour on the previous night. All the stories and admonitions with which her mother had peppered her adolescence rose up to haunt her. She had behaved like a wanton, had permitted intimacies which no unbetrothed woman should ever allow, while he had not uttered one word or promise for the future. She was ruined; he despised her. Had she not seen on the stage how a man should speak to the woman he loved? Hesitant declarations of love received with panic by women of remarkable innocence who are strangers to passion. No wonder Napier had not even said he loved her.

By the time the clock chimed half-past four, she was simply furious and reached up to massage her scalp, determined not to allow an inconsiderate brute of a man to bring about one of her sick headaches. When the doorbell clanged through the house at five minutes to five, she had to take several deep breaths to control the angry words that had been hovering on the edge of her tongue for so long.

His thunderous expression, the eyebrows winging upwards, the tight set of his lips, all caught her by surprise. Her own

247

anger evaporated in the face of his evident rage.

'I've spent an hour in the edifying company of Henry Watts. What does that suggest to you?' he said as the drawing-room door closed behind him.

'That you have discovered your mother's involvement in the theatre company,' she said promptly, 'and a good thing too. I'm pleased that it is now out in the open.'

'Watts is a thief who has defrauded the Sphere Assurance Company of seventy thousand pounds in the past five years. He never owned the acting company, which is the property of Mrs Mowatt's husband. By trickery, he took two hundred pounds from Mama. And then,' he paused for awful emphasis, 'with *your* help, he took two hundred pounds more. What have you to say for yourself?'

Sybilla had a great deal to say in her defence, but chose to attack instead. 'You say you spent an hour with Mr Watts. Why then has it taken you so long to arrive here? Couldn't you at least have had the courtesy to arrive at the time appointed?'

'Is that your answer? Why have I not returned on time? Good God, woman! You and my family have conspired to make a complete fool of me and all you can say is: where have I been? I have been driving around London considering my future, that is where I have been!'

'I see,' she said coolly. 'Just because I took the opportunity to help your poor terrified mother out of her difficulties –'

'How long ago did all this happen?' he interrupted. 'When did you lend the money to my mother?'

'The day after you paid me for the land.'

'I see,' he said with sudden insight. 'As a subtle form of revenge, because I didn't pay your asking price, you decided to give some of *my* money to my mother. Tell me, when did you intend to let me in on the secret? When were you going to tell me that the mother of the rich Napier Drummond had been forced to turn to a complete stranger to save herself from disaster? You've never told *me* about it. Whom *have* you told?'

'No one! I've not told a soul about it. What do you take me for?'

'It was revenge, wasn't it? You did it out of revenge. That was your object, not sympathy for Mama.'

There was a sharp intake of breath from the woman he had

thought he loved. He bore down on her with blazing eyes. 'Admit it. Tell me you wanted to revenge yourself on me for some imagined slights.'

'Well, yes at the time. You are so high-handed, Napier, and your mother is so afraid of you, that I thought it would serve you right if I – but later of course, I saw that I couldn't – it wasn't my secret.'

'Say no more. You've said quite enough. I understand you perfectly. Mad Drummond, the beast of Hertford! Well, now that I know your sentiments, there is nothing more to be said by either of us.' He searched his pockets for two hundred pounds which he could slap down on the table with a satisfying thump. But, of course, he wasn't carrying that kind of money on him. Denied his grand gesture, he informed Sybilla that she would be hearing from him in the future. A bank draft for two hundred pounds would be on its way to her.

'Don't be an idiot! That won't be necessary. I lent your mother two hundred pounds and you lent me two hundred pounds. We are even. Have the courtesy never to speak to me again. I find your temper totally unacceptable in any respectable drawing-room.'

In the sudden silence that followed his departure, she had an opportunity to reflect that she had just said goodbye to her future happiness. Why had she allowed herself to become so angry? A few soothing words, a sensible explanation of how it had all come about, and she could have had the man she loved for ever. He would have seen – he was a quick-witted man – that once she had lent money to his mother, the secret was no longer hers. She couldn't tell the truth without betraying a trust. Instead, she had fuelled his fury and sent him away to vent his spleen on his hapless parent.

She rang the bell, met Saul in the hall, and told him to bring round the gig. Then, calling to Mrs Potter to come upstairs and help her dress, she ran to her room, throwing off clothing as she went. It was hardly more than ten minutes before she was on her way in the gig.

This was not the best time of day to be travelling across Hertford Heath, although it was still quite light. She couldn't hope to reach Bailton Hall before Napier did, in order to give a warning of the storm that was about to break, but this was the quickest route. She would arrive soon after him and, hopefully, deflect his wrath from Mrs Drummond who would never understand his disposition.

The area was heavily wooded just past the green, but Sybilla had no thoughts to spare for any lurking footpads. She was probably travelling too fast to be chased by men on foot, in any case. The horse was galloping in an easy rhythm, faster than Sybilla had ever driven and very exhilarating, when she saw a phaeton approaching her at equal speed on the narrow road. She began to pull frantically on the reins. By the time her gig had slewed across the road behind a very fresh horse, Napier was almost upon her.

'You idiotic woman!' he shouted from his seat in the phaeton. 'Are you mad? Hertford Heath is no place for a lady at this time of day.' He jumped down from his carriage to go to his horse's head.

'I wanted to find you,' she said, still sawing on the reins in a fruitless attempt to bring her horse under control.

'Why didn't you stay at home? I was coming back to you to apologize.'

'Well, how was I to know that? You left the house like a madman.'

'I never behave like a madman. That is a rumour put about by people who have been unwise enough to arouse my reasonable displeasure.' Having tied his own horse by the side of the road, he now took hers by the head. In the meantime, Sybilla climbed down from her gig to lend a hand.

'I can explain everything, Napier. I did want foolish revenge at one time, but soon changed my mind. You have been so kind to me. How could I want to be hateful to you? As for your mother, she's a faint-hearted widgeon. Try not to be angry with her.'

Napier laughed, a joyful explosion that chased away all the ill-feeling between them. He gathered her in his arms and swung her round. 'I'm never angry with my mother. Whatever gave you such an odd idea? She and Farley are to marry and move to London. I thought it would be more pleasant to have the house to ourselves. Or would you prefer to move to a new house?'

'Whatever,' she said breathlessly just before he kissed her warmly.

It was at this tender moment that Jeremiah Cobbett, who had been watching the drama from the safety of a tall oak, chose to leap from his hiding place, an empty pistol in his shaking hand. 'Stand and deliver!'

Napier looked round at the man, who could not be more than twenty years old and clearly new to the game. With a sigh, Napier reached into his pocket, found a coin and tossed it into the dust of the road.

'Do go away,' he said irritably. 'Can't you see that I'm in the middle of a quarrel?'

Jeremiah gaped. He could see the man and the woman were in the middle of an embrace. He wouldn't call that quarrelling, not what they were doing. Crabwise, he sidled towards the half-hidden coin, all the while staring at these fancified people with a mixture of disgust and lonely envy that often afflicts voyeurs. A half sovereign! He melted into the woodland and tossed his useless pistol into the shrubbery.

Highway robbery was a hanging offence. This had been his first attempt at it, and he decided to retire while he could still boast of a profitable career. Glancing once more over his shoulder, he saw that the two nobs were *still kissing*. He shook his head in admiration of such single-mindedness and scampered off to spend his windfall.